A DEA[...]

"Do you give in, Bonds[...]

Horse was indignant. "Negative."

"You did not let me finish the rules." Howell chuckled. "You cannot ease out of this exercise by just letting your 'Mech run down or using any escape maneuver. You must run the gauntlet or be murdered dishonorably in your cockpit."

"How can you do that?" came another voice.

"Howell does not have to. But *I* can. I am allowed by the rules."

The voice coming suddenly from inside the cockpit startled Horse. He looked around. From the darkest part of the cockpit, a partition slid open and he saw a Smoke Jaguar warrior crouched inside. The hooded warrior held a laser pistol and it was pointed at Horse's head. . . .

Twilight of the Clans IV:

Freebirth

Robert Thurston

A ROC BOOK

ROC
Published by the Penguin Group
Penguin Putnam Inc., 375 Hudson Street,
New York, New York 10014, U.S.A.
Penguin Books Ltd, 27 Wrights Lane,
London W8 5TZ, England
Penguin Books Australia Ltd, Ringwood
Victoria, Australia
Penguin Books Canada Ltd, 10 Alcorn Avenue,
Toronto, Ontario, Canada M4V 3B2
Penguin Books (N.Z.) Ltd, 182–190 Wairau Road,
Auckland 10, New Zealand

Penguin Books Ltd, Registered Offices:
Harmondsworth, Middlesex, England

First published by Roc, an imprint of Dutton Signet,
a member of Penguin Putnam Inc.

First Printing, February, 1998
10 9 8 7 6 5 4 3 2 1

Series Editor: Donna Ippolito
Cover art by Bruce Jensen
Mechanical Drawings: Duane Loose and the FASA art department

 REGISTERED TRADEMARK—MARCA REGISTRADA

BATTLETECH, FASA, and the distinctive BATTLETECH and FASA logos
are trademarks of the FASA Corporation, 1100 W. Cermak, Suite B305,
Chicago, IL 60608.

Printed in the United States of America

Thank you to:

Andy Platizky, for support and general cheerfulness;
Blaine Pardoe, for so generously helping me to clarify
some BattleTech matters;
Eugene McCrohan, LAIRE Powerhouse, for his continuing
help and insights;
Rosemary, for kindness and understanding above and
beyond the call of duty;
Charlotte, for being such a good kid;
and Donna Ippolito and the FASA staff, for their
cooperation and encouragement.

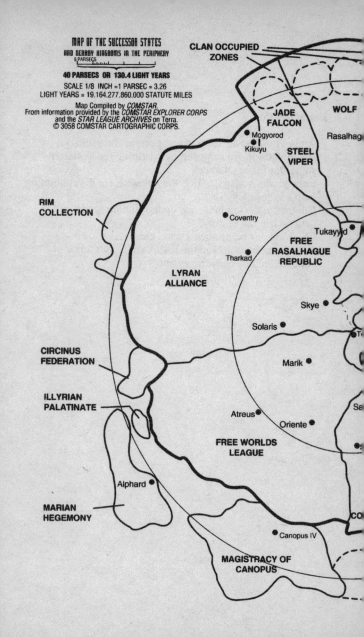

MAP OF THE SUCCESSOR STATES
AND NEARBY KINGDOMS IN THE PERIPHERY
8 PARSECS

40 PARSECS OR 130.4 LIGHT YEARS
SCALE 1/8 INCH =1 PARSEC = 3.26
LIGHT YEARS = 19.164.277.860.000 STATUTE MILES

Map Compiled by *COMSTAR*.
From information provided by the *COMSTAR EXPLORER CORPS*
and the *STAR LEAGUE ARCHIVES* on Terra.
© 3058 COMSTAR CARTOGRAPHIC CORPS.

CLAN OCCUPIED ZONES

JADE FALCON

WOLF

Rasalhag

Mogyorod

Kikuyu

STEEL VIPER

RIM COLLECTION

Coventry

Tukayyid

FREE RASALHAGUE REPUBLIC

Tharkad

LYRAN ALLIANCE

Skye

Solaris

Te

CIRCINUS FEDERATION

Marik

ILLYRIAN PALATINATE

Atreus

Oriente

Sa

FREE WORLDS LEAGUE

Alphard

MARIAN HEGEMONY

CO

Canopus IV

MAGISTRACY OF CANOPUS

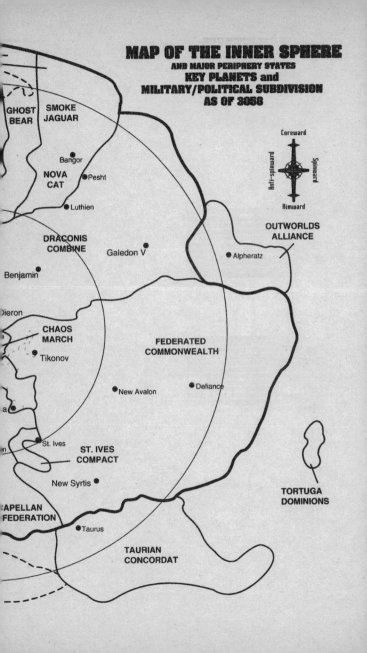

Prologue

They came from the far reaches of space, from beyond the Deep Periphery. The Clans. The most superior warriors ever known to mankind, genetically engineered to be weapons of destruction. The greatest threat ever faced by the Inner Sphere.

Three hundred years before, General Aleksandr Kerensky and most of the Star League disappeared into the unknown vastness of space. Then in the year 3050 they suddenly reappeared, so unlike anything ever seen that they were thought to be aliens. But they were the descendants of the Kerenskys come from the Inner Sphere and now they had returned to conquer the Inner Sphere.

They rolled mercilessly over world after world, moving relentlessly toward Terra, the homeworld of humanity. Then came Tukayyid. The scene of the bloodiest battle in the history of mankind. And it ended in the worst way possible for the Clans. A fifteen-year truce.

IlKhan Ulric Kerensky was called before his fellow Khans and accused of trying to destroy the Clans with the truce. In response Ulric and his Wolves fought a Trial of Refusal against the Jade Falcons, who battled in the name of his accusers. By the end of the Refusal War, Ulric was dead and both the Jade Falcons and the Wolves had been shattered.

And yet, the bloody battle was a victory for the Crusader faction of the Clans. By defeating Ulric's Wolves, they rid themselves of the Wardens, those who were against breaking the truce. By the end of 3057, Vlad Ward was the new Khan of the Wolves and Marthe Pryde the leader of the Jade Falcons. Neither one hesitated to do whatever was necessary to save their Clans.

When the Khans returned to the homeworlds to elect a new ilKhan, Vlad and Marthe formed an uneasy alliance. First, they plotted to get Lincoln Osis of the Smoke Jaguars elected ilKhan, knowing that he would not last long.

Now they wait. Osis is too short-sighted to ever successfully lead the Crusade to conquer the Inner Sphere. Vlad and Marthe's day will come, and when it does, the moment will be ripe for one of them to become ilKhan. They wait, forging the fires of their Clans. They wait for the day when the Clans will take back what is rightfully theirs.

1

Port St. William
Coventry
Coventry Province, Lyran Alliance
18 June 3058

"**W**hat the hell. The *hell*. This is one hell of a hellish hellhole, *quiaff*?" Star Commander Joanna shouted as she flung a rock down the slope of the hill looking down on Port St. William and its bay. She was, as usual, in an angry mood.

Horse grunted and squinted up at her. Joanna was instantly irritated by the relaxed way he lay in the grass, propped up on one elbow. Horse always seemed to sense when Joanna was ready to explode, and she suspected that was why he'd dragged her out for this late-morning hike into the hills and then insisted they stop to rest. Why rest? Especially when every Jade Falcon on Coventry was in the midst of packing up to return to the Falcon occupation zone?

Horse responded to Joanna's irritable moods by becoming even more laconic than usual. This time, though, through the use of the ritual interrogatory, *quiaff,* she was demanding a response.

"I said, *quiaff*!" She threw another rock, this time in his general direction.

"Aff, Joanna. Whatever you say."

"And what did I say?"

"Whatever you said."

"You do not know what I said. You were not listening.

"Whatever you say."

"That is on the verge of insubordination, Horse."

"I am always on the verge of insubordination. Do not take it to heart." He rolled onto his back and stared up at the sky.

Joanna sighed. An unusual trait among warriors, sighing. She sat down next to Horse, knees drawn in.

"We have the same conversations, Horse. Over and over."

Horse gave his gruff laugh. "We have known each other so long we are beginning to sound like coffin-mates."

Joanna shuddered. Coffin-mates was a term known to most of the seventeen Clans, though rarely used. By Clan standards it was one of the most obscene insults one Clansman could utter to another and still survive—which was why Horse had used it. It referred to two people who formed a lasting relationship. Such relationships, including legal arrangements like (ugly word) marriage, only existed among the lower castes, especially in the rural areas. Members of the Jade Falcon warrior caste, of course, found the idea of lasting relationships disgusting.

The archaic term coffin-mates suggested a relationship so permanent it would last to the grave and beyond. Jade Falcon warriors did not accept the notion of graves or any permanent sites for body disposal. Their desired fate was to be recycled after death for various uses. The highest honor for a warrior was for his or her genetic material to become part of the Clan's gene pool for use in the genetic engineering of new warrior sibkos. Thus, burial was un-desirable and even repellent to the warrior caste. The sight of a village graveyard nauseated warriors.

The burial custom harked back to a pre-Clan era on Terra, humanity's planet of origin. The humans of the past had been extremely wasteful when they buried their dead. Too much of the planet had been taken up with wasteful graveyards. But Terra had at that time been a wasteful planet, populated by wasteful civilizations whose greed and careless practices had nearly destroyed it in the time before her people made their way into space.

Space travel, with its tight confinements, and colonization, with its extreme hardships, made humanity alter its tendency to waste materials.

Sometimes Joanna wondered why there was such an urge among the Clans to reclaim Terra. Even if the first Clan to set foot victoriously on Terra would have the honor of becoming the ilClan, the Clan commanding all the other seventeen Clans, what would they be reclaiming? Terra held little allure for her, yet she knew it was the aim of the biggest military operation the Clans had ever undertaken—the invasion of the Inner Sphere.

After Horse had called them coffin-mates, she had an unwelcome image of the two of them being put to their final rest in side-by-side coffins, lids slipping open, skeletal hands reaching for each other and missing, winding up drooping from skeletal wrists. A bad way for a warrior to end. Her image of a good death was to go out in flames in the cockpit of her 'Mech, leaving in her wake about a hundred other smashed and burning 'Mechs.

Horse and Joanna had served together for many years, through many arguments. Somehow the arguing had brought them closer, but not too close. There had never been a sexual moment between them. Joanna, impatient when the need was upon her, generally chose the closest available male warrior, but she had never chosen Horse. He had never selected her, either, though she had not noticed him going off with anyone else. His apparent celibacy may have been governed by his caste. As a freeborn he could not easily approach a trueborn for the purpose of coupling, so his choices would have been limited to the few freeborns among the Falcon Guards or to members of the lower castes. Joanna, for her part, could not even bear to touch a member of any caste below warriors.

"You know, Horse, I always thought of you as a low freeborn bastard, but you are worse than that—you are beneath the lowliest of the low, scummier than dirty oil trapped in a 'Mech joint, lousier than—"

"Joanna, I get the point. This does not work anymore, this more trueborn than thou attitude."

"Well, of course I am more trueborn than you, lousy freebirth."

Horse stayed silent, gnawing on his lip, a gnawing that showed even under the abundant growth of hair on his face. Joanna squinted at him through steel-gray eyes. He simply stared back at her. She could only imagine what he saw when he looked at her. Freeborn warriors resembled trueborns in one way: both hated signs of age, in themselves and in others.

The signs of age were increasing for Joanna. She was already past the time when warriors got sent off to the trash heap of some solahma unit. She had just barely missed that fate six months back, when her orders to return to the homeworlds had been revoked at the last instant.

Clan warriors did not really expect to grow old. A true warrior did not fear death, but sought it by trying to go out in a blaze of glory on the battlefield. Those who did not die soon enough on the field battled a shame that grew with every passing year. Joanna had endured slurs about her age and her survival, snide implications that her skills were over-rated. Yet even her enemies had to admit that there were few warriors who rushed into battle so recklessly, who slew their quarry with so much ferocity. Her defeat of Natasha Kerensky of the Wolves, achieved by incinerating the fabled Black Widow in the cockpit of her 'Mech, was already legendary. It was for killing the Black Widow that Joanna had won the reprieve that let her remain here with the Falcon Guards. She had even won some lines in *The Remembrance*.

It was now rumored that she was so hated by Clan Wolf that many Wolf warriors had vowed to seek her out and destroy her the next time the two Clans met in battle. But that did not matter to Joanna. What had she to fear from the Wolves, or from death? What mattered was that killing the Black Widow had redeemed her from the shame of being shuffled back to the homeworlds as a canister nanny. Star Colonel Ravill Pryde was the one who'd given the order, stating that she was "past her prime." Joanna let out a low growl at the thought.

Horse did not often look directly at Joanna. When he did, as now, Joanna was sure that the lines radiating around her eyes and creasing her forehead were obvious, particularly in this bright sunlight. When she looked in a mirror, which wasn't often, she noticed the tight thin line her mouth had become, the sallow valleys in her cheeks, the mottled leatheriness of her skin, the half-hidden age-lines of her neck. A few warriors dyed their hair, as if to put off oncoming age, but Joanna could not abide such fraud. Her dark hair was now streaked with wide bands of gray.

Again, Joanna sighed and looked off into the distance, past the golden aspen on the hilltop and down into the valley. She watched where techs worked diligently on 'Mechs damaged in the brutal fighting on Coventry. By order of the Khan they had to work fast, so that the Jade Falcons could pull out in just three days. With the abandonment of Coventry and the expanse of repair (fallen 'Mechs looking like corpses, techs scrambling around them like insects), Joanna's description of Coventry as a hellhole seemed apt. The scene below even had specific hellish elements in it. Fires burned and sparks flew from 'Mech surfaces. Some fallen 'Mechs lay in distorted positions, like suffering sinners, with the repair crews in the role of minor spirits whose job was to torment them. Some techs roamed the battlefield, searching and supervising, discovering new ways to punish the sinners. Those who were not working on damaged BattleMechs were on salvage duty, making sure that usable parts of unusable 'Mechs were not being wasted.

Studying the scene, Joanna felt a familiar rage. Two days ago she, along with the rest of the Jade Falcon warriors on this planet, had been primed for battle against fresh troops arriving from the Inner Sphere. After the Jade Falcons lost half their numbers in the Refusal War against the Wolves, Khan Marthe Pryde had needed to prove to the rest of the Clans that the Falcons were as fierce and potent as ever. Otherwise, they risked Absorption by a stronger Clan.

Led by Marthe, the Falcons had thrust boldly into the Lyran Alliance, in just six weeks cutting a path across many worlds. But they did not try to hold any of those planets. All they wanted was to reach their target—the planet Coventry, which lay almost on top of the truce line.

In early March, they struck, first hitting Port St. William, Coventry's principal city. They took the city, then went on to defeat the planet's defenders in nearly simultaneous battles occurring at other key locations. Some of the most desperate, savage, and bloody fighting of the campaign occurred at the Coventry Metal Works, the single most valuable prize on the planet. Gyrfalcon Eyrie Cluster won the battle, but sustained serious casualties while Coventry's defenders withdrew to the hinterlands.

Joanna knew that Gyrfalcon Eyrie was one of five unblooded Clusters Marthe Pryde had poured into the conflict. It was, of course, not the way of the Clans to place untested warriors among the ranks, much less send them into combat. But Joanna thought she understood what Marthe was up to. How else could the Falcons be brought back up to strength without waiting ten or fifteen years for enough young cadets to come of age?

The Inner Sphere had dredged up reinforcements, including the hated Wolf's Dragoons—Clan traitors every one of them. By the end of May, the Falcons had fought them to the wall. The Coventry defenders were on the run, and Joanna was sure the Falcon Guards would be part of the final push to clean them up. But then Khan Marthe had done the unthinkable. She had allowed *safcon* to newly arriving Inner Sphere reinforcements—this time headed up by that cocky little Victor Steiner-Davion.

Safcon allowed Davion's force to land on Coventry's surface and join the planet's nearly defeated defenders without any sort of Clan retaliation. They had achieved this privilege because their leaders had invoked a revered Clan custom by which one Clan honored an enemy with safe passage onto the battlefield.

Joanna's eyes narrowed as she thought about it for the hundredth time. *How could Inner Sphere surats even know about the custom?* Perhaps Marthe had agreed to *safcon* because it had been invoked by Anastasius Focht, commander of the Com Guards and victor of the bloody battle of Tukkayid. Marthe was first and foremost a traditionalist. Honor was everything to her. *But was it necessary to be honorable with filth so low they do not deserve to live?* Joanna picked up the biggest rock within reach and flung it with a grunt.

What happened next was even worse, at least according to Joanna. Marthe had committed everything she had to the battle, and the newly arrived force made the two sides evenly matched. Any battle victory would be narrow, with serious losses on both sides. Marthe should have fought to the last Falcon, that was the way of the Clans.

But two days ago, she had met with the Inner Sphere commanders and accepted their offer of *hegira*! To Joanna this was even more shocking than the granting of *safcon*.

Hegira was another Clan custom, very much like the other side of *safcon*. By means of *hegira*, a victorious Clan could permit a respected enemy to withdraw from the battlefield with honor. It was rarely invoked among the Clans, for whom a fight to the last 'Mech was more venerable, and it had never been used before by any force that was not Clan. Horse had told Joanna that the word *hegira* came from ancient Terra, where it stood for some kind of flight. Flight for the enemy, Joanna assumed.

"Hegira!" she muttered.

"Not this again." Horse groaned and rolled away from Joanna, ending up on his stomach a few steps away, perusing the valley below. "You know as well as I do that it was the right decision."

She knew he was right but would never admit it. The official version of the incident was that Marthe Pryde saw no gain in the Falcons exhausting their ranks yet one more time. Coventry was, after all, a minor world on the truce line. And Marthe had already done what she came for. The Inner Sphere commanders could not know it, but her whole reason for attacking Coventry was to show the other Clans that the Jade Falcons were undaunted, and to blood scores of untried warriors.

At that she had succeeded. The Falcons were numerous and strong again.

Joanna had heard other rumors about why Marthe had accepted an end to the fight. It was said that that their speedy withdrawal from Coventry was necessary to meet a threat by Vlad of the Wolves against six Jade Falcon worlds in the Occupation Zone. Perhaps Marthe had been forced to choose between the disgrace of withdrawing from Coventry and the disgrace of losing six hard-won worlds to the Wolves. That would be a bitter choice, and Joanna knew it.

Joanna also knew that Marthe was the last person to ever run from a fight. The decision must have cost her dearly.

There had to be a spy somewhere, Joanna thought. It was the only way the Inner Sphere *surats* could know of these time-honored Clan ways. *No Jade Falcon would ever pass privileged information to the enemy. The traitor had to come from some other clan. The Wolves, maybe.*

Joanna, like most Jade Falcons, hated the Wolves. But even those dogs would never be so treacherous. Maybe the traitor was that former Wolf Khan, Phelan Kell. He was Inner Sphere in the first place, a lousy freebirth who had somehow been allowed status as a bloodnamed warrior within Clan Wolf.

No matter what the reasons, Joanna was enraged at the acceptance of *hegira,* enraged that the Falcon Guards had lost the chance to pay the Inner Sphere back for Tukayyid. It was in that desperate battle that Aidan Pryde had given his life and become a Clan legend. His genes had been accepted into the breeding pool early because his valiant acts had brought such honor to his unit, the Falcon Guards. Tukayyid was also where the fifteen-year truce had been forced down the throats of the Clans.

Joanna believed that *hegira* dishonored the memory of Aidan Pryde—the Khan's sibkin, after all. Joanna had been their cadet falconer back on Ironhold, and she had driven her charges mercilessly. Aidan Pryde had gone on to become the hero of Tukayyid and Marthe was now Khan of the Jade Falcons. They had been making history those many years ago, but no one had dreamed of it then.

Perhaps Joanna should not have been so surprised at what had happened here on Coventry. Deviousness and intrigue seemed to be infecting the Clans like a plague. Hadn't she been forced to endure the assignment of playing spy not so many months ago? If not for that mission, in which she had uncovered a hateful conspiracy among the scientists of all the Clans, she would probably be sitting on Ironhold right now holding the hands of a bunch of vat babies.

Joanna sighed for a third time, drawing a raised eyebrow from Horse. Now it was her turn to ignore him. She squinted off toward the bay, the brightness of the day hurting her tired eyes. The Falcon Guards had mostly been kept out of the fight here on Coventry. They'd been kept back at the staging area, while unblooded troops were continually poured into the thick of it. The arrival of Victor Davion and his reinforcements would surely have brought the Falcon Guards into the action. Except for the cursed *hegira*!

Joanna did not understand what was happening to the way of the Clans. She was seeing and hearing things that seemed to say that the rot was corrupting even the highest levels. Who else was to blame for creating the warriors she thought of as "the new breed," arrogant youngsters who never let up asserting their superiority over veteran warriors? Thinking about it nearly spiked her anger off the heat scale.

It was not so much their arrogance that bothered her— Jade Falcon warriors were *supposed* to be arrogant. What she despised was the way they set themselves apart from other warriors. Even more, she hated the hero worship they gave to the Falcon Guard commander, Ravill Pryde. Joanna thought the new breed much too cultish, especially with their attitude that the old warriors were outdated. And she despised Ravill Pryde for encouraging the division in the ranks with his obvious approval of the new breed.

Still, she would accept a new breeder before she would accept one of the sibbies, the name given to warriors who had been rushed from their sibkos directly into battle even before completing their cadet training. These half-formed creatures were not *real* warriors. To Joanna, the sibbies' arrogance was even less earned than that of the new breed.

And speak of the devil, she thought. Some sibbies had gathered at the foot of the hill, talking eagerly among themselves. That was one of their nauseating characteristics, eagerness. The group below probably saw themselves as seasoned warriors, merely because they had survived the bitter fighting on Coventry. She could see it in their easy manner and smug expressions. Who were they to have fought battles that should have gone to seasoned warriors like the Falcon Guards?

"*Eyasses,*" Joanna spat.

Now it was Horse's turn to sigh. "Calm down, Joanna." This was a conversation they'd had many times before. Horse insisted that the sibbies had served the Clan well, often bravely, in the brutal battles of Coventry, despite their lack of experience. Joanna thought it insulting even to use the term *warriors* for sibbies. It was wrong to rush unfinished cadets into battle, no matter how depleted the Jade Falcon ranks.

The more she thought about it, the more her anger spiked into the red. As she watched the cheerful sibbies below, her rage became unendurable and had to be released. Sometimes she attacked rooms of furniture or ripped branches off trees and punished them. This time, though, chairs and branches would not be enough. She needed to kick and punch and throw some real people. She needed to see blood on her freshly bruised knuckles.

Abruptly, she leapt up and started down the hill.

"Where are you going?" shouted Horse, sitting up, caught off-guard.

"I want to bash some sibbie heads."

"Joanna, do not be an—"

His insult was drowned out by the sound of rocks being kicked up as she ran so she would not have to hear him.

2

Port St. William
Coventry
Coventry Province, Lyran Alliance
18 June 3058

The sibbies were now moving away from her, walking in the direction of a severely damaged *Night Gyr*. One of the sibbies pointed toward the 'Mech, while another made a clearly disparaging gesture. What was being disparaged was not clear.

On the *Night Gyr,* a pair of techs were busily scavenging for usable parts. Joanna, in true warrior fashion, focused primarily on the sibbies, but also took in what the techs were doing with welding tools and an odd clamp-like tool known as the Peeler. The Peeler was a monstrous instrument, something like a pliers with exceptionally sharp teeth, used to peel off large sections of armor and metal from a 'Mech surface. It pulled off thick layers with minimal guidance from the tech operating it and could be recalibrated to peel off thin strips as well.

Joanna did not like this new type of 'Mech, the *Night Gyr.* It was too fancy for its own good. Equipped with the new laser-based heat sink technology that kept it going longer during a battle, it also had a distracting aura of light around it during night combat as laserlight bounced off cockpit viewports and other openings. In action it looked more like a walking monument than a BattleMech.

This particular *Night Gyr* had apparently seen some heavy battle here on Coventry. It was scarred, dented, twisted, and generally unfunctional. Good salvage, good riddance, she thought.

Joanna picked up her pace as she closed in on the sibbies. She tried to form a plan of attack that would not look like picking a fight. Cantankerous as Jade Falcons were, the idea of officers picking fights with subordinates was officially frowned upon. Some commanders might discreetly approve, but among them would never be the stiff-backed, by-the-book Star Colonel Ravill Pryde. She hated having to think so sneakily. It was too much like Pryde and his new breed. She *wanted* to smash a few sibbie heads, and that was that.

Near the bottom of the hill she spotted one of the small but heavy black rocks so common on Coventry. Picking it up, she tested it for weight and balance. It was said that black rocks rained onto Coventry during thick, swirling storms. As far as Joanna knew, this was just country superstition and not an observed phenomenon.

I do not know any of this bunch, she thought as she drew near the sibbies. *None of them are Falcon Guards, that's for sure. Good. Now I can get in trouble with their Star Commanders. Nothing like a little boil in the pot. Anyway, trouble clears my head, always has.*

"Hey, you!" she shouted.

The half-dozen sibbies all seemed to whirl around at once. Their faces copied each other's surprise. A couple of them stepped forward and eyed her up and down.

These stravags *look too clean.* Joanna could only imagine what they thought as they looked at her. Grooming was never one of her strong points. She had better things to think about.

She tossed the rock from hand to hand.

"What is it, Star Commander?" said the warrior on the right, a muscular young man with a face so childlike it reminded her of the fresh young cadets she used to train back on Ironhold. The only catch was, these *stravags* had left training before it was done, much less fought a Trial of Position. This sibbie even looked bizarre, since he had clearly ripped off his sleeves to show off his thick arms.

He looks like a baby in an overgrown body.

"No freebirths allowed in a repair zone," she taunted. "Too dangerous, *quaiff*?"

The other warrior in front, a woman with a long plait of blonde hair hanging almost to her waist, stepped forward and growled in a voice so low it was almost bass, "How dare you call us freebirths? Do you see the insignia? We are trueborn!"

This one really looks ridiculous. What is that braided long hair, some kind of sibbie fad? And she has on just enough uniform to satisfy battlezone dress codes. She looks disgusting, with that low neckline. How dare she show even the beginning of her breasts? Does she not know that warriors believe exhibitionism is foul?

Since trueborns were genetically engineered and birthed from vats, then nurtured by various devices that carefully measured their nutrition intake, some Jade Falcons believed that breasts were unnecessary and should be eliminated in genetically engineered female warriors. Clan warriors were neither nursed by females nor did one ever nurse a child herself. The argument given to this view was that not all trueborn warriors succeeded. Many failed training and later became freebirth mothers in their new lives. Even though it was difficult to overcome their natural revulsion, some of them did nurse their children. It struck Joanna that Peri, birthmother of freeborn Mech-Warrior Diana, must have suckled her, and the thought brought on a faint nauseous pain at the pit of her stomach.

As if reading Joanna's thoughts on the matter, the female sibbie rubbed the exposed part of her neckline. Joanna tossed the rock from her right hand to her left so hard it stung the palm of her hand.

"You are not warriors," Joanna shouted, "only half-warrior—and therefore the same as freebirth by my accounting. Later you will have the chance of claiming your trueborn heritage, when you succeed in proper Trials. You wish to argue with that?"

The woman took another step forward. "I do. I do wish to argue, Star Commander. I know who you are, and I know you to be an old woman. I can see the age in your face and it sickens me!"

Joanna wanted to lunge at the woman immediately, but she knew she would be at fault. By Jade Falcon custom, the sibbie woman was stating an obvious fact and had every right to say what she had. Were their roles reversed, Joanna might have said something similar to an ancient version of this upstart. This thought lessened her rage, and she had to struggle to maintain it. Fortunately, she was an expert at rage and, though it seemed illogical, she could even control its surges and falls. Horse had once accused Joanna of being the ilKhan of rage.

"Freebirth scum like you have no right to judge me!" Joanna shouted.

The woman continued toward her, but the muscular warrior rushed over and held her back. She struggled fiercely within his grasp. The man whispered something in her ear and she stopped. He let her go and she retreated toward the others at a gesture from him, not once taking her eyes off Joanna.

The man addressed Joanna. "We do not wish to do battle with you, Star Commander Joanna. As Carola stated, we know who you are, and we admire your defeat of the despised Wolf Khan, Natasha Kerensky. You are a hero to us, and we do not wish to battle our heroes, *quiaff*?"

How dare he be polite? How dare he show respect? Using the quiaff is despicable. It forces me to reply. If I do not reply, I will be at a disadvantage. I do not like that. I would rather just ram a knife into his throat.

"Aff," she muttered reluctantly.

The man nodded. "We are in this work area because we know that we are, as you say, still unformed. We believe we can learn from observing these techs working on our 'Mechs. We will become better warriors for it. We should like to remain in the work area, with your permission, of course."

This one turns my stomach. He is too well-mannered for his own good.

"What is your name, sibbie?"

"I am Shield."

As she stared into his cold eyes—cold eyes in a child's face—she realized that Shield was a good name for him. Underneath the shield of his politeness was a dangerous sibbie.

"You were not spilled from the vat with the name Shield assigned to you, I suspect, *quiaff*?"

He shook his head. "Neg. My given name was Shaw,

but I received the name Shield when I began cadet training, and I have taken it as my own. Shaw did not seem a warrior name to me."

"I am sure other warriors have borne it with honor, sibbie."

There was a ripple of annoyance among the group, but it was clear they deferred to Shield in most matters.

This child with the cold eyes might be a fine leader someday. Still, all this talk is not doing anything to give me a good fight.

Joanna rubbed the rock harshly against the skin of her hand. If she examined her skin, she knew she would find it raw and peeling.

"If it pleases the Star Commander, you may call me Shaw."

"I do not have to call you anything but sibbie scum, freebirth!"

"Scum, if that is the way a superior officer wishes to view us, but never freebirth!"

Joanna nearly smiled. *I have done it, riled this calm bastard. I can do more.*

"Scum *and* freebirth, if I wish it."

"I challenge your right to malign us."

Joanna felt almost joyful, a rare feeling for her.

"You would like a Circle of Equals, scum?"

"Aye!"

"I like to make children happy. What area shall we designate for the—"

"Right here, old woman."

Shield sprang at Joanna, who was quite ready for the move, who had longed for it. She did not even try to dodge him in order to make a calculated blow. Instead, she accepted him almost like a lover and allowed him to put his surprisingly powerful arms around her and push her backward onto the ground. He landed on her chest. It felt as if the pressure might have cracked a rib. The pain was sharp—and welcome.

She did not move within his grasp and looked up at him stoically. He was clearly puzzled and, with puzzlement, came a release of pressure that Joanna used to her advantage. She tightly gripped the rock, now in her right hand, and brought it up forcefully against the side of Shield's head. At the same time she kneed him in the crotch, for a moment glad of at least one physical difference between female and male warriors.

Both actions loosened Shield's grip further, and she was able to squirm sideways. She cast him off her body, but instead of jumping to her feet, she rolled toward Shield. Her right arm high, she slammed the rock even more forcefully against his cheek. She heard something crack beneath her blow and smiled. Shield had initiated the kind of fight she wanted—one where, according to all warrior tradition, she could punish her adversary as severely as she knew how. And, more than most, Joanna knew how.

Viewing the damage she had already caused, her rage abruptly subsided. From now on, she could function on warrior instinct. The fight no longer came from her desperate need; it was merely exercise.

Shield scrambled to his feet. His eyes were dazed. Apparently, though, his will was not affected. He managed a fairly weak kick against Joanna's side, and she laughed at him in response. Getting to her own feet, she stood calmly, not even egging Shield on. She did not have to. He vaulted toward her. She went into a sudden crouch, catching his stomach with her shoulder, then rose and flipped him past her. He landed on his back. In recoil, his head went upward, then down so quickly that it hit the ground hard.

Joanna decided to show him the kind of fierce warrior assault that an *old woman* could muster. She leaned down, picked Shield up by the collar, and yanked him to his feet. He had some trouble planting his feet and she had to keep holding him up. She ran forward with him, dragging him by the collar toward the *Night Gyr*. His feet finally managed a kind of drunken stumbling run.

When she reached the 'Mech, she gave Shield one powerful wrench and slammed him against it, so hard that the *Night Gyr* rocked a bit from the blow. Up above them, the tech holding the Peeler, who had been distracted by the fight below and come to the edge of the work area, lurched sideways, almost off the 'Mech. He regained his footing with obvious difficulty.

Joanna released the sibbie warrior, expecting to see him slide down the side of the 'Mech, unconscious. Instead, his eyes displayed a rage that mirrored her own. For a moment Joanna felt an absurd bond with this Shield.

He pushed himself away from the *Night Gyr* and at Joanna. She was not prepared for the sudden counter-attack, and he caught her with a strong roundhouse right to her jaw. The force of the blow was increased by the momentum of his rush at her. For a moment it dazed her, but before he could land another blow, she yelled with a voice that could rattle the armor off most of the 'Mechs in the valley and pushed Shield back against the *Night Gyr*'s side. The tech with the Peeler, who had barely regained his footing a moment ago, slipped sideways, off the 'Mech. As he fell, he lost control of the powerful tool and it fell straight down, right at Shield, who was shaking his head, trying to clear it. Joanna saw the falling Peeler and tried to leap forward to push Shield out of the way, but she was too late. It landed, heavy end first, on top of his head. Next to her, the tech landed a split-second later, just missing hitting Joanna by millimeters.

Joanna grabbed for the tool as Shield fell, trying to knock it aside. The end that resembled a large pliers locked onto the skin of Shield's forehead and began to peel it, raggedly, away.

3

About two hours after the debacle of Joanna's fight with the sibbies, Horse was summoned to the office of the Khan. As the guards posted at the door let him pass, he readied his version of what happened.

Marthe Pryde was seated at her desk as he entered and motioned for him to take a seat. Jade Falcon warriors usually paid scant attention to their own or anyone else's appearance, but Horse could not help but be affected by Marthe's presence. She was tall and striking, the pale skin of her face framed by long black hair. Even more remarkable was the way every part of her lithe body conveyed her power and intelligence. She got up from her chair and walked around to the front of her desk, surveying him with her trademark cool gaze.

"I have something of great importance to discuss with you, Horse," she said, sitting down on the edge of the desk.

Horse nodded. "Yes, my Khan, I am very aware of the seriousness of the incident."

Marthe smiled, then tried to suppress it. "No, it is not about Joanna, although that incident is troublesome in its own way. I have all the information I need about Joanna. What I wish to discuss with you is even more important."

Marthe stood and walked with measured steps back to her seat. She sat down and gazed at Horse for a moment, as if making some final assessment. "Nothing we say to one another here and now must ever leave this room, Star Commander."

Horse nodded, wondering what this could possibly be about. "As you say, my Khan."

Her tone was somber. "I believe the Clans have made a grave mistake in this invasion, one for which we could not have prepared. No, do not interrupt. With our Omni-Mechs and our superior warriors, we were able to make gigantic inroads with the first thrust of the invasion. But each time we made a deeper incursion, each time we lost 'Mechs and warriors in battle, we stretched our ranks thinner. Already far from the homeworlds, we weakened ourselves by gaining territory and removing ourselves further. It is a fairly constant problem in waging a war, particularly when you are the invading army. The damnable truce has weakened us even more, sapping our energies, leading us into wasteful skirmishes, spreading us thin."

She gazed distantly behind him, as though seeing something that lay beyond this time and place. "I believe that the Inner Sphere is up to something, though I have no evidence, no intelligence reports to justify my suspicions. I cannot help but think there is a major conflict coming and that, if we are not ready, we will lose it. The whole Clan invasion will go for naught."

Horse was startled by her words, but did not interrupt.

"I am sure the Inner Sphere leaders are as frustrated with this truce as we are. And I have surely provoked them here on Coventry. For awhile the Lyrans must have thought I was going to try to take their precious capitol of Tharkad." She laughed to herself and shook her head. "They will do *something,* but I do not know what. Perhaps they will retaliate here in their territory. Perhaps they even have grandiose dreams of driving us away, of chasing us to our homeworlds and defeating us there. I sense all this, but I cannot prove it. I have spoken of this in the recent meeting of the Grand Council and proposed that we deploy more trueborn warrior units in defense of the homeworlds."

Horse shook his head in disbelief. "The homeworlds?" he said. "They are not vulnerable."

Marthe's eyes were on him now. "Oh, but they are. I know, I know. They are light years away and it would take an Inner Sphere attack force many months to reach the Kerensky Cluster, even if they did know the route and could mount a large enough force without being detected. In theory, no invading force should even be able to find the homeworlds. The route back is not kept in any single location. JumpShips traveling to and from the Inner Sphere carry only a portion of the map and must dump one segment in order to obtain the next. It is one of our greatest secrets.

"But think about it, Horse." Marthe rested her forearms on her desk and leaned forward. "We Clansmen are shrewd and strong, but the way of the Clan is so different from that of the Inner Sphere that we cannot imagine the extent and depth of their perfidy. I have urged more lines of defense for the homeworlds, but the other Khans have scoffed. Worse, who is defending them now? I will tell you. The dregs of our warrior units are the sole defenders of many Clan planets. Solahmas. Maimed warriors. Disgraced warriors. Warriors who have made enemies, or should I say, political misjudgments."

Horse nodded. "Just before he was killed, Aidan Pryde warned of grave changes occurring within our ranks. He said we were becoming too devious, too much like the Inner Sphere."

"Yes." Marthe leaned back in her chair, slapping her long fingers on the desk. "It nauseates me to even speak of our noble people in the same breath with the barbarians of the Inner Sphere. But perhaps it is not too late. Aidan was right, and he would have taken action. As I shall. And you, Horse, will be among my first lines of attack."

He looked at her with as much admiration as respect. She was as forceful as any of her line. Who could refuse her? She was Marthe Pryde, one of the finest warriors the Falcons had ever produced. And now she stood at their head, highest among them. It was she who had brought the Jade Falcons here to Coventry to prove that the Falcons were still a force to be reckoned with, and she had blooded several galaxies of young warriors in one stroke. Freebirth, he was. Arrogant and sarcastic, he was. But he was above all a Jade Falcon warrior and she was his Khan.

"I am asking you to make a great sacrifice, Horse. You must leave the occupation zone and return to the homeworlds."

His protests sputtered out of him. "I cannot do that! I wish never to return there. As a warrior, even a freeborn one, my place is here. Back in the homeworlds, I would—"

Marthe held up her hand. "Horse, I am not asking you to remain there. I am merely asking you to travel there—on a mission."

"A mission?" Horse's tone was doubtful.

She straightened in her chair. "I am soon to return to Strana Mechty, where the Grand Council will convene to elect a new ilKhan—in the right way, in the Grand Chamber on Strana Mechty, the only lawful place for such a conclave." Horse knew that Strana Mechty was a special place among the homeworlds, one shared by all the Clans. The Hall of the Khans was there, as was the master genetic repository.

"I am not sure I follow your meaning. What am I to do there?" he asked.

"What I cannot," Marthe said. "I need you to be my eyes and ears in places where I cannot go unobserved."

To Horse this sounded suspiciously like spying, and yet he knew that Marthe Pryde was too much a traditionalist to sanction such activity.

When she spoke again, it was almost as though she had read his mind. "I must emulate the jade falcon and soar silently until it is time for my swift descent and attack. And in my silence, I must ready myself. It has become necessary for me to consider measures I would not normally condone. But, then, extraordinary times require extraordinary measures. I am learning that, Horse." She gave a short, bitter laugh. "And that is why I am ordering you to assemble an elite freeborn unit, a Trinary. You will be in command, with Star Captain rank." She stopped. "You are smiling. Why?"

"Nothing much. Those words sound very strange. Elite and freeborn thrown together in the same sentence."

Marthe merely nodded. "Extraordinary times . . ." she echoed. "I am not yet sure how I will deploy your new Trinary, Horse. But I will be your only source for orders. I am assigning you because you have proven yourself a worthy warrior, freeborn or otherwise. And I also require someone who can take the initiative and think independently. It may not always be possible for me to give you direct and specific orders." She leaned in toward him with great intensity. "Further, I want you to swear complete fidelity to me, no matter what happens. That is important. It may be hard for you, too hard. If what I ask and what the Clan demands differ, you will do what I ask—without question. Can you do that, Horse?"

Horse could not speak for a moment. He merely stared at Marthe Pryde as the import of her words sank in.

"I can do that," he finally said.

Marthe smiled slightly and nodded her head. "I am glad you stopped to think about it first. What I am asking of you is not easy. I know that. But what I ask is clear, *quiaff*?"

"Aff, my Khan. You are perhaps the only one to whom I can swear complete fealty, as I once did with Aidan Pryde."

"Good. It is done then. For all intents and purposes, the oath is taken and our bond is done. No other bond may come between us, until I release you from this one, understood?"

"Seyla," Horse said. It was the most solemn oath a Clansman could utter.

"Seyla," Marthe echoed softly. Then she rose from the desk and took Horse's hand, performing the Jade Falcon handshake that signified a bond of honor. At that moment, Horse felt a surge of pride that his Khan would place so much trust in him.

Marthe Pryde dropped his hand suddenly. She held her arm stiffly as if she did not want to show her disgust at exchanging a loyalty vow with a freeborn or her greater aversion at actually touching him to seal the vow.

"What we have said and done, and what more we will say and do, must remain sealed in our hearts, never to be repeated beyond the walls of this room, *quiaff*?"

"Aff, my Khan."

"Good. In a few days, you and your Trinary will begin the long journey home. I will be traveling via command circuit, and will be on Strana Mechty long before you reach the homeworlds."

Horse hesitated. "So the destination of my new unit is Strana Mechty?"

"Eventually. But first I want you to make one stop, on the planet Huntress."

Horse stared at Khan Marthe, momentarily confused. "The Smoke Jaguar homeworld?"

"Aye, the Smoke Jaguars claim all but one minor bit of that planet. The Jade Falcons have a presence there as well—a small station in a mountainous region on the planet's main continent. The station itself is mainly devoted to research and was originally a gift from ilKhan Leo Showers. It is so well protected by the high mountains that the Smoke Jaguars have never been able to attack it successfully. And the Falcon force there is too small to attack them, so we tend to cooperate rather than fight them. UnClanlike, but necessary. The station is called Falcon Eyrie. I am told that we keep a number of jade falcons there, for study. But that is not the only scientific research going on." Her blue eyes momentarily darkened.

"What force defends it?" asked Horse.

"Falcon Eyrie's warrior personnel is limited to an honor guard, plus a support defensive Binary composed of solahma warriors. The secrecy of the station's work is protected by Huntress's geographical circumstances."

Marthe stood up as she talked and went to open a window. The air that rushed into the room, with its odors of lubricants, welding, and fire, was indeed acrid. Horse liked it. It was the smell of BattleMechs.

She continued from the window. "What is not known about Falcon Eyrie is that it is a developmental research station. There is a Brian Cache there, one that the Smoke Jags would not be pleased with. In it are a Star of LAMs."

"LAMs?"

"Land-Air 'Mechs. An old Star League design for what are basically light 'Mechs that can change into aircraft when needed. General Kerensky brought some with him during the first Exodus, but they have never proved worthy for Clan combat. They still show up occasionally in the Inner Sphere, and two types, *Stingers* and *Phoenix Hawks*, were apparently used in the battle for Tukayyid. Our engineers became interested in LAMs some time back. Prototypes were built and tested, some with interesting results—not always successful, but interesting.

"This is where you come in, Horse." Marthe walked back to her chair and sat down in it. "The scientists of Falcon Eyrie have been refining the LAM concept and claim they have come up with potentially useful attack models. But they are like all those of the scientist caste, typically close-mouthed about their discoveries. The spec sheets they have supplied are intriguing but inconclusive. Supposedly, their experimental LAMs are an improvement over anything we have seen in the Inner Sphere.

"I want you to go first to Falcon Eyrie to learn exactly what is going on there and to evaluate it. If the new LAMs are actually an improvement over the useless old ones, I want to know of it. Inspect the things and see if you can learn what the scientists may be holding back." She paused and measured her words carefully. "The scientists always hold something back. And I have reason to have grave suspicions about them. Reasons to believe they may be overstepping the bounds of their caste."

Horse stared at her in confusion, waiting for her to explain. She obviously had no intention of doing so.

"One more thing," Marthe continued in a brisk tone, "and this also is for your ears only. Falcon Eyrie has, until now, had little strategic value to our Clan. It has been maintained purely as a research arm and to annoy the Smoke Jaguars. But our Clans must stop fighting among themselves if we are ever going to conquer the Inner Sphere. I need to know whether we should continue to maintain Falcon Eyrie or abandon it."

Again, Horse felt a flush of discomfort at the idea of spying. Marthe fixed him with her unsettling gaze and said, "I sense your discomfort, Horse. But I chose you because I can ask you to do things I could never ask of a trueborn warrior."

Horse could not resist one of his snorts of anger, an equine sound that was the reason for his name. His real name was so rarely used as to be all but forgotten. No one had addressed him with it since his training days as a freeborn warrior on Ironhold. It was an irony of this moment that his freeborn unit had trained at the same time as Marthe's sibko, and he and some of his comrades had served as their opponents in training exercises. When

Aidan Pryde had resumed his warrior training disguised as a freeborn, it was as a member of Horse's unit. They had won their Trials of Position together, and Marthe Pryde had been one of the warriors they had defeated.

Horse met Marthe's steady stare and then drew himself up, despite the sting to this honor. "I have sworn fealty and would swear it again, no matter what task you command. I will serve, my Khan."

Marthe nodded sharply. "You are dismissed, Horse."

He gave the Falcon salute, then paused just as he was turning to leave. "To get rid of *surats*, you must think like a *surat*."

Marthe Pryde gave a hard laugh. "Aye, Star Captain. And do not forget. I am counting on you." She returned his salute.

Horse did leave the room then, feeling her still watching him even as he went out and shut the door behind him.

= 4 =

Turkina Keshik Headquarters
Port St. William, Coventry
Coventry Province, Lyran Alliance
18 June 3058

Four hours had passed since the death of Shield, and the ensuing investigation was about to conclude here in the field headquarters of Khan Marthe Pryde.

"Well, Star Commander Joanna, you have created quite a mess this time," Marthe said as she came around the desk toward her battle-scarred warrior, who was standing at attention. Her very battle-scarred warrior, Marthe noted. Joanna had seemed old years ago when she had been Marthe's training falconer back at Crash Camp on Ironhold. Everything that had seemed old about her then was etched even deeper into her skin and joined by more signs of age.

Marthe exchanged glances with the man standing behind Joanna. Star Colonel Ravill Pryde was an officer of Marthe's own bloodline and Joanna's commanding officer in the Falcon Guards. Both women knew that he also detested Joanna.

Marthe suspected that Ravill Pryde resented the history she and Joanna shared. He belonged to what some of the older warriors called the new breed. What was more, he was a new breeder who had come to high command at a younger age even than most warriors. But if anyone doubted the stuff he was made of, he had proved himself in the Refusal War against the Wolves. On Twycross, in the same battle in which Joanna had bested Natasha Kerensky.

Marthe knew that Ravill Pryde had been obsessed with removing Joanna from his command. He had recently ordered her to return to the homeworlds, and then been forced to eat crow when the order was revoked as a reward for Joanna's work at Dogg Station.

Marthe Pryde also knew that Joanna was clearly at fault in the unnecessary death of the sibko warrior, Shaw. Joanna had shown equally poor judgment when she maimed Carola, the warrior who had attacked her in response to her sibmate's death. Carola had apparently leapt onto Joanna's back, been thrown off, and then crippled when the furious Joanna had flung the Peeler at her. Catching Carola in the torso with its heavy end, it had done serious injury.

Carola was in critical condition, and Marthe hoped the medtechs could put her back together enough that she would not lose her rank as a warrior. Any kind of waste was abhorrent to the Clans, especially to the Jade Falcons. Besides, Marthe could not afford to lose warriors for petty cause. Not after all she and the Falcons had just been through.

She folded her arms across her chest and suppressed a sigh. Seeing Joanna's jaw set in its usual arrogant thrust told her that this would not be easy. The logical thing to do about Joanna was to punish her severely for the wasteful killing. Shaw's death was especially grievous in light of the ban on duels to the death between Jade Falcons. One of the reasons Marthe had attacked Coventry so ferociously was the need to blood young warriors to rebuild the ranks of the Falcons. Losing warriors to infighting was almost unforgivable.

But Joanna had won glory in her time, including lines in *The Remembrance*. Marthe did not want to bring shame on the Falcons by humiliating a hero.

"You wish to explain yourself, *quiaff*?" Ravill Pryde said, surliness in his voice.

Marthe saw Joanna struggle to hold her temper. Knowing Joanna, this was perhaps even more heroic than some of her battlefield exploits.

"My Khan," Joanna said, refusing to address Ravill Pryde, "I regret the death of a potentially valuable Jade Falcon warrior and am sorry for my part in it."

Marthe's eyebrows raised, surprised to hear Joanna come that near to an apology.

"However," Joanna continued, "the fight was provoked by the sibbie and I was merely responding to—"

"Provoked!" Ravill Pryde shouted angrily. "I have interviewed those involved. The MechWarrior Shaw threw the first blow, to be sure, but we know that you egged him and the others on to the point where—"

"With all due respect, my Khan," Joanna said, her voice in control, "I wonder if Star Colonel Ravill Pryde may be forgetting what it means to be a Jade Falcon warrior. We are not tamed *surats* who deal politely with each other over biscuits and tea. We are aggressive, we address each other aggressively, and the sibbies, if properly trained, would have known this. We thrive on fights. It sharpens our talons, makes us better warriors in the true battles. It helps us to—"

"Spare us the training lecture," Ravill Pryde said, coming around to face Joanna. "Let us face facts, Star Commander. You have served the Jade Falcon well enough, at least most of the time, in spite of your—well, let us say you have done so *for many years.*" Marthe heard the small, almost inaudible grumble in the back of Joanna's throat. "But, like most warriors with whom time has caught up, you have gone on too long. Age is the problem. It has affected your judgment to such an extent that—"

Ravill Pryde must have known his diatribe would be interrupted, but he looked astonished that it was Marthe and not Joanna.

"Star Colonel, nothing is served by your own *provocations* at this moment. I wish to speak with Star Commander Joanna in private."

"But—"

"Star Colonel?"

Ravill Pryde nodded. "As you wish, my Khan."

He saluted and turned briskly, giving the door a sharp push to open it.

Marthe watched him go, glad that he was so easy to read. She had become more and more disturbed of late with the new trend toward deceptive dealings among the Clans. And it seemed to be infecting the highest levels. The two previous Falcon Khans, Elias Crichell and Vandervahn Chistu, had died for their attempts to manipulate events, both at the hand of Vlad of the Wolves, who himself was proving he had a taste for dirty games.

The thought of Vlad set her teeth on edge. She had been virtually forced to accept *hegira* from the Inner Sphere rather than fight to the last Jade Falcon on Coventry, and he was to blame for it. Marthe had bid everything she had in the battle for the planet, but no one outside of Coventry could have known that. Archon Katrina Steiner herself had blacked out all news coming off the world.

Yet, somehow Vlad had guessed. Just as the fighting reached a peak, Marthe received a message from him, informing her that the Wolves were in position to threaten six of the Falcon-held worlds in the occupation zone. It was Vlad's threat that eventually led Marthe to accept *hegira* on Coventry, a humiliation she was sure he relished. But he would never have dared threaten her unless he knew that she had committed her whole force to Coventry. And he could only have learned that in some kind of secret alliance with the Inner Sphere. The idea turned her stomach.

She pushed herself up from the edge of the desk and walked slowly around to her chair, an image of Vlad's ugly face in her mind. It was ugly too, the way his machinations had humiliated ilKhan Elias Crichell and caused his death. *Vlad claims I stick to outmoded ways.* She rapped her knuckles absently on her desk. *Maybe I do. But the old Falcon ways are the ways of honor. I will prove that. I will circle and soar and wait—wait for the opportunity to swoop down on my prey. A new ilKhan will be chosen soon on Strana Mechty. Vlad will be there too, ambitious as ever, but this time he will have to play by Clan rules.*

Marthe Pryde pushed the thoughts from her mind for now. This was not the time to analyze Clan political intrigues. Right now she had to do something about this warrior standing at uneasy attention in front of her.

"Star Commander Joanna . . ."

"My Khan," Joanna barked in military fashion.

Marthe suppressed a slight smile at the familiar harsh

ring of Joanna's voice. It took her back to Ironhold, to her cadet days at Crash Camp. She could still see Joanna standing there, barking out orders and punishing her into the warrior she was today. Joanna with her insults, her whip, her studded gloves.

"Have a seat, Star Commander," Marthe said, and gestured to a chair.

Joanna hesitated, apparently confused by Marthe's easy tone. That was not exactly common among Jade Falcon warriors. The freeborns among them sometimes appeared to have good times together, and there were rare drunken nights with native wine and stories of heroism, but most of the time Jade Falcons were as combative in their socializing as they were in battle.

"Sit, Joanna." Marthe pointed to a padded chair that looked dangerously comfortable. Joanna sat in it tentatively, as if defying it to do anything good to her body. As Joanna shifted her position, Marthe noticed her wince perceptibly, presumably from the injuries incurred during the fight with Shield. Marthe leaned against her desk, putting both hands on its edge.

"Joanna, I know what happened. I know the official version of why it happened. I just do not know why it *really* happened. What is the reason you provoked those sibbies? Do not tell me you did not provoke them. I know you, after all, *quiaff*?"

Joanna looked away, saying nothing for a long while. Finally she looked back and said, "Aff. I only wanted to work off my anger. The young warrior's death was an accident. I regret the death but do not mourn for the corpse." Her eyes flashed with defiance.

Marthe narrowed her eyes. "Joanna, the heart of the falcon still beats strong in you. I remember the first time I saw you, when I was just a cadet. Every member of our sibko hoped to survive the training, but only I and Aidan Pryde succeeded. Of course, he was not Aidan *Pryde* back then, any more than I was Marthe Pryde. Perhaps we proved the worth of our sibko later, when we both earned bloodnames. You also have competed for a bloodname, *quiaff*?"

Even though the subject of bloodnames—or the lack of them—was a sore one for Joanna, Marthe was the Khan and no warrior could deny her.

"Once I was in the final round and lost narrowly. Another time I made it to the next to last round. I always fought well and lasted well into the final bouts, but I did not—" Joanna stopped herself.

"A warrior like you—why did you not prevail?"

Joanna took in a deep breath and straightened her back. Again, Marthe noticed a slight grimace of pain. "It's not the way of the Clans to hash over failures. I failed and that's all there is to it."

"I know that you are prone to contractions, Joanna. But it is not the way of a warrior and I am your Khan, *quiaff*?"

"Aff."

Marthe pushed herself up off the desk in one smooth motion and stood at her full, impressive height. She walked slowly back around the desk as she spoke. "I have risen to high rank because my genes are superior. But I was also trained well, trained by you to attack swiftly and suddenly, to seize with my talons and vanquish my prey. You were a ferocious falconer, Joanna. And you helped instill the fierceness of the Falcon in me." Marthe turned back toward Joanna and nodded her head slightly in acknowledgment of so much.

"The rules say I should punish you severely. Intelligence tells me I cannot in any way waste one of my best warriors, one who has also won glory. What can I do?" she asked rhetorically. "*Surkai* is not an option, *quineg*?"

"Neg. I regret that the incident happened but am not sorry for it. Therefore, a rite requesting forgiveness is inappropriate."

Joanna was right. An admission of wrongdoing and a free request for punishment had to precede *surkai*, the rite that pardoned an offense and allowed the warrior to escape without blame.

Marthe sat down at her desk and stared into a corner of the room in contemplation, rubbing her fingertips lightly over her lips. Joanna sat unmoving. Suddenly, a solution materialized for Marthe, another in what was becoming a long line of swiftly made decisions. With an abrupt turn of her head, she focused again on Joanna, the slightest of smiles tilting the corners of her mouth.

Marthe spoke deliberately. "You are aware that Mech-Warrior Diana, Aidan Pryde's daughter, wishes to compete for a bloodname, *quiaff*?"

Joanna nodded. "Aff. Diana claims that she is more than a freeborn because she is the freebirth spawn of true-born warriors, a rare occurrence."

"Frankly, I find her argument a bit specious," Marthe said. "We both knew her mother, Peri. She is trueborn, but she flushed out of training." Trueborns who could not survive the rigors of Jade Falcon cadet life or who failed their Trial of Position were simply demoted to a lower caste. Peri had become a scientist.

"So, while genetically a trueborn, Peri lost her warrior status. Diana's birthparents are a warrior and a caste-bound trueborn, not exactly a situation of privilege. In fact, Aidan himself was a member of the tech caste at the time of her conception." Marthe made a face at having to pronounce that last word. "Nevertheless, it is true that while Diana is not a valid trueborn, she is something more than freeborn—a sort of in-between state."

Marthe steepled her fingers and tapped them together. "Many bloodnames have become vacant among the Clans, especially our own. Soon, all the Khans return to the homeworlds, where we shall meet in Grand Council to rightfully elect a new ilKhan. Now that we have purged the Wardens, a new wave of blooded warriors will bring life to the cause of finally conquering the Inner Sphere. I shall oversee many of the competitions myself.

"I have decided that Diana does deserve a chance at the Pryde bloodname. She has distinguished herself in battle."

Joanna looked shocked even though she attempted to conceal it. "But how—? It won't be allowed." Marthe's face went stony at the use of the contraction and Joanna quickly restated herself. "It will not be allowed."

"On the contrary, there is precedence. As in the case of Phelan Wolf." Even though it left a bitter taste in Marthe's mouth to use Clan Wolf as an example, she knew that times changed and with them their demands. Giving Diana a chance at a bloodname would let Marthe keep a fine warrior. And she needed such warriors.

Joanna flinched at the comparison to the Wolves, but again held her tongue.

"I am suggesting a way to remove you from the scene for a specified time, a way that will seem to others like a punishment," Marthe went on. "You will go with Diana to Ironhold, to train her to compete for a bloodname. Either she will prove herself now or forever fulfill her role as a freeborn warrior. No one could have a better trainer than you, Joanna. This will suffice as punishment for the killing of Shield, but will not force me to humiliate you unnecessarily."

Joanna's jaw clenched, showing that she was not entirely happy with this solution. "I suppose . . . if there is no other way. Anyway, there may not be a real war for a long while, especially if there are more *safcons* and *hegiras*—"

Marthe cut in abruptly. "Joanna, would you have found *hegira* more acceptable had you known that Vlad of the Wolves had his units in position to take six of our planets in the occupation zone?"

Joanna's eyes displayed her shock. "Yes. As I thought," Marthe said stonily. "I weighed the disgrace of losing on Coventry against the disgrace of losing worlds that I already possess and that I *need*. But I was prepared to fight to the last Falcon on Coventry. As it turned out, I did not have to. Instead, our Clan will survive to fight another day, on another world, in a greater war."

Marthe had no doubts about her decision on Coventry. Not only had she thrown five Galaxies of untried warriors into a bloody battle, in which many had proved themselves worthy and many others had died to buy victories, but she had decisively established her leadership as Khan of the Jade Falcons. Her own jaw tightened imperceptibly as she fixed Joanna with her eyes. "Do not speak about that of which you know nothing."

There was a long pause as Joanna seemed to collect her thoughts.

"I am Jade Falcon," Joanna began slowly, "but I am not Khan. My fate is tied to yours. We rise or fall by your decisions, Marthe Pryde, and I do not doubt you." Joanna laughed, but not as harshly as usual. "After all, I trained you."

"Aye," said Marthe. "What did not kill us made us stronger."

"And I will train Diana no less rigorously." Joanna nodded, almost to herself. "Yes, a bloodname contest—I have not seen a bloodnaming since Aidan won his. There is something, I don't know, *right* about Diana competing. She will not win, of course."

"I would not bid on that," Marthe said. "She is tough, that Diana, and an excellent warrior."

Joanna shrugged slightly. "But she will never be a trueborn—never."

"Aye," said Marthe. "But there is certainly room for her, for a good skilled officer, among our forces."

Joanna tensed as a thought clouded her face. "I will go to Ironhold with Diana, but I ask that you do not leave me to rot in the homeworlds, doing homeworld things and thinking homeworld thoughts." Joanna gave a shudder. "Had it been up to Ravill Pryde, I'd be on Ironhold right now as a nanny for sibkos fresh from the vat."

Marthe chose to ignore Joanna's use of yet another contraction. Joanna was right, after all. For a warrior, few fates could be worse.

"I will do my best, Joanna. But no one can predict the future. Who knows what will happen by the time you reach Ironhold? It is a journey of many months."

Joanna stiffened, but did not try to push. "There is still one problem," she said finally.

"And that is . . . ?"

"Ravill Pryde. He has to sponsor Diana, and he says it will be a cold day in hell before he will."

"Then he should prepare for icebergs sailing out of hellfire," Marthe said briskly. "Leave him to me."

She stood up behind the desk. "Star Commander Joanna, as your Khan I inform you that you will be detached from the Falcon Guards to accompany MechWarrior Diana to Ironhold in the homeworlds as her trainer for the upcoming bloodname contests. That is an order."

Joanna snapped to attention and called out her response smartly, though Marthe knew it must cost her.

"Aye, my Khan. We shall begin our preparations immediately."

"Good. You are dismissed, Star Commander."

After Joanna was gone, Marthe crossed to the window and stared out, reflecting on the events of the day. She shook her head slightly at all that had transpired—Horse's mission, Joanna's new assignment, Diana's chance at a bloodname. There was a time in her life when she would never have imagined herself making such deviations, even these slight ones, from the way of the Clan. But these are extraordinary times, she told herself, demanding extraordinary measures.

Marthe wondered what other surprises might be in store for her in the coming days, what more might be demanded of her before she was done.

5

Falcon Guard Command Center
Port St. William, Coventry
Coventry Province, Lyran Alliance
18 June 3058

For a command post, Star Colonel Ravill Pryde's office seemed too insulated, too stifling. No cooling air penetrated the room. Diana felt as if she had to struggle to draw a clear breath.

As she waited for Ravill Pryde to explain why he had so urgently called her to his office, she sat in silence and gazed out the window at the setting sun. He seemed angry about something, though Diana had not a clue as to what. When he finally spoke, his tone was sharp, his words clipped.

"I have called you here to say that I will sponsor you for a bloodname, MechWarrior Diana. But I do not approve, and I never will."

"You will sponsor me, Star Colonel?" Diana kept her voice deliberately neutral, fighting to hide her astonishment and her joy. She knew Ravill Pryde's mercurial temperament too well from her time assisting him as his coregn. She was sure that his many quirks must derive from his bizarre genetic background, about which only she and Joanna—among the Falcon Guards he commanded—knew the truth. The experiment, no doubt misguided, had combined Jade Falcon and Wolf genetic materials to form warriors like Ravill Pryde and some of the other new breed. The Wolf/Jade Falcon combination resulted, she thought, in a courageous warrior (the Jade Falcon part) with a talent for treachery (the Wolf part).

Nothing, Diana vowed silently, would get in her way now, not even Ravill Pryde's interference. Her hands moved actively, gripping and releasing, as if she were already in training for the bloodname matches.

Ravill Pryde seemed not to notice, squirming a bit in his chair, which made him appear physically smaller. He was already one of the shortest warriors holding a command rank. "Many warriors have become eligible in recent days, and many bloodnames have come open," he said. "Word that you may return to Ironhold to compete has just come down from Marthe Pryde."

Diana was startled. "The Khan herself," she said.

"Aye. I do not know why, and I tell you again, I am against it. This time it is the Khan's will and I cannot protest. But if you do not succeed, I promise that you will never get another chance."

Diana pulled herself up even more erect than before. She had not been born from a canister, but her genes were no less trueborn. "Once a bloodname is earned, no one can take it away, *quiaff*?"

"Not usually," Ravill Pryde said, glaring at her. "But I know of some cases where it was the only punishment suited to a warrior's crimes."

Then he shrugged, as though weary of the whole subject. "MechWarrior Diana, you will be relieved of your Falcon Guard duty from this moment and make ready to return to Ironhold. I will see to it that you are scheduled for a DropShip headed for the homeworlds at the earliest opportunity. Star Commander Joanna will accompany you as trainer."

Diana was even more surprised by that news than the announcement that the Khan had approved her request. Joanna had trained her father, Aidan Pryde, both as a warrior and for his own bloodname victory. There was something right about it all. She would become a Pryde, just like Aidan. Who could doubt it?

"Thank you, Star Colonel," was all she said.

"Do not thank me," Ravill Pryde said. "I have done

nothing." He did not hide his irritation and abruptly dismissed her.

After Diana was gone, Ravill Pryde grinned. Let her go to Ironhold. She would never succeed in the Trials. Her claim that she belonged to a special category as the offspring of two trueborn warriors did not convince him of her right. As far as he was concerned, she would always be a freeborn. Her father might indeed have been Aidan Pryde, but his genes did not truly qualify her as a trueborn, given that she had been so foully conceived.

Ravill Pryde, who believed deeply in the system by which bloodnames were contested and earned, knew that Diana did not deserve one. *But good riddance,* he thought. *Getting her out of my hair for a while suits me fine.* At least he would no longer have to listen to her continual hounding that he sponsor her.

Then an unsettling thought came into Ravill Pryde's mind. What if she *won* the bloodname? Not only would it violate his deep beliefs, but Diana would be in *his* bloodline.

The prospect sickened him.

Joanna could not sleep at all that night. She listened to every sound and tried to puzzle out those she could not discern well. She did not mind. For once she welcomed the noises of the night. For once she did not mind pondering the events of the day.

Diana had rushed to her with the news that Ravill Pryde would sponsor her, and Joanna did not reveal exactly how she came to be named Diana's trainer. She let the younger warrior think it came from some misguided belief in her. Let her think what she pleased.

Whether she won or not, Diana would compete. And Joanna found the prospect exhilarating, even though she would only be there as coach and not competitor.

Diana was so certain she would succeed. She had no sense of the odds against her. As her trainer, it would have been wrong for Joanna to caution her at this point. That would come later.

Now that she knew she was going, Joanna felt good about it. At least she would be in a place where life was not so complicated, where the future—to succeed or fail at winning a bloodname—was clear. The occupation zone, with its shameful truce, its galaxies of unblooded warriors, its leaders granting *safcon* and accepting *hegira* from Inner Sphere scum, had become repellent to her.

That thought, with its comfortable level of anger, eased her into her own comfortable sleep.

Night. Dreams. Dream-places.

Ravill Pryde dreamed of a large auditorium, with himself at the podium, holding the ceremonial robe that he would present to Diana as the winner of her bloodname, a smirk on her face as she came toward him to accept it. He woke screaming.

Horse dreamed of the village where he'd grown up. He was a child again, with his mother. Later in the dream he strolled by a river with a companion named Yasina.

Marthe Pryde dreamed of a Grand Council meeting where Khan Vlad of the Wolves demanded her execution. This was a recurrent dream and was not too bad, since she always killed Vlad in it.

Joanna dreamed of a fiery death in a *Summoner*. This made her smile in her sleep.

Diana dreamed of triumphantly winning a bloodname and being presented the ceremonial robe by an obviously fuming Ravill Pryde.

MAP OF HUNTRESS

CLASSIFIED

Northern Polar Cap

Path of The
Warrior
Peninsula

Dhundh Sea

Continent of Jaguar Prime

Liberation
Sea

Lootera (Planetary Capital)

Mt. Szabo

Black Shikari River

Continent
Abysmal

Dhuan
Swamp

Lunar Range

Myer

Bagera

Falcon's Eyrie
(Jade Falcon Base)

Pahn City

New Andery

Hatya Desert

Lake
Osis

Shikari Jungles

Bahg Jana
River

Frothing Jaguar
Straits

Sangram Sea

Southern Polar Cap

6

Russou Howell didn't know who he was anymore. Yes, he was a Smoke Jaguar warrior, genetically engineered to be the ultimate fighting machine, bred for no other purpose, and yet this was no fate for a warrior.

He pushed his chair abruptly away from his desk, noting the time. *On to yet another review of cadet training.* He paused for a moment and stared bitterly at the desk. It was a beautiful thing—large and imposing, its top made of gleaming black obsidian. A legacy from his predecessor on Huntress. And yet he hated it more than anything on the planet right now. *I shouldn't be sitting behind a desk. I should be sitting in a 'Mech, ending my days with an honorable death.*

He wondered if the former Galaxy Commander, Benjamin Howell, had felt as ashamed of being assigned to Huntress. Ah, well, no matter now. Benjamin Howell had been disgraced and purged from the warrior caste, his bloodname pulled from the Clan's breeding program. Proof that Russou's own fate could be worse.

Russou might never again fight in the Crusade against the Inner Sphere, but he would, at least, be part of arming and fortifying the Clan. He could also be proud that a

Smoke Jaguar would lead the renewed invasion. The Khans had gathered in Grand Council on Strana Mechty some months before and elected Smoke Jaguar Lincoln Osis as ilKhan. And now the Clans were gearing up to resume the war.

Russou Howell had replaced Benjamin Howell as both commander of Zeta Galaxy and of the whole planet of Huntress, the Smoke Jaguar homeworld. The previous Howell had gone rogue with a smuggling scheme to obtain better equipment for this planet garrisoned mostly by solahma units too old for combat. Russou Howell did not have to stoop to such measures. The homeworlds were humming with the war effort now, and the factories on Huntress were going full-tilt. He had just returned from preliminary reviews of the huge industrial complex at Pahn City and the big training base at New Andery. Their output would ultimately be sent off to renew the invasion of the Inner Sphere, but at last the war effort had brought new life to Huntress.

Russou leaned in on the desk and stared at the wooden cabinet directly opposite. Inside were flasks filled with the makings of a drink he had come to like very much during the nine long months of travel from the Inner Sphere. The JumpShip captain had introduced Russou to brouhahas, a concoction that had helped him pass the utter boredom of space travel in a dull blur. They had also helped him avoid thinking too much about the shame of being sent to command a bunch of has-beens on a backwater planet. And they had eased the other pain, the one that felt like some enormous weight in his chest. The pain that always came with the memory of the moment he had triggered the lasers that killed his best friend.

Right now, all Russou Howell wanted to do was take a quick drink, but he had made a vow never to touch a drop before the sun went down each day. He knew that Huntress had taken on some importance again, and he needed his wits about him. The Khans had set a fire under the homeworlds—settling interClan disputes, bloodnaming new warriors, sitting in Grand Council, and generally whipping things up into a fever for war.

And so that settled that. He put away the dark thoughts as best he could and strode quickly out the door of his office. *His office.* After only two weeks here, the words felt strange. He jabbed the elevator button and scowled at two passing officers on some routine business or other. He could not remember what it was like to feel normal, and would have given his right arm to be merely that again. In just a year, his entire life had turned upside down and inside out. Never to be the same.

The elevator arrived, and Russou stepped in. As it dropped with a soft whoosh, he had to steel himself against the terror of plunging down the many floors to ground level. Falling. It seemed to be the quality of his whole existence—physical and mental—since the dawn of that terrible day in the Shenandoah River Valley. It had been almost a year ago, but it seemed like yesterday. He had still been a real warrior then, in the thick of the action. He and the rest of Beta Striker Trinary, under the command of Star Captain Trent, were under serious attack during a raid on the Combine world of Maldonado. Trent and he had been sibmates and Trent was the only friend Russou had ever had.

They were seriously outnumbered and struggling to hold off the Twelfth Dieron Regulars from the top of a ridge leading down into a small valley, when a DropShip had suddenly loomed in the sky over the embattled foothills. Then came the unmistakable voice of Star Colonel Paul Moon, booming from the ship over a wide-band communications channel. Voice echoing over the ridge and across the valley, Moon called Trent a traitor to his caste and his Clan. He demanded that Trent surrender now or be destroyed.

Elementals dropped from Moon's ship, with the Star Colonel in the lead, and they deployed on the south end of the ridge, moving to engage Trent. Russou remembered the confusion as Moon ordered the members of Beta Trinary to break off their attack on the Combine defenders and turn on Trent. Meanwhile a Star of Elementals hit him with a barrage of fire.

Then the Com Guards 308th Division appeared over the top of the ridge and began firing on the Elementals. Through the smoke and confusion, Russou Howell and his Charlie Sweep Star approached Trent's 'Mech, and his friend had turned to meet them calmly. Then came Paul Moon's voice screaming, "Crush him. He is a traitor to you and your Clan." Russou remembered the sickening indecision that had gripped him. And Trent's final words: "You have no choice. This is how this must end." Russou had fired.

Paul Moon had been trying to get rid of Trent almost from the moment he first laid eyes on him. Too many Jaguars had died in the brutal, bloody fight on Tukayyid and that was the reason Moon hated Trent. If the battle was a disaster for the Jaguars, it was a catastrophe for the Clans as a whole. It was the Truce of Tukayyid, seven years ago, that had forced them to halt the invasion of the Inner Sphere for fifteen years.

Moon considered Trent a coward. He was the only one of his Binary to survive Tukayyid. A true warrior would have died fighting for his Clan and for the great goal of conquering the Inner Sphere. That was why Moon had wanted to get rid of Trent, and would not stop until he finally succeeded.

And at my hand. Russou glanced down at his hands and saw them clenched into fists. He punched the wall of the elevator and felt the sting spread across his knuckles. Moon had accused Trent of being traitor, but how could that be? Russou had never known another warrior truer to the way of the Jaguar. It was a doubt he had been wrestling with constantly over the past year. And the doubt had been winning.

Then, soon after Trent's death, Russou had found himself fighting a Trial of Position that was practically forced on him by Moon. He had defeated two others and won the new rank of Star Colonel. The victory had felt hollow. At the time he fought, he did not even know what his new command would be.

The elevator doors opened with the same discreet whooshing, and Russou stepped out onto the massive main floor of the Hall of Hunters. The Smoke Jaguar planetary command was embedded deep in the heart of the mountain that overlooked the capital city of Lootera. He felt dwarfed by the high-ceilinged chamber carved out of the rock of Mount Szabo. Boot heels clicking sharply against the stone floor, he hurried toward the natural light of the entryway. Being stationed inside a mountain had its advantages, but windows wasn't one of them.

Russou pushed through the security checkpoint at the entryway, giving a sharp nod to the soldiers on duty. They snapped to attention but not before Russou noted what seemed to be a typical laxness of military discipline on the part of the units stationed here. He tried to cover his annoyance and made a mental note to have the security guards drilled later in the day. Then he pushed out into the cool morning air.

He paused for a moment and raised his face to the sky. Another gray and hazy day on Huntress. It was typical weather, or so he'd been told. Two weeks had passed like a minute, and Russou still had not really adjusted to the fact that he was really here.

He was headed for the parade ground to review one of the many cadet sibkos on Huntress. He told himself it was important work, that the training of new warriors was essential, now more than ever. Very few cadets made it all the way through their training and even fewer would actually qualify as full-fledged Clan warriors by winning their Trial of Position. Someone had to make sure these new troops were the best the Clan had to offer. And that someone was now Russou Howell, whether he liked it or not.

He paused mid-stride and turned, looking up behind him at the lunging jaguar carved high into the rock of Mount Szabo. The Smoke Jaguar symbol could be seen from anywhere in the city of Lootera, and was lit at night in a most impressive manner. Someone had told Russou when he'd arrived on Huntress that Lootera was the Hindu word for predator. Now, gazing at the carving of the jaguar in mid-attack, he felt a familiar swell of pride. Here was the symbol of everything a Smoke Jaguar warrior must be—aggressive and lethal, quick and ruthless. It was what he lived for—to ride onto the field of battle in the cockpit of his *Mad Dog,* destroying the enemies of the Clan with this OmniMech's fearsome array of weapons. And then one day to die a proper warrior's death—to die fighting, to go out in flames if need be, and to take as many of the enemy with him as he could.

But, no, he thought, snapping back to the present, *now I sit at a desk.* He shook his head bitterly to think that he was merely a paper warrior now. Despite being the ranking officer for an entire planet—commander of the Iron Guard and The Watchmen, two galaxies—he felt somehow useless. Bloodname and all, a warrior genetically engineered to be the fiercest fighter on the field—now all he battled was red tape.

Turning a corner, he nearly ran head-first into a small group of warriors on their way somewhere. He felt a flush of embarrassment at not hearing their approach. Especially when he realized they had been laughing together. *Laughing. What is there to laugh about?*

He found himself face to face with Star Colonel Logan Wirth. The man had a mean, pinched face and a sallow complexion. His eyes were narrow slits that made his gaze even more inscrutable than usual for a warrior. Russou had hated him on sight. And for Logan the feeling seemed to be mutual.

Logan was commander of one of the Huntress Defense Clusters and had fought for the honor of temporarily filling the post of Galaxy Commander during Russou's long journey from the Inner Sphere. When Russou arrived, he and Logan had performed the ritual blooding necessary for Russou to officially take over command. Although the ritual was usually carried out more for show than to inflict actual injury, Logan had looked up at Russou with murderous rage after being punched hard enough in the face to draw blood from his nose. Logan was not outright insubordinate, but he and the rest of the troops on Huntress did not show the proper respect either to Russou or to themselves. At least, according to Russou.

Logan barked the order to attention, and the little group snapped to it. Russou had to give them credit for that much. There were seven in all, every one a cursed solahma. Russou recognized most of them and knew they shared the military sloppiness that seemed to characterize this place and that he so detested. One of them seemed to smirk. *What is his name? Too many faces in too short a time. It all feels like a blur.*

Russou stood in front of the warrior with the smirk, a tall, insolent-looking man. Young warriors were rare on garrison worlds. This one must have done something very wrong in his previous assignment. Russou made a note to look up his record later. "State your name," Russou barked in his face.

"I am Star Commander Cajuste."

"I think it is interesting that you have the energy to feel amused by anything, Star Commander. After your humiliating performance during the 'Mech drills yesterday, I would think all your effort would be devoted toward improving your performance as a warrior."

Cajuste's smile faded and his face grew hard. "I did nothing to humiliate myself yesterday."

"That only goes to show how low is your own standard. You are not worthy to be a Smoke Jaguar warrior. It is no wonder you are assigned to garrison duty at your age."

Cajuste's face flushed with anger. "You have no right to speak of anyone's age. You are past the warrior's prime. How is it that you did not die in combat, but managed to survive long enough to end up behind a desk and managing drills?" He sneered the last word.

Russou struggled to control the clenching and unclenching of his fists, a habit he had developed in recent months. "You words are arrogant, solahma, when you should feel shame at not knowing how a warrior should speak to his commanding officer. This is Huntress, and it is still the proud place that the Smoke Jaguars call their homeworld. Not only am I commander of two Galaxies, but I am responsible for this whole planet and everything and everyone on it. None stands higher than Russou Howell on Huntress. And I refuse to be insulted by a mewling, weak-spirited excuse for a warrior. You will pay for your lack of honor in a Circle of Equals."

The rest of group backed away to form a circle, leaving Cajuste and Russou in the center. Russou glanced at the faces around him and saw how eager they were for this fight. His anger grew as he glanced back at the smug look on the face of Cajuste, who was already raising his hand to begin the ritual that preceded the match. Russou walked to him and raised his hand in return, but instead of signaling his readiness, Russou made a fist and smashed it fiercely against Cajuste's nose. He felt a surge of energy even as he felt the bone inside the nose crack with his blow. Cajuste reeled backward, and Russou rushed him and pummeled his face mercilessly.

Everything that had been building in Russou since that day on Maldonado, all the rage, confusion, and despair, seemed to boil up and out of him. He was Jaguar through and through, so he had no qualm about vicious fighting, nor the least thought of giving quarter to any enemy. Yet he had never fought so brutally, or so mercilessly in his life. Within moments, the stunned Cajuste lost consciousness and fell at Russou's feet.

A profound silence hung momentarily in the air as Russou looked at the faces of the men around him. Now it was his turn to feel smug. He turned to leave.

"You violated the ritual of honor, Galaxy Commander," Logan said in a low, angry voice.

"So be it. This was not a duel of honor, but of discipline and duty. What honor is due any warrior so low in worth, in self-respect, that he forgets his place in the chain of command and forgets that he only exists to serve? Solahma or not, we are Smoke Jaguars and I will tear you apart and put you back together again if I have to. We are the defenders of the Jaguar homeworld, and cannot know when the day may come when we will have to do so. I have been assigned this command, and I intend to return you second-rate, slovenly misfits to the way of the Clans."

Russou Howell wheeled about and went on his way, leaving his warriors stunned.

═══ 7 ═══

Black Shikari River Valley
Huntress
Kerensky Cluster, Clan Space
21 March 3059

Solahma Star Commander Sentania Buhallin made her way down the steep hill in the late morning haze in her usual manner, through a series of quick maneuvers that belied her age. She would bounce off the bark of one of the thin trees scattered down the hillside, letting it propel her a few steps, then grab the slim trunk of another tree and swing around it, virtually leaping to another tree and then letting it slow her down so that she could catch her breath and work out the route she would follow. Bouncing, jumping, grabbing, sliding, dancing across thick roots, swinging on low-hanging branches, kicking her body from one branch to another, using bushes to brake speed. An observer might have thought he was watching a choreographed hillside ballet suitable for holobroadcast. Of course there was no holovid programming on Huntress, since the Smoke Jaguars had little feeling for entertainment or art.

It was unlikely, though, that anyone would observe Sentania Buhallin, who was skilled in stealthy movement. MechWarrior Stenis, one of the more ancient solahmas among the Jade Falcons here on Huntress, insisted that her ability to remain unseen was not skill but the art of invisibility and mind-clouding. Sentania never argued with him, believing that Stenis had been driven mad by his years at Falcon Eyrie. In fact, she thought most of Falcon Eyrie's solahmas were crazy in some way, including herself. They often assumed attitudes and said things one would never expect from a Clansman.

As Sentania skidded toward the bottom of the long hill, approaching what she already knew was a deep river cutting between the city of Lootera and the Eastern Mountains, she dove into a clump of bushes she thought would make a good hiding place. Sentania always scouted for hiding places even when she was in a safe place. It never hurt to have one ready in case she needed it.

She had been on Huntress for so long that she had an admirable knowledge of the general terrain for many kilometers in any direction from the mountaintop where Falcon Eyrie Station perched. Given the convolutions of this rough, mountainous region, she often had to travel at least twice as far as the direct distance between two points. As a result she had evolved the up and down, in and out, over and under, side to side series of movements that propelled her across country.

She was not usually in any hurry, however. And often she was merely exploring, so Sentania didn't mind being sidetracked at all. No one would particularly miss her back at the Eyrie, for there was little to do. Discipline was so slack as to be virtually non-existent, and her commander seemed more interested in hunting with his pet falcon than anything military.

Today the waters of the Black Shikari River surged and foamed, making it impossible to cross unaided. On other days they were calm enough to easily float to the other side. That was unnecessary, though, since downstream was a natural bridge made by a tree that had fallen there after being split by lightning. As usual, after resting, Sentania would cross the river at that point.

The trouble with being solahma, even one as energetic as Sentania, was that sometimes her body required rest. In her heyday she had never rested. She remembered many a time when she could have gone forward even when those under her command were too exhausted. That had only made her MechWarriors more proud of her, and they often bragged about serving under the toughest and gamest of all Jade Falcons. They would have thrown themselves on an about-to-launch rack of missiles for Sentania Bulhallin. Once, a warrior of hers had done just that.

She closed her eyes for a moment, ready to welcome a quick nap, then she jolted herself awake.

I won't become one of those solahma warriors who need to nod off in midafternoon. Too many like that at Falcon Eyrie—though that doesn't stop them from being just as crazy as the wide-awake ones. What is it Stenis is always saying? You have to be crazy to be solahma so it helps a lot if you are already a bit loony by nature. No wonder so many of the regular warriors look at us so warily.

The station's honor guard and the support Binary of solahma warriors did not mingle or communicate much outside of duty, and there was not much duty these days for the Falcon Eyrie forces. The Jaguars mostly left them alone, little concerned with this scientific outpost. The only way the Falcon warriors joined together was against the scientists, whom both regular and solahma warriors believed to be the craziest Falcons of all. Sentania did not completely endorse that attitude since she was one of the few who admired the efforts of the scientist caste to improve the warlike capacities of the Clan.

Hungry, she shoved aside some leaves that had fallen onto the ground and saw, as she expected, some of the hard-shelled round insects indigenous to Huntress. The Smoke Jaguars called them berry ants. They made a nice snack, crunchy and slightly sweet, with a hint of orange flavor.

She scooped up three of the insects and popped them into her mouth. The orange flavor was especially strong for this trio. It seemed to drift up into her nose. She had never expected to savor insects as delicacies, though she'd eaten her share of them during the grueling survival training of her cadet days. Since coming to Huntress, however, she had developed a taste for them. When she was roaming the land and starving, insects were easy to find.

Huntress was less bountiful in edible vegetation, but there were enough good pickings that could be made digestible. What Stenis could do with a pot of karna leaves off the bizarre, skinny trees that grew all over Huntress was quite remarkable, especially if flavored with berry ants.

Rested and ready to resume her scout, Sentania stood up. After she had walked a few steps toward the river, she heard a faint noise in the sky. She looked up. There was nothing visible at first, then a DropShip appeared over the hill she had just descended and drifted across the sky. Usually DropShip flight, in descent, was direct and straight. This one wavered and seemed almost wobbly. Then she saw smoke streaming out from several areas along the ship's rim. The smoke was the last thing she noticed about the ship as it disappeared beyond the line of trees toward some point beyond the river. Sentania guessed that the ship might have been headed for the spaceport at Lootera, which lay to the north.

Something is wrong, she thought. Her view was reinforced by a loud explosion that shook even the ground beneath her feet, followed by another tremor that she assumed was the DropShip crashing.

Surprising events excited Sentania. She was off quickly to the natural bridge downstream. She ran across the fallen tree with sure, small steps. On the other side she was able to sense the direction of the crash site by the acrid burning odors and the sounds of cracking metal.

Before she reached the crash, she sensed something else and stopped. Through the ground she felt one of the most familiar sensations to any warrior—the earth-shaking tremors of BattleMech movement. Kneeling with both hands on the ground, feeling the vibrations through her legs, she determined that at least a full Star of five 'Mechs was also lumbering toward the crash site. From the rhythm of their giant footfalls, she concluded that they were moving fast and were, at best, no more than three or four kilometers away, to the northeast.

Now she moved more cautiously toward the site. The last thing she wanted was to be discovered by any Smoke Jags. The tales of their sometimes harsh treatment of prisoners were numerous. It wasn't that she never dared trespass on their ground. That was actually one of her favorite pastimes, and she was good at the game of not getting caught. It was the reason her commander indulged her absences and eccentricities; she often brought back interesting tidbits of information on Jag activities in the capital of Lootera and environs.

The relationship between the Jaguars and the Falcons on Huntress was uneasy. The small base of Falcon Eyrie had been awarded to the Falcons by ilKhan Leo Showers prior to the start of the invasion of the Inner Sphere. The Falcons kept to themselves up in the Eastern Mountains, and the Jaguars apparently felt that challenging them to a Trial to drive them out was not worth the trouble. But hostilities did occasionally break out, which was not unusual when two Clans got anywhere near each other.

Not long ago a group of Falcon solahmas had ambushed a tired patrol of Jag warriors just to embarrass them by liberating their insignia, which they then dispatched by messenger to Zeta Galaxy Command in Lootera. It was just one of several Falcon activities designed to welcome the new Galaxy Commander to Huntress. The Jag commander had subsequently vowed to deal severely with any Falcons who made the mistake of trespassing on Smoke Jaguar territory.

No surprise, Sentania thought. The Jaguars went overboard on everything.

Life on Huntress was not particularly exciting for a warrior, but the planet itself was significant enough to the Jaguars. Not only was it their homeworld, but there were weapons and 'Mech production plants and many sibkos in training. It was also the location of the Jaguar genetic repository. Their attitude toward the place amused Sentania. You would think the repository was some kind of shrine the way they fluttered around it. She knew the gene pool was sacred and could understand the solemn meaning of such a place for a Clansman, but did Jags have to carry everything to extremes?

Sentania continued to lope toward the crash site, managing to stay out of sight while paralleling the track she projected for the Jag 'Mechs. Ahead of her, some of the forest was on fire. She heard Huntress tree-monkeys, a particularly annoying species known for their narrow faces and nerve-shattering screeches, creating a cacophony as they fled the scene. Looking up, Sentania saw a group of them. They were moving so fast they seemed like a gray cloud above the trees.

Hearing a BattleMech coming dangerously close, she

dove between two large-rooted trees. The sounds of the 'Mech footfalls grew in volume. Some frail trees bent, and she saw a single 'Mech foot, angled and looking like it was precariously attached to bent ankles. From the fleeting view, she could tell that it was a *Warhammer IIC,* one of many second-line Jaguar BattleMechs refitted for garrison duty to free up the fearsome OmniMechs for use in the Inner Sphere. This foot was scorched, scarred, and dented. Its green surface was so dirty it was virtually colorless.

The shaking of the ground beneath Sentania increased, as did the vibrations in the root she clutched. A *Warhammer IIC* could tear up and even destroy a whole lot of forest as it proceeded through the trees, especially if it used the long barrels of the PPCs on each arm to push intrusive growth aside.

To Sentania a BattleMech was one of the most awesome sights in the galaxy, though she no longer logged any time piloting one. She would never forget what it was like to sit in the cockpit of her *Mad Dog* during battle. She had fought many a *Warhammer* from that vantage point, and knew without seeing this one what it would look like—a twelve-meter tall monster ready to mow down any enemy as it thundered forward with its considerable paunch stuck out.

As soon as the *Warhammer* had passed, Sentania slipped from her concealment and followed the 'Mech the short distance to the crash site.

Luckily for its passengers, the DropShip had been flying low enough that its crash had been comparatively gentle. Crouching behind a tree, Sentania saw only minimal damage to the ship's superstructure. Across the front of the craft a wide gash belched smoke and an occasional lash of fire.

She recognized the ship as a *Union-C* Class, designed to carry a Trinary of BattleMechs. The possibility that the ship might actually be carrying 'Mechs excited her, though Sentania knew they might have been damaged in the crash. Falcon Eyrie had no real 'Mechs. That included the feeble Land-Air 'Mechs that the station's scientists had been trying for some time to fashion into effective fighting machines. Like most other Clan warriors, Sentania considered the LAM an aberration, worthy neither of a Mech-Warrior nor a aeropilot.

The weight of the DropShip had rammed it into the ground fairly deep. With its great bulk and rounded design, it looked like a small hill of refined metal added to the landscape, albeit one with several fires along its slopes. Squinting to see past the smoke, Sentania noted with surprised satisfaction that the DropShip bore the swooping falcon insignia of the Jade Falcons.

Unfortunately, a Star's worth of Smoke Jaguar Battle-Mechs was lined up along the ship's rim. Their weapons pointed down at the crash survivors, who were in no condition to offer any resistance. Some staggered and fell onto the ground while the rest dragged others out of the ship to safe places. In the midst of all the activity was a brawny warrior with a thick beard. He seemed familiar to Sentania. Edging in closer, she recognized him. According to the insignia on his fatigues, he was now a Star Captain. She also knew his name. Horse.

Unusual, she thought, *a freeborn commanding a Trinary, even if that freeborn is a warrior of some renown.* She couldn't recall ever seeing a freeborn in such a position. Of course, this Horse had quite a reputation for valor. He had even earned some lines in the Falcon version of *The Remembrance,* the epic poem every warrior knew by heart. *Still, it looks odd to see a freeborn shouting orders when a trueborn should be in charge.*

Then she was disturbed by another detail that began to sink in. *What happened to the trueborns? These warriors all have the freeborn piping on their outfits. No trueborns here at all. Is it possible that all the trueborn warriors were killed in the crash?* She realized Horse must be in charge. She recognized the command voice. And the command arrogance.

Sentania had not been off Huntress in almost a decade, disqualified from participating in the Clan invasion because of her age. She had not even been fortunate enough to get assigned to one of those sacrifice missions that could buy a solahma at least the semblance of a warrior's death. By now, she would have heard any astounding news about the status of freeborns being different. A freebirth in command of a Trinary—what other strange sights she could expect in her last years?

She recognized Horse because she had met him once before when both had participated in a raid against the Wolves. Horse had been a MechWarrior then, in a Star led by the even more famous Jade Falcon warrior, Aidan Pryde.

   . . . *She had recently won her bloodname in a fierce competition. Her BattleMech, a* Mad Dog, *was backed against a free-standing brick wall. The rest of the building lay in rubble around it. Her* Mad Dog's *legs could barely maintain balance, a problem complicated by the fact that its left arm had been rendered useless by missile fire. The elbow joint was so badly damaged that the lower arm hung ineffectually, connected to its fire-damaged upper arm by tangled strings of myomer fibers. Its lasers were still operative but could do little more than shoot off her own 'Mech's foot.*

   An enemy 'Mech, a Dire Wolf, *bore down on her. Very few missiles remained in the two shoulder-mounted missile racks of her* Mad Dog. *Only the right-arm lasers were usable, but there was something wrong there, too. The weapons responded, but too slowly.*

   She tried to eject, but the eject mechanism jammed. Swallowing hard, she readied herself to accept her inevitable death in the calm manner of a Falcon warrior. Just then, like a rude suitor, a Summoner *swung around the wall and began blasting away at the enemy 'Mech. The attack was so unforeseen and the* Dire Wolf *so damaged, that the laser shots from the* Summoner *penetrated the last armor layers and destroyed the fusion engine inside. The* Dire Wolf *exploded, with its pilot just managing to eject first. Lucky for him his eject mechanism responded,* Sentania *thought.* Dire Wolf *shrapnel flew at the* Mad Dog *in a dense cloud. The shrapnel storm nearly destroyed her 'Mech. It survived, but had required many days of work by techs before she could take it into the field again.*

   Climbing down from the cockpit of the Mad Dog, *using all the new holes in its leg as footholds in an easy descent, she saw the* Summoner's *pilot swinging down from his 'Mech, also with ease. She jumped down and prepared to thank him. After two steps she halted abruptly when she saw the green piping on his combat fatigues, the green*

*that marked him as a freeborn. Sentania had never frater-
nized much with freeborns and had tended to sidle away
when one was in a wardroom group or other recreational
situation. Besides, most freebirths also seemed to prefer
staying apart.*

*This particular freeborn, however, had saved her life.
She could not snub him nor ignore her obligations, even
for strong reasons of caste. She strode forward to greet
her rescuer, who nodded casually and asked if she was all
right.*

"No wounds?" he asked.

"None. Your name, warrior?"

"I am Horse."

"Horse?"

He smiled, and she noted the amiability of his smile. "It
is not my real name, of course. It was given me long ago."

"A freeborn custom, to be careless with names?"

"Not at all, Star Commander Sentania Buhallin."

"You know my name?"

"Your exploits have been on many lips in recent weeks.
They say you treat war frivolously."

"You are forward, freebirth!"

"I tell the truth. You take little seriously, quiaff?"

"Well, aff. But it is a defect, not an admirable trait, and
you—as freeborn—are out of line in mentioning it."

"I am told I am often out of line. But do not think I
judge you. I am sometimes said to lack seriousness
myself."

"I acknowledge my debt to you, MechWarrior Horse,
but I cheerfully remind you that, in certain circles at
least, a direct comparison between trueborn and freeborn
is considered offensive."

"Yes. Usually by the trueborn. Are you offended?"

She paused, then had to succumb to the smile. "Well,
no. Just uncomfortable. Perhaps we should merely exchange the vow of debt and go our separate ways."

"As you wish."

*Sentania stood at attention and tried to remember the
words of the vow. They came to her in a rush, undoubt-
edly in some scrambled fashion, and she spoke the vow
quickly:* "Jade Falcon warrior, noblest of all Clan warriors, I am in profound debt for the honor you have
afforded me. The rest of my life has been granted me by

your valorous act. I take note of the debt I owe you. When you require return, I will grant your request with dispatch. Praise the Clans."

"Praise the Clans. I acknowledge your vow and will remember it forever."

The vow completed, Sentania started to walk away. Horse said, "There should be no need for such an exchange of rede. The honor of defeating a Wolf Clan BattleMech happened to fall to me, and that is the upshot of it. That I saved you was incidental and should require no special gratitude."

"Who said I was grateful? The rede is my duty."

"I think I will never have to present a request to you."

"That may be. I know little of your freebirth customs nor how they affect honored warrior ritual."

"I am a warrior like you and—"

"Again I acknowledge my debt to you and again I must caution you against comparing yourself to trueborns. You are brave, MechWarrior Horse, and I hope that we may meet again."

"I hope so, too."

She strode off . . .

In the ensuing years Sentania had remembered the incident from time to time when she heard about another of the freeborn warrior's courageous exploits. From that time to now, she had not seen Horse again, nor fulfilled her vow.

Recalling the incident, she marveled at how correct Horse's perception had been. She had, indeed, rarely taken things seriously. As a result she had risen no higher than the rank of Star Commander, even though she never performed less than valiantly in combat. She often suspected that her solahma assignment had come about in part because her attitude was considered unbecoming, or at least questionable, to her superiors.

Well, that was all coolant left on the battlefield. She had been on Huntress for nearly a decade now. The young warrior part of her life had happened to some other Sentania Buhallin, one just as reckless and frivolous as she was now.

Her reflections on past glories were interrupted by the

eerie, booming, deprived-of-humanity voice that emerged from speakers located in the chest of the *Warhammer IIC*.

"Identify yourself, Jade Falcon warriors."

"I am Star Captain Horse," Sentania heard Horse say, then, "I serve Ravill Pryde, Cluster Commander of the Falcon Guards, but am now detached and in command of this Trinary currently undesignated by number or title. We are on our way to Strana Mechty, but wish to stop first at the Jade Falcon research station, which I understand does not interfere with Smoke Jaguar dominion over this planet. We came in under the neutrality signal, which is generally honored by all Clans. But your Smoke Jaguar fighters ignored it, diverted our DropShip from its course and attacked it, forcing this crash landing. May I have the honor of knowing who asks the question?"

"You will not merely have the honor. We will discuss matters face to face."

The speaker clicked loudly as it was shut off. Sentania slipped sideways for a better view of the Smoke Jaguar officer, who was now out of his cockpit and climbing quickly down the side of his BattleMech.

8

**Black Shikari River Valley
Huntress
Kerensky Cluster, Clan Homeworlds
21 March 3059**

The Smoke Jaguar leader had taken off his helmet, and Sentania recognized him immediately, due to his receding hairline and the few dark-haired strands brushed meticulously across his bald pate. Galaxy Commander Russou Howell had apparently tended to his grooming in the short time between removing his neurohelmet and exiting his cockpit.

Sentania could recognize the Smoke Jaguar commander because she had seen and talked to him during one of her clandestine trips into the Jag capital of Lootera. A natural actor, she always went in some disguise or other and was able to portray members of even the lowest Jaguar castes with ease and what her fellow solahma warriors (but not Stenis) had described as some flair.

The day she had talked with Howell, she had been disguised as a tech, dressed in one of the many uniforms she had stolen, then stashed in a hollow tree trunk in the forest just outside Lootera. Anyone getting too close might have smelled the forest on her, but Smoke Jaguars, throughout all their castes, rarely got close to each other. Forbidding types, these Jags, cold and cruel.

Before encountering the Smoke Jaguars, Sentania might

just as easily have characterized her own Jade Falcons as just as distant, cold, and cruel. Her people certainly were that when necessary, but Falcons also had moments of humor, camaraderie, and even some warmth. Such moments might be rare, but they were plentiful compared to the way of the Jaguar.

The day she had met this balding Smoke Jaguar warrior, she was seated at a table in that rare phenomenon, a Jaguar rec hall. This one was obviously intended for the tech caste or lower, as it was not in the Warrior Quarter of Lootera. Scientists and warriors had their own rec halls. At least she thought so.

She sipped at a Jaguar version of a drink called the fusionnaire. *Jade Falcon fusionnaires are more potent than this anemic brew*, she thought. It was all right with her, though, that this one had no kick. She did not want her disguise exposed through casual drunkenness.

Russou Howell strode into the rec hall with a determination characteristic of all his moves. He looked around as if his presence among techs at leisure was natural. Sentania at that moment did not know he was an officer, and there were no insignia on his fatigues. But she had no doubt of his caste. All warriors were arrogant, and rightly so.

"I will sit with you," he said brusquely. "Get me one of those—whatever it is you are having."

She resisted an impulse to tell him to get it himself, but kept her mouth shut. Maybe she was too startled by the fact that a Jaguar officer did not even recognize a fusionnaire. There was, after all, no other drink that looked like it.

She studied him surreptitiously as he downed the potent mixture, but guessed it was not his first drink of the evening. Beneath the receding hairline, she saw that he was obviously of solahma age, and that he had endured much in his time. She usually thought of older officers still active in warrior ranks as solahs. The word was her own, kept in her mind so she could own it. There were a number of words that were her sole possessions.

"You know who I am, *quiaff*?" Howell said, after downing an abnormally big gulp of the drink. His eyebrows were thick and dark, even against his tanned and weathered skin. They made his small eyes even more pronounced and intense.

"Neg," Sentania said. "I do not know you. I do not mingle much with warriors. I am a tech—sanitation repair."

Since she was improvising, she did not know whether the designation was accurate. She counted on the typical warrior tendency to care little about the niceties of the caste system.

"Oh," he said, taking a shorter sip. He seemed to let his tense face relax. "A worthy post indeed. I am Russou Howell."

She raised her eyebrows. He was clearly pleased by the deference in her look. Of course she had *heard* of Howell.

"I hope you are enjoying your refreshment, Galaxy Commander," she said. "And that my presence does not disturb you."

The movement of his lips was almost a smile. *This is one bizarre Jaguar,* she thought.

"Enjoy, what a strange concept," he said, almost to himself. "Perhaps I should travel among the castes more."

"You do this often?"

"What?" he said, as though the words caught him by surprise. "Ah, no. I have sometimes visited warriors in disguise and heard their thoughts spoken freely, but, well, never within the lower castes—and of course I am not now in disguise."

His words affected her in diverse ways. She was at first impressed with the strangeness of a Smoke Jaguar warrior even considering disguise, and oddly pleased by the irony of his sitting with her while she was indeed in disguise. That he visited his troops on the sly also impressed her, but she was most astonished by the idea that he would deign to move within the haunts of the lower castes.

"You wonder why I am here, *quiaff*?"

"Aye, Galaxy Commander." His words again took her by surprise.

"I do not know either." He took another sip, and it seemed to loosen his tongue even more. "I can tell you this, and I can tell it to you because you will not understand it. There are moments when even the most devoted Smoke Jaguar has a doubt or two, even a bitter thought.

This is one of those moments. You do not understand, *quineg*?"

I understand more than you think. I recognize a warrior who's become weary—weary of life, weary of his fate. A solahma, especially, can see that, Russou Howell.

"Neg," she replied.

"Good. Drink with me, Tech—?"

Sentania did not want to give him a name, and no warrior would really notice. "Aye, Galaxy Commander. I am honored."

"Get us two more."

He downed the second drink rather quickly, and much too silently. As a fake tech, Sentania could not ask probing questions to try to learn the source of his strange mood. But in his eyes she read a bewilderment, like one who has suddenly begun asking questions to which there are no answers.

Then Howell said very softly, "Guilt. Can a Clan warrior feel guilt?"

"I do not know, Galaxy Commander."

"Of course you do not, Tech."

Sentania waited to hear more, but he fell into silence, then abruptly slammed his glass down, stood up and left without saying anything more.

Now, watching him glance around the field after stepping energetically off the bulky foot of his *Warhammer,* she was impressed at the fierce clarity in eyes that she had last seen as troubled. His walk toward Horse displayed the extreme confidence of a Clan commander.

"I am Galaxy Commander Russou Howell," he said.

"Why did your ships shoot at us?" Horse asked angrily. "We clearly broadcast the beam of neutrality, which is to be honored throughout the Clans."

"Do you think Smoke Jaguars care about anyone's beam of neutrality?" Howell said. "We have no respect for neutrality. It is weakness."

"It is the breaking of a bond, a—"

"You Jade Falcons are no strangers to the breaking of bonds, when doing so is to your advantage. And this is to our advantage. Jade Falcons have recently conducted a dishonorable skirmish against us, solahma warriors stealing insignia and then sending them back to us to flaunt their victory. The Falcons are here on Huntress only through the continued good will of the Jaguar. We cannot permit such an insult."

Horse shrugged. "I agree, even though you say the perpetrators were from my Clan. Such an action is foolish and not particularly honorable, even though it may be understandable as—"

"Then you agree that punishment is due. That is why you and your force must bear the brunt of our vengeance."

"Your vengeance. For a raid performed by Falcon Eyrie troops? We were not even here then. You must have noticed, since you shot us down, that my Trinary and I have only just arrived on Huntress."

"You are Jade Falcon, *quiaff*?"

"Aff."

"And equally answerable for any dishonorable deed done by any member of your Clan."

"No honorable warrior covers up the misdeeds of others, no matter what their Clan."

"Let us not split hairs. I would not dispute this matter even with a trueborn, but I recognize the markings of the freeborn caste on your uniform—and, for that matter, on the uniforms of your warriors. I do not see any trueborns present even. So, you see, I need not even deal with you, although I will, since you are at least a warrior. Star Captain Horse, I require vengeance on the Jade Falcons. Your enslavement is my vengeance."

"Enslavement? That is—"

"Sufficient to satisfy my vengeance. You earn the punishment for your puny Clan's gnatlike antics. I have recently handed down an edict that my warriors are free to deal with Jade Falcons any way they like. No truce, no bargaining. I will not attack Falcon Eyrie, but I will not tolerate attacks on Smoke Jaguars. The Falcons are on Huntress only because the Jaguar tolerates them."

Horse surged forward to attack Howell. A pair of warriors stopped his progress and held him back.

"Do not bother to fight, Star Captain," Howell said. "You have no rights here. You see now, do you not, that by forbidding you entry to Huntress and by attacking you for trespassing into our territory, I have merely obeyed my own edict by downing your DropShip. If you recall, we did send out a message that you could not enter our skies, right after you initiated your beam of neutrality, *quiaff*?"

"I did not captain the DropShip."

"Bring out the DropShip captain to testify!" Howell shouted to the nearest Smoke Jaguar officer.

"Do not even attempt it," Horse said. "She was knocked unconscious when we crashed. It is serious. She may have a concussion or even skull fracture. She is being attended to."

"All right then. Star Captain Horse, you violated our ban against your entry into our space. We forbade the landing your DropShip captain requested and you came on. We had no choice but to fire on you, *quiaff*?"

"Neg. That is twisted logic. We were merely on our way to our own outpost on Huntress. We would have passed over your territory only momentarily. Your attack on us was vicious and unwarranted, and your tale of reprisal is a mockery! There are agreements among *all* the Clans that—"

"Stop! No Jade Falcon can judge a Smoke Jaguar. You do not tell us what we must do. Much less what we *can* do. We have treated you fairly, *stravag* freebirth!"

Horse struggled within the grasp of his captors. Russou Howell turned slightly. One of his Star Commanders emerged from a hole in the side of the DropShip.

"There are BattleMechs inside," the Jaguar reported, her loud voice carrying across the clearing. "A full Trinary's worth."

Howell turned back toward Horse. "A Trinary? See? I was right to forbid you landing here. Obviously you have come to Huntress to attack us. Another reason why we are not obligated to obey your neutrality beam—your false symbol of neutrality. These 'Mechs show you intended an act of war, and the rules and customs of war apply."

"You cannot make that assumption. We are here in peace. We were not even taking the 'Mechs to Falcon Eyrie. They would have remained in the DropShip."

"You lie, freebirth Horse," Howell spat out. "I am Galaxy Commander Russou Howell, and I claim your BattleMechs, your warriors, and all else we choose from your ship of deceit. Your invasion of our territory has failed and—"

"You have no right to, to confiscate. According to Clan—"

"Silence!" Howell yelled.

Sentania had moved to a spot from which she could view Howell better. He now stood at full attention as he bellowed, "Jade Falcon, you may not claim any rights here. To speak truly, I need your BattleMechs, no matter what their condition or their age, and I have no qualms about confiscating them in response to an act of war."

Horse struggled against his captors. "By Clan custom, you may not do this. First, you must allow me to contest you in a Trial of—"

"You cannot demand a Trial of anything, Star Captain Horse, although you show an admirable audacity in even suggesting it."

"The Clans—"

"Silence!" Russou barked. "This is not a matter of Clan custom, particularly when it involves freebirth scum. Know this well, Star Captain Horse, as freebirths you and your people have no rights here. Smoke Jaguars do not, like the Jade Falcons, allow freebirths within their warrior ranks. From this moment on you are Prisoner Horse, and you and your entire Trinary have no rights but those few accorded prisoners within our Clan. Do not even try to resist."

Howell made an expansive gesture toward the edge of the forest, from which a fully armed contingent of Elemental warriors appeared and started marching forward. Howell ordered the Elemental Star Commander to take charge of the prisoners and march them back to Lootera.

To the Star Commander who had searched the Drop-Ship, he gave the command to start collecting the Battle-Mechs and take them to the repair bay for examination. He allowed the DropShip crew to stay with their ship and begin repairs on it. They would be allowed free passage off Huntress if they managed to get their ship working again.

Sentania watched Horse carefully. He clearly wanted to kill Howell, but he was smart enough to recognize odds that were against him. When he was released, instead of going toward Howell, he wheeled around and began to tend the wounds of his fallen comrades.

For the next few minutes, Sentania had to dodge around the area, keeping out of the way of discovery.

When Horse's Trinary and its support techs were all finally assembled, they were led out of the clearing by the Elementals. On an impulse that she could not rationally justify, Sentania slipped from the forest and inserted herself into the ranks of the prisoners. None of the guards noticed her. She had no worry. She knew she could escape again. No Smoke Jaguar facility could hold Sentania Buhallin.

9

Warrior Quarter
Lootera, Huntress
Kerensky Cluster, Clan Space
21 March 3059

After being forced to travel two hours on foot, Horse and
his unit were brought by their Jaguar guards to the
Lootera city limits, which they entered through an
impressive, free-standing arch that served as a kind of
ceremonial city gate. There, they were met once more by
Howell, who came to officially greet his new captives. He
ordered everyone but Horse taken to the detention center,
then led Horse over to a hovercar.

Whisked through the city of Lootera, Horse observed
the streets through which they passed with great curiosity.
He caught glimpses of a river as the car passed along
smoothly. From what he could ascertain, the river bordered one side of the city. After going a short distance,
they turned into a sector with a distinctly different feel
from what he had seen so far. Horse guessed by the suddenly weighty look of the architecture that this was the
Warrior Quarter.

The main boulevard of the Quarter was impressive. It
was quite wide and lined with massive, inscribed gray
stone pillars on either side. This ponderous look was
especially pronounced in the enormous monument to
General Alexandr Kerensky, leader of the Exodus and

father of Nicholas Kerensky, founder of the Clans. Over-large and unnatural, the statue was circled by a fountain whose waters surged in a series of miniature waterfalls. Opposite the Kerensky monument was a pyramid, standing almost at the foot of a large mountain that loomed over the city. The structure was surrounded by a wide stone parade field lined with stone sculptures of Battle-Mechs, all facing away from the pyramid. The 'Mech statues appeared to be inscribed along the bottom, but the hovercar did not pass close enough for Horse to be able to read the writing. Horse found the whole scene oppressive.

"Fine work, *quiaff*?" Howell said, obvious pride in his voice, as they came to a halt.

"If you like big statues."

Howell seemed to ignore the sarcasm. "I meant the pyramid. It houses our genetic repository. An impressive architectural achievement, *quiaff*—majestic and simple at the same time."

"I can see what you mean," Horse said carefully. He conceded the impressiveness, but simple and majestic were words that did not really seem to apply. A decade ago Horse might never have made such distinctions. In the time since, he had read most of Aidan Pryde's secret library, plus a few volumes that he, in a strangely insatiable search for more useless knowledge, had picked up elsewhere. His studies had revealed to him a great deal about what humans beyond the Clan homeworlds considered art. Much of what the Clans produced would certainly not be called art by those who cared for such things, but Horse admired the sense of the human spirit and living heroism often captured in Clan creations. However, Lootera's bombastic and sterile displays were not, according to either standard, art.

"I can tell that you do not agree," Howell said, glancing over at Horse.

"It is not agreement or disagreement," Horse returned, noticing something odd in the intensity of the Galaxy Commander's gaze. "I feel differently about such things, I suppose."

"Explain."

Horse knew he was venturing into dangerous terrain, a discussion of how two different Clans expressed what they valued and admired. He ventured anyway. It was his nature.

"We Jade Falcons have our own approaches to heroic display. I cannot judge yours."

"Tell me your thoughts."

"I saw a statue somewhere. On a Clan Jade Falcon world, I do not remember which one. It depicted a hero, I do not remember whom. It was made of some material or other, I do not remember what. What I do remember is that it showed a Jade Falcon warrior in action. Veins of effort stood out on the surface of the arms and legs. I know it was all stone, but it looked real. There was something, a fierceness maybe, in the way the sculptor chiseled the eyes. They made me uncomfortable, they were so much like a falcon's. A true Falcon warrior. Well, it stirred in me an excitement that was surprising. At the time I thought my reaction indicated weakness. Now I know that I was stirred by the—I do not know what to call it—I guess the craftsmanship of the statue."

"And you do not see the craftsmanship here?"

"I see it. But it does not stir me."

Howell seemed angry, and his own eyes shifted back to the statues.

"I can assure you that I am stirred by them, Prisoner Horse. To a great sense of pride in my Clan. And I am even more stirred by that—over there. Our tribute on Mount Szabo."

Howell pointed up and Horse's eyes followed. On the southern face of the mountain was carved out the massive form of a smoke jaguar. The animal crouched, looking as if it would pounce on the city at any moment, as if it would crush it beneath its great weight. Horse caught his breath. The carving was indeed different from the rest of Lootera's architecture and monuments. In his opinion, its details had been created by a real artist.

"What puny opinion do you have about that, freebirth?"

"That is what I mean. It lives, breathes. Its pose seems realistic."

"And what do you think of it?"

"I like it."

Howell smiled. "Of course you do. You will learn to like the statues, too, if I have anything to say about it." He signaled the driver to stop the car. "Come with me."

* * *

To Horse, Russou Howell's office was as cold as the
rest of Lootera. In spite of a rather impressive black desk
at one end and a polished wooden cabinet against the
opposite wall, the room was severely functional, meticulously arranged, and devoid of decoration.

Horse was accustomed to simple rooms. Most Jade
Falcon offices and quarters showed not much more adorn-
ment, though he had seen the occasional framed painting
on a wall. Even the notoriously neat office of Ravill Pryde
was not as severe as this one. Yet, the Smoke Jaguars
seemed inconsistent. Their city was, after all, a mixture of
styles, even garish in places. The only actual link between
this office and the rest of the city was its *emptiness*.

Howell crossed to his desk and sat staring at Horse for a
moment. Apparently, he could not resist the urge to convince Horse of the artistry of the Smoke Jaguars. "Those
stone BattleMech statues we saw surrounding the repository commemorate the deeds of our greatest warriors,
whose genetic materials are kept there. We naturally contemplate our Clan's present and future warrior strength
when we see the pyramid and go within to honor our legacies. Here in Lootera is the largest and most significant
preserve of Smoke Jaguar genetic legacies."

Howell fairly glowed with pride. "And there is our
crowning glory, Mount Szabo, the most famous peak on
Huntress."

Horse thought he perceived something hollow in the
Smoke Jaguar Galaxy Commander, some straining to
convince himself that his words were more than mere
braggadocio.

Howell rubbed his balding pate, disturbing the few
hairs he had combed across it. "The mountains of Huntress are formidable—as are, for that matter, its heavy
forests and thick jungles. Most of the planet's other hemi-
sphere is a scorching desert without significant habitation.
The Huntress oceans are small, but there is no lack of
water, due to this continent's plentiful springs and rainfall. Geography, in fact, plays a major role on Huntress.
Your Jade Falcon station, Falcon Eyrie, paltry as it is,
enjoys natural protection because it sits on a rocky
plateau among the high peaks of the Eastern Mountains. I

assume you know that, and I assume you and your Trinary had some purpose in going there."

"Assume what you will. As a captive, I am bound to remain silent." Horse kept his gaze steady.

"You are not required to remain silent on your former Clan associations. We claim prisoners for the Smoke Jaguar Clan. It is your Clan now."

"That sounds suspiciously like being a bondsman."

Howell laughed uproariously. Horse tried not to stare at him, but the man's violent swings of mood were jarring.

Howell leaned casually forward on his desk. "No worries along those lines. None of you can be bondsmen, Horse. You and your Trinary, you are all freeborn scum. Unlike the misguided Jade Falcons, we do not allow freeborns among our warriors, nor do we ever make them bondsmen. The idea itself is revolting."

Horse's face reddened, his fists clenched.

"You will understand eventually. I am sure of that." Howell looked smug. "As our prisoners, you are bound by the rules and customs of Clan Smoke Jaguar. You must serve us. We do allow freeborns to serve us."

"If we do not?"

"We excel at punishment."

"You steal our BattleMechs, then expect us to do your bidding."

Howell steepled his fingers on his desktop. "If you were trueborns, the response would be different. You would be made bondsmen, or returned to your Clan, or honorably killed. Honor is not, however, due freebirth prisoners. We will use your warriors honorably, but as prisoners. Prisoners serve us in the maintenance of our streets, the cleaning of sewers, the polishing of metal surfaces like statues and plaques. We can always use more maintenance techs in Lootera, for the city must shine—it is the capital of the Jaguar homeworld, after all. I am sure you Jade Falcons will do very nicely."

"You plan to use warriors in tech roles? And you consider that honorable? It is abominable." Horse fairly sputtered.

"By the rules of warfare, I have every right to use you Falcon freebirths as I wish."

"Is this warfare then?"

"Do not question wording. I have captured your 'Mechs and your Trinary and—"

"I demand release for all! Your seizure of a Jade Falcon Trinary and its BattleMechs was unlawfully accomplished under the signal of neutrality and—"

"As a freebirth you may not even put forth such claims."

"I demand free passage to Falcon Eyrie!"

Howell smiled and tapped his fingers on the desk. "You do not understand, that is clear. It does not matter what Clan you formerly belonged to. I have claimed you and your people for the Smoke Jaguars. In our Clan all free-births are fair game—unless, of course, they are properly under the command of a trueborn. There is not even a trueborn among your Trinary, proof of the decadence to which the Jade Falcons have descended, *quiaff*?"

Howell did not even pause to wait for Horse to agree. "The Falcon victory over the Wolves in the Refusal War helped purge the traitorous Ulric and his mewling Wardens from the ranks of the Clans, but look at your heroes—this Star Commander Joanna, for one. It is true she killed the Black Widow on Twycross, but the two of them should have been thrown onto the trash heap long ago. What were either one of them doing in battle anyway? And what glory can there be in one old solahma warrior shooting down another?"

Howell seemed to be watching Horse for a reaction. Horse was angry, but he'd be damned if he would let this truebirth see it. Howell seemed to be prodding and poking at him purely for the fun of it.

"And do not imagine that the puny forces on Falcon Eyrie can help you either," Howell said. "They can barely mount a raid. And their present leader, a certain Bren Roshak, a Star Colonel, I believe, is not known for daring leadership. Besides, you are freebirth. No warrior would waste time or resources contesting for your freedom."

"You insult the honor of the Jade Falcons."

"These are not insults but statements of fact. Do not contradict me again, Horse. You are *freebirth* and have no rights here."

Howell paused and studied Horse's face, which Horse kept totally impassive.

"You hate that word, do you not, freebirth?" Howell said, leaning into the word.

"When you are freeborn, *freebirth* is always an abhorrent word," Horse said coolly. "You know that well enough. That is why you use it. On the other hand, my kind has heard it used against us all our lives."

Horse refused to tell Howell that, as he had grown older, he was actually more and more enraged by such insults.

Howell gave a small unreadable smile. "Yet—it must be difficult for even a stoic warrior like you to endure. Of course, your whole life is an insult."

Horse responded angrily. "What I know is this. I have proved myself as good a warrior as any trues I have met."

Howell's face became cold with fury. "You are out of line in comparing freeborn exploits to those of the true warriors."

Horse held out his wrist to display the bracelet that contained his codex. "My codex proves it. It shows more damage inflicted on the enemy, more kills, more brave acts than in the codexes of the average trueborn warrior, even some of the above-average ones."

"Even in your freeborn-loving Clan, not much weight is given to a freeborn's codex. They are rarely examined."

"That is, unfortunately, true, Galaxy Commander Howell." Horse stepped forward boldly and flattened his palms on Howell's desk as he leaned across toward the other man. "But, whether you know it or not, I have won a place in the *Remembrance*. How many lines do you have in the Smoke Jaguar *Remembrance*, Galaxy Commander?"

As Horse had expected, Howell reacted instantly. His arm whipped out, backhanded, to slap Horse hard across the cheek. The blow stung but, since Horse had known it was coming, he smiled broadly. He straightened up slowly, holding Howell's eyes with his.

Horse was sure he was right. This man Howell, he was sure, had never been a hero. The look of fury on Howell's face gave it away. Besides, he was old enough to be solahma, and would not be assigned here, removed from the action in the Inner Sphere, if his Clan still valued him as a warrior. There were no lines in anyone's *Remembrance* for Russou Howell, and there never would be.

Let Howell deride him for being a freeborn. Horse knew who he was and what he had achieved. He had trained and fought alongside the Jade Falcon hero Aidan Pryde. Later, after Aidan was killed, Ravill Pryde had kept him as a member of the Falcon Guard Cluster Command Star, freeborn or not. And now Horse was on a mission for the Khan herself. Nevertheless, wherever he went, whomever he met, whatever he achieved, he would always be nothing but a freebirth in the minds of the trues. The word trueborn was the highest honor, while the word freebirth was so low it was even used as a vile curse word.

Freebirth.

He would like to take the word, turn it into corrosive poison, and shove it down Russou Howell's throat. Then he would sit back smiling and watch the man's death throes.

But there was nothing to be gained from goading this Jag officer. Horse knew he was responsible for the safety of his Trinary and their BattleMechs. He must gain control of himself for the sake of his men and his Clan and his mission. He shrugged slightly. "All right, then, I and my men are your prisoners."

"You will be my personal prisoner. That infuriates you, *quiaff*?"

"Neg, Galaxy Commander. It is duty. Even freeborns understand duty."

"Good," Howell said. "You and the others will be housed in our detention center for the time being. Your eventual disposition will depend on your various work assignments."

Howell stood up then with amazing quickness, and though Horse never saw where it came from, a whip suddenly appeared in the commander's hand. He did not open it up, but leaned across the desk and hit Horse in the face with the handle in almost precisely the same place he had slapped him earlier. Perhaps there was already a bruise there serving as a target.

Horse wanted to snatch the whip away and beat Howell with it himself. But he had his Trinary to think of and his mission. He couldn't help anybody while he was Howell's prisoner, so the smart thing would be to pretend submission until he could figure out how to get out of this mess. If this Jaguar wanted to play master and slave, Horse would just have to go along until he could find a way out.

"Be careful of your words, freebirth. You are not a warrior now and cannot behave like one."

"Aye, Galaxy Commander."

There was a long uneasy silence as the two men stood staring at each other across the gleaming obsidian of the desktop.

Then Howell spoke again. "Let me tell you something else, freebirth. As you know, Huntress is defended by solahma units, two Galaxies of them. The young warriors will be shipped immediately to resupply the front lines almost as soon as they have tested out. I suspect the same is true of your former Clan. The homeworlds are not endangered, and my Galaxies can certainly defend against any attack by the Ice Hellions or any other Home Clan who seeks to bury their shame for not participating in the invasion. My troops may be solahma, but they are still warriors. And I intend to make them even better ones, whether they want it or not. Discipline, obedience, and duty are the order of the day around here, and you had best remember that."

Horse recalled Marthe Pryde's premonition that the Inner Sphere might one day discover the location of the homeworlds and try to attack them. At the time he had considered the possibility totally absurd. Now, he realized that the homeworld defenders—used-up solahma warriors at best—might turn out to be easy prey. And yet, how could the Inner Sphere possibly invade the homeworlds? They had no idea at all of their location, and no way at all of finding out. Had Horse not been in this sober room with this sober Smoke Jaguar officer, he might have laughed out loud.

"And freeborn warriors, you have none, *quiaff*?"

A hint of disgust came into Howell's face as he spoke. "As I said, we Jaguars do not allow freeborns into the warrior caste. We believe it is unproductive to train or employ freeborns as warriors. We tolerate your kind in the professional and tech castes, but a freeborn warrior is a contradiction in terms."

"Then you will not use me in a warrior capacity, even as a prisoner?"

"I could not possibly. A prisoner *and* a freeborn? That would be a grave insult to my Clan."

"And our BattleMechs, you will use them, even though they are tainted by our former presence in their cockpits?"

"They will be refitted and decontaminated as Smoke Jaguar 'Mechs, and no doubt improved in the process. Our tech caste is infinitely superior to that of the Jade Falcons."

"I may conclude then that you do not have sufficient materiel for a proper defense of Huntress, or even Lootera."

Howell looked ready to use the whip handle again. "What are you, Horse, some kind of spy?"

Horse shook his head. "Neg," he said mildly. "I am merely hoping that you will find a way to use me effectively. The Clans abhor waste, and I wish to be useful, even as a prisoner."

"Spoken like a true Clansman."

"But not a true*born* Clansman."

"That is obvious. Why do you say it?"

"In my former Clan we had an unusual trait we called humor, and sometimes a sense of humor. I will have to purge myself of it."

"Please do, freebirth."

Before dismissing him to be taken to the detention center, Howell explained the rights and rules of Jaguar prisoners. It was as though he were recounting the formal bonds of some ritual.

"As a prisoner," he said, "you are the property of the Smoke Jaguars, and thus you become a member of the Clan. Although only a trueborn may be a bondsman, our prisoners must show allegiance to the Clan. In that respect, they are like bondsmen, but without the honors that may be awarded bondsmen.

"If you and your freeborn Trinary do not maintain loyalty, or if you try to escape from us, we will kill or torture immediately. There are no judges or judgments. Killing or torture is automatic, and may be administered by any Smoke Jaguar. Not just warriors, but *any* Smoke Jaguar. You could be executed by a mere laborer, Horse, if your acts warranted it. An ignominious end, *quiaff*—to be executed by a freebirth lower in status than yourself? I will win your loyalty. Soon, former Star Captain Horse, you will become a Smoke Jaguar, fully committed to our Clan."

Horse wanted to laugh in Howell's face, but he knew that for the moment he must tell the man exactly what he wanted to hear.

"Aye, Galaxy Commander."

"Excellent, freebirth. You and your freebirth Trinary will gather in the repository square this afternoon to acknowledge your prisoner status and its concomitant agreements."

Horse hated Howell's repeated use of the word *freebirth*. It was, of course, proper, but it made him furious.

≡ 10 ≡

Warrior Quarter
Lootera, Huntress
Kerensky Cluster, Clan Homeworlds
21 March 3059

After his interview with Russou Howell, Horse was taken
on foot to the detention center, a short walk from Mount
Szabo. The afternoon air was muggy with the threat of
rain, but Horse was so lost in his own thoughts that he
barely noticed. He went over in his mind the bizarre conversation he'd just had with the head man on Huntress.
Everything Russou Howell had said and done in the few
short hours since he'd shot down Horse's DropShip was
baffling. Except for one thing—the man obviously
intended to break Horse's spirit, or at least make his life
miserable. Horse had dealt with worse in his time as a
freeborn warrior, and he would take anything Howell
might dish out.

Now as he came into the large wardroom where his
men were being held, MechWarrior Croft beckoned him
over to share some food their captors had provided. Croft,
a strange bird, had previously been assigned to overseeing
a mining colony of Inner Sphere prisoners on one of
the Falcon-occupied planets, definitely not an assignment
for a top-echelon Jade Falcon warrior, especially in the
occupation zone. Croft had been so glad to be relieved of
that duty that he'd bear-hugged Horse with considerable

strength the moment he got the news. Normally, warriors detested such displays, and were especially repulsed if the contact was executed with vigor. However, freeborns from some villages were brought up with more customs that involved touching, and even the most aloof of Jade Falcon warriors might have to endure such contacts from time to time. Still, Horse had dodged the burly man's company from that point on.

"This food is not much," Croft commented as Horse approached the table, "but it sure beats DropShip chow, *quiaff*?" Horse could not figure out why the man seemed positively jovial.

"I am not very hungry. Croft, does your enjoyment of the food mean that you *like* being a prisoner of the Smoke Jaguars?"

Croft's joviality immediately vanished. "I am Jade Falcon and will always be so. I will not challenge you, Star Captain Horse, because I believe you are joking. You are joking, *quiaff*?"

"In my way I suppose I am."

Horse walked away, leaving a less cheerful Croft in his wake. Sometimes, Horse decided, that was what leadership was all about, shaming a warrior back into his senses. But could he shame this whole Trinary of freeborn warriors, all of whom seemed to be enjoying themselves at this moment?

Star Commander Pegeen, commander of Beta Talon, strode up to him. Because she was smaller and not as muscular as the typical Clan MechWarrior, others believed that she could be easily subdued. Quickly—dazzled by her array of combat techniques—most challengers had to admit the error of their judgment.

When Horse had collected his Trinary and assigned rank and role to these freeborns who had been consigned to him by Marthe Pryde, some of the group were disgruntled about him giving Pegeen Star Commander rank. Four of Horse's special Trinary challenged Pegeen for her command and won only humiliation as the result. Pegeen knew more about combat, including a vast array of dirty tricks, than any other freeborn warrior Horse had ever known—excluding himself, of course.

As she came up to Horse, her face displayed a curious and mysterious amusement. She touched his arm briefly as a signal for his attention, and Horse noticed that hers looked more like a child's limb sticking out of some adult's too-big clothing. Her straw-colored hair was, as usual, unkempt, with several strands hanging down over her smiling eyes.

"We may have a spy among us," she said quietly.

"A spy?" Pegeen's words took Horse totally by surprise. "Where?"

"Look over there, near the wall, the woman eating alone. She is wearing a Jade Falcon uniform, but not like ours. Hers is a field uniform, worn on duty. They are not fatigues like ours, and she is not part of our unit. See, there is no freeborn piping on her uniform."

"Perhaps she was one of the ship's crew. I know they left most of them behind for repair duty, but some were—"

"No, I know all the ship's crew. She was not among them. She was not even on the ship, I am certain. She is a warrior, that much I can tell. Warrior's eyes, a warrior's bearing. She looks trueborn."

"How could you possibly discern that?"

"She has that swagger you see in all truebirth louts."

"I take it you despise trueborns."

"Always. As they despise us."

"I understand. Why would there be a warrior among us, wearing a Jade Falcon field uniform? Is she Smoke Jaguar, do you think?"

"Possibly. Are they so inept they would plant such an obvious spy?"

"No. Humorless and overdisciplined, but not inept. I doubt they would stoop to spying either. Let us see what we can find out. Accompany me, Star Commander Pegeen."

"Of course."

They went directly to where the woman sat. She was picking at the food on her plate and examining the rest of the room surreptitiously. *She moves her eyes like a spy,* Horse thought, *but if that is her purpose, why conduct the business so blatantly?*

"I am Star Captain Horse," he announced, standing over her. Pegeen edged in closer to the woman, as if to protect her commanding officer from sudden attack. This was Pegeen's peculiar virtue, he thought, to be so loyal she would protect someone who did not especially need protection.

"I know who you are," the woman responded. Standing up, she looked directly into Horse's eyes. She was tall, just slightly shorter than Joanna. She also resembled Joanna in her obvious age and the steeliness of her gaze, but there was none of Joanna's anger. Actually, this woman seemed even older than Joanna. Though the look in her eyes was youthful enough, the wrinkles around them were the accumulations of many years. Not only that, he also noticed the tiny creases one often saw at the corners of the mouths of ancient warriors.

"I have to say, Horse, that I was a bit shocked to see a freeborn in command of a Trinary. How do such wonders come about these days among the Jade Falcons?"

"You speak as if we know each other."

"We have met. I expect you do not remember. My name is Sentania Buhallin."

"A bloodname. You are trueborn then?"

"Aye, but it seems that none of these Smoke Jaguar scum noticed a trueborn among you freeborns. Best place to hide, out in the open. They perceived nothing, though I would have checked codexes immediately. They are dense, these Jaguars. Dangerous, but dense. Watch out for their new leader, though."

"Russou Howell?"

"They say he has seen some fierce fighting in the invasion. And he has shown toughness in his new role. He fought one of his warriors who questioned his right to command, and the man ended up in the hospital. They say he's a bit erratic, but he's only been here a month. Meanwhile, he's been shaking things up, calling inspections, running drills, stepping up field exercises. Guess he wants to shape these Jaguars up."

"How is it that a Jade Falcon should know so much about Smoke Jaguars?"

"I get around. I can never sit still for long. You would be surprised at the places I've been to."

"Star Captain," Pegeen said, "this woman has to be a spy. How did she even get here, if not planted?"

Sentania smiled. "I came in with you. Straggling unnoticed at the end of the line, but with you nevertheless. I was in the forest when your DropShip crashed. I joined your ranks as you were being led away."

"You *voluntarily* became a prisoner?" Pegeen's eyes widened with incredulity. "That is hard to believe, Sentania Buhallin—if that *is* your name."

"Of course it is. And I am no prisoner. I can slip away as easily as I came. As long as I am unaccounted for in your ranks, I can become invisible. As soon as I see a codex check coming, I will be elsewhere."

"That is—"

"Enough, Star Commander Pegeen," Horse interrupted. "I believe her. The more I look at her, the more I seem to remember seeing her before. Leave us."

Pegeen accepted the command calmly, as always. She moved off.

"All right, Sentania Buhallin," Horse said, gesturing her to a wooden chair and pulling up another one to sit beside her, "I need to know more. If you are Jade Falcon, what is your rank and where do you come from?"

"I am Solahma Star Captain Sentania Buhallin and my unit is stationed at Falcon Eyrie. It has been a dull life there, but now that you are here, Star Captain Horse, I suspect that our boredom may be relieved."

Russou Howell's encounter with Horse had unsettled him. He sat at his desk, staring off into space at the spot where, less than an hour ago, he had attempted to tame Horse's spirit by hitting and humiliating him. It was not the man's freeborn status that bothered him. He had been around freeborns often enough. But this Horse—he was different. Clearly stubborn, clearly confident, clearly bold, the man did not allow his inferior birth to interfere with his independence of spirit. He would be more trouble than he was worth—to Howell or to the Smoke Jaguars. Howell would probably have to kill him eventually.

Russou Howell had never been a warrior of great ambition, beyond the burning desire to serve his Clan well. He had not even minded when his friend and sibmate, Star Captain Trent, had beaten him in the Trial of Position for command of Beta Striker Trinary of the Beta Galaxy. Howell had been one with himself and his existence, reveling in the exhilaration of combat, satisfied with his role as a respected Smoke Jaguar officer, overjoyed when

Trent miraculously returned from an assignment to the homeworlds and won a new command. Russou never wanted anything but to honor the way of the Clans, and he was Crusader through and through. The conquest of the Inner Sphere seemed to him right and just. Then, in a short time, everything about his life changed.

He had suddenly been nominated for a bloodname contest and had earned the bloodname, followed by an abrupt battlefield promotion to Star Captain. After that, his world had radically changed. He had been forced to kill his only friend, made to think that friend might be a traitor.

As happened so many times in a day, his mind drifted back to that day on Maldonado, the heavy fighting, the failure of the plan of attack, the Trinary on the run from the Combine defenders and their ComStar allies. The order to destroy Trent from Star Colonel Paul Moon, an order Russou had no choice but to obey. Moon had done everything possible to break Trent. But Trent had prevailed.

Then came Maldonado. He would never forget Paul Moon's voice booming over the battlefield, but another voice haunted him even more. The voice was Trent's, coming over the commline to Russou in his *Mad Dog*.

"You will have to destroy me, Russou. You know that."

The memory chilled Russou. Their long years of comradeship flashed before his eyes. Times in the sibko, times of serving together, times of sharing the kind of secrets one warrior rarely revealed to another. He had told Trent he did not want to kill him.

"You have no choice. This is how this must end."

At that moment Russou had reverted to what he had always been, a loyal Smoke Jaguar officer. But his eyes had filled with tears as he ordered his Star to attack Trent. At the same time he saw the Com Guard forces also rushing in at his old friend. Russou could not remember the last time he had cried—or if he ever had in his life—but the tears streamed down his face as he watched Trent's 'Mech disintegrate and his mind's eye watched his friend die a terrible death within the cockpit.

Afterward, Star Colonel Paul Moon rewarded him for making the right choice, the Smoke Jaguar choice. Moon had insisted that Howell fight a Trial of Position to

attain the rank of Star Colonel. Yet, it had been only
a short time since he had been an unbloodnamed Star
Commander. The promotions were coming too hard and
too fast; as a result, he did not see the subterfuges of
Moon's plan.

Always one to follow orders, Russou fought the Trial of
Position and won it easily. He came away from the fight
feeling barely tested and with a strange feeling that the
event had been rigged. Further, the disturbing thoughts
about Trent continued to haunt him. It was as if the road
forward was stained with Trent's blood.

Star Colonel Moon had hardly pinned the Star Colonel
insignia on Howell's uniform when he informed him of
his new orders. He was to be shunted homeward, back to
the Kerensky Cluster, to command of Zeta Galaxy and the
planet Huntress.

On Huntress he had first encountered resistance from
what he perceived as inferior subordinates, weaker troops.
He had taken care of that for a time with his easy victory
over Cajuste, but now the warriors were again showing
signs of restlessness, again seeming to show a lack of
confidence in Howell as a commander. That must not
continue. Huntress was part of the great Crusade, for
it would provide both men and materiel to conquer the
Inner Sphere once and for all. Indeed, a Smoke Jaguar
would lead the crusade again. Lincoln Osis had been
elected ilKhan, and Russou considered this right and
just. The original thrust of the Crusade had been commanded by another Smoke Jaguar, ilKhan Leo Showers.
The next ilKhan had been a traitor, but he was dead now.
With a Jaguar again in the lead, the Clans would prevail
once more.

Howell rose uneasily from his desk and crossed aim-
lessly to the window. But none of this could ameliorate
the fact that his life had been shaken up, and all he held
dear become a mockery. Why had he, a line officer content with his status, been suddenly allowed to compete for
a bloodname and then, a surprise even to him, earned it
and a promotion to star captaincy? Why had he been so
conveniently there where Moon could order him to kill
his friend? Why had the Trial of Position even taken
place? Why the sudden rank of Star Colonel and, above
all, why Huntress, where he assumed the rank of Galaxy

Commander when he had been only a Star Colonel for such a short time?

Russou Howell stared out his window at the genetic repository, then up at the stirring sculpture of the springing smoke jaguar. *I am probably where I am supposed to be. Yet, what have I just said? I used the word probably. I rarely needed that word before. To me everything was set, ordered, unchangeable. And now—I have become a pawn. Paul Moon used me in a plan that I could not perceive because he wanted to retire an old officer and send him back to the homeworlds. He saw to it that suddenly an undistinguished but good officer would rise through the ranks, be set up, accomplish his devious purposes, and then be gotten out of the way. A pawn, yes, that is the right word. I have been used for what I have to assume is the greater strategy. But, how could I have killed Trent, my sibmate, my only friend, no matter how justified it may have been? For once I could have disobeyed an order. I did not. And now—now what? I am no longer the same. I was never bitter, now I am bitter. I was never a leader, now I have my own command. I once was a necessary warrior, now I am commander of a solahma garrison. I have to accept it all. I do. I must. What else can I do?*

Howell began to clench and unclench his fists. A nervous habit now. He watched his hands, but kept doing it. He had never had a nervous habit before. It was worth study.

Horse sat back and stared into the eyes of Sentania Buhallin, who stared right back with a defiance that amused him.

"You amaze me, Sentania. Are you sure you are solahma?"

"Look at my face."

"It is attractive."

"It is also old. Look at these lines. They have been growing there like weeds, faster all the time."

Horse smiled. He could not figure out what interested him in this solahma warrior's face. And then suddenly he knew just what it was.

Years ago he had passed the tests given to freeborns for recruitment into warrior training. He was the only one from his town who had succeeded and—so far unfamiliar with trueborn attitudes toward freeborns—he was elated at the prospect of earning a chance to pilot a BattleMech. His village was proud of him. No one was prouder, though, than Yasine, the daughter of a laborer. She was a bit below-caste for Horse, whose family were of the merchant caste, but such things did not matter so much among freeborns.

Yasine had a round face and wide eyes and looked nothing like Sentania Buhallin. But there was something in the eyes of both, an eagerness, an animation that they did share. They also spoke similarly—quickly and with energy.

Yasine may have loved him. She would never have said so. Open expression of affection was discouraged within all Jade Falcon castes, although it was rumored that the scientist caste was looser and more likely to violate caste traditions. He liked Yasine, but he was going to be a Jade Falcon warrior and could not love her because warriors did not love. He had heard that most warriors looked down with disdain at village matters, and he was already in training to absorb warrior beliefs.

Just before they parted, Yasine and Horse had taken a walk beside the river that skirted the village. He had been excited that he would soon leave for Ironhold and warrior training, and he could not stop talking about it. Even though Yasine had taken the tests and failed, she listened without resentment.

Horse abruptly stopped talking about his future when he saw Yasine smiling. "Why do you smile?" he asked. "I am happy for you," she said. She put her arms around him and gently embraced him. It was one of the few times in his life when an affectionate gesture had not disturbed him.

Back in the village they said goodbye. Next morning he left. He never saw Yasine again.

Horse blinked his eyes twice, trying to shake the superimposed image of Yasine's face over Sentania Buhallin's face. He supposed that the only real similarity between the two was that, at different ages, they both represented humanity's ancient ideals of beauty. Neither of them probably ever realized that. So many people in his life—

Diana, Yasine, even Joanna, and now Sentania Buhallin—were viewed by him for their physical attributes. What, he wondered, was wrong with him?

"So, Sentania Buhallin, you are concerned with age?"

"Are you an idiot, Star Captain? You do not seem like one. The only solahma warriors who are not concerned with age are either brain-numb, brain dead, or just dead."

"I apologize."

"Apologies? Are you sure you are a Jade Falcon warrior?"

"I merely meant that I spoke, as you say, idiotically. I have always pictured solahma units as . . . I do not know how to put it, but—"

"As mere fodder walking into weapons fire in order to buy time for the real warriors? As upright dead people?"

"Something like that. You can be quite blunt."

"I am Jade Falcon."

Horse laughed. The laughter startled some of the free-born warriors around them.

"I meant bluntness above and beyond the call of duty, Sentania Buhallin."

"I was like that before I was assigned to a solahma unit."

"I believe you."

"Why would you not, freebirth?"

Horse realized that her use of *freebirth* should have angered him. Somehow, when spoken by this vigorous solahma warrior, he was not disturbed by its use.

"What, then, do solahma warriors do here on Huntress?"

"Our duty."

Horse smiled. "And your duty, what is it mainly?"

"You are inquisitive—and you called me the spy."

"You know I am not. I and my warriors wish to find our way to Falcon Eyrie. Russou Howell does not intend to let us leave, and there is little chance of a rescue mission coming from the JumpShip. None of the crew are warriors. I can only hope they can get a message to someone. For the time being we are trapped on Huntress." *And who knows when or if Khan Marthe will bother trying to find us,* he thought sardonically. "Myself, I would rather be trapped at Falcon Eyrie than Lootera. I would rather be a freeborn among solahmas than a prisoner. I would—"

"I can see you hold no respect for solahmas. It is the way of the Clans, freeborns and trueborns, to sneer at the solahma warrior. Oh, lip service about courage and valor, that is all right. But, once you assign us to our solahma units, you forget about us. We are so insignificant that, like now, even a freebirth may insult us. Well, ease your mind. There are several others at Falcon Eyrie, as you already know."

"What do you mean?"

"You know more about Falcon Eyrie than you pretend, Horse. After all, why are you here in the first place? Clearly your mission was not to go to Smoke Jaguar territory and get yourselves captured. You intended to drop onto Falcon Eyrie in the first place, you and your Trinary. But why?"

"I heard the food in your mess hall was good."

"I should challenge you to an honor duel for that rudeness, freebirth."

"Perhaps you will have that chance, away from Lootera."

The moment of tension silenced them briefly.

"All right, Sentania Buhallin. I cannot speak freely about my presence here on Huntress. Suffice to say that I am here and that is that. I wish to get to the Jade Falcon station."

"That is all I need to know."

"To tell the truth, I like you, Sentania Buhallin and I do not wish for us to be angry with each other."

"Are these plain words or do you merely see me as a means for your escape from Lootera?"

"I will escape with or without you. But with you may be simpler. You will help us, *quiaff*?"

"Well bargained and done."

Sentania Buhallin offered a handshake. Horse took her hand. Its skin felt rough and weathered. However, he noticed there were few wrinkles on the back of her hands. His hands had more wrinkles, in fact.

Several other members of the Trinary noticed the ritual and looked puzzled.

"Lootera is well guarded," Sentania said in a low voice. "Getting you out of here may take time. With the Smoke Jaguar reputation for torture and punishment, an escape will have to be well-planned. Best to do it within their rules. Abide well and do not risk anything. I will find a way."

"Why are you taking it on yourself to help us, Sentania Buhallin?"

Her smile was gleeful. "You do not remember me, *quineg*?"

"Neg."

"Long ago we exchanged the vow of indebtedness. I owe you, Horse."

Horse suddenly recalled the incident of the vow, although he could not remember the events that led up to the making of it.

He would have asked her for more details, but a warrior interrupted their conversation to tell Horse that he and his Trinary had been ordered to assemble outside in an hour—for duty assignment, they said. The words chilled Horse, and he turned back to complain to Sentania, but she was no longer there.

He searched the room for her, but she was gone.

11

Lootera
Huntress
Kerensky Cluster, Clan Homeworlds
5 April 3059

Sometimes *life made little sense,* Horse thought. He hated every moment of the past weeks as a prisoner, especially since he had been detached from his Trinary to become little more than a valet to Russou Howell. Like his own warriors, who were continually grumbling about the demeaning work the Jags made them do, Horse detested the menial labor. A warrior was never averse to cleanups after a battle, no matter how unpleasant and messy, but the idea of doing manual labor that had no connection to their identity as warriors was repellent.

In spite of his distaste for the work, even worse were the little chats Howell forced upon him almost every evening when he called Horse to attend him. For the first few days, he could not understand what Howell was up to. Then one night Horse was there, shining Howell's shoes. Howell had apparently downed one too many brouhahas—a Smoke Jaguar drink similar to the Jade Falcon fusionnaire, but without the latter's terrific kick. The Galaxy Commander was flopped in his usual chair in the corner of the room, cradling his glass.

"I do not have many friends among my own people, Horse." Russou Howell's voice was blurry, his words thick. "I had a friend once, or at least I thought he was a friend, but he—well, that is a story of betrayal that I do not choose to tell." He waved his glass and shook his head drunkenly. "I have spent my life being the best loyal officer I could be. I tried to be an exemplary Smoke Jaguar, and rarely touched alcohol. Fact, I prob'ly have drunk more brouhahas here than in my whole entire life. But what am I supposed to do with this command? I'm saddled with grouchy, second-rate officers and a bunch of aging, incompetent warriors who want to sleep away the rest of their lives. Meanwhile, the Clans are preparing to renew the Crusade. The ilKhan himself is on Strana Mechty, and I do not know how many other high officers are scrutinizing the war effort here on Huntress."

Horse continued his silent polishing.

"*Stravag,* I am not supposed to talk like this," Russou mumbled. "Denigrating fellow officers—it is not the Smoke Jaguar way. But these solahmas do not seem like any Smoke Jaguars I have ever met." Howell leaned out unsteadily from the chair. "They would not have been assigned here, would they, while their betters continued the fight in the Inner Sphere? They are not outstanding, not outstanding, not at all, not one of them, well, maybe that Star Colonel who detests me, I like his courage, that, what is his name, that Star Colonel Logan."

This surat *can certainly babble on,* Horse thought. *He will regret this little speech, if he remembers it at all. I'm not sure where his mind is, or if it's in little pieces, drifting off in different directions. On the one hand, he proclaims the wonder of the Smoke Jaguars, then he turns around to complain about the quality of his warriors. Something's wrong with him. Something happened before he came here . . .*

Horse had been lost in his own thoughts for a moment, and had missed Howell's last words. But Howell was looking at him now, as if he might expect a response soon. "Like to talk with . . . I like to talk with you, Horse. Like me, you came here fresh from battle and all that is going on in the Inner Sphere. You have not been moldering on the homeworlds like the rest of these fools. Too bad you are from the wrong Clan."

Horse decided to play along. He was too tired for much

else right now. "I do not catch your meaning, Galaxy Commander. The wrong Clan?"

"The Jade Falcons and the Jaguars have been long-time allies, both Clans in the lead as Crusaders for the Clan invasion. Both our Clans have a love of war, but you will never be Smoke Jaguars."

"That is true, Galaxy Commander." Horse finished the first shoe and began on the second.

Russou seemed to be in another world, almost talking to himself. "Yes, the Falcons and the Jaguars are not so different. You Falcons are straightforward, you are skilled in combat, you are quick to fight anyone who crosses you, and you hate Clan Wolf, whom we also despise both for being Wardens and for being so underhanded. But we Jaguars can never accept the Falcon tolerance of your freeborns. The concept of freebirth warriors has been tested by us, but it simply does not work, ever. Yet freebirths flourish within the Falcons."

Horse laughed, aware that he was not hiding his sarcasm. "The Falcons are too tolerant of their freeborns? Commander, had you been born a freeborn Jade Falcon, I don't think you could say that."

For a moment Howell's eyes seemed to clear and grow a bit cruel. "I forgot for a moment that you are freeborn, Horse. Your use of contractions reminded me. And I remind you that Smoke Jaguars allow no contractions. I will let it pass for this time, *quiaff*?"

"The difference between our Clans is that the Jade Falcons have found a way to employ their freeborns sensibly, and Smoke Jaguars have not."

"Hmmm," Howell muttered, "maybe we *should* learn to exploit our freeborns. Might be a good solution for the defense of a homeworld station like this one, at least it would provide personnel without using any of those damned solahma warriors. And, you know, it just might show my insolent and grumbling warriors something, might shake them up, at least."

Howell's head slumped back against the chair, the brouhahas obviously making him drowsy.

After a protracted silence, he began to mutter again, "Somehow, I cannot, cannot cotton to the idea of freeborn Smoke Jaguar warriors. It would weaken the Clan. I am sure it has weakened the Jade Falcons. I can see it."

"The Jade Falcons are doing well enough. We beat the Wolves in the Refusal War, and on Coventry we showed that we are as fierce as ever."

"Maybe, maybe, but—but, seems to me there is a seed of destruction growing in that Clan. Sorry if you do not like me saying so. I like you, Horse, but you are freeborn so it is all right."

Horse chose not to argue. It was wasteful to attempt logic on a drunk. He rubbed harder at the boot in his hand.

"Freebirth," Howell slurred and fell asleep in his usual way, twisted up in his chair.

Horse reacted as the captive he hated to be. Gently, before it tipped out of Howell's limp hand, he removed the cup containing the dregs of the brouhaha and placed it on a side table. Those parts of Howell's uniform that he had cast off, Horse folded neatly, as Howell had shown him, and placed on the table. Howell did not like to be awakened to be sent to his bed, and so Horse left him in the discomfort of sleeping in a chair. Sometime during the night Howell would wake up, stagger off to bed, and recall very little of the previous evening. Horse washed the cup before returning to his quarters.

In his room, Horse wondered, as he always did, how long he would have to endure this. His people were getting restless. Some of them had been in minor trouble, trouble that showed up as bruises and new scars on their skin. Pegeen had told him that the only thing keeping the Trinary in line at all was their respect and admiration for Horse. They had faith he could find the way out.

Faith, he thought, *what a dangerous idea. Marthe Pryde brought me to this with her faith in me, despite my freeborn status. I have sufficient faith in myself to believe I deserve the honor she bestowed. I have faith in the warriors of the Trinary to know that they will respond bravely at my command. But it all can break down with a shaking of that faith, some heresy that could cause any of us to lose faith. All avenues of escape seem closed to us at the moment. Lootera is too well guarded. The way through the mountains is difficult and too obvious. They would pick us off like flies. Sentania Buhallin promised escape, but where is she? Well, one thing I've learned as a war-*

rior is that patience is often the most explosive weapon of all. Especially when the enemy has none at all.

And Horse was sure of one thing. Though his Khan was only a jump away on Strana Mechty, she would surely not raise a finger to save him. His freebirth status would taint her, and nothing could be done about that.

The next day Howell announced that he and Horse would visit the genetics repository. As they approached the entrance seemingly guarded by the towering stone BattleMech statues, Horse began to feel edgy. There was something not right about a Jade Falcon going into the place where another Clan stored its genetic legacies. He couldn't imagine the Falcons ever allowing a Jaguar to get that close to their sacred gene pool.

A warrior emerged from behind one of the statues and hailed Howell. Horse recognized the man as Star Colonel Logan. Logan glanced at Horse with the usual hate-filled expression. Most of the Smoke Jaguar warriors made no secret of how much they despised Horse's presence among them.

"Star Colonel Logan," Howell said irritably.

"Wish respect, sir, I see that the filthy freebirth scum is with you."

Howell glanced toward Horse. "That is true. I take it you object."

"With vehemence, sir."

"You do much with vehemence, Star Colonel Logan. I suggest you perform your regular duties with such vehemence. But I appreciate your words of respect and will not perceive your interruption of our goal as insubordination. Dismissed, Star Colonel Logan."

"But, sir, a freebirth cannot be taken to—"

"DISMISSED, Logan!"

Logan threw another venomous glance at Horse, then wheeled around and walked away.

Howell watched Logan for a moment, seemed to consider a comment to Horse, then thought better of it. He resumed his path toward the repository. Before entering the building, he stopped and stared up at the smoke jaguar carved out of the mountainside. Horse looked up also.

Howell's eyes seem almost reverent. More than reverent.

In awe. It's an impressive sculpture, I can't deny that, impressive in its simplicity, the fact it looks so real. But perhaps it stands out because the rest of Lootera is so cold and forbidding. I do not like its pose, though. A predator about to attack, fine. It reminds me of the Jade Falcon insignia, the falcon in flight, sweeping across the sky.

Howell glanced toward Horse, apparently detecting the puzzlement in his expression.

"Horse, it is our custom before entering this honored ground to stop and contemplate a smoke jaguar. It helps us to maintain the proper mind of a warrior. A smoke jaguar, the animal, and the smoke jaguar, the warrior, are essentially the same. Ferocity is the main characteristic. Just as the jaguar seizes the enemy's neck in its mighty jaws, so the warrior tears into battle until the enemy falls. We do not retreat, we Smoke Jaguars. Jade Falcons retreat, *quiaff*?"

"*Aff*, as a tactic of battle, but not on principle."

"That can never be the Smoke Jaguar way. We remain in combat until we either fall or prevail. No retreats."

"Not practical."

Howell's eyes flashed with anger. "Horse, you keep forgetting you are Smoke Jaguar now. I have instructed that you may not judge Smoke Jaguars, your Clan now. Anyway, I further instruct you to stop and contemplate the Smoke Jaguar there as often as you can. Our Clan is based on the virtues of the Smoke Jaguar and on Nicholas Kerensky's vision of the true way. To be a member of our Clan, even a prisoner, you must extol the Smoke Jaguar. Otherwise, I will be forced to kill you. It is as simple as that."

Horse never intended to succumb to the way of the Smoke Jaguar, nor did he intend to be executed for it either. He would bide his time until Sentania Buhallin returned. Once the escape attempt was made, he knew his life would be forfeit if he were captured by the Jaguars again. He could not comprehend the Smoke Jaguar attitude that a prisoner must submissively accept a new role, especially a subsidiary one, within the Jaguar Clan.

The Jade Falcons would expect prisoners to try to escape once in a while. They even looked forward to it, so they could retrieve the escapees and beat them to a bloody pulp. The Jag rules could not apply to Jade Falcons, especially not to Horse. He was, to use the foul word, a freebirth. Sometimes being a freebirth meant that you could violate the customs of other Clans, and sometimes even your own.

Howell gestured Horse through the doors of the genetic repository. Horse took note of the eternal laser at the pyramid's base before entering the repository. Looking back, he saw that Logan had resumed his place alongside one of the BattleMech statues, glaring with disgust.

Once inside, they came to a massive chamber, its marble floors tiled with black, gray, and white shapes of running jaguars. An aged scientist in a flowing white robe came forward, flanked by a pair of Elemental guards.

"I am the Keeper of the Jaguar kin," the man said. "Who dares disturb the blood of our warriors? Who disturbs this most sacred of places?"

"I wish to honor my legacy," Howell said.

Horse had some trouble looking at the Keeper. The man was so old that Horse felt a slight nausea at the sight of the unbelievable network of wrinkles and the eyes buried behind the thick lenses of his eyeglasses. Howell extended his wrist toward the man and gestured for Horse to do the same. The scientist verified Howell's identity with a portable codex scanner. Then Howell indicated the prisoner bracelet on Horse's wrist and informed the Keeper that the prisoner was with him.

"This is most unheard of, Galaxy Commander."

"This man is being instructed in the way of the Jaguar," Howell said. "What better place?"

"As you say, Galaxy Commander." The Keeper nodded and even gave a slight bow, then moved off through the incense-filled chamber, flanked by two dark-cloaked Elementals.

The repository chamber was enormous and quite dark, lit only by laser candles at various points of the room. The light given off by the candles was intense but focused on a small area. The walls all bore dozens of seals. Each showed a name and a digital code, each was the holding place of a giftake. Horse observed an attendant taking one of the candles out of its holder and carrying it a short distance to put it in another holder. Like everything else in this room and in the Smoke Jaguar society, the movement had a strong ritual appearance to it.

"There are thousands of giftakes in this room and its side chambers, Horse. Genetic materials are regularly selected from this store for the formation of new sibkos. This repository is the source of more than one-third of all Smoke Jaguar bloodlines. The best of the Smoke Jaguars, the legacy of the Clan. In here are the originals rather than the genetic copies maintained on Strana Mechty. Come, I wish to show you something."

They headed toward the rear of the massive room. They neared a door that was bordered with panels of interlocking golden warriors, each one posed like the mountain sculpture. Three Elemental guards, in full regalia, converged to block the path of Horse and Howell. Then the Keeper suddenly reappeared. Horse could have sworn that the man had been heading in the opposite direction when he left them previously. How could an old man have gotten to this side of the chamber so quickly?

"Galaxy Commander, why head you toward the Hall of Heroes?"

"I wish to pay my respects, as I do every week, Keeper."

"Aye, Commander. But no freeborn may enter the Hall. It is against custom."

"Custom does not always stand with a commanding officer, *quiaff*?"

"Aff. But no warrior rules within this repository. Galaxy Commander Howell, you are allowed free entry here as a privilege, but the privilege can be revoked . . ."

"You allow your scientists to order you around?" Horse muttered, just to make trouble. Howell's face reddened slightly.

"Why would you violate a sacred chamber?" the Keeper asked Howell. "To taint its air with otherClan presence?"

"I wish this freebirth scum to know the majesty of the Smoke Jaguar Clan. He is a former Jade Falcon who must ultimately concede the genetic superiority of our Clan."

Horse suppressed a fair number of available sarcasms as the Keeper of the Jaguar kin considered those words.

"Well bargained, Galaxy Commander. This time you

win permission, but I request that this be the last time. If we allow freeborn otherClansmen such a dispensation, we violate the honor of the Jaguar. There will be no record of this man's visit, and you must both take the oath of secrecy regarding this matter."

"Agreed," Howell replied. "As does Horse."

The Keeper himself escorted Howell and Horse into the Hall of Heroes. Howell looked remarkably satisfied, but Horse doubted the wisdom of breaking the sanctity of the repository. And the place *was* sacred from his point of view. All genetic repositories were, even those of other Clans.

At first glance the lighting seemed stronger within the hall, which was about a third of the size of the huge chamber outside it. The lighting here was like that in the outer chamber, rows of laser candles. But there were more of them. Clustered together in what appeared to be decorative arrangements, they caught the light on the golden seals of the giftake holding places.

In the center of the room was a large circular column that rose impressively toward the high ceiling of the Hall. There were more golden plaques on the side of the column. The golden glow from the laser candles radiated strongly from the column.

Howell marched straight for the column. Horse matched him, stride for stride.

At the column, Howell proudly announced, "This is where the most significant giftakes are stored, those of the greatest heroes and those who have risen to the highest positions. Up there is the giftake of ilKhan Leo Showers, killed so unexpectedly when an Inner Sphere warrior crashed her fighter into the bridge of his flagship. We honor him especially on the column of great heroes. There are regular ceremonies conducted here in his memory."

Howell gazed reverently upward at Leo Showers' plaque, while Horse studied the plaque itself. As a freeborn, he could understand, but not particularly sympathize with, the trueborn compulsion to revere as icons what was merely a package of meticulously preserved genetic materials. To them the material was, in some way, the individual, as if the package containing the genetic strands of Leo Showers were transformable into the great man himself.

DNA could be used to form inherently great sibkos, but was still only coding. Horse did believe that the Clans' genetic engineering programs created warriors whose potential in warfare was destined. But everyone knew that more members of a sibko failed than succeeded at their Trials of Position. Not only that, but freeborns without all that genetic advantage had contributed mightily to Jade Falcon military efforts. None of this altered his essential beliefs about his Clan (his *real* Clan), but it did soften any tendency toward veneration.

Horse did not venerate anything. Watching the emotional commitment of Russou Howell toward a leader whose demise had been a matter of fate rather than an act of personal courage disgusted Horse more than it impressed him. In Aidan Pryde's library he had found some works on Terran religions, and he wondered if genetic repositories had become, for the Clans, some twisted kind of religion. He did not care much, but he did regard it as a curiosity, one of many he had detected in his curious life. Curious, in more than one sense of the word.

Those books have ruined me. Once I was a stupid warrior, stupid but content. No, that is not true. I was never content.

Later, after Horse had returned to the detention center, a fight broke out between MechWarrior Croft and Star Commander Pegeen. Horse sat on his cot and let it happen.

It was certainly a strange-looking fight, with the burly Croft squaring off against the small, frail, almost dainty Pegeen. The few prisoners in the room had formed a rough Circle of Equals, pushing away furniture and clearing floor debris. They seemed grateful for the fight, no matter what it was about.

Horse turned to the Jade Falcon seated near him and asked, "What's going on?"

The warrior, a MechWarrior named Millat, a man so tall among warriors that some of his comrades had nicknamed him Elemental, leaned back against the wall and rubbed his scraggly beard. Horse, who trimmed his own beard regularly, found uneven and badly groomed beards an eyesore.

"They were each on a maintenance patrol. You know,

the kind of duty where they practically dare you to find some dirt or litter in this place. This is the only place I ever saw where you could rub your finger over a surface and it comes away looking cleaner. Anyway, this piece of paper comes drifting down from a window and the both of them jump for it, bumping heads. The way I was told it, the paper fell onto the ground, which really angered the Jag in charge. You know how they are—the way they cannot stand the slightest bit of litter." Millat snorted in disgust, and Horse nodded in agreement.

"Then Croft and Pegeen both go for the paper. Croft pushes Pegeen out of the way, then he has the paper, but she kicks him in the leg and grabs the paper out of his hand. I guess the paper goes back and forth between them for about a minute before the Jag guard snatches it from them and stuffs it in the garbage bag himself. Then, when they got back here, they started arguing over the whole thing. Croft issues the challenge, Pegeen accepts and now they are busy busting each other up. That is life here in Lootera, I suppose, *quiaff?*"

Horse, aware that the man's sarcasm might just be meant as a veiled insult to him, nodded again and went on watching the fight. Croft managed to push Pegeen to the floor and jump on her. His sheer weight advantage should have crushed her, but her toughness prevailed. She squirmed out from under him and, grabbing his hair, pulled his head back. He elbowed her in the stomach, which did not seem to faze her. Still grasping the hair, she kneed Croft in the back. He grimaced in pain, but managed to fling her off.

Pegeen fell away, still clutching a few strands of his uprooted hair. Springing to his feet with surprising agility for such a burly man, Croft charged at Pegeen and attempted to put a bear hug on her. She slipped out of it easily and, with quite an extraordinary jump, kicked him in the face. Growling with rage, he grabbed her the instant she landed and picked her up over his head. He was about to hurl her against the nearest wall, which would have violated the parameter of the Circle of Equals, when Horse shouted, "Stop!"

Croft whirled on Horse. "You cannot stop an honor duel, no matter what your rank, Star Captain."

Horse stepped into the circle and, with a punch to the jaw delivered so quickly that the others later confessed they never saw the blow, he sent Croft reeling backward against a stone wall. Croft released Pegeen and she fell into Horse's arms. Horse set her down, then stepped between the two.

"This is unconscionable, Star Captain—to interrupt an honor duel is to—"

"Quiet! Honor duel? This is no honor duel. The two of you are using the tradition to fight over a scrap of paper! What will that prove about Jade Falcon honor? That litter is a goal worthy of competition? You make absurd all that the honor duel stands for. And, yes, you are right that I should not step across the line of the Circle of Equals into your battle. I will step back now and, if you wish to continue the fight over garbage, that is your option, but I will no longer watch."

Horse strode out of the circle without looking back. If he had, he would have seen two fierce Jade Falcon warriors with all the fight gone out of them.

Outside, he tried to slow down his breathing. It was not like him to show his anger, especially so quickly. In combat he could be terrifying in his rage, but in other situations he was the cool one, the one who could calm down the wrath of others. Now he was ready to smash a fist through a wall.

He looked around him. Evening came slowly to Huntress, and there was a long twilight that caused eerie shadows on building surfaces. Darker buildings seemed superimposed on the real buildings. As the shadows moved across and lengthened, the unreal city became surreal. The pristine streets seemed to contain pockets of shadow litter.

The air, as always, was clear. The mountains in the daytime were incredibly vivid, and the trees in the nearby forest a notably rich green. Nothing stained Lootera, littered Mount Szabo, or made Huntress ugly. Yet there was little beauty either. All the richness, vividness, clarity only made clearer the planet's sterility. It needed a good Jade Falcon mess, he thought.

Storming back into the center, Horse started picking up paper, spoons, cups, bits of food left behind on tables, whatever he could scoop up easily. Returning to the entrance, he flung it all out into the street. He realized he was just hurling garbage, an act no more meaningful than fighting over garbage, but he had to do it, and somehow he felt better afterward.

12

*Falcon Eyrie Research Station
Eastern Mountains, Huntress
Kerensky Cluster, Clan Homeworlds
5 April 3059*

Star Colonel Bren Roshak, head of Falcon Eyrie Research Station, had a peculiarity that was exceedingly strange among Jade Falcon warriors, or warriors of any Clan, for that matter. He cried. He did not know why he cried. It had nothing to do with any stupid lower-caste emotional trait or reaction. He did not cry *at* anything or *about* anything. He did not cry in pain or laughter. But at any moment, at any time, he could break into tears. It was sometimes embarrassing. For most circumstances, however, he had contrived many disguises, many gestures with which to camouflage his weakness. It riled him to cry in moments of command, but his most loyal subordinates had long ago learned to turn their own tearless eyes away from the extraordinary and sometimes ugly sight of Roshak's sudden tears.

The trait, however, did not win him points with the station's chief scientific officer, Peri Watson. Talking to her now, he knew his eyes were watery. He hoped she would attribute his condition to something else, even that she might think he was drinking too much. Addiction to drink was fairly rare among Jade Falcon warriors, although not unknown among commanders of backwater garrisons.

However, Roshak drank little and not to much effect. His teary condition almost made him wish he did. Being drunk was preferable to this humiliation.

Peri peered at Bren Roshak. She had often wondered why this warrior so often looked on the verge of tears. After all, he was dour in so many other respects.

"So what have you to report today, Peri Watson?" he said now, in a slightly stuttering way that reminded Peri of a child choking back tears.

He spoke her name in a derisive tone. Usually he elided the name by slightly flattening the "i" sound, so that it became Periwatson. Many of the Jade Falcon warriors, the largest group at the station, spoke derisively when they addressed the lower castes. Peri was a trueborn, had once been in warrior training herself, but she had flushed out and been demoted to a lower caste. Caste privilege was the way of the Clans, and she had no choice but to accept it.

Warriors especially resented the scientists, despite the fact that the latter enjoyed some prestige. The scientist caste had even been allowed to adopt surnames. They were merely honorary and never used outside the caste, nor were they drawn from the list of bloodnames handed down from the days of Nicholas Kerensky. But the use of any surname sounded too much like the theft of the bloodname tradition to warriors. They despised a surname on anyone outside the warrior caste.

"Nothing to report, Star Colonel Roshak. All phases of experimentation are progressing as well as can be expected, very well in some cases, but we have no new findings as yet. As you know—"

"Yes, yes. You scientists only wish to report successful findings."

And keep insufferable commanders in the dark, Peri thought. *Anyway, what can I tell him? I have almost as much difficulty getting my own scientists to report anything to me. They guard their findings like precious metals, informing me only when it does them credit. The naturalists do their work as if it were a sport. The 'Mech and weapons specialists bicker so much among themselves that it's a wonder they accomplish anything. And*

*the geneticists—forget the geneticists. The gods them-
selves could not pry out their secrets.*

"Our methods of reporting are traditional for us, sir."

"You need not lecture me on Jade Falcon traditions."

Roshak quickly brushed back a tear with a backhanded
gesture that appeared to be quite practiced.

"See if you can tell me this," he said, voice dripping
with sarcasm. "Will there be falcons available for sport,
or are your naturalists testing them for feather texture or
some such thing?"

Peri, assigned now to Falcon Eyrie for the last four
years, had never gotten used to Roshak's abusive manner
with subordinates.

"There are several birds available for sport, sir. Just
ask—"

Another habit of Roshak's that infuriated Peri was his
predilection for interrupting in mid-sentence.

"I know the procedures. Hunting is one of the few
reliefs from boredom I have in this assignment, as you
know."

Peri had heard this litany before and wished Roshak
would give it up. Everyone knew that the warriors of
Falcon Eyrie had little to do. The Jaguars mostly left the
Falcons alone in their high mountain eyrie, but the Falcons did not dare test their patience too severely. Chal-
lenges for genetic legacies had been banned by mutual
agreement, and neither side had much else the other
needed. Sometimes there was a minor contest, like the
insignia-stealing episode, just to stretch combat muscles.
Peri abhorred the waste of the skirmishes, but not much
harm was done. After all, Huntress was hardly in the thick
of the Crusade.

"I must say," Roshak continued, "that one of the few
highlights at Falcon Eyrie is the genetic work your naturalists have accomplished to improve and refine the skills
of the jade falcon."

"We are proud of our achievements in genetic engineering, Star Colonel."

"The falcon named Jade Rogue is a particularly fine
creation."

"We do not call them creations, sir. They are merely
genetically altered forms of—"

"As always, you speak freely for a scientist. You should remember your caste, freebirth."

It was all Peri could do to subdue her anger and reply in a calm voice. "I am not freeborn, sir, as you well know. I am trueborn."

"Oh, yes, I forgot." He had not forgotten, that much she knew. "You were in a sibko, took warrior training, failed, wound up a scientist. Not much to brag about, Watson."

His use of her surname alone, an unusual practice among warriors, was sneering and clearly intended to rile her. Others would speak her first name by itself, but rarely addressed her by surname only.

"If you flushed out of warrior training," Roshak continued, "your failure should mark you as no better than a freeborn."

"Most scientists are trueborn, sir. We serve the Clan just as much as—"

"Spare me the lecture, Watson. I want you to bring me Jade Rogue and accompany me to the mountainside for the sport."

"Sir, I have work to—"

"I am your commander, Watson, *quiaff*?"

"Aff."

She knew what he would say next and again her response was subdued.

"And you must obey my order, *quiaff*?"

"Aff."

"We shall leave now."

Peri noted that the tears in his eyes now could be regarded as tears of rage. As such, they seemed appropriate for a warrior.

Even with the hunting hood over his noble head, Jade Rogue looked regal perched on Roshak's wrist. The wrist was protected by a soft leather glove because the bird's sharp claws could easily have dug through the man's skin to the bones. Indeed, Jade Rogue's thin, attenuated legs seemed already stretched for flight. Its black feathers shone as if oiled, an effect the slight genetic manipulations had enhanced.

The Jade Falcon was, of course, a genetic enhancement of a bird native to faraway Terra, and it was the creature most admired among the Clan that bore its name. The experiments on Falcon Eyrie were further elaborations of the genetic engineering that had produced the superb predator. The experiments verged on insignificance, but the naturalists themselves loved them, mainly because they took such pleasure in studying the various magnificent birds collected from their habitats in the Falcon homeworlds and transported to the Huntress research installation. Ironically, Roshak was not the only one who took special interest in the work. Every trueborn at the station eagerly followed the falcon research. That did not bother Peri, who was happy to have the warriors stay out of her hair as much as possible. There was another project of the station that interested her more.

Occasionally Jade Rogue spread its wings. Their span cast a shadow so deep, it momentarily blotted out Huntress' sun. The naturalists had bred for the broadest wingspan possible while keeping the wings aerodynamically sound.

Roshak's current tears seemed fitting, with such a fine specimen on his arm. He puffed up with pride. Clearly he felt some ownership of the bird, although Peri couldn't see why. She only knew he had plenty of time to indulge in falconry—too much, in her opinion—and it seemed to give him great pleasure.

In a grand gesture, he tore off Jade Rogue's hood while simultaneously releasing the bird to flight. Jade Rogue soared into the sky with such speed that, to Peri, it looked as if the falcon itself was struck with joy at being free. Roshak's wet eyes followed the falcon's magnificent arc steadily, with total concentration. It flew toward a passing flock of birds, a type of Huntress avian species that the Falcon Eyrie naturalists had dubbed skittishes, a name derived from the apparent aimlessness of their migratory travels.

For most Huntress birds the traditional migration was from northwest to southeast and was accomplished in a relatively straightlined fashion. However, skittishes would sometimes veer east or west, north or south, and sometimes even reversed their flight for several kilometers, as if their real desire was to return home so they could endure the wonders of the colder weather. But then they would resume their original direction for a while, usually before veering to one side or the other for a distance. One of the naturalists had observed that occasionally there was a definite danger ahead of them and that perhaps their apparent skittishness was more logical than it seemed. However, none of the scientists had been able to turn the observation into anything conclusive.

The skittishes would be no match for Jade Rogue, though. A jade falcon was too quick. The skittishes could not sense its flight toward them. Peri resented Roshak's release of Jade Rogue to attack skittishes. They were much too easy prey. It was no longer sport. But then, nothing in Roshak's behavior ever indicated a true sportsman.

She turned away from the coming carnage and stared down at the forest below. Even as Roshak was whooping over some hunting feat of Jade Rogue's, Peri saw a movement in the foliage at the edge of the forest. A figure emerged from the timberline and started sprinting up the relatively steep slope. Peri recognized Sentania Buhallin, her one friend here at Falcon Eyrie.

Sentania had been gone for a long while this time, over a month. She must have been on one of her excursions into the Huntress lowlands, probably to Lootera, where she derived a perverse enjoyment from passing among the Smoke Jaguars without being detected. Peri was cheered at the prospect of listening to Sentania's accounts of her adventures. Sentania did liven up the dull days at Falcon Eyrie.

Peri glanced back at Roshak. He was also watching the solahma warrior's run up the mountainside. He snorted, his usual reaction at seeing Sentania Buhallin. Long ago he had learned he could not control her. Since he did not like *any* of the solahmas, he decided to maintain the illusion of control by allowing her to roam, but then requiring a full account of all that she had seen and heard. Mostly it was insignificant, but Sentania was the one who had reported the disgrace and banishment of the previous Galaxy Commander, the arrival of the new one, and his recent efforts to instill some discipline into the solahma slush the Jaguars had defending their homeworld.

Peri strode down to meet Sentania, who nearly stumbled to a stop.

"That was some excursion." Peri said. "MechWarrior Stenis is getting downright surly about your absence."

"That is just his excuse," Sentania said with a laugh. "But, Peri, I have so much to tell you."

While Bren Roshak sported with his jade falcon, Peri and Sentania found a perch on some large rocks on the hillside. Then Peri listened spellbound to Sentania's breathless account of the DropShip crash and its aftermath.

"Howell merely confiscated the 'Mechs and then took the freeborn warriors prisoner?"

"Aye."

"Those 'Mechs and warriors were coming to Falcon Eyrie, which is independent of the rest of Huntress. Did the ship not broadcast the beam of neutrality?"

"Aye, I heard the Falcon commander say they had."

"Then the Jaguars violated our sovereignty."

"Russou Howell is a new commander, so tell him that."

"I would if I had his neck in my hands just now."

Sentania laughed. "Always a warrior, Peri. No matter how long you have been a scientist, you think, talk, and react like a warrior. I cannot see how you failed your sibko trial."

Peri frowned. "I never even made it that far. I flushed out of training."

"That is even more puzzling."

"Our training falconer was very tough."

"I know. You told me. Star Commander Joanna, the slayer of the Black Widow."

The news about Joanna's victory over Natasha Kerensky had reached Falcon Eyrie only recently.

"At any rate, I still see you as more warrior than scientist, even though you are good at what you do."

"So comforting to hear praise from a solahma."

"I can always irritate you, *quiaff*?"

Peri smiled, her brief anger instantly vanished. "Aff. You molting falcons disgrace Falcon Eyrie."

"I will drink to that. But I did not tell you the best part. The warrior in charge of the freeborn unit may be known to you. He has some fame. His name is Horse, the freeborn hero of Tukayyid, the friend to—"

"I know well enough whom he was friend to, Sentania Buhallin, you wrinkled karna leaf. And I have told you more than I should have about myself and Aidan Pryde."

"Did you know Horse, too, at Ironhold?"

"Neg. I saw no freeborns there, except in the occasional

training exercises. But Horse did train at Ironhold in a freeborn warrior group. Before earning his Pryde blood-name, Aidan disguised himself as a freeborn and took another man's place in the same unit. I understand that Aidan and Horse took their Trial of Position together. That is the legend, anyway, you know it well enough."

"The legend of the Jade Phoenix, *quiaff*?"

"Aff."

Peri's eyes momentarily dimmed as she reflected on those long-ago times, then she forced her attention back to the present.

"The Jaguars took the Falcons to Lootera, and Howell made Horse his servant."

"*Servant?* That is—it is unacceptable! The man has violated our sovereignty, illegally confiscated Jade Falcon 'Mechs, unfairly taken warriors prisoner, freeborn though they may be, made a Jade Falcon hero a servant when Smoke Jaguars hate freeborns! It is not only unacceptable, it is so far beyond the way of the Clans that it shames the Jaguars. This Russou Howell must be some piece of work!"

"I would agree. From what I have seen of him, that Howell seems to have gone beyond the Periphery."

Peri nodded. "Yes, way beyond."

"And maybe even crazier than that. There is something odd about this Russou Howell, something . . . bizarre and unClanlike. He wanders among his troops, spends nights in lower-caste rec halls getting drunk. He says strange things. He tries to instill discipline and encourages stronger training for his force, but get him off-duty and he seems to collapse."

"How can you even know all this?"

"As you well know, I get around. Wherever I am."

"I forgot, sorry. But what about Horse?"

"He wants to escape."

"You have talked to him then—in your wanderings?"

"Of course."

"Of course." "The problem is that the Jaguars really believe that their prisoners are bound by rules very similar to those of bondsmen. They even have rituals and oaths for prisoners. Horse and the others have been put through them. But there's more. Horse and his Trinary are most certainly here on a mission."

"Mission?"

"Why else come here? Nobody comes to Falcon Eyrie. We are the misplaced station, and you scientists seem to want it that way."

Peri frowned. "Careful, Sentania."

"I know, I know. Do not question the secrecy, it is necessary. No pun intended, but this Horse is chafing at the bit. And I think we should help him."

"Help him scape? I doubt Roshak would approve, especially not to aid a freeborn."

"Forget Roshak. I intended to bypass him anyway."

"I gather you have a plan."

"You might call it that. I need your help."

Sentania lowered her voice, even though there was nobody else near to listen to her. Briefly and eagerly she told Peri what she had in mind, a plan she had been formulating all the way up the mountainside. At first it drew laughter from Peri. She said it was extravagant and impossible.

"There are no BattleMechs at Falcon Eyrie," she protested.

"There are the LAMs."

Peri again laughed. "True, but you know that so far the tests have shown them to be unpredictable. And you know about all the failures. And there are no proper pilots, only a pair of converted warriors who were probably not very good warriors. And—"

"I guess I was wrong. I thought there was still some warrior in you. Now you sound all scientist."

Peri gave a good loud laugh, suddenly realizing that she had not felt this good in some time. "Ah, Sentania. You know just what to say to get what you want from me. Aye, let's do it. Let's help these Falcons escape."

13

It had been three weeks since Horse first came to Huntress, but not much had changed. He was constantly at Russou Howell's beck and call, and on this afternoon, like every other, he was making the Galaxy Commander his cup of karna tea, a concoction that revolted Horse but was a favorite of Howell's.

Howell sat staring at Horse for a few moments, then ran a hand over his nearly bald head as though checking to see if the few strands were still there. "So, Horse, how do you like this new life? This is a fine end to a glorious career, *quiaff*?" Howell said suddenly. He leaned toward the brewing liquid and took a sniff. The act made his face relax.

"I was not bred to be a serving man," Horse said. Howell was always baiting him. Horse had gotten so used to it that it simply rolled off his back. He knew who he was, and insults from this useless old has-been amused him more than anything.

"You were not really bred at all. You are a filthy freebirth. You are somebody's accident."

"You know what I meant. I have been a warrior all my life. They say I was a warrior in the cradle."

Howell blanched and started, almost dropping his mug. Trueborns did not like to hear any word associated with free birth. Cradle was akin to a curse word for those whose natal origins were the genetic engineering vats of the Clan laboratories. What was known in the vernacular as iron wombs.

"If you despise freeborns so much, does it not bring shame to you and your Clan to keep one so close by?"

"No, it does not. And I savor your captivity all the more for that, Horse. You have a clever tongue, but I have not merely made a freeborn my servant, I have taken a Jade Falcon hero into the Smoke Jaguar ranks and humbled him. You do feel humbled, *quiaff*?"

"Neg. No matter where I go or what I do, nothing can take from me my Jade Falcon pride."

Howell laughed. "What a mouthful! Most warriors can barely communicate in grunts. You have given me my challenge then."

"Challenge?"

"To humble you, Horse. To humble you totally. You are Smoke Jaguar now and must realize that."

Howell laughed quietly to himself as he took delicate sips of his karna-leaf tea. Horse thought he must have had something stronger to drink earlier, for he fell asleep soon after.

The next morning, in his office, Howell called Horse to him and greeted him with an expansive enthusiasm. Howell was in uniform, the garment carefully brushed and creased, his gloves spotlessly white. On the collar tabs of his uniform was the leaping jaguar insignia.

"It is all arranged, hero," he said.

"What do you mean?"

"Today, once and for all, I plan to make you into a Smoke Jaguar."

"That is impossible. I am Jade Falcon. And always will be."

Howell smiled grimly. "Such a response shows your freebirth origins, Horse. A trueborn Clan warrior would see the wisdom of becoming part of the Clan that bound him. But no, you freeborns do not like to follow rules. You are rebellious. That cannot be, not if we are to fulfill the vision of the Kerenskys. Here, wear this."

Howell held out a plain robe. It was made of thick, stiff cloth. Such a garment had denoted the lowest castes back in Horse's village.

"I cannot," Horse said. "No warrior would."

"But you are a prisoner. Put it on."

"I refuse."

Howell nodded. "I expected that. It is direct disobedience of a lawful order and must be punished." He tapped the communicator on his desk and lowered his head slightly as he spoke into it. "Warriors, come forward."

Six Smoke Jaguar warriors in dress uniforms immediately filed into the room. They had obviously been given orders, since they now awaited none from their commander.

Two Jaguars seized Horse by the arms, while a third used a long baton to slam the back of his ankles hard enough to make him lose his footing. At the same moment, his two captors pushed him backward onto the floor. Two more seized his flailing legs and held them down. One of the Jags still standing produced a long, sharp knife and leaned down, the blade end of his weapon aimed toward Horse's neck. Horse felt a tightening in his throat as he waited for it to be cut. Instead, the warrior twisted the knife sideways, grabbed the collar of Horse's tunic, inserted the knife and began ripping downward in a smooth motion. Soon his tunic and trousers were ripped open. With a few more deft knife slashes, the warrior had cut open the entire garment so that the remaining Jaguar could, with his baton, flip the clothing off Horse's body, leaving him in his plain warrior undergarments.

"Let him up," Howell ordered.

The guards pulled Horse roughly to his feet.

"Free his arms," Howell said as he offered Horse the robe again. Horse spat upon it.

"Just the response I would expect from a filthy freebirth," Howell said as he brushed away the spittle with the side of his gloved hand. He leaned down to pick up a piece of Horse's torn clothing and, tucking the robe under his arm, wiped the side of the glove with a nervous thoroughness. Taking the garment again in his hands, he offered it to Horse, saying, "Will you wear this robe, Horse?"

Horse's response was to elbow one his guards and

then, with the same arm, swing it around to land a punishing blow to the mouth of the other one. The remaining four rushed forward. Two grabbed his arms while the baton-holder slammed his baton brutally into the small of Horse's back. As Horse's body bent backward, the warrior deftly flipped the baton to his other hand and slammed it into Horse's stomach. Horse groaned. He vowed to show no more physical reaction, no matter how much worse the torture got.

"The robe, Horse?"

"Sprinkle lye on it and eat it for breakfast, Jaguar!"

Howell held the robe up, as if to display it for his warriors. "See? The captive resists an order, an unconscionable offense." He tossed the robe to one of the warriors. The throw was so fierce it seemed carried by a sudden burst of wind. The warrior who caught it let it unroll.

"Dress him in it," Howell ordered and strode out of the room.

It was quite a struggle, but the six warriors finally managed to force the robe over Horse's head and then tied it at the waist with a thick cord. The moment it fell over his shoulders, Horse started pulling at it.

"Do not bother, scum," one of the warriors said. "You cannot remove the robe. It is fastened at the back with a device that can only be opened by one of us. You will wear this garment until you humbly ask us to remove it, freebirth, or die in it, whichever comes first. We hope for the latter. It is what you deserve."

As they shoved him roughly toward the door, Horse suddenly saw the truth. These warriors hated him for exactly the reason Howell should. The Jaguars abhorred the idea of freeborns among them as warriors. What must they feel about a freeborn in constant contact with their commander?

As they pushed him through the door of Howell's office, it was clear that none of these Jaguars particularly wanted to see Horse survive whatever filthy plan their commander had in his mind.

Horse didn't understand Russou Howell's obsession any more than they did. And he liked it even less.

≡ 14 ≡

Lootera
Huntress
Kerensky Cluster, Clan Homeworlds
13 April 3059

The robe felt scratchy and too tight. Horse moved his shoulders while pulling at the cloth to try to adjust the garment to a better fit. Nothing helped. It was as if tiny metal threads attached to the cloth rubbed against his skin. He wondered how it was even possible to weave with threads so stiff.

He'd been shoved and dragged here into the repository courtyard where a pack of Smoke Jaguar warriors had been assembled. Most stood with crossed arms and aggressive, wide-legged stance, and Horse thought all of them looked pleased at his plight. The BattleMech statues to Horse's right cast long shadows across the open space, making him feel that even these gigantic 'Mechs were witness to his ordeal.

Howell stood in front of Horse. He had now added a long cloak to his uniform.

"Horse," Howell announced in a voice addressed as much to the crowd as to Horse, "you are accused of violating acceptable behavior from a Smoke Jaguar prisoner. We Jaguars hold that all prisoners must honor our Clan regulations, traditions, and customs. We demand that prisoners devote their whole existence to the way of the

Clan, a duty as binding to the lowest among us as to the highest. Sometimes it happens that a prisoner cannot quite shed his or her ties to a former Clan, requiring us to remind that captive of his obligations."

Horse held up his arm and pointed to his prisoner bracelet, which had been attached to the bracelet containing his codex records. "This is not a bondcord. It makes me your slave, but it does not make me one of you."

Some warriors in the crowd snarled at the insult, but Howell held up his hand to silence them. "In one way you are right. You will never, as you say, be one of us. You are no more than freebirth scum. But we have claimed you to serve the Smoke Jaguar Clan and that bracelet you hold up guarantees it. It does not accord the honor of a bondcord, but it implies serious obligations for a prisoner."

"I have properly fulfilled the procedures required."

"You have not satisfied me of your loyalty, Horse. Or your obedience. Today you will undergo a ritual, one that is venerable among the Smoke Jaguars, though rarely invoked. It is called the Ceremony of Kinship. It is used to eliminate deviations of any kind."

Star Colonel Logan Wirth stepped forward ominously from the gathering of warriors. When he spoke, it was partially to address Howell and partially the crowd behind him.

"Ceremony of Kinship? I know of no such ceremony, Galaxy Commander."

Howell turned to stare hard at Logan, as if daring him to insubordination. "As I noted, the ritual is little used."

"Freebirth! I know all the Smoke Jaguar customs, and there is no Ceremony of Kinship."

"We will speak of this later, Star Colonel Logan."

"We will speak of it now!"

The other warriors began to mutter, echoing Logan's words.

Howell took a step toward Logan and lowered his voice. "Hear me now, Logan Wirth, and hear me well. There may or there may not be a tradition for this ceremony. But if I say it is a tradition, it is one now, *quiaff*? *Quiaff*, Star Colonel?"

Logan looked around, as if seeking support. Horse

wondered if this would turn into some kind of revolt, but then Logan shrugged. A commander was a commander, and a warrior must obey.

Satisfied, Howell pulled himself up to his full height and smoothed those few strands of hair across his bald pate. Then he turned again to Horse. "The way of the Clan is clear and none must deviate from it. That is the reason for this special rite. It is a way of maintaining the Smoke Jaguar ideal, of strengthening all that the Smoke Jaguar stands for!"

Howell pointed up at the jaguar sculpted from the rock of Mount Szabo.

Horse leaned toward Howell and whispered so that none of the others could hear. "Sounds to me like you should put yourself through this stupid rite."

Howell bellowed in anger and rushed at Horse. Horse sidestepped, forcing Howell to run past him. At the last moment he stuck out his foot and tripped the Galaxy Commander, sending Howell flat on his face into the dirt, his long cloak ballooning up and settling down slowly. Then Horse stepped back to face a trio of Jaguar warriors who were approaching him menacingly. He went into a defensive stance. At the same time, he noticed the confusion among the other warriors. Nobody seemed too sure which side they were on.

The weight of his cloak made it difficult for Howell to stand up. With a massive swing of his arm, he threw the cloak off his body and rose to his knees. Seeing the warriors running to his aid, he gestured them away.

Now on his feet, he addressed the warriors. "You see, fellow Smoke Jaguars, the need for this Ceremony of Kinship in this pitiable case. This prisoner, a Jade Falcon freebirth, scorns the honor of becoming one of us."

"Why talk?" somebody shouted. "Kill him now and be done with it."

"Yes, kill him," called another warrior, and it became a chant as several more joined in. Horse saw that Howell had managed to whip them up enough that even Logan had joined in.

Howell held up one hand to quiet the crowd. "No. I demand that he submit to the will of the Jaguar and acknowledge the honor of becoming part of us. I initiate the Ceremony of Kinship!"

As he spoke the last words, he whirled around and gestured toward another warrior, who wore a knife. The warrior flipped the knife toward Howell, who caught it by the handle. Howell advanced toward Horse, then, swiftly, he raised the knife and in one graceful sweep sliced it lightly across the side of Horse's neck.

Horse blinked a few times, but resisted the impulse to reach up and touch his neck to make sure his head was still on. Glancing at the knife, he saw that the blade was bloodied, but it had only nicked his flesh.

"Hah!" Howell said. "The blade is, of course, symbolic—to remind even a warrior of how transitory is life, mere light and shadow, so easily swallowed up by sudden darkness. But no warrior fears death for death brings hope that his genes might be accepted into the sacred gene pool or become ashes scattered into the nutrient solutions of the vats."

Howell threw the knife back to the warrior who had first passed it to him. Gradually, cued by Howell's gestures, the warriors formed a circle around Horse.

"You belong to us," Howell said. "You are Smoke Jaguar. We own you, but you also own us. We are one. We will die for you, you will die for any one of us. You must accept this, Horse. Do you accept this?"

Horse glowered. "You must be mad, Russou Howell. I will not become Smoke Jaguar. I will perform the duties expected of me as your prisoner, but I am Jade Falcon. I will always be Jade Falcon."

Howell sighed. "Those words should be your death warrant, Horse. But we Smoke Jaguars are magnanimous with our lessers. Since you not only originate from another Clan, and are freeborn, we excuse your ignorance. The Ceremony of Kinship will continue. Stage two."

Again Howell prompted the warriors, who caught on to what he seemed to want. They took a few steps forward, forming an unbroken circle. Howell remained outside the circle and began moving around it. The warriors looked confused about what was happening or what they were supposed to do next, but Howell seemed almost in a trance, going from on outlandish deed to the next without missing a beat.

"This is the circle of loyalty, Prisoner Horse," he shouted. "An unbroken circle like the interlocking bloodlines that form the perfection that is the Smoke Jaguar Clan. It is not a Circle of Equals since you, as a freebirth, are never equal to any one of us. In this circle, you are offered the chance to be part of the circle or to break through it."

"What if I stay where I am?"

"Star Commander Mikel, raise your weapon."

Mikel, whom Horse knew slightly, raised a laser pistol and pointed it at Horse.

"Star Commander Mikel will kill you if you do not join us or take the challenge," Howell intoned.

"Very well. I welcome challenge."

Suddenly, Horse rushed toward the line. At the last minute he veered sideways and slammed his body into Star Commander Mikel, knocking him backward. Briefly, there was an opening in the line. Horse jumped toward it, but the line closed quickly and denied his escape.

Horse only laughed and began to pace around the inner circumference of the circle. After about five measured steps, he took a sudden step back and elbowed the warrior behind him in the neck. The woman choked but held her ground. Horse swung around, in a crouch, looking for his next opportunity. A warrior raised his left leg high and kicked Horse in the face with his boot. Horse reeled back, pain going up and down the struck side of his face. Briefly his hand went to his throbbing cheek, but, when the warriors' yells became joyful, the hand just as quickly returned to his side. He did not want these Jaguars to realize his pain.

For the next few minutes, Horse attacked individuals in the circle, many of whom he hurt seriously, causing them to break out of the circle and stagger off. Whenever one left, the circle closed in further and the grunts and growls of the warriors grew more intense. Soon the circle was about half its original size. As the ordeal continued, Howell kept pacing around them, calling to his warriors not to break the circle. Maintaining the circle, warriors occasionally kicked out and dealt damaging blows to Horse. Once in a while one would slightly disengage and punch him. His responses were quick, and he either sent the warrior back to the relative safety of the circle or right out of the circle, making it even smaller.

Slowly, after he had made several rushes at the still-intact circle, Horse suddenly got an idea. He would have to do it now, before the circle became any smaller. At a smaller circumference, he realized, the remaining warriors could pummel him at will.

He calculated the pace of Howell around the circle's exterior. It was regular, unvaried. He kept his face turned toward the circle, looking pleased at every well-landed warrior blow, irritated by any successful move from Horse.

Suddenly Horse backed violently into the warriors behind him, surprising them but not breaking the circle. He had not intended to break it there. Rebounding off the warrior immediately behind him, he ran the short distance toward the other side of the circle.

Timing his move precisely, he leaped upward as he reached the edge. His feet straight out, he kicked the warrior in front of him in the stomach, doubling him over. Horse first fell to the ground, then leaped up quickly and dove over the warrior, who was still bent over, clutching his stomach. He was able to somersault to his feet, in spite of the way the stiff robe threatened to confuse his legs. He landed directly in front of Howell.

Now he faced Howell in a slight crouched pose, ready to do battle with the Galaxy Commander, if Howell chose. From the expression on his face it seemed as if Howell might choose. Instead, he smiled slowly.

"Not a bad move, Horse," he said. "For a freebirth. But freebirths do have cunning, *quiaff*?"

"Tell me, Russou Howell, if I am only a freebirth, and freebirths have no value in Smoke Jaguar eyes, why are you so determined to make me a Smoke Jaguar?"

Horse's words came in short, breathless bursts.

"Perhaps I would like to show that once a freebirth, always a freebirth. Perhaps I would merely like to crush you. Perhaps I wish to take a freebirth of no value and turn him into a Smoke Jaguar of supreme value. Or perhaps I only amuse myself and the warriors of my command. Life can get very predictable here on Huntress."

"I will not be one of you. Kill me now."

There was another round of angry rumbling among the

nearby warriors. Howell turned toward them and again held up his hand to still them. "See, Horse, they would like to kill you. Only I stand between you and death. You may be a Smoke Jaguar or you may die."

"I choose death then."

"You do not have that choice. I have it, but you do not."

"I will not be Smoke Jaguar."

Howell turned toward his warriors and said, "Very well then. Stage three."

15

Near Lootera Wood
Huntress
Kerensky Cluster, Clan Homeworlds
13 April 3059

A short while later, they arrived at a large stretch of open ground that lay between the stone arch that marked the southern end of Lootera and the nearby forest. A trio of Jag warriors from the squad who had marched him to this place grabbed at Horse's arms to hold him in check. Horse waved them off.

"I am going nowhere," he said. "Not just now, anyway."

The warriors backed off a few steps and left Horse standing in the middle of the clearing contemplating his predicament.

Maybe Howell wants me to escape. This is a pretty small squad to assign to me. Or maybe it is to humiliate me by showing how few are needed to guard me. These stravags are certainly milling about uselessly.

What is Howell up to, anyway? After I broke out of the circle, his eyes got even crazier. What he should've done is just kill me from the start. There's no point in me being a prisoner and even less point in expecting me to accept his rules as if I was a trueborn. It's hard for freeborns to think like trueborns, even though we fight side by side with them. Freeborns can be warriors, can honor and live the way of the Clans. What the truebirths never realize is

*that, for all the accepting freeborns do, we remain free-
born inside. I don't even want it that way. It just is. My
loyalty to the Jade Falcons is indestructible. I can't be a
Smoke Jaguar. Howell's all wrong. This Horse cannot be
broken. Silly joke. But true enough.*

Horse surveyed the squad surrounding him. *A lot of
these Jags look as confused about all this as I am. They
keep saying they've never heard of this Ceremony of Kinship. Maybe Howell's making it up. But they're loyal to
their commander even when it seems like he's crazy. For
the moment, anyway.*

*It's all Howell, this ceremony. They don't even want me
in their Clan. They want me dead.*

Horse was wrenched out of his reverie by the eruption
of a fight between two of the Jaguar warriors in his squad
of captors. The blows came so rapidly and fiercely that
the faces of both were covered in blood within seconds.
The officer in charge, a Star Commander named Keyre,
moved in to break up the fight and received some harsh
blows to his own face before he could break it up.

When Keyre asked one of the warriors what had started
the fight, the man mumbled a response. Horse took a
couple of steps toward them and, almost comically, a pair
of his captors slid that way with him.

"You must not question the Galaxy Commander's decisions," Keyre was saying firmly. "You understand that,
the both of you, *quiaff?*"

The pair of affirmatives that followed the question
seemed hesitant and unsure.

"Keyre." A MechWarrior Horse had heard addressed as
Merkad stepped between Keyre and the two squabbling
warriors. "You are right in quashing this, but you have to
admit that everyone is confused. This ritual Howell has
invoked out of nowhere does not exist. You heard Star
Colonel Logan. He is right when he says that—"

"Silence, Merkad. This disloyalty is not fit, especially
in front of freebirth scum like this one."

Horse tried to look like he had heard nothing.

"What do you mean, disloyalty? Logan Wirth says—"

"I will hear no more."

"But you agree with—"

"I will hear no more of it, *quiaff?*"

"Neg. This ceremony does not bring honor to anyone."

"Merkad, we will settle this between ourselves in a Circle of Equals," Keyre said firmly. "For now, shut up."

Merkad strode off, angry. Keyre waved the two squabblers away. Horse noted that, although they started walking in a different direction than Merkad, they slowly made their way toward where he stood.

A BattleMech was now visible, approaching from the direction of Lootera. A *Stormcrow*. Horse knew it to be one of the most versatile of Smoke Jaguar 'Mechs. Although it clearly had seen abundant service, bearing proud scars all over its metal surfaces, it was one of the better 'Mechs among Howell's motley group. Like most garrison posts, this one's BattleMechs were older and sometimes Inner Sphere refits. However, the 'Mechs on Huntress represented somewhat less than the norm for garrisons. When he had first accompanied Howell to the 'Mech storage area and seen the collection assigned to the planet's pair of Galaxies, he saw why Howell had broken protocol to steal the BattleMechs of Horse's Trinary. They were not top-line either, but were more advanced than most of the hulks in Howell's command.

Following the *Stormcrow* came Howell on foot, leading what looked like several dozen warriors. He spoke loudly, addressing them all.

"Horse, we Smoke Jaguars do not kill or destroy wastefully. We have discerned your worth and see a place for you among us—not as a warrior, of course, but in some valuable tech role. No more repulsive freebirth views or behavior will be allowed, though. You accept, *quiaff*?"

Horse took a deep breath to support the bellow that followed. "Neg! Never!"

Some warriors rushed a few steps toward him, ready to annihilate him right there, but Howell's warning stopped their progress.

"Horse, you may enjoy this next little task. It at least gets you inside a BattleMech." Many of the Jaguars raised their voices in protest at those words.

"I know, warriors," Howell said, "that you are offended at a freebirth violating the inside of a 'Mech cockpit. I have considered that. Horse will pilot an out-of-commission 'Mech." The rumbling of the ground would have already warned them, but Howell also pointed at the machine now approaching.

The 'Mech lumbered through the gate, and Horse recognized the type right away. It was a *Mackie,* an ancient example of BattleMech manufacturing, an extremely heavy and boxlike Inner Sphere contraption that might once have been admirable but was long past its prime. Low in heat-sink capability, with an impractically weighty engine, a *Mackie* was thought to be no longer used anywhere. Even among the Clans, *Mackies* had not seen regular combat for centuries. Horse had seen one only once before, in the Strana Mechty BattleMech Museum.

Howell now spoke softly. "This *Mackie* has apparently been around on Huntress ever since the Jaguars first took over the world. Its record shows it served the Clan well. At one time. But it is a bit out of the habit of combat now. What do you think, Horse? A worthy 'Mech for a freebirth scum prisoner, *quiaff*?"

"You wish me to pilot this antique?" Horse demanded.

"Affirmative. What do you think, Horse? Your evaluation as a Clan warrior?"

"All right. It is heavy tonnage without much compensating mobility. The weapons on this one look like they have not been used in decades. It heats up dangerously almost as soon as you get it going. Compared to our OmniMechs, its heat-sink technology is farcical. Anyone piloting it would have to spend more time checking the thing's heat levels than in combat. Actually, there would not even be time for that because this machine would not last ten seconds against an Omni."

"With your piloting skills, it would last longer, I suspect. Twenty seconds, maybe even thirty. However, your evaluation is quite accurate. The *Mackie* is a fossil, but it is your fossil, for the moment."

"You wish me to fight in this—this fossil?"

"Correct. But do not despair. The weapons in both the *Stormcrow* and the *Mackie* are powered down. We do not wish to unnecessarily harm a perfectly good BattleMech for the sake of freebirth scum, not even a worthless *Mackie.* You must get past your opponent, the *Stormcrow,* and get back into the city. The trial will be over when you reach the arch or you fall. You have the right to start the trial when you are ready."

"This is your way of making me a true Smoke Jaguar? To put me in a clumsy, high-tonnage vehicle against a much more maneuverable 'Mech and then watch us dance around like two puppets? All right, Galaxy Commander, let me get up into this godforsaken 'Mech and see what I can do with it."

"Very obliging of you. See, you are becoming more cooperative already. Oh, and did I tell you that the pilot of the *Stormcrow* is Star Colonel Logan? I understand he is not exactly a fan of yours, Horse."

"Seeing his ugly face in my mind will only make this exercise in madness more acceptable."

Howell smiled. "Good."

The warrior who had piloted the *Mackie* into the clearing climbed down the 'Mech looking relieved to be out of its cockpit, then stood to the side, inviting Horse to ascend. As Horse climbed up to the footholds, he scraped his hands on shards that stuck outward from the 'Mech's battered surface. Near the top he looked down and saw how heavy-limbed and big-footed the *Mackie* was. Its weapons, old fashioned in design, looked more like plumbing pipes than instruments of firepower. He turned toward the cockpit and the one-way glass that was a unique *Mackie* feature. The glass looked eerie, as if forbidding him to enter. Well, whatever he did, at least his opponents would not be able to see him do it.

Inside the cockpit, he was struck by how primitively equipped it was. The command couch did not seem contoured to anything human. There was a single screen clearly undated to present sensor techniques. There were misshapen controls. The neurohelmet looked like it might electrocute you before you could use it correctly. Horse would need every bit of skill he could muster for this one. There was nothing worse than taking over a new 'Mech and seeing that it did not suit you. This *Mackie* did not suit Horse, but he would have to show Howell and his Smoke Jaguars that a Jade Falcon could handle any machine you gave him and could do it well.

Easing himself into the seat, he found it surprisingly comfortable. Perhaps the unnatural contours he had earlier noted corresponded to the unnatural contours of his own body. Even the neurohelmet, so ineffective-looking, felt right when he put it on.

"We will allow you a few moments to familiarize yourself with the controls," Howell said over the commline after Horse had connected its archaic headphone.

"No need. I am ready."

Even over the commline the incredulity came through in Howell's voice. "I may be trying to teach you a lesson here, but I do not wish for you to deliberately place yourself and your machine in jeopardy."

"I am not doing that. I can handle this contraption as is. Practice would only put me in jeopardy. I do not want to know any more about it than I have already seen."

Horse peered through the viewport and saw Howell and the other Jags gathered at the edge of the clear ground, where the forest began. *Get a good seat, friends. The games are about to begin.*

The commline went silent for a surprisingly long while. Horse adjusted the controls while he waited. Turning the scanner console on its axis, he pointed its screen away from him. Its resolution was inadequate and he did not want to be distracted by it. The view out of the cockpit's one-way glass was just fine. Horse brought the *Mackie* about to face the city. He would just proceed on what he could see with his own eyes. What was behind him, what was to either side, was not important. He would focus on the city limits in the distance ahead of him and whatever placed itself in his way. Which, at the moment, was the *Stormcrow.*

Howell's voice broke the silence. "Very well then, we will apply the following rules. First—"

Horse made the *Mackie* take a step forward while firing his left-arm PPC at the *Stormcrow.* The shot caught Logan off-guard and, for a moment, the sleek-looking 'Mech seemed to reel from the hit. Simultaneously, Horse bellowed into the commline: "Forget your *stravag* rules! The game begins now!"

Horse kept the *Mackie* heading toward the *Stormcrow* and the city while firing quickly with the PPC and the center-torso lasers as he went. Although he did not stop often to aim, he could see that many of his shots were hitting the mark. Unfortunately, the heat level of the 'Mech seemed to be rising just as quickly. The *Stormcrow* scored some mild hits, causing the *Mackie* to rock from side to side. There was apparently no stabilization adjuster for the cockpit because Horse was frequently getting bounced in his seat. Once it felt as if he would actually hit his head on the cockpit ceiling.

His assault almost worked, but the *Stormcrow* was holding its ground and now headed toward the *Mackie*, firing cautiously. Even with low power, it was doing some damage. Horse stared now at the skyline of Lootera that seemed too far away.

The 'Mech's heat level had soared past the halfway mark. If he fired much more, or used more energy to force the *Mackie* forward, he would wind up immobile and still on the wrong side of the city. Beaten. In his mind he heard Howell's scornful laughter, his demand for capitulation. Thinking of Howell's victory squawks seemed to fire Horse all the more.

He would beat them. There was a way.

"Do you give up, Horse?" Howell said.

"Neg."

"Let me tell you one rule that you did not give me a chance to state, if we judge your efforts to be insufficient or even cowardly, we may execute you. It is the Smoke Jaguar way."

"Do not worry. The Jade Falcon who is a coward does not exist."

Howell's fury was obvious in his raised voice. "You refuse to acknowledge that you are no longer a Jade Falcon. You are Smoke Jaguar now! That is what this is all about. Resume!"

I will not die in the ignominious manner these Jags would like. If I die, I will go down fighting. And fighting well. Forget the heat levels, forget weapons. I'll move as fast as this clunky 'Mech will carry me.

The *Stormcrow* continued to fire and the *Mackie* felt the brunt of its attack. Still the *Mackie*'s bulk worked to Horse's advantage. He began to think that Howell might have miscalculated the deliberate insult of his 'Mech selection. Because Horse's opponent was burdened with powered-down weapons, shots that might have devastated the *Mackie* did only minimal damage. The barrage did little to slow the *Mackie* as Horse pushed forward, closing the distance between the two 'Mechs. It was simply too big and thick to reel much from a blow. In a way it was a solahma 'Mech, here being used as cannon fodder on the whim of a commander who might just be losing his mind. As this thought crossed his own agitated mind, Horse smiled, a smile whose confidence might have rattled his enemies—except that, of course, they could not see through the one-way glass.

The *Stormcrow* surged forward, clearly intending to finish off this upstart and his out-of-date 'Mech. Horse stepped up the pace of the *Mackie* instead of stopping for it. He would force the *Stormcrow* to retreat or step aside, a maneuver that would not automatically give Horse a clear route into the city, since the *Stormcrow* could easily catch up. Logan shot at the *Mackie* with his right-arm medium laser. The shots missed the *Mackie* entirely, slicing just past its left shoulder in crossfire.

Good. Maybe we're rattling him, me and the Mackie! *I'm beginning to enjoy this. And why not? Being in a 'Mech cockpit is what it is all about,* quiaff?

Horse smiled, amused at his own use of the rhetorical quiaff. He was thinking that Howell was losing his mind, and now instead he was talking to himself.

Horse did not hesitate but kept on going. When he reached the *Stormcrow,* he realized that it seemed runty next to the thick-bodied *Mackie.* He brought the *Mackie* to a sudden halt and, simultaneously, swung its left arm, connecting with the *Stormcrow* cockpit. The *Stormcrow* was edged backward by the blow. Horse followed it up with a right-arm punch, again to the cockpit.

"Horse!" Howell's angry voice came through the commline. "You know we detest physical attacks by a 'Mech. Stop it at once!"

"This is not a battle. It is an exercise. You said so yourself, Howell. I will use any tactic I can."

Horse had deliberately avoided Howell's rank in addressing him, knowing how much it irritated him. He was right. Howell screamed into the commline shrilly: "Scum! Freebirth!"

The two blows had rocked the *Stormcrow.* Without allowing the *Mackie*'s left arm to swing backward, he slammed it forward again for a third smash against the cockpit. This time the blow cracked the cockpit glass. Raising the *Mackie*'s left arm, then bringing it down at a slight angle, Horse was able to send the *Stormcrow* tottering. What in a human would have been a comparatively weak left nearly toppled the smaller 'Mech over.

Horse did not even watch the *Stormcrow* stagger, but slipped past it and started on his run toward the city. He was sure that its run was hardly graceful. No doubt it was lumbering. But the move was his only choice.

He sensed the *Stormcrow*'s pursuit. There was no way he could outrun it. In a way, Horse was glad of that. He was uncomfortable running away from an enemy, but he needed to close the distance between himself and the city.

The next *Stormcrow* shot, from its left-arm PPC, hit the *Mackie*'s right arm, sending armor flying and—according to the primitive diagnostics of Horse's cockpit—disabling the limb.

A harsh and cruel voice that Horse recognized as Star Colonel Logan's came over the commline now.

"You will not be able to land any of your fancy punches with that arm, Horse. Now, the other one."

Horse reacted quickly, swinging the *Mackie*'s left arm away from the torso. Logan's shot slipped between the arm and the torso.

The *Stormcrow* caught up to the *Mackie,* all weapons firing. Anger had reduced Logan's caution. Only a few shots caused damage. The *Mackie* was rocked, shaken, and battered, but never fatally. Either Logan was not a very good 'Mech pilot or his anger was affecting his skills.

The *Stormcrow* caught up with the *Mackie* alongside its disabled arm. Even if Horse could maneuver his awkward machine toward the *Stormcrow* while both were in a run, he realized he could not use that arm to shoot at the oncoming 'Mech or land a backhanded punch against the *Stormcrow*. On the other hand, the *Stormcrow*'s weapons were still powered down and they were doing little harm to the *Mackie,* no more than the BattleMech equivalent of tweaks and nudges.

As abruptly as he could manage, Horse brought the *Mackie* to a halt, allowing the *Stormcrow* to surge past it several steps. Horse then held the *Mackie*'s body as still as possible. Logan managed to turn the *Stormcrow* around with some difficulty to face the *Mackie* again. Then he began firing his weapons almost wildly, apparently satisfied that his maneuverability and firepower could win the day easily. In spite of the hits the *Mackie* was taking, in spite of the rain of armor now falling around his cockpit, Horse held off firing and set the *Mackie* on what might have looked like an easy pace toward the *Stormcrow*. Calculating as well as he could through dead reckoning that was now his only recourse, he took the *Mackie* close to the *Stormcrow*, while getting off some weak blasts from his own powered-down center-torso lasers. His assaults left thin scars on the *Stormcrow* but caused no real harm.

The *Mackie*'s heat was spiking close to the red zone.

"Freebirth coward," Logan said. "Do you think you can land another punch now, with only one arm and with me ready for it?"

"I would not insult a good trueborn Clan officer by repeating myself, Logan."

Deliberately Horse started the *Mackie* moving again slowly. When he neared the *Stormcrow*, he angled the *Mackie*'s body a bit to the right so that its left side leaned away from the *Stormcrow*, then took a step in with the *Mackie*'s right foot. In his mind he saw the maneuver as resembling one of the movements in a traditional Jade Falcon village dance. Raising the *Mackie*'s left leg and using the right foot as a pivot, he swung the *Mackie*'s left side toward the other 'Mech. If he had miscalculated by as little as a few millimeters, the two 'Mechs would not have made contact. As it was, however, since the old war-horse *Mackie* outweighed the *Stormcrow* by so much, he could use the *Mackie*'s shoulder to push solidly against the *Stormcrow* torso. Horse surprised Logan enough to tilt the *Stormcrow* backward.

Now, he reversed the dance. Using the left foot for pivoting, he brought the *Mackie* around and smashed it into the wavering side of the *Stormcrow*. The impact was strong enough, and the *Mackie*'s edge in weight large enough, to nudge the *Stormcrow* off-balance and make it stagger backward. Horse considered employing another smash for insurance, but he realized that winning Howell's bizarre little trial was more important.

Putting as much speed into the *Mackie* as seemed possible and ignoring the increasingly disastrous heat levels, he headed the 'Mech toward the city while Logan tried to regain the balance of his 'Mech. It was a struggle for Horse to recapture the *Mackie*'s balance, but he really did not need steadiness. He slipped past the *Stormcrow*, narrowly missing another collision.

Checking his secondary display, he saw the fuzzy outline of the *Stormcrow*, which was still stumbling a bit backward. It regained its balance quickly, and Logan was able to swing it around to begin pursuit. Horse felt the impact of several hits against the back of his 'Mech. That would not add anything to his reputation among the Jags, he knew. Few things were worse among Clan warriors than taking rear hits, which were often interpreted as a sign of cowardice.

The *Mackie*'s heat level was almost to the point where the 'Mech would simply shut down. Horse looked ahead, toward the stone arch that was his goal. It seemed as if he could not possibly make it.

Then Logan, probably frustrated by Horse's tactics, stopped the *Stormcrow* in its tracks and let go a barrage of weapons fire that rocked the *Mackie*. Unfortunately for Logan, it also gave Horse's 'Mech the necessary push forward to send him through the arch on uncertain feet. Just as he entered Lootera, the heat sinks failed. Horse realized that without Logan's rear attack, the *Mackie* would have shut down at a point just short of victory.

For a long while, Horse could not stop laughing. And he made sure the commline was open so Howell could hear him.

16

Lootera
Huntress
Kerensky Cluster, Clan Homeworlds
13 April 3059

Horse climbed halfway down the *Mackie,* then looked around. Howell's warriors were moving toward him, their eyes angry, their fists clenched.

Logan had brought the *Stormcrow* to an abrupt halt and was now leaping off the 'Mech's foot. He ran toward Horse, with the others gaining ground behind him. By the time they reached the *Mackie,* Logan was just ahead of them.

"Scum!" Logan yelled. *"Surat! Stravag!"*

Some of the other warriors echoed Logan's chant. Horse waited for the din to grow fainter, then came the rest of the way down the 'Mech. Standing in front of Logan and staring into his eyes, he said calmly, "You are displeased?"

Logan took a swing at Horse, who ducked neatly under the punch. He came up, ready to fight, but others held Logan back.

"You ignorant Falcon freebirths might not know about honorable tactics," Logan said, "but Smoke Jaguars would never stoop to using their 'Mechs for purely physical attacks."

Horse nodded and again spoke calmly. "I know more

than you think of honorable combat, Star Colonel. On a
battlefield I would smash you in some other way, but this
was, as your commander said, an exercise. If we Falcons
believe in anything, it's winning. Maybe winning is not
so vital to the Jaguars. It is—"

"Freebirth! You are the lowest scum from the sewer. I
will fight you again!"

"Count on it, Logan!"

"And I will beat you to a—"

"Do not count on that, Logan," Horse said, stepping
forward.

Howell also took a step forward, a strange smile on
his face.

"Star Colonel," he said. "We will argue the point no
further. This was purely an exercise. The weapons were
powered down. This time we shall give Horse the benefit
of the doubt. After all, he is only a freebirth."

Howell followed the words with a scornful laugh, but it
was obvious that the other Jaguars gathered around were
not satisfied with the decision. Howell turned to Horse.
His face was surprisingly placid.

"You are lousy freebirth scum," he said, "but you also
showed skill against one of my own Jaguars. I ask you
again, do you acknowledge Clan Smoke Jaguar as your
own?"

Horse stared at Howell a long while, wondering whether he had already been drinking today. More worrisome
was what the other warriors standing around might do.
They were calling out protests, insults, and some of them
shook their fists in menace.

Howell, although outwardly calm, held himself stiffly.
The fingers of both his hands were held close to his body
and spread apart. Horse sensed that he would like to
clench and unclench them, as he did so often when edgy,
but such a nervous habit would not look good in front of
his warriors.

"Galaxy Commander Howell, I must respect another
Clan's beliefs and customs, even when they do not make
sense to me. But how do you call for me to acknowledge
the Smoke Jaguars when your warriors are so easily
beaten by a mere freebirth? I—"

With angry shouts, several warriors standing nearest
moved toward Horse, as if they wanted to rush him now.

Howell stopped their progress with the same imperious upraised hand he'd used previously. Horse took advantage of the pause to continue his little speech.

"I am only a freebirth and a prisoner to you, and that is all I can ever be among your Clan. I am Jade Falcon and cannot be Smoke Jaguar. By your own customs, I should be sentenced to death, but know this—I will fight any of you who come forward to execute me and I will fight to the death."

Howell listened with apparent calm, but Horse could see the fury in his eyes. He tensed, ready to meet any attack, even if it might be his death. He found comfort in the fact that he would die a Jade Falcon warrior.

"Well spoken, freebirth," Howell finally said, his anger making his voice tremble slightly. "Ordinarily such a speech would surely be punished by death, but this is a Ceremony of Kinship. Some fates, however, are worse than death. The Ceremony of Kinship continues. Warriors!" Howell motioned to several Jaguars, and they reacted almost without thought.

With screams like those warriors often gave when charging into combat, they converged on Horse. The first one to reach him was running with his arms up and head bent forward. Horse kicked him in the groin and followed the kick with a flat-handed chop to the back of his neck, knocking him to the ground. Another warrior jumped at him with her feet aimed at his face. He abruptly dodged his head to one side, forcing her to fly over his shoulder. As she came by, he grabbed her arm and twisted it. He heard the sound of breaking bone, which he might have enjoyed except that he had to react to the next attacker, who came in with his fists flying. He punched Horse in the chest and landed a dizzying blow to the side of his head. Horse feigned a counterpunch but instead stepped aside and, with a mean sweep of his leg, tripped up the attacker. When he had eliminated the first few, more joined the fray.

In all, at least ten Smoke Jaguars got to Horse, and he dealt with them all. But then they kept on coming, until there were too many of them and Horse was pinned to the ground, an astoundingly heavy warrior lounging on his stomach and forcing the breath out of him.

"That is enough!" Howell screamed, then pointed

wildly to several warriors. "You and you and you, string this man up."

"What?" Horse whispered with what little voice he could recover after they forced him up. "You are going to hang me?" He struggled to regain his balance.

Howell smiled bitterly.

"We will not kill you. Death can never be humiliation. The Ceremony of Kinship demands capitulation—although it can result in your dying from, oh, natural causes. We cannot, after all, help it if you are not warrior enough and expire before the end of the ceremony."

"I am warrior enough. And more."

"We shall see, Horse. We shall see."

The warriors Howell had called to grabbed Horse's arms, and despite his struggling, began dragging him back toward the forest.

An hour later, Horse did find himself strung up. Strong, exceptionally bulky ropes attached to his arms and legs had been secured to the thick branches of a pair of trees that he was now suspended between. The trees were just at the edge of the wood, and Horse could easily see Lootera across the open area between here and there. The robe given him earlier had been ripped open in several wide gashes, the rending accomplished methodically with a special cutting tool normally used for slicing open the innards of 'Mechs. The ropes on his arms were so secure that they stretched and strained his muscles. The ropes on his legs were looser, but tight enough to keep him from bringing his legs together. His head was held straight because of a cushioned metal collar on his neck.

"This particular punishment is quite primitive, I admit," Howell said with some pleasure in his voice. "But it has ancient precedents. I want to give you ample time to consider your present plight.

"We will send emissaries to feed you once a day. For an hour each day, your bonds will be loosened sufficiently for you to take some food and to exercise your cramped muscles. We would not want you to miss our excellent meals or to die of starvation or from atrophy. You will have to work to find a way to die. Perhaps you can summon one of your jade falcons here and it could peck you to death."

The Jaguar warriors standing at the foot of the trees were evidently amused by the remark. They laughed heartily, nastily. Horse tried to spit at them, but the collar prevented him from aiming well. Most of his spittle dribbled down his chin onto the collar.

"And you will not be lonely, Horse. We will visit you, to heap taunts upon you and to hear your feeble responses, responses that will no doubt become feebler as the days pass and you foolishly resist.

"You may avoid all this by capitulating now. Do you?"

Horse grunted.

"Be glad you are allowed this ceremony, Horse. You are a filthy freebirth, and you always will be! You are Jade Falcon scum, as long as you resist! Think of the honor we offer you. Think of it. Think of it all night.

"I believe a storm is developing in the mountains and is heading this way. Perhaps the winds will be violent. Such a storm could conceivably shake the trees enough to pull your arm out of its socket, to break a leg. Perhaps the cold will numb you and your limbs will become fragile and snap off. Perhaps a branch will crash out of the trees and collapse your skull. Much could happen. You might prefer to end your life in one of these ways, but I certainly would be sorry to see you die so ignominiously. There is nothing sadder in legend or history than the final humiliation of a dead hero. There is still time, Horse, for you to accept our Clan now. Think of the honor—"

"There is no honor possible for me within your Clan," Horse said.

Howell snapped out his hand toward one of his warriors. The woman immediately produced a whip.

"Horse, this whip is not electronically enhanced, nor is it equipped with any special features. It is an ordinary whip, like those used throughout history. You have reduced us to primitive actions through your obstinacy."

Holding the whip high, Howell flicked it at Horse's body. The end cracked in through a rent in the robe and stung Horse's chest.

"Your fate is in your hands. You could die of the elements by doing nothing or you can capitulate."

Horse, still feeling the sting of the whip's lash, said with as much volume as the circumstances would allow, "I will not capitulate."

"Very well. Warriors, we shall leave him now."

Before walking off, some warriors strode up to where Horse hung and showed their contempt. Some spat, some struck him, some merely uttered foul oaths. Horse tried to kick at several of them, but there was not enough slack in the ropes to allow more than a brushing contact.

Then they were gone, leaving him alone as they returned to Lootera.

Howell was right about the weather. A prodigious storm began not long after the departure of Howell, his 'Mechs, and his warriors.

First the sky darkened with ominous, heavy gray clouds, then the wind started suddenly with tremendous velocity. Hanging from the ropes, Horse felt the bursts of wind as more severe and painful than Howell's whip-blow. Sometimes a sudden barrage of wind would throw his body forward, tautening the lines to the tree branches, then stretching the branches to possible breaking points. Horse could not figure out how his arms and legs survived without breaking.

As Howell had suggested, the pain from the wind was brutal, at times making him feel as if his spinal cord would crack. When the wind died down just as abruptly as it had arisen, he bounced back almost as strenuously, ending with the ropes pulling at his limbs over and over as their tautness diminished. At other times gusts of wind came from different angles, stretching Horse one way and then another.

Then the rains came.

Like the winds, the rain's strength varied. Most of the time it came down in thick pummeling drops. He was grateful that the abundance of trees often weakened the rain's intensity. Throwing his head back as much as he could with the collar restraining the movement, Horse managed to capture enough water with his tongue to satisfy his heavy thirst.

He looked back toward the outskirts of Lootera. In spite of the low visibility, he saw 'Mechs and some ground cars gathered like an audience, their occupants no doubt amused by his bouncing like a puppet. He wanted to shout epithets at them, but knew the storm was too noisy. Anyway, he needed to conserve his strength.

Water dripped and surged down his face and body. He kept wanting to wipe some of it away with his hands. Unthinkingly, he pulled at the ropes, but he could not budge them. Relaxing, he tried to sink deeper into the collar and let the water wash over him, let the wind work its will with him. He could not adjust his head much, but the relaxation helped to reduce the pain.

A lull in the storm. The wind eased down and the water hitting him was no longer rainfall, just drops from leaves and branches.

There were no longer any 'Mechs or other observers in the distance. It was probably storming in Lootera now. Perhaps the rain had chased his tormentors away. That made Horse feel as if he had won somehow. He had endured the storm while they had been driven off.

He tested the ropes, trying to see if the storm had loosened them or perhaps stretched them to a point where, with a jerk of his arm or leg, he might have loosened them more, even split one apart.

"*Stravag,*" he muttered, realizing they were as tight as ever. As they dried, they would become even tauter.

"*Stravag* seems a good word for your situation," said a voice. It seemed to emerge out of the tree to his left. Horse managed to turn his head slightly, in spite of the collar, but he saw nothing. However, he had recognized the voice.

Speaking as low as he could, he whispered, "Sentania Buhallin, where are you?"

"I think it is better if I do not show myself at this moment. I can peek out at you quite easily from my perch here."

"How long have you been there?"

"I only arrived during the storm. I was headed for Lootera, expecting to see you there. Instead, here you are, strung up like a hock of meat intended for tomorrow's supper. The Smoke Jags have not turned cannibal, *quineg*?"

"Neg."

Horse, his voice made hoarse because of the elements and his collar, told Sentania all that had happened. But he stopped trying to look toward the tree, as the effort only intensified the pain shooting down his spine.

"Seems that garrison duty is getting to Howell," she said quietly when he was done.

"You think Howell is doing all this out of boredom?"

"Or rage. I have been watching him and he seems, well, unbalanced."

"You mean crazy."

"Or well on the way. They say he was a good enough warrior, but only recently bloodnamed, only recently thrust into command, only recently assigned to garrison duty. Garrison duty is always some kind of punishment, *quiaff*?"

Horse knew she was right. Especially assignment from the front lines of the invasion back to the homeworlds. It must stick in his throat to be one of those involved in arming and preparing the Clans for another thrust at the Inner Sphere, with no hope of true combat for him.

"This Howell is about to explode, Horse. And when he blows, more than just you will get hurt. He may be out to humiliate anyone who crosses his path, just to ease his own torment. He may even try to attack Falcon Eyrie. I hear he's whipping up discipline among his troops."

A gust of wind slammed Horse in the back, and his body was thrust forward, while his arms stretched back. His shoulder ached with pain. He grimaced from it.

"Eventually this little game of Howell's will kill you, Horse. What good is that to you? You are on Huntress for some reason. I'm sure the great Falcon hero didn't just decide to drop into Falcon Eyrie for a visit?"

"I am only here to have a look-see for the Khan. A kind of informal inspection."

"Forget it. I do not care why you are here. You may be here to torch the Eyrie for all I know or care. Whatever your reason, you might as well throw it to the wind for all the good you are doing it."

"I cannot let Russou How—"

"Jettison that, Horse. It's no more than surat droppings. Here you are strung up in a tree in the midst of one of those Huntress storms the Jags call the rage of Kerensky. This one is not finished, and it will leave you one dead warrior. Not much value there to either the Jade Falcons or the orders you rode in here with."

"So I am a dead warrior. Warriors die. I will not bend

my knee to this Howell. He is trying to turn a prisoner bracelet into a kind of unofficial bondcord. I will not be bound to him in any way."

"That is right. You should not be. You should remain a Jade Falcon warrior, which in this case means a dead Jade Falcon warrior."

"You could cut me down."

"I would not even if I could. It is a good possibility that the Jags would be here before I split the final rope, even if I had the tools to cut through that nearly indestructible Huntress fiber, which I do not. And even if I were successful and got you down, you will barely be able to move, *quiaff*?"

"Neg. I can—"

"Your every joint is in pain, *quiaff*?"

"What does that have to do with it?"

"I like your bravado, Horse. They would catch us in a minute."

"Your caution is unClanlike. Cowardly."

"Perhaps, but only planning will get you out of this."

"You are a strange breed of Jade Falcon, Sentania."

"One who is alive. That is my virtue and my curse. I was too clever a warrior and could not manage to die in battle. But my cleverness may be of some use now. The Jags are not stupid or inefficient. We must outwit them."

She parted some of the leaves in front of her. Horse twisted his neck through shocks of pain to look at her. He was surprised to see how young and beautiful she looked with just this small part of her face framed by the leaves.

"Horse, I know how you feel about honor. I, too, am Jade Falcon. But there are times when honor becomes an obstacle. Pretense then becomes the honorable pursuit."

Horse relaxed his head forward again, the strain of trying to look at her too painful. "What are you suggesting?"

"I am suggesting that, instead of dying here, you do exactly what Howell asks. Capitulate."

Horse jerked his head toward her again, the suddenness of the movement sending spasms down his back. "You ask too much. That would be a violation of my honor."

"Maybe. Dishonor yourself now and you can redeem

yourself later. That has worked for generations of heroes."

"You are crazy, Sentania Buhallin," he spat.

"Some do say that. But, as an old Terran saying goes, I am crazy like a fox. Look, Horse, I see our goal as teaching Howell and the Jags a lesson. And that we will do."

"How?"

Sentania explained her plan to him. When she had finished, Horse said, "A good plan, but do not underestimate Howell."

"Then you will do it? Come on, Horse, at worst we keep you alive but dishonored." Horse grunted his disagreement with that option. "At best, we return to Falcon Eyrie and you perform whatever mission you came for."

After a long and tense pause, Horse sighed with frustration. "I cannot do it. I cannot, as you ask, pretend."

It was Sentania's turn to be silent. In the distance there were ominous rumbles indicating the return of the storm.

"Well, die then, Horse. Die, hero. But remember this. Your own great Aidan Pryde spent years pretending. Disguised as a lousy freebirth. And he went on pretending until a chance came to reclaim his trueborn status. And then what happened? Nothing much, he merely won his bloodname, became maybe the greatest Falcon hero, died a glorious death, was accepted into the gene pool way ahead of time. So, go on, criticize Aidan Pryde for being a fraud. For risking dishonor. For being a freebirth at heart!"

Horse strained at his ropes but succeeded only in making intense pain shoot up and down his arms.

"I would kill you if I could get free now!"

"Then capitulate, Horse. I will fight you later."

Horse strained again to see the circle of face in the leaves. She looked even younger, her questioning eyes almost childlike.

"All right. I will do it."

"Good."

"And I may never feel right again."

"Horse, you think too much. But, you know, after all these years at Falcon Eyrie, I kind of like it."

Then the leaves she had been holding apart shivered as

she released them. Sentania was gone, with only the slightest rustling of the brush.

She certainly knew how to appear and disappear quickly and quietly.

17

Falcon Eyrie Research Station
Eastern Mountains, Huntress
Kerensky Cluster, Clan Homeworlds
13 April 3059

On the morning of the day Russou Howell decided to put
Horse through his Ceremony of Kinship, Peri Watson
was winding her way through the Falcon Eyrie complex headed for her morning rounds. Set on a rocky
plateau among the Eastern Mountains, the base was a
collection of small, camouflaged ferrocrete buildings
nestled together under one of the surrounding high crags.
It always struck her how much the construction of the
research station resembled a human brain. Its conscious part was the few installations, living quarters, and
other buildings on the mountainous surface of the station,
all of which constituted less than ten percent of the
station's usable brain. There were a number of crevices
between the sections of the station, and the station
was studded with bridges, comparable to synapses.
From above the activity, people crossing the synapse-
like bridges and into the containers of knowledge that
were the various buildings, would have seemed as busy,
and sometimes as idle, as thoughts going through the
brain.

In spite of the surface busyness, most of the station—
like a person's unconscious—was hidden. Below the sur-

face, a complex hive of passageways and caverns led to the secrets of Falcon Eyrie. The analogy possibly failed when the traveler came out of the tunnels and discovered the huge cavern that was the Eyrie's Brian Cache. Still, a case could be made for the Cache representing the Eyrie's true subconscious, that part which, because entry into it was restricted, was mysterious and forbidding to those whose duties were performed above it. All together, the brain of Falcon Eyrie, they functioned to make the place a much more complicated unit—something like a human being.

Even Peri, in her position as chief scientist, was not privy to all the experimentation that went on in the depths of the Eyrie. Now, as she entered the genetics laboratory section, whose passageways twisted in a complex web that occasionally left new arrivals lost among the maze, she thought again of the secret experiments that had been transmitted via secret channels to certain specialists. These specialists, although ostensibly under her supervision, were not accountable to her. When she had expressed concern to the central station on Ironhold, she had received a reply that the specialists were appointed and supervised by the Scientist General, a bloated, sallow, mean-eyed man named Etienne Balzac. Their research and findings were to be reported back to him exclusively.

Peri had worked with Balzac for a while as his principal assistant back on Ironhold and had grown to despise him. He had ascended to the position of Scientist General by surreptitiously ruining the careers of those ahead of him in the strictly regulated scientist caste. And he had forced Peri to help him do it. When an assignment elsewhere, with less prestige, had come up, she had jumped at the chance to get herself sent to Falcon Eyrie, as far away from the main station as possible. It would be just like the vengeful Balzac to slap her hand by saddling her with secret research specialists so that she would not feel in complete control of her assignment.

Though she found it rewarding to work with the naturalists and with the designers of weapons and LAM modifications, Peri knew that the geneticists considered her little more than a paper-shuffler. Especially ironic because genetics had previously been her specialty. At that time, the secrecy had not been so hermetic. Scientists exchanged discoveries in the interest of the higher good. Now there was a secrecy within the secrecy, and Peri—who made no secret of her objection to it—had been shut out as a kind of punishment.

She sighed as she keyed in her security clearance to enter the inner sanctum of the genetics section. Those outside the caste, even the trueborn warriors, had no idea that the scientist caste had a leader with such a military title as "General." The position must have evolved before Peri's time, when the covert fellowship among the scientists was formed. Secret organizations needed a hierarchy to keep their plotting organized, and the Scientist General represented the secret pinnacle. Etienne Balzac was the latest of the ambitious, clever individuals to reach it. Another would take his place in time. Peri vowed to stay as far removed from these intrigues as possible. It was not the way of the Clans, and she could not even imagine how it all began.

The heavy door buzzed and cycled open. Peri pushed her way through.

To outsiders, Balzac was merely the head of the Ironhold Science Research and Education Center. No one suspected the clandestine network that rayed out beyond the center and, Peri had heard, even beyond the caste. There were odd things going on—among the scientist caste, among the warriors of the Clan, perhaps even in the other Clans. But Peri was stranded on Falcon Eyrie, and only knew her little part of it, no matter how much she tried to find out more.

Such thoughts always brought to mind her few nights with Aidan, when she had still been assigned to Tokasha. He was only an astech himself at the time, but destined to return to the warrior caste as a bloodnamed warrior, even a legend, of the Jade Falcons. But before all that happened, they had coupled and even in that short time managed to conceive a child. Their daughter Diana. Even in his disgrace, Aidan had never lost his passion for all that was embodied by a Clan warrior. Though Peri had come to accept her new life and her new caste, Aidan's belief in everything they'd been raised to believe had reawakened in her the importance of the way of the Clans. Now she wondered if it was merely the way of Aidan Pryde.

Thinking of Aidan made her a bit sad. She had named their daughter Diana as an anagram of his name, though he had never realized Diana was their child until just before his glorious death on Tukayyid. Before that time, Diana had been merely one of the MechWarriors in his Falcon Guards. Diana had written to tell her mother all that had happened, and reading that letter was the only time in her life that Peri cried. They were momentary tears, easily wiped away so no one could see, but she could still recall her sorrow. Then she had folded up the letter and never looked at it again. She had kept it, though, and it was packed away with her few belongings stored on Tokasha.

Peri turned down the corridor that led to the genetics lab. She had not heard from Diana in a long while. The last she knew, Diana was still a member of the Falcon Guards and still a MechWarrior. Given her origins, it would be difficult for her to rise in rank. Perhaps she would eventually be a Star Commander, since some freeborns did reach that rank, but there was a good chance she might not. And there was nothing wrong with that. Merely to be accepted as a warrior was sufficient honor for a freeborn. The trueborn Peri could not help regretting that she had failed to make it through cadet training. She still dreamed of what it would be to live as a warrior, and it was one of those dreams from which she never wanted to awaken.

Gashi, a blue-eyed and rather pretty lab tech, saw that Peri had entered the room, and she came forward.

"Star Colonel Roshak has been looking for you," the young woman said in an expressionless tech voice.

"Oh? Is he down here?"

"Aff. He just left for the weapons research lab."

"I will find him. Thank you, Gashi."

Peri picked up a noteputer and began half-heartedly scanning the latest readings on the jade falcon experiments. *So Roshak is looking for me? What useless thing does he have on his mind now? Something to do with his sporting life probably. I should strangle or poison Jade Rogue. No, that would be wrong. Jade Rogue has done nothing. I should strangle or poison Roshak, if anybody.*

She glanced up, sensing Gashi observing her out of the corner of her eye. Gashi immediately dropped her eyes and pretended to be intent on her work.

She is probably wondering why I do not go out immediately and find Roshak. I'll see him when I'm ready to.

Peri set down the noteputer and headed for the locked storeroom on the other side of the lab. She was one of the few with a key for it. Unlocking the door and entering, she ignored all the containers of genetic materials arranged on refrigerated shelves around the room. Each one was logged, with its information and history recorded on one side of the container.

Peri knew that these cylinders contained copies of the genetic legacies of Falcon warriors who had shown exceptional ability. Two of the missions of the genetics unit at Falcon Eyrie, as at many research stations, were to study and experiment with the legacies. The goal of such work was to refine and improve the genetic makeup of Jade Falcon warriors. The originals of the materials had no doubt already been used as the genetic foundation of new sibkos, which was the closest a warrior came to being a birthparent. That word was, of course, a repulsive one among trueborns, who took great pride in the fact that they were the products of genetic engineering—and, for that matter, the highest the Clan had to offer. The work of the geneticists was to make each new generation of trueborns even better.

Many of the experiments were under Etienne Balzac's aegis and were kept secret even from Peri. She had deduced the nature of some, but was baffled by others. She stood motionless, letting her gaze take in the whole room.

Even the records of the secret research are kept from me. That is not right. I could protest, but Etienne Balzac will see to it that it comes to nothing. At least, as Chief Scientist, I am allowed to enter into any of the labs and storerooms.

She walked to the shelf where the container she regularly visited was placed. The container was still sealed, and there was no sign that it had ever been opened.

The side of the container displayed a sequence of clas-

sification numbers based on a code Peri knew well. The
first time she had decoded this particular information, she
had gasped as she realized that the genetic materials
copied and placed in this container belonged to Aidan
Pryde.

It should not have been a shock. She knew that such
copies were used for experimentation. Yet, it was an eerie
feeling to pick up a container containing a copy of
Aidan's genes. Perhaps it was not eerie. Perhaps it was
corrupt. The gene pool was sacred. If Peri had been taught
anything in her life, she had learned that much.

As a Jade Falcon, she knew that if she opened the
cylinder, it would be an act so irreverent she couldn't
even see herself doing it. Yet the scientist in her knew
that the contents were merely genetic stuff that looked no
different from whatever was in all the other containers.

And yet coming here and knowing that some bit of
Aidan's essence was within reach brought back the
memory, as it always did, of her last night with him. They
had been entwined in each other's arms when they heard
the VTOL skimming along the top of the nearby forest.
Coming for Aidan that night were Falconer Joanna and
the tech Nomad, both sent by a high-ranking Falcon
officer to find Aidan and return him to Ironhold. Only
later did Peri learn that he would return there to pose as a
freeborn and train with a freeborn unit of cadets, in order
to receive an unprecedented second chance to qualify as a
warrior.

Except for those final moments, the rest of their brief
time on Tokasha had mostly faded from her memory. *It's
that way with memories. You cannot put them in some
computerized corner of your brain, then call them back at
your ease. When the precious moments actually happened, you didn't realize you would want desperately to
remember them.*

The container still in her hands, Peri stared off into
space for a moment, back in another place and time. Then
she quickly placed the cylinder back on the shelf and
turned away, vowing never to come near it again. She
always made that vow and usually considered herself
morbid for breaking it.

Leaving the storeroom, she returned down the aisle and

headed for the door of the lab, conscious of Gashi's discreet and watchful eye. Surely the tech wondered why she made such regular trips to the locked room. Peri gave her a curt nod as she walked past, not caring whether the tech returned it or not.

18

Falcon Eyrie Research Station
Eastern Mountains, Huntress
Kerensky Cluster, Clan Homeworlds
13 April 3059

When Peri entered the research and development lab, Star Colonel Bren Roshak was standing at the head of a long table, casually rubbing his right eye with the back of one hand. The lab was located in a room that had been dug out at the end of a long tunnel. The stone walls had been smoothed out, then paneled to make it feel more like a conventional room. Fake sunlight, which brightened and darkened according to work cycles so that workers would have a sense of time passing, shone through apertures in the walls. Tiny fake landscapes were set into windows that hid the cave walls.

The intention of the room design was to give workers the sense of being in an above-ground building. For Peri the effect was unsettling because, unlike the outside, the light here was too uniform and scheduled. Recently Roshak had ordered that outdoor scents also be fed in through vents. Pausing at the door, Peri noted the odor and felt her usual annoyance that anyone would bother. The place still felt and smelled like an underground lab being fed a chemical undercurrent of mechanical and faintly malodorous scents.

Roshak looked up and saw Peri come in, but the

scientists and technicians seemed not to notice, so absorbed were they in watching the activity on the holotable's surface. Hanging back from the table but also watching carefully were two aeropilots, the only two attached to Falcon Eyrie. Their names were Geoff and Gerri, and they were as peculiar as most fighter pilots, even though they had not been originally bred and trained for that role. They were, in fact, former Mech-Warriors so injured in combat that they had been re-assigned to serve in the Clan's experimental aeropilot program. Fine tracery around their eyes and foreheads revealed the neural interfaces that had been implanted to help them master the control systems of aerospace fighters, but they lacked the genetically bred bigger heads and smaller bodies of Clan aeropilots.

On the table were tiny, glowing holograms of Land-Air 'Mechs engaged in a mock battle. As Peri walked toward Roshak, who had beckoned her forward, she could hear the whispered conversation among the others.

"These 'Mechs are simply not maneuverable on rough terrain. Their gyro balance is much too delicate," pronounced one engineer near the head of the table.

"That is *exactly* what I have been telling you," another responded. "We should install the gyro differently. It is much too vulnerable when compared to the mounting in an OmniMech. These LAMS can be knocked out too easily, even when it takes the advantage in a battle. It's the physical location of the gyro."

"You can't put it anywhere else, *stravag*. Anywhere else and you get poor distribution of weight in flying mode, almost uncontrollable maneuverability."

"You call me *stravag* one more time and I will—"

"You will what?"

"Come now," one of the scientists broke in. "We are here to solve technical problems, not create personal ones. And watch those contractions. Star Colonel Roshak is present."

"But he—"

"It does not matter. If you have not noticed, we are losing this mock battle."

When Peri got closer to the holotable, she saw that the two LAMs in BattleMech mode stood motionless at the

center of the mock battle. They were out of commission.
The other LAMs were in full retreat from some Omni-
Mech, as potent here in hologram as in real life.

Roshak stepped back from the table and joined Peri.
He held his arm crookedly, as if he were expecting a
hunting falcon to swoop down and perch on it at any
moment.

"Will these freebirth things ever be useful in real
combat?" he asked Peri. She suspected he was feigning
scientific detachment in order to chide her for the continued glitches with the LAMs.

"They do have potential for superiority on the battlefield. That is why I proposed the project."

"But we simply cannot get them to work well. Perhaps
you should swallow your pride and notify your superiors
that the experiment is a washout. Close down the research
and report that our experimental LAMs would be disastrous in real combat."

"No. Even with the malfunctions and the other problems, we have significantly advanced the efficiency of the
Land-Air 'Mechs."

"I am not sure efficient is a valid word for your little
toys."

Peri ignored the sarcasm. "I am still not convinced we
have failed. The performance of the machines has been
mercurial so far, I grant you that. But that is the nature of
research, *quiaff*? We discover what can go wrong and
what is needed to correct it. I have kept headquarters on
Ironhold apprised of our progress—"

"Or lack of it."

"Yes, lack of it." Peri swallowed the angry retort that
almost slipped out. "My orders are to continue all phases
of our research here, not only work on the LAMs."

Roshak pulled her a step farther away from the group
still observing the dismal tabletop battle. "Can you be
sure everything gets reported to the highest levels of
command?"

Peri looked over at him sharply. "Have you any reason
to doubt it?"

"I have already been assigned to garrison duty at
one kind of station or another, and I have learned that
wherever you see a bureaucracy, you see an organization

committed to the perpetuating of itself. Some of our, let us say, lesser bureaucracies have not always been honorable in the dissemination of key information."

"I am surprised to hear you say that, Star Colonel," said Peri, but she knew only too well that he was right.

"Is that so?" he retorted. "Well, on every research station where I have been assigned, the scientists seem always to cloak their efforts in extreme secrecy. What is to stop them from exaggerating progress reports on various projects just to puff up their importance or to keep from being sent on worse assignments? The scientists already have too much power as it is. Secrecy breeds intrigue, while intrigue breeds politics. And politics breeds lies."

Peri couldn't help but think of Etienne Balzac.

Roshak seemed to read her thoughts. "You know that I am right, *quiaff*?"

She didn't like the way he was peering at her. It made her think of a suspicious little weasel. "Neg. That is not the way of the Clans."

Roshak laughed abruptly, a short, grunting laugh. "I am not sure any longer what is the way of the Clans. I thought I did once, but much is changed since the start of the invasion. Perhaps our leaders are being corrupted by contact with the Inner Sphere."

"Does not this conversation border on treason?" Peri hissed, not wanting to be drawn into some new intrigue. Etienne Balzac had been bad enough.

"If reported, I suppose you are right. But no one cares much about the babblings of a pair of forgotten functionaries."

She looked back toward the table, where the scientists and techs continued to bicker. The mock battle had come to a halt. The miniature OmniMechs had clearly triumphed over the Land-Air 'Mechs.

The sight distressed her for more reasons than one. She knew this did not bode well for Sentania's plan.

"You believe our work to be useless?" she asked Roshak, distractedly.

"Perhaps—with the exception of the wonders our naturalists have performed in perfecting the hunting abilities of our jade falcons."

"And that, too, is a disputed project. Some think we should not tamper with the jade falcon, after all."

"Not many know we do, but I believe we have brought them as close to perfection as possible—and anyway the hunting is so much better."

Him and his hunting. "Did you summon me here to discuss speculative matters or was there a purpose?"

"Yes, Peri Watson," he said, his voice taking on a snide tone. "If you insist in continuing this LAM research, then I must insist that you create a real test of these freebirth vehicles, one that will settle once and for all their value. If we declare the project a failure, we can at least get some of these people reassigned to another station where they can bicker about something more useful and I will not have to listen to them anymore. If successful, then perhaps the work will also get me assigned to more useful duty. You can do this, *quiaff?*"

Peri did not tell Roshak about Sentania's plan for the LAMs, even though it was, in its way, just the kind of test he wanted. If she told, she was sure he would glitch it up by trying to stick his own crooked talons into it. Anyway, there were too many variables already. Although Sentania, in her confident way, believed that the uniqueness of the strategy would give her the edge. Peri was not so sure that the Smoke Jaguars would fall into the web Sentania was weaving.

Roshak's eyes were very watery.

"We must do something about the light in here," he said, as he wiped away the moistness with his finger.

"It is the sunlight reproduction you ordered, Star Colonel."

"I know that," he replied irritably. "It just needs a little . . . adjustment. Make it more natural, Peri Watson." He turned to go, then stopped and said, "And I will be waiting for your test proposal for the LAMs."

"I will get right on it, Star Colonel Roshak."

He stared at her with watery vision, probably trying to decide if her words were mocking or sincere. Then he turned on his heel, walked over to the table and, with a dramatic gesture, switched off its holographic machinery. Two dozen 'Mechs seemed to snap out of existence in an instant. The gesture also shut off the chattering engineers and scientists, and an unusual silence descended over the large, lit-like-early-dawn, room.

=== 19 ===

Falcon Eyrie Research Station
Eastern Mountains, Huntress
Kerensky Cluster, Clan Homeworlds
13 April 3059

Before going back up to the surface, Peri briefly visited
the underground facility's central cavern, which served as
a bay for all their large equipment. Two ancient Battle-
Mechs lay prone and forgotten in one corner, while the
five LAMs at the center of the current experiments occupied most of the space. Near them were a few piles of
parts that had been salvaged over the years from wrecked
or otherwise ruined LAMs. The test models were being
tinkered with by techs, who crawled over the big machines like hungry insects looking to take out a bite. A
couple of the LAMs themselves resembled overgrown
insects, especially the ones adapted from the old Star
League Wasp and Stinger designs. From their names,
their designers must have thought so too.

Even though the Land-Air 'Mechs often tested well
enough for a while, usually something would go wrong
toward the end of the test. Not necessarily something
major, just an unsettling, ditzy little malfunction that prolonged the LAM's time on the field or affected its maneuverability or simply made it look foolish. No wonder the
LAM researchers were getting so testy.

There was a rumble from above, and an open elevator

descended into the cavern. On it were more techs, probably going on shift. On the massive platform of the elevator, the techs looked like insects, too. Two elevators served the cavern. Each one could transport a single LAM to the surface. That was all right, since there was only about enough level land overhead to hold a pair of LAMs. Only two could be launched at a time, and drills had shown that it took awhile before another pair could be brought up and made ready.

Before leaving the bay, she glanced back at the two forgotten BattleMechs. At one time or another, some regular 'Mechs had been dropped onto the research station, but they took up too much space in the underground bay and there was not enough level space to keep them outside. The Falcons had tried keeping them parked at the foot of the mountain, but they had been too tempting a target and the Smoke Jaguars captured most of them in a raid. Judging that 'Mechs were too precious to risk, the Falcon commanders sent a DropShip to carry off the few that were left. Peri had no idea why this pair had been left behind.

She stepped off the elevator and began taking deep breaths as the outside air rushed into the exit tunnel. After all the bright artificial light in the laboratories, she was happy to step out into the natural hazy light of a typical day on Falcon Eyrie.

As she came out of the tunnel, she saw MechWarrior Stenis at his outdoor cooking fire, stirring something in a large iron pot. Stenis often did his cooking outdoors, said it added to the flavors. Whatever it was he was concocting had started to bubble, and tempting aromas came to her on the strong breeze. Stenis beckoned her over.

"How is my favorite chief scientist?" he said. His voice was scratchy, the voice of old age. He pronounced his words well, and there was vigor in his tone, but he could not make the sound of his voice young.

"I am the only chief scientist you know and probably have ever known."

"True. But you would be my favorite if you were a bandit out to steal my fingers."

"What a revolting image. You *are* crazy."

"That is nothing new, is it? Everyone calls me crazy."

"But you cook well."

"That I do. A taste?"

He held out a wooden spoon. The liquid in it was an ugly yellowish color and there was something insectlike sitting in it, but Peri knew not to be repelled by the sight of anything Stenis cooked. She took the spoon from him and put it gently in her mouth. As she tilted it, the liquid settled like velvet onto her tongue, and the flavor of the solid content was an odd mixture of subtle spice and the taste of karna leaf. She let it slide down her throat and shut her eyes, savoring it.

"Is it right?" Stenis asked.

"It is fair, I think, Just fair."

"You are as bad as Sentania Buhallin. You would lie to me so that the doubt your falsehoods caused would make me strive for better."

"Oh? Let me try another spoonful. Perhaps I missed something the first time around."

"No. Suffer. I do not feed the unappreciative."

"I would really like another."

"Beg."

"All right. Please, MechWarrior Stenis, cook extraordinary, I would like another taste."

"Granted, peasant."

Stenis sometimes spoke in royal tones. It was part of his craziness. Peri noticed that he looked more tired than usual. His heavily lined face seemed to droop in several places, and his skin was yellower than the concoction he was cooking. He always seemed to fade a bit when Sentania Buhallin was gone for a while. She would return and he would be revived. Peri thought the two of them needed each other to grouch at.

The second taste was even better than the first, and it lingered in the palate for a longer time. She chewed on some of its ingredients and was sure it was an insect, but it was definitely not berry ant. Anyway, Stenis—who protected his recipes as a warrior protected his 'Mech—kept the ingredients of his creations secret.

"You admit it was delicious?" Stenis asked.

"I think so," Peri replied, "but the mountain air affects our taste."

"Do you not think I plan my dishes that way?"

"I am sure you do. Anyway, I thank you for allowing me to taste, MechWarrior Stenis. Is there anything I can do for you in return?"

"Yes. Bring me the corpse of Sentania Buhallin."

"I do not even know where she is. And, as you know, no one can kill her, *quiaff*?"

"That is unfortunately true. She and I must hold some record for surviving as solahmas. Of course, I am allowed only to cook, and there are no real military duties for solahma at Falcon Eyrie."

"You would prefer to head some forces into battle as cannon fodder?"

Stenis stopped his stirring for a moment. "Nothing would make me prouder than to die for the Clan. I would perform any Jade Falcon duty with honor."

"That is fine to hear, but I am a scientist and am not intrigued by all the honor codes of warriors."

"You were a warrior once, I hear."

"Almost a warrior, perhaps, but never a warrior."

Stenis narrowed his eyes. "You know what I see in you, in your deliberate and methodical manner?"

"Neg. What?"

"A warrior waiting to emerge. A fighter ready to clench her fists. A surat longing to bite into a predator's neck."

"You are getting too fanciful, Stenis. No wonder people call you crazy."

"I am crazy."

"And proud of it."

"You bet, Chief Scientist Peri Watson. One other thing?"

"Yes?"

"I love you."

The stupidity of the words made her laugh heartily. Stenis stared at her as if wondering what she was laughing at.

"I lied," he said. "Who could even care a *stravag* about a do-nothing like you?"

He went back to stirring his pot. But his final words bothered Peri as she walked away. There was an old saying about truth being contained in joking, or something like that. His words made her wonder if he was right. Had she been at Falcon Eyrie for so long that her existence had no value? Was she indeed a do-nothing, trapped in the self-perpetuating bureaucracy that Roshak had described?

She shuddered and walked on.

Hall of the Hunters, Zeta Galaxy Command
Lootera, Huntress
Kerensky Cluster, Clan Homeworlds
15 April 3059

Howell sat at his desk, his face flushed red, both from his meeting with his officers and the quick pair of brouhahas he had downed as soon as he returned to his office. The officers, still enraged by the admission of Horse into the Clan, argued that he should have been executed after being cut down, despite his vow of allegiance to the Smoke Jaguars. As usual, Star Colonel Logan Wirth was the spokesman in these continually escalating arguments.

Horse was a *freebirth,* they claimed, and a freebirth vow was a waste of words. Howell had countered that Horse's glorious exploits during the Crusade brought honor to all Clans and that he was a mere vassal to the Jaguars, one who would be humiliated daily by the duties that were now his lot.

That humiliation, along with the ordeal of the Kinship ceremony, had taught Horse his place in Jaguar society, Howell insisted. Star Colonel Logan wanted to know why this arrogant freebirth was being favored, and despite all Howell's arguments, the other Jaguar commanders objected strongly to having a freebirth among them one instant longer. No matter what he said now, they believed he had mocked the Jaguars. Nothing could make up for that.

Howell had abruptly adjourned the meeting and returned to his office, not caring what his officers thought. On the way, he'd passed Horse doing his daily rounds of delivering papers and hardcopies of messages to various offices in the command center. After ordering him to report to his office within the hour, Howell decided he would spend the time working with his favorite companion, the intoxicating brouhaha.

Now, fortified and relaxed by several drinks, he prepared himself for Horse's arrival. Howell believed he had broken him, yet something about Horse still made him angry. He remembered the first time he had seen him, almost a month ago now. The sight of a freebirth in command of a Trinary had been inconceivable. How could the Falcons allow such a thing? The filth of the universe allowed to fight and command. And now, as he thought back on it, he realized it was that which had disturbed him most. That they would allow a freebirth to command. It went against everything that the Clans stood for—the orderly stratification of society, with warriors at the pinnacle. A warrior should be the very best of the best, genetically bred for war.

Howell snorted with disgust and looked around his office as he leaned his elbows heavily on the desk. He was a trueborn, genetically engineered with the best of them, but what battles did he fight these days? His only struggles were with the mountains of paperwork, the increased inspections of factories and mines and sibkos demanded by his own superiors, and petty arguments with his officers.

He shuddered at the thought and considered having another brouhaha, one that would probably change his present comfortable glow to a stupor. He was spared the decision by Horse's arrival.

As usual, Horse tapped on the door and waited for Howell's permission to enter. When he stepped into the room, Howell observed that Horse seemed to be in good shape, in spite of his recent ordeal. His bruises had faded quickly, and he wore that air of calm that frequently made Howell want to blow it to smithereens.

"Your wish, Galaxy Commander?" Horse asked.

His voice was subdued though not servile. Howell could see in Horse's steely eyes that the man would resist indefinitely, no matter how much humiliation he was made to suffer. Howell felt that familiar odd mix of admiration and anger that Horse always aroused.

He felt his lips tighten in what passed for a smile these days. "Once I promised you better quarters. There is an unused pair of rooms on the floor above. You may move into them."

Horse hesitated. "I would prefer to remain in the detention quarters with my Trinary, Galaxy Commander. I have a comfortable nook there."

Although irritated, Howell chose not to show it. As if speaking to a child for whom the same lessons must be repeated constantly, he intoned, "They are no longer your Trinary. You are Smoke Jaguar now, as you vowed back in the forest. You must not remain among the Jade Falcons, even in your mind. You must be separate. The members of your Trinary are not good enough to be Smoke Jaguars. You should realize that."

Howell saw the anger in Horse's eyes and felt a ripple of satisfaction.

He switched back to command voice, "It is necessary that you move into the command center, and I require it, *quiaff*?"

With seeming difficulty, Horse muttered, "Aff." Then he added, "But I wonder if this will only anger your officers more. Allowing a freeborn to reside in the Hall of Hunters?"

"That is my prerogative."

"I have overheard some of your officers questioning—" Horse stopped himself and seemed to consider his words.

Howell sat up and narrowed his eyes. "Questioning what?"

"I have heard them say that although you are doing an exemplary job training the troops and overseeing the new production schedules"—Horse paused for a moment—"your erratic behavior in other areas is cause for concern."

Howell slammed a fist down on the desk. "I am the ranking officer on this planet. I will do as I please. You will move into the quarters I have assigned at the conclusion of this meeting." He glared at Horse, daring any further response.

When there was none, Howell sat back in his seat and decided he deserved another brouhaha.

Horse had to fight the urge to leap across the room and pummel the smug expression off Howell's face. There were moments when he felt he would explode with the strain of this charade. Sentania had persuaded him that the game was necessary and that it would not be prolonged, but he felt like choking with every obsequious word he uttered to Russou Howell.

Howell ordered Horse to mix him a drink.

As Horse picked up the empty glass from Howell's desk and crossed to the liquor cabinet, he wondered what his own warriors would think when they heard he was being relocated to the Jaguar command center. Sentania had insisted that Horse must not let them know he was only play-acting, that they had a plan.

"They would not understand," she had said. "They are not practiced in the arts of tactics and strategy. All they know is that a warrior rushes in and hammers left and right."

"They will see me as a traitor."

"Perhaps."

"That will be difficult for me."

"Of course it will. But it will build your character, too."

Sentania's comments frequently irked Horse. But she was his best hope right now, and even he—warrior that he was—could see that tactics and strategy definitely beat hanging by thick ropes from trees during a violent storm.

Horse mixed and poured a brouhaha and carried the glass over to Howell's desk. Howell had that hazy look on his face that he always got from the alcohol. Horse suspected another long rambling diatribe was about to begin.

"You will get used to all this, Horse. It may not be the life of a warrior, but duty is all. Once you grasp that, being a Smoke Jaguar is easy. Have you contemplated the jaguar carved out of the mountain?"

"Often." Horse set the glass down and moved off a few steps, then stood and awaited further command, as usual.

Howell spoke with relish. "In its fierceness, its readiness, its ability to spring without warning, the smoke jaguar represents the goal of all our warriors, as a Clan totem should. It is the highest honor to be a member of the Smoke Jaguars, and the ultimate pinnacle to be a Smoke Jaguar warrior." His face darkened momentarily. "To serve the Clan, to further the way of the Clan, is the reason we are here."

Horse watched as Howell's face sent slack and he seemed to retreat into some inner space. Then Howell shook himself and turned to Horse with that condescending expression Horse despised so much.

"But come now, Horse. I require some entertainment. It is many months since I have known combat. Perhaps you can help me pass the time with stories of valor and war. We have all heard tales of the Falcon Guard hero, Aidan Pryde, and I know you fought alongside him. I would like to hear about him from you, a prime source, after all."

As Howell waited expectantly, Horse thought that this was the first true test of Sentania's plan. *I am not some trained dog, here for his amusement. And I am not going to use the exploits of one of the Jade Falcons' finest to entertain this drunken lout.*

But, in his mind, he could hear Sentania egging him on. *Play the role, Horse. Give the audience what it wants. That is the essence of the play-actor, the deceiver. Do it.*

Then something occurred to him. *I don't have to tell the truth. If I'm playing a part, why not say what I choose? I can make up whatever I want about Aidan Pryde.*

"Horse, I gave you an order."

"Of course, Galaxy Commander." *Such a good servant.* "I was just gathering my thoughts. The stories I could tell are many."

"Be spontaneous. Take me away from here. Take me back to the acrid scent of 'Mech coolant, the stinging fog of war, let us recall the days when our throats were raw with the shouts of battle."

Howell closed his eyes.

Horse restrained the impulse to slap him out of his drunkenness and instead took a seat in an adjoining chair.

"As you wish, Galaxy Commander," he said, "And once upon a time . . ."

≡ 21 ≡

Hall of the Hunter, Zeta Galaxy Command
Lootera, Huntress
Kerensky Cluster, Clan Homeworlds
22 April 3059

These Jaguars really believe in doing it up sparse, Horse
thought. *Not that the Jade Falcons are fancy. Far from it.
Still, this is—what did they call it?—the Great Assembly
of the Hall of the Hunter, the place where command decisions are made on Huntress. All it's got is that small, low
stage and these hard wooden chairs. Hard, that is, except
for Howell's. No surprise there. He plays the king more
and more as time passes. He gets to sit in that high-
backed, cushioned chair. Throne, really. I wonder where
he found it? And here I sit on a stool next to the throne.
The court jester. He never stops the humiliation. Half the
time, I don't think he even knows he's doing it anymore.*

*I hate sitting here, hate having to look up at him. I can
see his damn earwax, for Kerensky's sake. I'd point it out
to him, but he'd probably order me to dig it out.*

Howell had just called the assembly to order. His warriors were slow to obey the command, milling about and
looking surly. Howell had to stand and bellow for them to
take their seats. Even then, there was a great deal of
grumbling among the seated warriors.

*Something's wrong here. These aren't the Smoke
Jaguars of legend. A Jag is, at the very least, obedient*

*and respectful. Rough, yes. Cruel, yes. But at bottom they
are disciplined warriors who follow rules and respect traditions. Not disrespectful and insolent like these warriors.
Howell is losing his hold over them. And he knows it, I
can see it in his eyes. He is looking for a way to regain
control. He should take them in hand, make them respect
him. But he just sits and glowers. That is his main
problem, sitting. He sits in his quarters and downs more
and more of those brouhahas. Sits on his throne, letting
his commanders revile him.*

Howell sat and stared at the gathering of warriors
without speaking, and perhaps it created some discomfort
because the din they were making diminished. Even when
the room was quiet, he continued to stare fiercely for a
while, then said in a controlled but loud voice, "Assembled warriors, for now we will dispense with ceremony. I
know you all have much on your minds. That is the reason
I have called this meeting. I want you to speak freely. I
wish to hear your complaints."

At first there was chaos, many voices babbling at once.
Howell sat back on his cushioned chair and watched
them. His hands clenched and unclenched.

*That hand clenching, it's a tic that comes only when
he's agitated. Sometimes it's the only way to tell that he is
agitated. Listen to me. I'm even thinking like a servant,
noting and cataloging the master's habits. It's been
barely a week that I've had to put up with this, but I don't
know how long I can go on living this fake life. Sentania,
wherever you are, let's make things happen. And where
are you? What if her real purpose is to make a fool of me?
What if she intends never to come back, leave me here to
rot in my own self-disgust?*

Howell raised his hand. The grumbling voices quieted.
Then Star Colonel Logan Wirth came forward, urged on
by the others.

"With all due respect, Galaxy Commander, we cannot
proceed with this assembly, we cannot speak openly, as
you command—not with that *freebirth* present."

He pointed at Horse, who rose from his stool and took a
threatening stance. "If you have something to say," he
shouted angrily, "say it to me directly, *savrashri!*"

Logan rushed toward the stage, and Horse also moved
forward a few steps, ready to meet him with his fists.

Howell grabbed Horse's arm and held him back, while other warriors did the same with Logan. Apparently a brawl was not allowed to break out during a warrior's assembly.

Howell stood and spoke in his command voice: "You forget that Horse is a Smoke Jaguar now. He has taken the oath in your presence."

"That may be," Logan called out. "But he is not a warrior and he *is* a freebirth. We do not wish him to taint a gathering of trueborn warriors."

"I have ordered him here, though he is present in a purely subservient role. You challenge my decision, Logan?"

"With all respect, I do."

"Then you must challenge me. You do, *quiaff*?"

"Aff."

"Then let us settle this in a Circle of Equals. Your choice of combat mode?"

As Logan opened his mouth to respond, Horse interrupted the proceedings with a jade falcon war cry. Intended to duplicate the sound of a swooping jade falcon, at least within the limitations of the human voice, the cry was one he had learned during cadet training. It began with a screaming sound that rose in pitch, then broke into a series of five whoops, followed by a descending shriek. He bellowed it at the top of his voice. The cry silenced the warriors and left Logan with his mouth still open.

As Horse finished the cry, he was astonished by how good it had made him feel. He had not let loose with a falcon scream, outside of combat, since he was a cadet. At that time it had signified an excess of good feeling, sometimes brought on by the defeat of an opponent.

Horse addressed Howell, turning his back on Logan.

"I am the insulted one here, Galaxy Commander, I respectfully request the opportunity to mangle this *surat* in a Circle of Equals. I believe it to be my right."

Some warriors broke out into raucous laughter, while others shouted angrily.

"You cannot even step into a Circle of Equals," one warrior called out, and another shouted, "No freebirths in any Circle of Equals!"

"Freebirth!" screamed a third. "You may be Smoke Jaguar, but you are not a warrior."

"In my life I have won more battles than you have dreamed of, whelp." Many warriors protested, but Howell held up his hand, then gestured to Horse that he might continue. Horse knew him well enough to see he was enjoying the trouble he had provoked. "I am not a warrior among you, it is true, but I am willing to take on this entire roomful of warriors within the Circle, one by one if you wish. You are failures and old-timers, sent to the scrap heap where you can do no harm, away from the real action of warrior life!"

The entire roomful of warriors suddenly seemed to surge toward the stage as one person, but again Howell stopped them.

"Galaxy Commander, I petition you to allow me to engage this warrior in an honor duel," Horse continued, gesturing angrily toward Logan Wirth. "And, after that, I will take on any others who wish to test the mettle of a freeborn warrior!"

It took a full minute for Howell to get the room quiet, to stop his warriors from killing Horse right on the spot.

"Horse," Howell said, in regal voice, "you are correct in stating that you are the injured party in this dispute. However, my warriors are correct in refusing to fight you, as you are neither a Jaguar warrior nor a member of the warrior caste. As a prisoner, and especially a freeborn prisoner, it would be dishonor for us to allow you into a Circle of Equals. To put it simply, you are not equal."

Howell looked around the large room. Satisfaction showed on the faces of the Jaguars, too smug a satisfaction for Horse's taste. "However, there is another custom that may be applied to these circumstances, if all will agree to an unorthodox procedure. A Khan has the right and privilege to name a warrior to fight for him within the Circle. It is a custom that the highest-ranked officer of a large military unit may also occasionally invoke. Star Colonel Logan challenged me first, an act of sheer audacity when directed at a commanding officer. Still, the Circle of Equals has been designed to achieve order and harmony in unusual situations."

Now the warriors were confused. Some began to mutter

among themselves, while others called out insults against Horse.

"You all honor my right of command, *quiaff*?" Howell said. "That command includes the privilege of naming individuals for a particular duty and endowing that person with the rank necessary to accomplish it."

"What are you trying to say, Galaxy Commander?" demanded Logan, whose wrath had increased so much his face was a bright red.

"This was once called naming a champion. For this occasion I am selecting a champion. Horse, I give you the temporary rank of MechWarrior. No matter what rank you enjoyed in the Jade Falcons, this is more than you deserve as a Smoke Jaguar and a freebirth. Do you accept the role of champion, MechWarrior Horse?"

"Aye, Galaxy Commander," Horse growled.

"And know this: MechWarrior is a rank I will take away from you after the Circle of Equals, but with the rank comes the duty and privilege of defeating Star Colonel Logan in my name."

"I am eager for it."

"Even if we accept this logic," Logan called out, "how can I fight a *freebirth* within the honorable confines of a Circle of Equals? It is degrading, insulting. And it has no meaning. The Circle of Equals is an *honor* duel."

"Are you afraid of me then?" Horse shouted.

Logan leaped onto the stage and grabbed Horse by the neck before Horse could react, then began to squeeze. For moments Horse could not breathe, but patiently, adeptly, he gradually broke Logan's grip and forced the man's arms far apart while he head-butted him. Logan stumbled backward, off the stage and into the arms of another warrior.

"That is just the first blow of our battle," Horse shouted. "I am taking you on without 'Mechs, without weapons. To the death, surat!"

Before Logan could attack again, Howell stepped between the two warriors.

"Enough," he said. "I am willing to stage this unorthodox Circle of Equals because we all need whatever meaningful exercise we can get. That is the issue. It is not one of rank, nor is it really a question of Horse's genetic origins. In this case it does not matter whether the Circle of Equals is sanctioned or not. The fight itself is necessary. Remember, Horse is a warrior who has won glory before all the Clans, and now we can show this hero what Smoke Jaguars are made of. If, indeed, we are worthy of the name of Smoke Jaguar."

The protests burst out again, but Howell's voice, made stronger by the excitement, carried over the din.

"Look at you. You are becoming a mob! This is not the Smoke Jaguar way. We are the most disciplined of Clans, the most aggressive, the most tenacious, *quiaff*! *QUIAFF*?"

The voices grew louder, but the sound had changed. There was in it a sense of renewal, a sense of purpose.

That certainly ups the ante, Horse thought. *Now I not only fight a highly trained enemy, but Howell's put them all on a mission. Well, no worse than what I've faced before. And I always did savor a good challenge. Not only that, this will be good practice. Howell was right about that much.*

Howell ordered everyone to reassemble in the parade ground adjacent to the genetics repository. The Jaguars quickly filed out of the room, slapping each other on the back and already congratulating themselves on what Logan would do to Horse.

When Howell and Horse were alone, Horse asked: "Why?"

Howell shrugged. "Perhaps just one of my whims. Logan needs a lesson and I would like to see him learn it. They all need a lesson and, while it disgusts me to see a freebirth provide it, this Circle of Equals will reestablish order within this command. No matter how it goes, I can gain from it. The defenders of Huntress may never have to fight a major battle, but it could come and we might not be ready.

"I must find a way to keep my warriors sharp. As much as you may hate us, your own sense of honor overcomes any resistance you might have to fighting for me."

Horse shook his head firmly. "I am fighting for myself, Galaxy Commander."

"Fine," Howell said. "At any rate, however this Circle of Equals turns out, I will be satisfied. If you win, Logan and the others will see that I am right in trying to teach them discipline. If Logan wins, well, nothing may be changed, but at least we Jaguars will have the satisfaction of seeing a bit of freebirth scum shown his worthlessness, and that can only help raise the morale. Not a bad decision on my part, *quiaff*?"

"It is disgusting."

"Oh, well, but it is going to happen, *quiaff*?"

"Aff. I am eager to fight Logan. I am eager to fight anyone."

"You do have the sound of a warrior in your words."

"More than just the sound," Horse said. Then he turned and began moving toward the door, so eager he could not help but break into a run. Close behind came Russou Howell, running after him.

$$=\!=\!= \mathbf{22} =\!=\!=$$

Parade Ground, Mount Szabo
Lootera, Huntress
Kerensky Cluster, Clan Homeworlds
22 April 3059

As Horse lay on the ground, staring up first at the smoke jaguar carved into the mountain, then twisting his neck to view the pyramid of the genetics repository, it struck him that most of Smoke Jaguar life on Huntress revolved around these works. Ceremonies and rituals, bravery and honor, honor duels and fights—they all took place in the shadows cast by the jaguar and the towering statues of BattleMechs.

Horse was on his back, struggling to catch his breath, due to a lucky but wicked punch to the stomach administered by Logan. From his fallen position, Horse had just kicked Logan backward, but the other man had quickly scrambled to his feet and was walking, almost strolling, to where Horse lay.

Horse did not feel particularly like standing up or even moving at all. This Logan put up quite a fight. He used every part of his body skillfully and efficiently, arms and legs, elbows and knees, kicks backward and forward, head-butting, head between two fists smashing, forearm slamming, ear and nose pulling, biting, spitting, bumping and shoving, leaping and colliding. Horse was able to answer each blow, counter each move, but as the fight lengthened along with the shadows, he realized he was tiring.

I shouldn't be surprised that he is fighting so fiercely. He is like me. We both have our own missions. Overwhelming missions. Perhaps I should have selected some kind of weapon as the mode of this contest. I just thought a free-swinging, no-holds-barred fight made more sense when both fighters were propelled by anger. What if I was wrong?

Even as the doubts rushed through his mind. Horse was springing up to meet Logan's assault. Logan took one big jump and used the momentum from his landing to leap upward. He virtually flew toward Horse. Horse ducked under the leap, twisted sideways, and shoved his right fist into Logan's abdomen. The man's legs flailed as he hit the ground to Horse's left. Groaning, Logan rolled away, his body rotating three times before he gathered himself into a threatening crouch, only to realize that Horse was not coming toward him but was standing motionless near the center of the Circle.

The Jaguar warriors, gathering tensely around the Circle, seemed to alternate between euphoria and despair. They cheered their comrade every time he seemed to prevail, but their voices faltered whenever Horse took the advantage. Then they rallied with more raucous cheers as Logan seemed once more on the verge of victory.

Horse glanced around the Circle. The one silent individual, standing a bit apart from the rest, was Russou Howell. His arms were crossed, his body relaxed, and he looked very satisfied with the progress of the fight. As he had said, he could not lose, no matter how this Circle of Equals turned out. Howell seemed to be enjoying it as some kind of entertainment.

Logan slowly came out of his crouch. When he straightened, he winced slightly. No wonder. He and Horse had inflicted so much pain on each other that both were suffering multiple aches.

Logan gestured toward Horse. "This is no Circle of *Equals* as long as you are in it, freebirth, but I can see that you might once have been a worthy warrior in your better days. Your proximity to old age has not slowed you down, it seems. I must speak the truth, no matter how difficult—and the truth is that you have fought well and bravely. Nothing more can be gained from this fight. You have won my respect, but you cannot take my honor from me because you are neither trueborn, nor a warrior. No more can be accomplished here because this is not a true Circle of Equals. Come, let us put aside our differences and walk from this Circle together."

Horse sensed that this was no trick, that Logan meant what he said. With his muscles aching, and his head a bit dazed, he was tempted to accept the man's offer of a draw. He could walk through the edge of the Circle of Equals, the Smoke Jaguar warriors clearing a path for him, and he could go back to his quarters above Howell's office, where a decently comfortable bed awaited him, and he could drop off into a curative sleep. At this moment, standing near the center of the Circle, he could almost sense the dreams of his village that would come to him.

It was tempting.

He glanced at Howell, who gave a slight nod. Horse could walk out of the Circle right now.

Tempting.

But not possible.

He was Jade Falcon and could not quit. They might say he was not their equal and thus a fight within a Circle of Equals proved nothing, but he neither granted nor accepted quarter in any battle. Especially not from a Smoke Jaguar.

"No," he said quietly and tensed his body. He would not attack Logan first. He would await Logan's next move.

Logan again used his phenomenal leaping ability. It was as if 'Mech jump jets were attached to his legs. The leap was high and his legs were already executing a kick. But something—fatigue or a miscalculation—put the kick off-line. Horse was grateful for that, since his own weariness made his move to dodge sideways too slow. The kick would have connected and Horse might have had his brains oozing out his ears. Instead, the leg just missed Horse, who was quick enough to grab Logan's leg at the thigh, and swing Logan around a half-rotation. He let go of the leg, and Logan smashed head-first into the ground. As his body settled, his head lifted for a moment, then he passed out. Horse came to him and kicked him in the side to make sure he was not feigning.

Glancing around, he was not surprised by the fury on most of the Jaguar faces surrounding him. But they were also shocked into silence and stood staring at their fallen comrade.

Horse was about to claim victory when Logan came to and reacted instinctively, grabbing Horse's leg. But the grab was weak and Horse was able to squirm out of it.

Logan got to his knees. "I will kill you, freebirth scum," he muttered. Springing to his feet with surprising agility, he rushed at Horse. Catching Horse off-guard, he landed several punches to his face and body.

Horse went nearly berserk at this. Screaming, he repelled Logan's next blows, and then himself began raining blow after blow at the other man's bruised face and body.

Seizing Logan by the neck, he used all the strength he had to squeeze. Logan's arm went limp and his eyes closed.

Horse released the hold just before Logan might have died. The man staggered a step, then fell into Horse's open arms. Lifting the body onto his shoulders, Horse glared at the onlookers, then began running toward the edge of the Circle. A pair of warriors ran at him, but he pushed each away with his free arm, without substantially breaking the pace of his dash toward the genetic repository.

He tried to calculate what he had to do to achieve his goal. Picking up speed, a difficult accomplishment with the weight of Logan on his shoulders, he raced toward the foot of the building.

Without breaking stride, he started running up the pyramidal slope of one side. With each step, he seemed to gain in strength. Logan began to feel weightless.

His fierce running got him nearly halfway up the slanted wall. As he slowed, he discovered there were small footholds built into the stone, and he was able to keep his balance and get a little bit further.

Finally he had to stop. Twisting his body and shifting Logan's weight on his shoulder, he was able to look down. He was astounded by how high up the wall he had managed to get. The warriors below looked tiny. Those beginning to scale the wall clumsily were so far down that it would be a while yet before they got to him. He did not choose to wait.

He saw Howell at the base of the pyramid, staring up at him. All the fury he felt toward the man welled up within him. He needed to demonstrate to him the way of the Jade Falcon. Lifting the limp body of Logan above his head, with almost no effort, Horse hurled the body downward. His thrust was so strong that Logan sailed in an arc until he struck the stone halfway down and began bouncing and rolling down the rest of the wall.

The pursuing warriors were unable to react. Logan's body crashed into several of them, and soon there was a mass of bodies hurling down the wall like an avalanche. When they reached bottom, most of the warriors got to their feet holding some part of their anatomy, no doubt feeling breaks and sprains. Everybody got up except Logan, whose body was angled so unnaturally that it was clear immediately to Horse, even from this height, that Logan was dead.

Parade Ground, Mount Szabo
Lootera, Huntress
Kerensky Cluster, Clan Homeworlds
22 April 3059

Horse stood with his legs spread wide apart. Although the stance was arrogant, triumphant, it was also the only way he could stand without falling. Weak-limbed, head dizzy, he was not sure he could make it down the side of the wall he had so energetically scaled only moments ago.

For him victory always brought sadness along with the sense of exaltation. He had shown that a freebirth could prevail, yet it was done at the expense of a brave life. Logan had fought well, and Horse could have left him thrown down in the Circle of Equals. But the lust for vengeance had been too strong.

His death or mine was destined, right from the challenge. I could not accept Logan's offer of a draw. A draw is a loss. Proof lies only in victory. That is the way of the Clans.

Dizzy, he thought he might pass out. He closed his eyes for a moment until the feeling went away.

When he opened them again, he was surprised by what he saw.

Russou Howell was laboriously making his way up the side of the slope. Until that moment Horse did not realize how difficult the climb had been. The slope was steep, a strenuous climb when not assisted by the kind of burning hatred that had driven Horse upward.

Horse wondered what Howell was up to. Perhaps he thought he could punish Horse by throwing him off the wall. Instead, he held out his hand when he got near enough.

"You are going to need help getting down," Howell said.

Horse nodded, too exhausted to speak. All he could think of was that this Russou seemed to flip from one extreme to another in the blink of an eye. After all the ordeals he'd been orchestrating for Horse, now he wanted to *help*?

"I want to show my gratitude," Howell said.

Horse's eyes widened. "Not a trait much prized among the Jaguars, *quiaff*?" *But he was too weak to make the words come out with sarcasm.* Horse realized that he did need Howell's help. His feet felt glued to the wall. Not only could he not move his legs, he did not *want* to move them.

He accepted Howell's assist, and the two started slowly down the slope of the pyramid. Howell's steps were steady. Horse's were not.

Howell had no trouble holding forth as they went. "You have vastly improved my situation here, Horse. Which is why I am grateful. Logan was becoming a trouble-maker. He was starting to question every move I made, and who knows where that might have led? We have our work cut out for us on Huntress these days, and I need the cooperation of my officers, not their interference. Besides, it is not the Jaguar way for an officer to dispute his commander's decision. Perhaps my own superiors would have criticized me for putting up with his antics. Now Logan is dead, thanks to you, and I can resume bringing order to my command."

"I am honored to serve, Galaxy Commander," Horse mumbled.

Howell glanced over at Horse and almost smiled. "And now you are truly one of us, Horse. You proved it today. Not only did you fight well in the Circle of Equals, but you showed how much you are already a true Smoke Jaguar by hurling Logan off the side of the pyramid. A Jade Falcon might have finished off his enemy within the

Circle, even slit his throat or crushed his head. But a Smoke Jaguar warrior punctuates his killing with bravura. I am most satisfied with your progress."

Again, Horse did not answer, but Howell's gloating over his "progress" was enough to make him want to spit in the man's face.

"But one thing you must realize, Horse, is that in the Circle of Equals, you lost."

"Lost? I do not understand, Galaxy Commander."

"Certainly. Logan may have been unconscious when you carried him out, but the fight had not been declared over and you were the one to cross out of the Circle, signifying your defeat. A competitor in the Circle of Equals must not willingly cross that line until the fight is clearly over. So, you lose. As the old saying goes, you lost the battle but you won the war, something like that."

"Are you sure you are Smoke Jaguar, Commander?" Horse muttered. "You think like a Wolf."

Howell laughed. The laughter struck Horse as a bit too loud, almost hysterical. "Well, Horse, I am a true Smoke Jaguar but I have seen more than most."

Horse was sure of that. And whatever it was had definitely twisted Howell's mind. He had never heard of a Jaguar, a Falcon, a Steel Viper, a Wolf—or any other member of all the seventeen Clans who thought or behaved like Russou Howell.

Once they reached the foot of the wall, Howell broke away from Horse and ordered the angry warriors to reassemble in the great hall. Horse started to walk in the opposite direction, but Howell shouted at his back.

"Horse, I have not released you from your duty to me. You must attend."

In the hall, Howell waited patiently by the podium while the warriors filed into the meeting room. They were talking angrily among themselves, a dull roar that probably would have erupted into open revolt anywhere but among the Clans. He leaned over and whispered to Horse, who he had next to him on the stage, "See the ferocity, the intensity of their complaints? They are finally coming together as a unit. I knew I would find a way."

Horse made no comment, sarcastic or subservient. The glittering of Howell's eyes showed his excitement. It was as though the man was seized by something warped within him, rather than actually aware of the reality around him. He certainly did not seem conscious that his troops were on the verge of dragging him up to the pyramid and then throwing him off as well.

But they were still obeying somehow, and gradually the room filled up. Many of the Jaguars did not take their seats, however. They remained standing, a sign of belligerence as well as a failure of respect.

Again, Howell seemed oblivious as he began to speak. "Warriors of Zeta Galaxy, Star Colonel Logan died fighting bravely. He was defending what he thought was the honor of the Smoke Jaguars, and I will make sure the codex of his genetic legacy is annotated properly to show the import of his final combat. It is true that he had not won the right for his genetic legacy to be accepted into our sacred gene pool, but I will personally see to it that his ashes are used in the nutrient solutions of our genetic engineering vats. His genetic code will also be placed in our genetic depository."

Honors, yes, Horse thought, *but they are the same that would be accorded to any loyal warrior. Only cowards or those judged failures would receive less.*

He realized suddenly what Howell was doing. Howell was trying to pacify his warriors by seeming to glorify a warrior who was tainted by dying at the hands of a free-born from another Clan. Logan should have been due no honors, but Howell was manipulating hallowed Clan custom for his own ends. The whole thing was diabolical, yet impressively clever.

Howell turned toward Horse, a look of sheer elation on his face. He was right. Horse had served his purposes no less than Logan had, in a contest that Howell had arranged and manipulated like some kind of maestro. *This madness has much sense,* Horse thought, remembering a line from his forays among Aidan's secret library.

"An opening has been created within the ranks. Star Colonel Logan's command will go to Star Captain Arias, who for now bears the rank title until such time as she may properly qualify. MechWarrior Horse, you have shown us today your worthiness as a Smoke Jaguar warrior. Your victory today over a fine warrior will stand as your Trial of Position for acceptance into the ranks.

"MechWarrior Horse, we take note that you have shown us that we can open our ranks even to a freeborn. As respecters of the old ways, the Smoke Jaguar Clan is not usually open to change, You are released as a prisoner and, after a period of indoctrination and study, you will go through the proper ceremony, at the end of which you will be assigned a BattleMech."

Horse was stunned, but the Jaguars standing around listening to this outrageous announcement must have thought they were dreaming. Horse knew he was trapped for now. He had to go along with anything this filthy scum ordered him to do. But what was wrong with these Jaguars? They just stood there gaping. Logan surely would have protested, but he was gone forever. The whole group had just watched with their own eyes as Horse flung him to his death from the heights of the pyramid.

Howell dismissed the meeting, then ordered Horse to accompany him to his office. Howell said not a word all the way there, until they entered the room and he was seated behind his black obsidian desk.

"Horse, what I said was true. I can use you here."

"Using me is exactly what it is, *quiaff*?"

Howell's eyes darkened for a moment. "Blunt and sarcastic as ever. I can even use that. The way I see it, you have no choice but to accept the inevitable. You are Smoke Jaguar now, and that is that. It is not likely you will ever go beyond the position of MechWarrior, but that will not prevent you from serving us loyally. I do not know if we will ever have honorable warfare on Huntress, but I can use any warrior with strong combat experience."

"What about my Trinary?" asked Horse. "My Battle-Mechs?"

Howell again laughed his peculiar laugh. "You do remain stubborn, *quiaff*? Get this into your head. You no longer have a Trinary. You are not in command of anything. Your 'Mechs are being refitted as Smoke Jaguar 'Mechs. You are now a MechWarrior of the Smoke Jaguars, and I believe that is the greatest honor you may achieve in your life. Unless you have something to add, you are dismissed, MechWarrior Horse."

For once in his life, Horse was uncertain of what action to take. He could murder Howell right now. It would be dishonorable and would be his last act as a warrior, but he was severely tempted.

"You are dismissed," Howell said softly.

Horse stood for a moment then remembered to salute even though he thought it would have been more fitting to spit in Howell's face.

Howell returned the salute, then nodded his head and smiled. The smile grew broader, and by the time Horse had turned and reached the door, the Galaxy Commander was laughing uproariously.

≡ 24 ≡

Warrior Quarter
Lootera, Huntress
Kerensky Cluster, Clan Homeworlds
22 April 3059

Horse hung his head as he returned to his quarters after Howell's most recent display. *MechWarrior. Smoke Jaguar. Freebirth,* he thought glumly.

For the time being, Howell wins. The bastard wins. This is the final disgrace. I looked for physical torture, and received it. That didn't humiliate me. I endured service as his servant. That didn't humiliate me. I accepted the role as Howell's champion in the Circle of Equals. That didn't humiliate me. Now I am made a MechWarrior of the Smoke Jaguars, and I am properly humiliated.

"Nice going, Horse."

Sentania's voice, coming suddenly as it generally did, startled him. He stopped walking and looked around. At first all he saw was the meticulously clean street, darkening with shadows as night came on. What little light there was seemed to bounce off the immaculate surfaces.

Then Sentania stepped out from a dark doorway. She was wearing a tech uniform as pristine as this street in Lootera's Warrior Quarter.

"Are you being sarcastic, Sentania Buhallin?"

"Not at all. I think you have done well."

"Well? As what? A liar and deceiver? A Smoke Jaguar champion? A vassal of Russou Howell? A full-fledged MechWarrior? A freebirth?"

"Yes. In all of those respects."

"Are you sure you are Jade Falcon?"

"An aged one. Something you may not know about solahmas: with age comes a certain freedom. If you are not soon disposed of as cannon fodder, sent to the front to save the young warriors for a better fight, you wind up with the kind of duties that leave you free to be as crazy as you like. That is the kind of crazy I am, and it is going to get you to Falcon Eyrie with your Trinary and your BattleMechs."

"You *are* crazy, Sentania."

"Or are you the crazy one? You have trusted me this far, *quiaff*?"

"Well, aff. What choice did I have?"

"You had many. You could have thrown yourself off that wall instead of that filthy Jag scum. You could have run a rampage before being killed. You could have murdered Russou Howell."

"I considered that."

"Good for you. Howell is right about one thing. You are one admirable freebirth, Horse."

"You were there? You heard his words?"

"I manage to be anywhere I choose. The Assembly in the Hall of Hunters is a cinch. I have even been inside the repository. I will take you there soon."

In the growing darkness, the shadows played over Sentania Buhallin's face. She was, Horse decided, a phantom. He would not have been surprised to see her rise into the air and float down the street.

"What now, Sentania Buhallin?"

"You have a unique position here, Horse. Exploit it."

"Go on with the deceptions, you mean?"

"That is exactly what I mean. Use your advantages with Howell. Use him. He is ripe for it."

"Odd that you should say that. He claims to be using me."

"I know. I heard."

"You heard? He said it in his office."

"I know. I was in a duct, not far above your head. But

for a grate I could have reached down and tweaked your beard."

Horse stared at Sentania. He recalled what he had observed about village ways when he was a child. In the village, people met and fell in love. As freeborns, they could do that. Horse had chosen another way, the way of the Clan warrior. Was it possible he could feel love or something akin to it? For a moment he felt as if he could love this Sentania Buhallin, take her back to his village and live out his days with her. But no, that was not possible. It was just an unfortunate thought, one of those disgusting and forbidden thoughts that could easily pass through the mind of someone like him, a freebirth.

"I have just come from listening in on barracks chatter. They hate you more than ever, but they hate Howell even more. Logan was constantly stirring them up, telling them that Howell was either brainless as a berry ant or going truly insane. The man has gone off the deep end with all these so-called rites and customs that he pulls out at the drop of a hat. But he's the top man, and without Logan, they just aren't sure what is the right thing to do. So much the better for us. The more confused everyone around here is, the more we'll use it to our advantage."

Horse shook his head unconvinced. "I don't know if I can do all you say, Sentania."

"Trust me. You will not be in Lootera much longer, I promise."

She wheeled around and walked away. Although her feet definitely touched the ground, it seemed to Horse that the fluid grace of her stride looked like floating.

Howell summoned Horse to his office the next morning.

"That was your last night in the quarters upstairs. But you expected that, *quiaff*?"

"Aff."

"You will take your place in the warrior barracks."

"May I take leave of my former comrades in the detention center?"

"No, I will not allow that. They are much too insignificant for the attention of a warrior. You must show them, too, that you are now a Smoke Jaguar warrior. They are no longer your comrades, *quiaff*? *QUIAFF?"*

"Aff."

Horse had not noticed at first, but now he could see that Howell was drunk. He had never seen him drunk so early in the morning.

Before he dismissed Horse, he asked, "Well, Horse, you have been a full-fledged Smoke Jaguar for several hours. How does it feel so far?"

"Feel?"

"Do you sense the pride, the honor, the tradition?"

"I cannot say yet. I think I do."

Howell smiled. "That will do. Some things take time, *quiaff*?"

"Aff."

Like learning not to choke on my words, on my lies. Like learning to deceive and being comfortable with it. Like suppressing the urge to challenge you and cut you to pieces within the Circle of Equals.

Howell blinked several times, evidently trying to blink away his intoxication.

"Horse, you are relieved of your servant duties now that you are no longer a prisoner . . ."

Not that kind of prisoner, anyway.

". . . but you must continue to come to my quarters in the evening. We shall talk, just as we have until now. Command has its hardships. I need to keep perspective . . ."

To keep sober, you mean.

". . . and I have not finished instructing you on the ways of our Clan . . . "

I have learned enough, thank you.

". . . and you will help me, *quiaff*?"

Lie, deceive. I can almost hear Sentania Buhallin egging me on.

It was difficult for Horse to speak the lie. "Aff. I am at your service, Galaxy Commander."

After Horse had left, Howell pondered what he had done. He had made an example of Horse, but he had also shown the troops that he, and only he, knew what was best for them and the rest of his command on Huntress.

Order is returning. My warriors are less resistant, I feel it. My command can function smoothly. I like things to be smooth. But what if . . . ? Forget it. Where did I leave that brouhaha I was sipping at? Horse used to mix a fine brouhaha. I will miss that. Where is my glass? It must be here somewhere.

≡ 25 ≡

Falcon Eyrie
Huntress, Lootera
Kerensky Cluster, Clan Homeworlds
23 April 3059

Peri Watson sat on an isolated cliff to which she had
climbed in order to get a better look at the Land-Air
'Mechs that were being tested below. She imagined herself piloting one of the LAMs, a thought that made her
briefly laugh, then she imagined herself in a regulation
BattleMech. She did not often imagine herself in a 'Mech.
After she had flushed out of cadet training, she had forced
herself not to think about warrior matters any more. But
sometimes memories returned unexpectedly.

She could never forget her first day in a BattleMech
cockpit—not a real 'Mech, just a cockpit simulator connected to a virtual reality device. Getting used to the
neurohelmet, keeping track instantly of the constant
data being fed to her from various displays. She had
not performed well on the test, only managing to knock
some virtual armor off the virtual image of an attacking
Timber Wolf.

The very next instant she had been blind-sided and rendered ineffective by what the display identified as a *Summoner*. Although all of it was pure imagery of one
simulator cockpit against another, that was the day she
sensed that she might not make it through her cadet

training. Aidan and Marthe received praise for running up high scores before they, too, endured simulated defeat. Their falconer, the ever-harping Joanna, commented that the two did not seem to have the makings of a warrior, but had at least shown a bit of skill.

Peri wondered what Joanna thought now, since one of her charges had become the hero of Tukayyid and the other was now Khan of the Jade Falcons. Joanna herself had won glory by killing the notorious Black Widow. Even Horse had won fame.

Sometimes I wish I could go back to those days and try again. What if I'd somehow gotten a second chance, the way Aidan did? What if I hadn't flushed out and was now a warrior instead of a scientist trapped up here in a scientific research outpost?

I was not so dissatisfied before ... before I was assigned this Falcon Eyrie duty. Well, I brought it on myself. If only I could find a way to get posted elsewhere, get back to the kind of research that truly excites me.

The two LAMs below the cliff stood in the mountain air as if unaccustomed to the outdoors. In a way, that was true. Except for the occasional, very rare exercise, the LAMs were kept underground where they were tinkered with by techs who believed that their destiny was to be forever frustrated by these unwieldy fighting machines. Sometimes, though, a LAM was put on a lift and brought to the surface, where it seemed like a bat suddenly released from the comfort of its cave.

A Land-Air 'Mech, in theory at least, had once been considered an advanced concept. A BattleMech that combined features of the aerospace fighter with the traditional 'Mech. The theory was that, in an instant, a fighter weaving in and out of aerial combat could reconfigure into a war machine that could battle on the ground as well as any normal 'Mech. It could be quite an awesome spectacle, watching an aerofighter apparently grow legs while losing wings as it descended. Using the jump jets on its legs to slow the fall, a LAM would appear to settle gently onto the ground, looking as if it would never do any damage. A skilled pilot was often triggering pulses from his laser weapons even before the LAM landed.

However, as with many promising technological

developments, theory and practice did not mesh. Land-Air 'Mechs had not lived up to their promise. While effective on occasion, LAMs were more often down with glitches and outright mechanical failures. Some believed that the internal machinery was too complicated. After all, they argued, the reason a BattleMech was such a successful fighting machine was that its design was relatively simple and its technology emphasized flexibility and maneuverability, two features apparently diminished in most of the LAMs. Either a LAM had the assault finesse of an aerofighter or the maneuverability of a 'Mech, but most lacked one or the other and some lacked both. One explanation was that too many sacrifices were made in each component of the machine and the result was a weakening of either the aerofighter or the BattleMech capability.

Another objection made about the LAM was that it was too difficult to train a warrior to operate both its aerofighter and its 'Mech phases. Whoever sat at the controls seemed to lack skill in one operating mode or the other. Some pilots, of course, could do neither effectively.

The LAM had never been used much among the Clans. Peri, however, had thought that the Land-Air 'Mech concept still represented the ultimate in efficiency—if it could be made to work. She had managed to present a proposal convincing enough that the scientist hierarchy approved her request to study and test the possibility of putting two pilots into a LAM, one skilled in the aerofighter configuration, the other in the 'Mech configuration. As a geneticist, she had not expected to implement the project and then been astounded to be selected for it.

Someone among the scientist leaders, Etienne Balzac no doubt, had demanded that the project be secret and conducted at a remote station. Falcon Eyrie, secure in its mountain stronghold, was their choice.

Why the project had been approved Peri wasn't sure, because her superiors refused to approve the use of any properly trained aerospace pilots. Instead, she'd had to work with warriors who had been recalled from regular 'Mech duty and converted into aerospace pilots. The two presently assigned to her, Geoff and Gerri, were skilled enough, but they lacked the "oneness" with their machine that a 'Mech or aeropilot trained from youth generally exhibited. The pair were exactly like almost ever other warrior at Falcon Eyrie—just a pair of solahmas.

But she had to work with what she had to work with, that had always been her philosophy. Pragmatism was the crux of a scientist's work—anything to get to the goal. Just one more contrast with the way of the warrior. No Clan warrior believed in compromise.

The LAM below her, one of the pair she had named the Evil Twins, had just failed its mechanical inspection. Its gyro had shown signs of operational imbalance, which the chief engineer had reported would result in about a forty-five percent chance of the 'Mech toppling over at the moment the fighter-'Mech changeover was completed. At the very least, the LAM would sway impressively, the man had said calmly. To an enemy it would seem as if the 'Mech was mounted on wobbly legs.

And this was the 'Mech that Sentania wanted to use for her little adventure against the Smoke Jaguars. Peri wondered for the tenth time about the wisdom of agreeing to it, especially since agreement meant not telling Roshak. He would find out eventually, and who could predict what might happen then. It was no small matter, stealing a pair of 'Mechs for an unauthorized mission. Even though they were only Land-Air 'Mechs and Roshak hated the sight of them.

Well, time would tell.

"Time will tell," said a voice near her.

Peri was not surprised. She had seen Stenis laboriously climbing toward her along a gentler slope. He surprised her because she'd been so lost in thought.

"You reading minds now, in addition to your other talents?"

"No, but I could see the doubt in your face. You do not have much faith in those—what do you call 'em?"

"The Evil Twins."

"Odd name."

"Well, there are two pilots, one for the ground, one for the air. We can call them anything for now, rename them later. Why do you pester me with these questions, Stenis?"

"Pester you? Far from it. I bring you a message. A message from that old hag, Sentania Buhallin."

"There is an old saying about a pot calling the kettle black."

"I know it. I am old, but at least my wisdom is measured out on my face. Do you want to know the message?"

"If it is the only way I may get rid of you."

"Sentania says to make sure that Mary and Mary are ready. She will be asking for delivery soon."

Peri nodded.

"You understand all that?"

"Very well."

"Good, then."

Stenis worked his way back to the easier slope and laboriously began making his way down it. Peri was surprised that he had not tried to get her to explain the message. Perhaps he hadn't because he already understood it. Not so hard, really. Sentania had suggested the codewords, something to do with some old rhyme. Mary had a little lamb. Or LAM. The two Marys were, of course, The Evil Twins.

Down below one of the twins had suddenly stalled. Peri sighed. Stenis could not possibly have heard the sound of her sigh. Nevertheless, he turned around and looked back up at her. The man was spooky. She longed for a battle in which he would be needed as cannon fodder. That was not a cold or cruel thought. If the man was crazy it was because he had been cheated of his chance to die for the Clans, which was the only fate befitting a Clan warrior. If he was going to be solahma, then he deserved the fate of one.

26

**Prisoner Detention Center
Lootera, Huntress
Kerensky Cluster, Clan Homeworlds
1 May 3059**

Horse nearly laughed in triumph as he saw the thin line of blood emerge from the mouth of Star Commander Croft, then become a small stream trailing down his cheek.

"You asked how I deal with insubordination, *quiaff*?" Horse asked.

"Aff," Croft replied weakly.

"That's how I deal with it, scum."

Glancing coldly around the room, Horse saw that the warriors and techs of his Trinary, those who were off-duty from their usual menial assignments, looked on in shock. The last thing they expected from Horse was a sudden sucker punch to the jaw of one of them. Pegeen, especially, looked sick.

Horse had come to the detention center out of a deep craving to be with his own freeborn Jade Falcon warriors. He could no longer bear the stifling presence of the aloof and unfriendly Smoke Jaguars. Croft had interrupted Horse's attempt to initiate small talk by saying that Horse had forgotten who he was. He might not have hit Croft if the man had not added that Horse was becoming a Smoke

Jaguar in every way. The words infuriated Horse, and he had decked his accuser.

He could hardly look the others in the eye, yet he could also not dispel the urge to kick Croft to oblivion. Frustrated, he started to walk away, thinking to return to his new quarters. Pegeen grabbed his arm to stop him.

"What's happened to you?" she asked, concern in her eyes.

"Nothing," Horse said. "I don't know what you mean. He insulted me, I decked him, that's the Jade Falcon way, *quiaff*?"

"No, it isn't. We get into fights, aff, but not to blows over petty spats."

"Spats? You're mistaken. Let go my arm, Pegeen."

"No."

"Now."

"No."

With a violent swipe, Horse virtually lifted the body of the slight Pegeen with the arm she clung to and hurled her backward, breaking her hold. She stumbled and nearly tripped over the prone Croft. Only some fancy footwork kept her on her feet. The concern had vanished from her eyes and she glared at Horse with true Falcon fury.

Knowing he couldn't tell his warriors the truth and unable to abide their antagonism, Horse swung around and stomped out of the room.

He did not know why, what urge prodded him, but the instant he passed through the detention center doorway, he began to run. He raced down to the end of the street, made a sweeping right turn, just managed to dodge a maintenance vehicle (from which two other members of his Trinary looked down in bewilderment), picked up his pace down the new street, then turned into a side street, where suddenly his breath gave out, and he leaned and crouched against a wall.

Trying to catch his breath on what looked like an empty street, he was startled (but not surprised) to suddenly hear the voice of Sentania Buhallin.

"You are hard to keep up with. If you had not stopped, I would never have caught up with you."

She came over and knelt down beside him. "Can I get

you something, old man? Some water? Resuscitation injection?"

He nearly laughed. "You . . . you chased . . . me?"

"I tried. You set a mean pace."

He struggled to get his breath. "But . . . but you . . . you're not out of breath."

"Conditioning, I guess. I have walked, run, swung, jumped, dodged, even tripped and stumbled through most of the terrain between here and Falcon Eyrie. I can run halfway up the side of a mountain before the first stage of exhaustion. Pretty good for a solahma, *quiaff*?"

"Aff. I'm impressed. I was once . . . once able to run a great distance."

"When was that? Last month? Before you became a Smoke Jaguar warrior?"

There was no sarcasm apparent in Sentania's words.

Horse bent his head down. The street and everything around it was spotless. It seemed to gleam even in the shadows.

"I am no Smoke Jaguar. You know that. You're the one who put me up to this . . . this ruse. You told me to take the Jag oaths, and you would have told me to become a MechWarrior when Howell ordered it, *quiaff*?"

"Aff. Definitely. I was pleased with the way you dealt with that."

"I heard you in my mind, goading me on."

"It's the neural obedience chip I implanted in your brain while you were asleep."

Horse stared at her for a moment, almost believing she could have pulled that off.

Sentania chuckled. "Come, Horse, pull yourself together. You know I'm only joking."

"What a weird bird you are, Sentania Buhallin. A Jade Falcon, and yet so skilled at deception."

"I was not always so. Only since being consigned to solahma duty, sent here. I don't know what changed. Maybe it is something in the mountain air. Maybe it is the futility of the duty itself. The Falcon Eyrie warriors are mere decoration, necessary only to fulfill Jade Falcon regulations requiring guard at all installations. But I should not complain. The lack of real duty has freed me to roam the region, discover knowledge and information, and bring it back to the Eyrie. Some of the information turns out to be useful."

"I can see then why you are as you are. You have taken to spying."

"And you disapprove of such deceptive activity?"

Horse smiled. "Yes and no."

"Yes."

"Deceit is not true to the way of the Jade Falcons. And yet I am also a kind of spy. Only the Khan knows why I am here."

For a moment they shared a silence, then Sentania spoke. "Then you will be prepared for what I am to offer you now. It is spying, but I don't think you will object."

"Tell me."

"We are going to make a little visit to the Jaguar genetics repository."

Horse's eyebrows raised. "Are you truly mad, Sentania? The place is guarded more heavily than any other in the area."

"Not if you know the secret entrances."

"What is this all about?"

"I am not ready to tell you all. You must trust me, that is all I ask. Will you come?"

How could Horse refuse at this point? He had already gone along with Sentania this far, to the point that he felt deeply shamed by how well he was succeeding in his pretense. It was too late now to say that he felt he was betraying the Falcons with this game. The die had already been cast. What Horse did not tell her was that even though he had killed many an enemy in his life, the only individual he had ever wanted to murder was Russou Howell.

"Our chief scientist asked me to investigate," Sentania added. "She also asked me to identify herself to you. She is Peri Watson."

Horse was startled to suddenly hear that name. He hadn't thought of Peri in a long time. "I know of Peri Watson. I also know her daughter, Diana."

"Yes, she said you would. And that's why I can tell you there are more strange things going on around Mount Szabo than just the madness of Russou Howell. When I told Peri what I had seen, she said we had to find out more. When you see what it is, you will be glad you helped me. You will come, *quiaff*?"

"Aye, Sentania. I will. I need to be doing something useful, something other than this shameful game of playing Smoke Jaguar."

"Tomorrow night, then, by the *Rifleman*."

"The *Rifleman*?"

"The statue of the *Rifleman*, of course. It is the easiest statue to hide behind. And do not look at me like that, of course we have to hide. Spies do that sort of thing. I will see you then."

She walked out of the side street swiftly. Horse tried to run after her, but when he got to the main avenue, he looked up and down and could not see her in either direction.

Of course not. I am not surprised.

It was several days later that he heard from Pegeen about Croft's attempted escape from Lootera. Croft had used the distraction of some BattleMechs returning to the city from a training exercise. While the 'Mechs lumbered toward the command center's 'Mech bay, he had slipped out through the legs of the same *Mackie* Horse had used in the gauntlet trial.

Unfortunately, Croft did not even make it to the edge of the forest before a Jaguar *Rifleman* ran him down and crushed him under one of its enormous feet. The order could only have come from Russou Howell. Croft's body was dragged back to the Mount Szabo parade ground and all the other prisoners were marched out to view it.

Croft's death only increased the resentment against Horse among the members of his Trinary. There was nothing Horse could do about it, however. He regretted Croft's death, and respected him for the courage of his escape attempt, but there was little time to mourn.

First of all, he had to make good his own escape. If anything, what had happened to Croft made it even more imperative that he not only escape, but provide his people with the leadership they needed. Not to mention the vengeance he would wreak.

Second, he had been to the genetics repository with Sentania and had seen the puzzling abomination inside.

≡ 27 ≡

Genetics Repository at Mount Szabo
Lootera, Huntress
Kerensky Cluster, Clan Homeworlds
2 May 3059

The bright light of Huntress's moon fell on the smoke jaguar sculpture with the kind of brilliance that made its edges all the sharper. As Horse leaned against the base of the *Rifleman* statue, he gazed at the Jags' greatest work of art. The shadows cast by the moon and the overall force of the sculpture itself made the jaguar seem to come alive in its graceful leap downward, perhaps with the intention of seizing Horse in its jaws and tearing him to pieces before returning to its rightful place on the cliffside. The jaguar's eyes, also moon-brightened, peered down with a baleful stare.

Horse shuddered and tried to look away, but could not keep his eyes off the sculpture.

"Yes, I am impressed by it, too."

"Materializing out of nowhere again, Sentania."

"Don't be foolish. I am just careful. The Jaguars outdid themselves with that carving, *quiaff*?"

"Aff. It is wonderful, awesome. Look at its eyes. Doesn't it make you feel that it is warning us away?"

"What is this, Horse? Superstition? Is this some kind of freeborn trait?"

"Not at all. But I am sensitive to omens, and that certainly looks like an omen to me."

"They planned it that way, I suspect. Anyway, this is too bright a moon for us to stand around waiting to be spotted by the next patrol. Let us go inside."

"You are not in awe of the sculpture?"

"Oh, I am awed all right. That is why I insist we get away from it right away."

Horse was surprised to find that Sentania's secret entrance to the repository was not located in any of its walls, but was a small hatchlike door several meters away from the main body of the repository and a short climb up the incline. After they squeezed themselves through it, they entered a cramped, narrow tunnel through which they began to crawl along.

"I think this is an escape tunnel or a place to hide genetic materials in case of attack," Sentania said.

At the end of the tunnel, there was another small door. Sentania slid it open, looked around, and gestured Horse forward.

"We are going into a corridor that is normally entered from the Hall of Heroes. It is often deserted, but we have to be careful, since there are guards on duty in the main hall itself at all times. If we see anyone in the corridor, well, you are in warrior garb but I am wearing this tech outfit, so we'll have to think fast and come up with some kind of story, *quiaff*?"

"Aff. I'll leave that you, Sentania. You are the one who is a master of deception."

"I will assume you do not mean that sarcastically. Do not forget that I am still a Jade Falcon, and deception is no more than a useful tool, not a way of life."

"I'll have to think about that."

"You do that, freebirth."

Again Horse noticed that she seemed to use the insulting term without malice.

In the corridor, he followed Sentania through several doors, past several rooms, and into a new passage. They saw no one, but Horse thought he heard activity behind some of the doors. At one point, he not only heard things but smelled something—a harsh, heavy, chemical odor.

"That is certainly foul," he whispered to Sentania.

She glanced back over her shoulder. "Oh . . . scientists, you know."

The new passage was darker, and the only door was just ahead and dimly lit. Sentania slowed Horse down as they came toward it. She listened for a moment at the door, then turned to him.

"I can hear voices. Distant. Probably scientists. Could be trouble, but usually not. When we go in, we will veer to the left and take the aisle there. Do not act suspicious. Chances are, nobody will pay attention. They do not expect intruders back here. Except for me, I doubt that there have ever been any. When there is no trouble, guards tend to grow complacent.

"My tech uniform could cause problems, so I will have to duck out of sight. But they might not look as closely at you. Still, we would do well to stay out of anyone's way if we can. Nobody will know we have been here. I've done it before—explored several sections of this pyramid without ever getting caught. The place is honeycombed with levels and chambers. Maybe that is the reason for all the secret passageways. To discourage thieves. In fact, I have never penetrated the most secret levels, though I think I've heard people talking about them."

"Why do you come here?" Horse whispered. "Why take these risks? The Jaguars would kill you if they found you prowling around their gene repository."

"It is my nature. Let us go in. Put on your Smoke Jaguar face and demeanor."

Horse decided not to dignify the comment with a response. They slipped into the room Sentania had indicated.

Once inside, Horse was amazed at its enormity. High-ceilinged and wide, it seemed to contain many aisles, some with tables festooned with scientific devices and equipment, others with tall cabinets, with and without drawers, on which he saw all manner of paraphernalia and stacks of disks and hardcopy. They ducked to the left, which took them into more aisles filled with cabinets. A group of people were gathered around a table down the nearest aisle, but Horse was sure none had noticed them.

When I came here with Howell the place seemed overrun with security, he thought. *But in this part of the repository, security barely exists.* It was odd, but Horse could only chalk it up to Smoke Jaguar arrogance. He smiled to himself.

Sentania walked ahead of him down an aisle. Her pace was rapid, and he had to keep racing to catch up after falling behind. Part of his slowness was the distraction of trying to see what might be on the shelves and drawers they passed. At first, much of it seemed like no more than routine clerical equipment, but then he began to see more complicated devices of the kind usually associated with genetic research.

When he paused to look closer at one, Sentania stopped abruptly and beckoned him on impatiently. Horse did as she bid, but if Sentania Buhallin thought she could order him around indefinitely, she was wrong. This was just for now. She had some strange ways, but he wouldn't tolerate them forever. One day he might have to challenge her to a Circle of Equals over it, but for the moment, she knew her way around this place, and he did not.

At openings in the aisles, Sentania took abrupt left turns into other aisles. As they progressed down more and more of these rows, Horse became completely lost and disoriented. He would have found his way out of here only with difficulty. If at all.

The further they went and the darker the aisles got, the more it seemed Sentania was leading him into a labyrinth. Finally she stopped at a place that had no light at all except the illumination coming from hundreds of glassed-in, floor-to-ceiling shelves. On each of the glassed shelves, in temperature-controlled environments that hummed as they worked, were containers apparently containing preserved materials.

Containers of what? The labels on them are obviously coded.

"You have never been inside a genetics research facility, *quiaff*?" Sentania asked.

"The only time was when Howell brought me to where the Jaguars store their genetic materials."

"The official ones, anyway. The renowned warriors and Clan leaders. Even then I am not sure each contains what it is supposed to. Some of the materials that are allegedly in that area may actually be back here."

"Why would the Jaguar scientists do that?"

"Research. From what Peri Watson tells me, scientists are a secretive group, to the point that they conceal information even from the warrior caste. If that's true, imagine what the Jaguar scientists might be up to."

"What could be mysterious or suspicious about genetic research?" Horse asked. "It is a normal aspect of the way of the Clans. That is the work of the scientists, to continually create better warriors. Each Clan's sibkos must be created from the most superior genetics possible. There are no finer warriors in the galaxy than those created by our scientists in their laboratories."

"Is that so?" Sentania said. "Strange talk from a free-birth, particularly one so prone to sarcastic criticisms. Did you read all that in a manual?"

"As a matter of fact, yes."

"I believed in manuals once, but now I am not so sure. As you say, genetic research within each Clan is admirable, but Peri says the scientist caste seems to be involved in interClan experimentations that may be part of a conspiracy by the scientists to seize more power for themselves."

"I too have heard of such things, strangely enough from Diana, Peri's own daughter. She once worked as an aide to our Falcon Guard commander, and discovered computer records proving that Jade Falcon scientists had apparently experimented with certain sibkos by adding Wolf genetic materials to their formation. Another warrior, Star Commander Joanna—"

"The slayer of the Black Widow, *quiaff*?"

"—discovered that Wolf scientists had initiated a project intending to dilute our sibkos with the genetic materials of techs."

Sentania looked disgusted. "What you say makes some of the things I've discovered around here a little less mysterious. Let me show you something particularly curious."

She strode down the aisle. Stopping at a shelf, she pointed to the container on it. "I have checked the code on the side of this container with files in another section. See the letters at the bottom? They say 'JF-Pryde.' And the date underneath, do you recognize the date, Horse?"

Horse leaned toward the container and read the numbers. He grunted his surprise.

"It is the day Aidan Pryde was killed in the Battle of Tukayyid. But why?"

"Curious, huh?"

"Aye," Horse said.

"I was here once before and when I finally figured it all out, I must confess that it shocked me considerably. Inside this container is a copy of the genetic materials of Aidan Pryde. It appears to be one of several Jade Falcon containers housed at this research facility."

"That can't be. Aidan's materials—in a Smoke Jaguar research lab?"

"Aye, Horse. I fear that it is so."

"I'm appalled. It is, well, disgusting." At the same time the idea that some part of Aidan was, in a way, just within the box he stared at did fascinate him. He shuddered. "Disgusting that the Smoke Jaguars would illegally possess another Clan's genetic materials, especially Aidan Pryde's."

"I know. Peri has suspected something like this for a long time. It was she who asked me to investigate the repository."

"But what does it all mean?" Horse said, almost to himself. "Why do they have this copy here?" He touched the glass, as if he might actually make physical contact with the cylinder. "The Jaguars are using these somehow. Aidan is part of some internal experiment, a Smoke Jaguar experiment."

"Aye," Sentania said, almost as though testing him. "What else do you see?"

"I am not sure. What would the scientists use them for?"

"Does it matter? They are Jags, and they have somehow gotten possession of giftakes that are part of the sacred gene pool of the Jade Falcons. Copies perhaps, but they carry the same import as the originals. And the conclusion is obvious. Scientists from outside the Falcons should not have them. Like Peri Watson said, it seems like some kind of conspiracy. I am sure that the Jade Falcons do not have any other Clan's genetic heritages in our own storage areas."

Something in her eyes, something in her tone, told Horse that Sentania was not as certain of that statement as she sounded.

"What is worse, Sentania, is that these are not just some warrior's heritage—this container holds the genetic legacy of Aidan Pryde. A Jade Falcon hero."

"One of our greatest heroes," Sentania said.

"But what does it all mean, Sentania?"

"I am not knowledgeable about genetics, to be sure, but this seems to be something more than mere experimentation. And it suggests secret cooperation among the scientists. It sickens me to think of it. If we do not preserve our individual Clans, the Clans as formed by the great Nicholas Kerensky, what will become of us? I am unnerved by the thought of interClan experimentation. You are right, Horse, it is disgusting. All of this, disgusting."

On impulse Horse crashed his forearm against the glass, which shattered in several places. Blood seeped out from several cuts on his arm.

"Why in Kerensky's name did you do that, Horse?" Sentania hissed, as though she had only just barely contained herself from screaming out the words.

"I cannot allow them to have Aidan Pryde's heritage, even if these genetic materials are just a copy. He was my friend, and nobody should—should—they cannot use them. I can't allow it, I can't—"

He reached into the cold environment. It stung the cuts on his arm. As he reached for the container itself, a voice behind him said, "Do not even touch it."

Horse whirled around and saw—standing calmly, his white robe brushing the floor—the Keeper of the Jaguar kin. The old man's smile seemed like another of the wrinkles on his heavily lined face.

Horse drew back his arm.

The Keeper took a step forward, stretching his neck to examine the damage Horse had caused.

"You must be quite strong. That is very thick glass. I was sure you would bring us trouble from the first time I saw you inside this building. Howell was wrong to bring you here, and he is even more wrong in this travesty of proclaiming you a warrior of our Clan. Well, I doubt that sponsorship will go on for long. Spies are not welcome in the Smoke Jaguars."

In the weird light the Keeper's features had become spectral. "But do not pride yourself that you have done any real damage here, young man," the Keeper continued. "What you see here—the preservation of genes—is no more than a formality, an extra protection. The containers themselves are insular and the contents virtually indestructible, especially since they are easily replicated if something *does* happen to them."

"There are other Aidan Pryde copies here?" Horse asked, as calmly as he could. He wanted information, not an argument.

"At the moment, no. The experiment in which these materials will be used has not yet begun. But, whatever it is, it will be wondrous. We are on the threshold of a new era, an era of even more superior Clan warriors. There will never be another Twycross or Tukayyid. That container contains potential miracles."

Horse reached again into the shelf. "Then I will remove this container from temptation."

The Keeper smiled. "You may not do that. Even if you try, we will catch you immediately and retrieve it. There is a tracer located inside the container, which you would not be able to recognize, and so we will find it wherever you choose to hide it. We do not even have to seek you."

Horse picked up the cylinder. It was surprisingly heavy, considering its size. He took it off the shelf and stood holding it, staring at the Keeper.

"You may not take it," the Keeper said and reached for it.

Horse raised it up, then smashed it down heavily against the Keeper's skull. The old man dropped to the floor immediately. The blood on his forehead clotted almost instantly.

Sentania knelt down and touched his neck. "He is dead, Horse."

"I know."

"This is not just a killing, but an act of war. This was the Keeper of the Jaguar kin."

"I know."

"They will execute you."

"Perhaps."

"It will be a dishonorable death for you."

"It will."

"Then why?"

"Why not?"

"That is cold, even for a Jade Falcon—or a Smoke Jaguar."

"Do not call me Smoke Jaguar again. Not if you wish to live, Sentania Buhallin."

Sentania stood up again. "All right. Explain."

"We had no choice. Left alive, he would have informed on us. I don't even know why he revealed himself. He had to realize that, by doing so, he was bringing his own death down on himself."

"You are naive, Horse. This is the Keeper. He had no reason to fear that anyone would kill him. No matter how warlike we of the Clans may be, we do not kill someone like the Keeper. Their status makes them virtually inviolable."

"Well, apparently this one was not."

Sentania shook her head sadly. "The Jaguars will go on the warpath over this. They will be shamed at not being able to protect their own Keeper even in the depths of Mount Szabo."

Horse smiled. "That is good. Any shame I can bring to this Clan is worthy."

"You are crazy, but I like it. I'm crazy, too, after all. Just don't go too far. Meantime, the man is dead. What now?"

"I wish to dispose of this container."

"I suggest that you do not. Leave it here. He said there is a tracer in it. Even if you find it and get rid of it, their suspicion will be drawn to you. In fact, I think that, not only should you put it back on its shelf, you should break up some more glass here, so that this particular damage will seem less connected with the killing. Maybe they will think it was only some kind of vandalism. They are not exactly bright, these Smoke Jaguars. We should get out of here as quickly as we can. I would not like to see you executed, Horse. I have wasted too much of my time on you."

Horse reluctantly replaced the container and quickly wrought havoc on several other glass partitions in the aisle. Sentania kept lookout, it case anyone heard the noise.

When he was done, Horse said, "I will return and retrieve Aidan's."

"What good would it do?" Sentania asked. "If there is

one copy outside of the Jade Falcon Clan, there can be others."

"I know. But I cannot allow the Smoke Jaguars to possess even this one."

Sentania held a finger to her lips. "Wait, I hear something. Someone may be coming. I know another way out. Let us go."

Before heading down the aisle, Sentania looked down at the corpse of the Keeper of the Jaguar kin.

"If it is any consolation, Horse, I would have killed him, too," she said. "But with a bit more finesse."

≡ 28 ≡

Warrior Quarter
Lootera, Huntress
Kerensky Cluster, Clan Homeworlds
5 May 3059

The body of the Keeper was discovered within hours, but Sentania had managed to sneak back into the repository and had planted some fake clues that suggested that the death was connected to a Jade Falcon raid. She had even snagged a piece of a Falcon uniform on a nail and left it hanging there, as if a sleeve had been accidentally ripped away during the raid. She also left a small dagger of the kind frequently used in hand-to-hand combat, the Falcon insignia etched into its handle.

Horse was beginning to believe that Sentania was something of a miracle worker who could do anything she said she could, no matter how impossible the task seemed. Not only that, but the daring, the audacity of casting the blame on the Falcons to save one individual, amazed Horse, and troubled him a bit. Each step of his experience on Huntress, much of it stage-managed by Sentania Buhallin, seemed to isolate him further from the life he had known, especially his place within the Clan. Expediency had dictated his alliance with Sentania, but was it, in any way, wisdom? The situation had become complicated and nothing in his life before had ever been all that complicated.

At any rate, Sentania's ploy worked. No one seemed to suspect that Horse was involved.

The days following the Keeper's death were a difficult time, one that had tested him in many ways. He had learned to play stupid by not acknowledging the taunts and insults thrown at him by other warriors. They had obviously not accepted him, though no one openly dared defy Galaxy Commander Howell. Horse probably fooled them most of the time, but the Jaguars were by nature suspicious. No matter how much fake evidence Sentania planted, and no matter how much Horse played the fool, they might put two and two together at any time.

On the day after the death of the Keeper, Howell had summoned Horse to his office. "This is monstrous," Howell ranted. "Who would dare commit such an outrage?"

"It is despicable, a horrendous act," Horse agreed calmly.

"Do you see now the abominable inferiority of your former Clan?"

Howell stared at Horse piercingly. He knew his answer had to be carefully worded. After all, the Jags' reactions were understandable, since murder was rare among all the Clans. Knowledge gained from the invasion had shown murder to be more common in the Inner Sphere, where it was even formalized into political assassination.

"I see dishonor," Horse said firmly. "I see the devious act of conspirators. I see the violation of what is intended by the way of the Clans."

In a way, I mean every word. Under other circumstances I would not be so deceptive. If I could be open, if I could freely proclaim myself a Jade Falcon, I would declare the killing of the Keeper openly—and proudly. The man was meddling with Falcon genetics, an odious act, one deserving of death. If I could take the Keeper's genetic legacy, grow him in a vat or artificially inseminate a woman, I would let his offspring grow to adulthood and kill him again.

Howell stared at Horse for a long moment, then said: "Noble words—I am almost convinced by them."

"Almost?"

"Aye, you are still new as a Smoke Jaguar warrior. You

understand this desecration in principle, but in time you will feel it to the bottom of your being."

It will be a very short time, stravag. Just long enough to finish you off.

For the rest of their conversation Horse provided terse, by-the-book comments to whatever Howell said. Howell expressed further satisfaction with his responses, and Horse marveled that the man could be so easily fooled.

He never knew when Sentania would materialize. She usually stepped from a dark place, although sometimes it would turn out she was merely the tech who had been working nearby for some time. As it happened now.

"Horse?"

"You startled me, as usual."

"I have been here all the while, repairing that heating unit."

"I never noticed. Tell me, is it true you can change shape when you need to?"

"Not really, but I have, well, certain manipulative skills."

"You are right there. What do you have to say to me now? Do you realize that your meddling may cause retaliation against the Falcons?"

"I know of that, and I expected it. Do not worry. What can they do? They cannot storm Falcon Eyrie, even the Jaguars know that. I am surprised that they did not make some sort of example out of your Trinary. That has been my main concern."

"Well, if you want to know what happened, I talked Howell out of it somehow. But only in exchange for a promise that the Trinary will become Jags, too."

"Smart thinking."

"You are crazy. You are just plunging me deeper into your web of lies."

"Be calm, Horse. Not much more time. We will work all this out at Bagera."

"Bagera? As usual, I have not a clue what you're talking about, Sentania."

"Bagera is a mining outpost to the south. It is rich in industrial-grade ores and certain important minerals. Looks different than Lootera. Even uglier."

"Uglier than this place?"

"Well, it's the kind of rough place populated by rough sorts, the kind you usually find in mining towns. I like it there."

"Not surprised. You fit in easily, I suspect."

"That is a sarcasm?"

"It is."

"Anyway, convince Howell that he should take you along on his upcoming inspection tour of war-production facilities."

"And just how do I do that?"

"Oh, you'll think of something, Horse. You always do. Look at the way you handled the Keeper."

Horse gave her a fake swat that she easily ducked, but again he told himself she wouldn't be ordering him around forever. He might be a freebirth, but he was no solahma. He was only going along with her now because for the moment he needed her help.

Howell, it turned out, was pleased that Horse showed so much interest in the productive capacities of Huntress. He seemed proud of the way the Jaguars were gearing up for war, almost as though he could claim the credit for it.

"I inspected Bagera once before, when I first arrived," he told Horse. "That time they knew I was coming. This time they will not."

Horse told Sentania about the projected trip the next time she appeared as if by magic.

"We will be accompanied by some BattleMechs, but will make some other stops along the way. That suit you?"

"How many 'Mechs?"

"About four, I think."

Sentania mulled over that for a while.

"Workable," she finally said. "Two too many, but we will make the best of it somehow. So, Bagera it will be. In a few days, Horse, you will be free, and it will be done with honor."

"Why not do it here, in Lootera?"

"Too many variables. Too many people. Howell's advantage. Out there, things become equal, or relatively so."

"What about my Trinary? We cannot free them in Bagera when they are here."

"I told you, the Trinary stays. Once you are a Jade

Falcon again, we will mount some kind of raid to retrieve your warriors. For now, we do it my way."

"And just what is your way?"

"Less you know, the better."

"You assume too much, Sentania."

A quick smile came to her face, and just as quickly left. "That is what they used to say about me in my warrior days. Anyway, Horse, be logical. The Trinary is here, but we can only do what we need to in Bagera. Howell will have only four BattleMechs. Maybe fewer, if certain things work out.

"There are already many obstacles to the mission of freeing you, Horse, and you have to accept that your Trinary cannot be freed, not now. I mean, listen, Horse, I know this will anger you, but they are only freebirths—I am sorry, I promised not to use the word—they are freeborns. As a trueborn, I am not about to risk all for them. I am only willing to risk for you. Accept that or remain here as Russou Howell's lackey for the rest of your life."

Horse glared at Sentania, then raised his arm to hit her, this time in earnest. She saw the gesture, but remained still, as if daring him. Horse dropped his arm.

"It is hard for me to say this, Horse, but I know I misstepped. You have confused my mind about freeborns, something you have been doing all your life as a warrior, from what I can see. We will go one step at a time. We succeed at Bagera, and I then discuss the fate of your Trinary, *quiaff*?"

"Whatever we do," Horse said, "it cannot be dishonorable. My return to the Jade Falcons must be accomplished as honorably as Howell's treatment of me has been less than that."

"Or even logical, for that matter. You are disturbed, I can see that."

"Angry is the word. Anger at what has happened, regret at what I have had to do until now. This deception—I do not know how to say it, but somehow it has drained something out of me. What I am, perhaps. The killing of the Keeper of the Jaguar kin, which seemed necessary at the time, seems too great a price to pay for my freedom from the Smoke Jaguars. I regret it."

Sentania bit her lower lip as she listened. "Acts of war are acts of war, and that is all. The Keeper's death was an act of war, nothing else. Remember, Horse you came here on a mission. Those who get in the way are expendable, and must suffer the consequences."

"No, Sentania, none of this was part of my mission."

"You are too idealistic, Horse. But we cannot talk more of this now. There is still much to do. I may not see you again until Bagera."

She started to walk away, then turned and said, "There is still my vow of indebtedness to you."

"That will be fulfilled at Bagera."

"No, that is duty," Sentania said. "To fulfill the vow properly, I must do something I need not do, as you involved yourself in my fate to save me that day."

"Then I release you from the vow."

"That is unacceptable. Here is my vow. Once we have accomplished your freedom, I will do what I can to help you free your Trinary. That is beyond necessity and so it is a deal, *quiaff*?"

"Aff."

"Good."

She turned suddenly and walked away. Without another word, just as she always did.

After she had rounded the street corner and was out of sight, Horse thought about their meeting, about all their meetings. He had put a lot of faith in this Sentania, and he wondered if he had placed his fate in the hands of a crackpot.

But her vow had invigorated him. He knew he was ready and would have his revenge.

Now, they were beginning their journey to Bagera. Horse watched as the quartet of BattleMechs, each being piloted by a Smoke Jaguar warrior, passed majestically out of the city.

I wish Howell had let me pilot one of them, especially since two are from my confiscated 'Mechs. His explanation was feeble, that he wanted me to accompany him in a ground car so he could show me the fine Huntress countryside and explain the great achievements of the Clan. I don't need to hear about any of their achievements. I can match him, Jade Falcon accomplishment for Jag accomplishment.

It is a reasonable claim, but I don't believe it. He does

not want me inside a BattleMech yet. He doesn't trust me. Maybe I haven't fooled him as much as I thought, but my hands fairly itch to get around the controls of a 'Mech.

"Smell that air, Horse. It makes Huntress' mean weather seem worth it."

Howell took a deep breath, enjoying the freshness of it as they neared the wood.

"This will be a fine trip, Horse, *quiaff?*"

"Aff, a good trip."

Better than you even suspect, surat dropping! Bastard!

While the word *bastard* was perhaps more meaningful when uttered, or thought of, by a freeborn, for a trueborn it was a foul term that became a deep insult when applied to a vat-born warrior. Horse hoped to say it directly to Howell. Soon.

=== 29 ===

**Falcon Eyrie
Eastern Mountains, Huntress
Kerensky Cluster, Clan Homeworlds
9 May 3059**

The second of the LAMs intended for the mission, dubbed Evil Twin Two, appeared—brought to the surface on the platform of the BattleMech elevator. It was based on a design for the old *Stinger* LAM, and it did not look formidable, not at all. Peri knew that a BattleMech should induce terror just by its very presence, but these LAMs were too slim with brittle-looking limbs. They looked almost like machines bent with age. In a way, Peri thought, they are solahma 'Mechs.

Geoff piloted Evil Twin Two off the platform in its BattleMech configuration, and it only emphasized how unthreatening the machine looked. Evil Twin Two seemed to come forward in something like a stagger. Of course, Geoff was more comfortable in the AirMech mode, and he generally protested the times when he had to operate one of these two-seaters alone. He now sat in the cockpit, which was not much larger than the original *Stinger* LAM's had been, and Peri could easily imagine him staring down at her with the usual sour look on his face. Geoff had more varieties of sour expression than anyone she had ever known, with the possible exception of Star Commander Joanna, when she had been falconer for Peri's sibko.

Evil Twin Two, which had been modified up from 30 tons to somewhere between 40 and 45, still looked fragile, like a jittery servant awaiting instructions. Its legs had been thickened, which slowed it down on the ground, and its fuselage was longer and narrower, which made it faster and more maneuverable in the air. It was easier to handle in AirMech mode, but Fighter mode was still erratic. No matter, in the fight Sentania had planned, AirMech mode would predominate.

She had added machine guns to the *Stinger* model's standard medium lasers, though the techs warned that too many stress points on Evil Twin Two's intricate superstructure would weaken its structural integrity. That was only one of many doubtful aspects of this LAM, but Peri had more confidence that its companion LAM on this mission, Evil Twin One, showed more promise. Evil Twin One now waited as Evil Twin Two made its unsteady way to the testing field. Peri was not certain why she had begun calling them twins, since they did not look much alike. Perhaps it was because they were linked in her mind as being a pair of research headaches.

Evil Twin One closely resembled the original *Phoenix Hawk* LAM, only slightly reconfigured to accommodate the two-pilot situation. Peri and her team had decided not to tinker too much with the basic *Phoenix Hawk* design. Its 50-ton weight could not be enhanced appreciably, and they had cut corners to keep it close to its original tonnage. The weight at the front had been reduced and, in contrast to Evil Twin Two, its fuselage had been shortened, even though sleeker. Peri's team had added machine guns to Evil Twin Two, but replaced them on Evil Twin One with an extra large laser and the capacity for SRMs. The current Evil Twin One had some SRMs mounted in its center torso. Peri had more faith in this LAM, if only because it had performed significantly better on tests.

But what good were the damn tests? They had shot a few missiles up the mountain and managed some good tight patterns on targets set on a cliff above. But flying around and engaging in some feigned attacks had not proven much either. The flight tests were too limited, because Roshak did not want the Jags to see the LAMs. Peri knew that the only real way to test this kind of contraption was just what they were now doing, sending it on a mission. *And Kerensky help us!*

She began to wonder if the whole operation was folly. Of course it did not really matter, since nobody would be passing judgment on it. Any report written would be cagey, with enough double-speak that no one would bother questioning any part of it. Peri detested the bureaucratic nature of reports within the scientist caste. As the caste seemed more and more to become one, huge, self-serving bureaucracy, its language sank further and further into incomprehensible jargon.

But words were not Peri's only problem at this moment. There was Sentania, too. Sentania had planned most of the operation, but Peri knew she was too wild to be trusted out in the field. Sentania was so certain of the advantages of surprise, LAM maneuverability, and the consequent Jaguar unpreparedness for what would hit them, that she had convinced Peri that the plan might work.

Now, looking at the Evil Twins exhibiting all their flaws in intense sunlight, Peri had trouble imagining them prevailing against real 'Mechs. The more she considered the plan, the more she was sure it was really not feasible—which was why she intended to go along personally. Somebody had to be there in case the unexpected occurred, and—in her experience—something unexpected intruded on a regular basis. Peri was not sure what she could actually contribute, but at least she was sane—or at least (she thought ruefully) believed she was.

She also wondered whether, in implementing Sentania's plan, they had been too deceptive. It was true that Peri had gotten Bren Roshak to approve a real test of the LAMs because he was virtually demanding one these days. That had been easy. It was also true that the raid would be carried out against a small group of Smoke Jaguars and would probably not raise much ruckus even if news of it ever reached the higher-ups.

Roshak himself had been irate to learn that the Jaguars were accusing the Falcons of the repository murder, when there had been no Jade Falcon unit anywhere in the vicinity. He had not been told of Sentania's presence

there, of course, or that only she could have master-
minded penetration of the repository. He also had no
knowledge of Horse's involvement with either the mission or the fact that he was the one who had killed the
Keeper of the Jaguar kin. Informing Roshak of these
details just might have dampened his enthusiasm for the
present test.

Roshak did say he understood Howell's need for
vengeance. Had it been a Smoke Jaguar who had killed a
Jade Falcon Keeper, his own thirst for revenge would be
insatiable, he claimed. Peri pointed out to him that he
need not worry since there was no Jade Falcon genetics
repository on Falcon Eyrie. What she did not say was that
if he were the Jag commander, he probably would find
nothing here to become enraged about. Roshak took little
interest in any of the goings-on at the Eyrie, except of
course for the work that produced a superb specimen
like Jade Rogue. Roshak's main response to the repository incident was to double the guards around Falcon
Eyrie, just in case the Jags found a way to penetrate its
impenetrability.

Sentania and Peri had sold the present raid as the first
step in a series of operations designed to retrieve the
BattleMechs that Howell had appropriated from Horse.
Roshak would not have approved the mission had its aim
been merely the rescue of Horse. Roshak was blithely
uninterested in any of the visiting Trinary. They were
mere freebirths, but the 'Mechs he wanted back. He had
no place to store them and would have to load them onto
the next DropShip for transport elsewhere, but retaking
the 'Mechs had become an issue of principle for him.

However, for all his fervor, he was not willing to
commit key personnel to the operation. He was satisfied
that solahma warriors and converted pilots should make
the attempt. That way, if anyone wound up dead, they
would be sufficiently expendable. Peri thought the logic
understandable to his particular type of garrison men-
tality, but it did not accomplish much in the way of
shoring up defense and providing offense. She tried to
argue for more experienced warriors, but Roshak had
sneered at the request, and she had backed off.

Had I been a warrior, I could have argued with him. He

only listens to arguments from warriors. But sometimes she wondered at the castebound minds of warriors. *Roshak is sometimes so blind he might as well be wearing a hood like his beloved Jade Rogue. But at least Jade Rogue flies with grace and kills with graceful cunning.*

For the next hour Peri strode back and forth between the Evil Twins, checking the checklists that the techs had already completed, making them go through them again. She briefed the BattleMech pilot assigned to Evil Twin Two, a grizzled veteran just on the verge of becoming solahma named Wyatt. He was a bit too confident for Peri's tastes. He nodded perfunctorily at her instructions, clearly offended at having to listen to orders from a member of a lower caste. Warriors did have difficulty cooperating with scientists, who often held nonmilitary authority over them. They did not like it, and few tolerated the indignity with much courtesy. MechWarrior Wyatt was no exception. He shifted his feet often, looked away from her frequently with boredom in his blank gray eyes, even appeared to stifle a yawn from time to time.

Have I doomed the mission by choosing this stravag *from the meager list Roshak provided? This fellow has no commitment to the mission, it is clear. Of course he will put forth an effort. No Jade Falcon warrior could do otherwise, but he may not have the skill to overcome the odds we will face. Stop the gloomy thinking! This can work. I know it can.*

Wyatt seemed relieved when she dismissed him. He walked away briskly.

"A fine loyal warrior, that Wyatt," said a voice behind her. She was not even startled. She was used to Stenis coming up behind her and speaking abruptly. It always seemed as if he were conducting a conversation in his head that he suddenly spoke out loud somewhere in the middle.

"Stenis, are you being sarcastic?"

"I never know. I just speak."

"I have noticed."

Wyatt touched the leg of Evil Twin Two, perhaps checking to see if it would topple at a touch. It did not, and he seemed satisfied. Then he headed toward the warrior hut, apparently to don battlegear.

"Wyatt is a good pilot," Peri said. "He has a pretty good

record at piloting a LAM in 'Mech mode, which is why I chose him."

"I notice you said 'pretty good.' Hardly a ringing endorsement."

"Are you saying, Stenis, that not all trueborn Jade Falcon warriors are the finest ever to come out of vats?"

"I would never say that. I believe in the Jade Falcon way and I know that all our warriors approach perfection, even those shuffled off to garrison duty. Even the solahmas."

"Aye," said Peri.

"I wish you good luck on your venture," Sentis said.

"It is only a test."

"Of course, only a test."

"There is the sound of doubt in your voice."

"Sentania Buhallin is involved, *quiaff*?"

"Aff. She will participate in the—"

"Then I have good reason to doubt. I wish you both well."

Peri was stuck for a response. It did not matter anyway, for Stenis was already walking away, his pace suddenly looking old, his shoulders bent.

It is a pity, but that man does not look as if he will survive much longer. That is the sadness of garrison duty. It can sap the life right out of good warriors, doom them to boredom, inertia, sometimes an early death. Well, with Stenis it will not be an early death, but it will not be the death of a warrior, and it looks to me as if it may come soon. No sense in continuing gloomy thoughts. I have to get ready for the flight.

Sentania was the assigned BattleMech pilot for Evil Twin One, and she was to meet the LAMs near the mining town of Bagera. For now, Peri had assigned herself the BattleMech seat in Evil Twin One. The other pilot, Gerri, could handle both modes and help her out if anything untoward happened. It was not likely that anything would, but it was best to be prepared. Anyway, Gerri would pilot the LAM all the way to the Bagera region, and all Peri would really need do was land the thing on a pair of jump jets, something she had done thousands of time, if only in a simulator.

Of course, Roshak had no idea Peri would be in the LAM for the test. He did not even know it would take place near Bagera. She had placed the name of a dead warrior on the flight roster. He had not recognized it, or perhaps not even looked, and he had signed off on the document.

She disguised herself as a warrior with the proper battlegear, and then took her place in the LAM.

The ploy worked, and soon the Evil Twins were in the air. Now she only had to sit back and let Gerri fly the machine. And fly it he did. She was thrilled as it cruised over the tops of the forest, casting a broad, ever-changing shadow onto the treetops.

Bagera was not too far away on a direct line, but they took a somewhat roundabout course, to keep from being spotted. Even if they were detected, it was unlikely anyone down there would figure out what they were up to. No one on Huntress had ever seen the Falcon Eyrie LAMs. A spotter would probably spend most of his time trying to identify the strange-looking vehicles. Still, it was better to be cautious and fly undetected.

As they neared the landing site, Peri began to get nervous. What if she botched the landing, ended up ruining the LAM? Then she laughed to herself. The thought of carrying out a procedure she would have done routinely had she qualified as a warrior excited her tremendously.

She needed to brief Wyatt and Geoff before they reached their destination. Switching on the comm channel to Evil Twin Two, she got Geoff's surly response. She gave him the few instructions that occurred to her, to which he responded with grunts instead of words. Then she asked to speak to Wyatt.

There was a long silence after Geoff's "Aye."

"What is wrong?" Peri said into the mike of her neurohelmet. "Do you read me? Geoff? Wyatt?"

"I read you," said a voice she dreaded to hear.

"Stenis?"

"Aff."

"What are doing there?"

There was a long pause before Stenis responded. "Wyatt, you see, was somewhat indisposed. I volunteered to fill in for him."

"But—but I saw him mount the Evil Twin Two. It was not your walk, it was Wyatt's. It could not have been you, it—"

"I too am skilled at deception, Peri Watson—"

"Stenis, we will have to turn back, we cannot—"

"And I was a better warrior than Wyatt ever dreamed of. I am your best chance, not Wyatt. Trust me. I care, he did not. There is no reason to turn back."

Something in Stenis' voice reassured her. And he was right about one thing. They could not turn back. The mission would not be possible a second time. The figures in the little drama Sentania had arranged would be together in one place only at this time. It might be months before anything like it could be arranged again. If at all.

In the background over the commline, she could hear Geoff cursing. He was uttering some of the worst oaths known to Jade Falcons. He came on-line and requested a return to base.

"You will continue on to Bagera," Peri ordered and switched off the comm channel.

A pair of pilots who know their machines only through tests, a pair of solahmas in the cockpits, and a pair of 'Mechs whose destiny as fighting machines is questionable. How can we lose?

Peri felt for a moment that she could imitate Roshak and let tears come out of her eyes. But she was too much Jade Falcon and the situation too risky to start crying about it now. Her next impulse was to laugh, and she resisted that, too.

They flew on. Below, the shadows of the two LAMs wavered over the trees like the drawings of a child.

Highway to Bagera
Huntress
Kerensky Cluster, Clan Homeworlds
9 May 3059

"**B**elieve me, Horse, Bagera was virtually useless when I first got to Huntress," Russou Howell said as the light APC bumped along a rough dirt road. The vehicle's wheels bounced off the ground so often that Horse expected to become airborne at any moment.

"Rowdy miners, bad management," Howell continued, sounding as if he enjoyed the sound of his own words. "And too many violent incidents—meaningless violence, that is. I took one look and then assigned a Star to restore order and discipline. They had to kill a few people, but the town is under control now. And the mine is going full-tilt, right on schedule. There is even a project to clean up the buildings and rebuild streets. One day soon it will be as fine a city as Lootera, just as pristine and filled with fine architecture."

Horse wasn't sure that modeling anything on Lootera was such a good idea, but he said nothing. Turning in his seat, he looked back down the road. In the distance, to the right of the road, two BattleMechs kept pace with Howell and their vehicle. The other two had gone ahead, to alert the officer in charge at Bagera that the Galaxy Commander would arrive imminently. "That is the secret of an inspection, *quiaff*?" Howell had said. "Give them as little warning as possible."

The vehicle, hitting a bump in the road at high speed, rose into the air for what seemed like a long time before coming down hard on the other side of the bump. Howell whooped with enjoyment, while Horse winced in pain. He got no thrills out of bouncing along a road in a car, and would have preferred the cramped but predictable seat of a BattleMech cockpit.

The longing was especially fierce because of the *Summoner* plodding along behind them. Although he hated this pretense of being a Smoke Jaguar, he hated even more this state halfway between prisoner and warrior that Howell had assigned him.

Two days ago he mentioned it to Howell, who answered, "It is not a halfway state at all. You just need some training in Smoke Jaguar customs, rules, and traditions. There is no regulation anywhere stating that a warrior must be assigned a 'Mech. But do not look so angry, Horse—you will have one soon, I promise."

Each side of the road leading to Bagera displayed a different geographical terrain. To the right, where the Battle-Mechs were kicking up dust, the land was barren—an expanse pocked with extensive patches of dry land, interrupted by insignificant areas of grass, much of which was almost completely brown and the best of which was speckled and scrawny. Horse wondered what had happened to so devastate the terrain. On the right, however, was a forest like the one near Lootera, but denser and looking almost as lush as a jungle. Loud, sometimes screeching, bird calls emerged from it. At one point a flock of the oddest-looking birds Horse had ever seen flew out of the forest and took an erratic path toward the distant mountains ahead. Howell commented that they were called skittishes by the locals because of their strange flight patterns. "An indigenous species that could be eliminated without environmental loss, I am sure," he remarked.

They continued to bump along the road in silence for a long while, with Howell seeming unusually pensive. Occasionally he glanced quizzically over at Horse. It made Horse edgy, and he glanced away, toward the forest. He could hear the rumbling sound of the *Summoner*, which had nearly caught up. The 'Mech's thundering steps vibrated through his body even through the car's cushioned seat.

Horse stared at the 'Mech and wondered if it was his *Summoner*. It did not appear to be. Its surface was too smooth, unmarred by the dents it had earned during many battles in the Inner Sphere invasion.

Howell noticed Horse studying the 'Mech.

"You may not believe this," he said, "but that *Summoner* is the one I took from your DropShip. It was yours, I think."

Horse was astounded. "I was just thinking—but it cannot be," he said. "Mine was, well, it was—"

"It was not in such fine condition, *quiaff*?"

"Aff. It has not gleamed so much since the day of its first shakedown run."

Howell gestured toward the *Summoner,* which had slowed to match the speed of the car. "Well, hard to believe maybe, but it is yours. Shows the superiority of Smoke Jaguar refitting and reconditioning technology. Our 'Mechs are always in fine repair. I am very proud of that, as are all Smoke Jaguars. You will see more and more of our superiority as you remain with us."

Horse said nothing. All he could think about was that his 'Mech was so close, but it might as well have been back in the Inner Sphere for all he could do with it.

"I have been giving the Smoke Jaguar attitude toward freebirths, a great deal of thought," Howell said, then stopped.

Horse struggled to repress his reaction to Howell's use of the foul term.

"The way we dismiss them as warriors, for one. You, Horse, are a different sort of freebirth and it would be wasteful not to use you properly. All Clans abhor waste."

Horse suppressed a laugh. If Howell suspected how ridiculous he seemed to Horse at that moment, his sponsorship of him might end. That would not be bad, but he did not want to upset the plan now, just when he was so close to freeing himself honorably.

"I have been thinking," Howell said, "that you deserve your chance with us. When this trial period is ended, I intend to give you a chance at a Trial of Position as a Star Commander for the Smoke Jaguars. You may fight me in the Trial, if you wish, instead of the normal trio of combatants."

Horse's astonishment at Howell's offer nearly made him reveal how much he would like to fight Howell in a Trial of Position and how much he would like to kill him in it. Aloud, he simply said as sincerely as possible, "I would be honored to fight you in a Trial of Position." The man had grown so unpredictable, so outrageous in his thoughts and behavior, that Horse barely knew what he might blurt out next.

"Very well then. As soon as we get back, I will set things in motion. It may take time. My own people will surely object. But I intend to win on this one, even if it means both of us must fight the others. You may have your chance at a position sooner than you expect."

Or never, Horse thought, *if Sentania's scheme works out. If not, I'll be dead anyway—also sooner than I expect.*

= 31 =

Bagera Forest
Huntress
Kerensky Cluster, Clan Homeworlds
9 May 3059

Howell's exuberance was irritating. The man could not stop talking, especially about matters of Smoke Jaguar pride.

The only pride I want to think about, Horse thought, *is the bloodline of Prydes in the Jade Falcons. Aidan Pryde, Marthe Pryde—stravag, even Ravill Pryde. If Diana succeeds in her Trial of Bloodright, she'll be another one. Diana Pryde. I wonder how she's faring? Has she already had a chance to fight in the contests, or is she in some long queue, awaiting her chance?*

"Time for a break."

Howell ordered his driver to halt and then got on the commline to tell the two accompanying BattleMechs to stay where they were until he returned. Their driver made an abrupt turn off the road toward the forest and pulled the vehicle to a stop. Howell leapt out lightly, motioning for Horse to follow.

The two of them climbed up a short hill covered with dense underbrush and finally stopped by a large tree in a natural clearing. Howell leaned casually against the bark and pulled a small flask out of his pocket.

Horse stood there, amazed at Howell's lack of shame.

He should have been used to the man's antics by now, yet Howell continued to astound him. Howell took a deep drink from the flask and closed his eyes while the liquor slid down his throat. When he opened his eyes, he smiled and said, "It feels good to be out of the city, Horse, *quiaff*?"

"Aff," Horse replied in a neutral tone, but he was on guard. The more unpredictable Howell had become over time, the more Horse had learned to be vigilant.

From their position, a rise slightly above the road, they had a view of the surrounding area through an opening in the lush growth. Nothing of much note showed from their vantage point, which was mostly a view of the desolate terrain on the other side of the road. But Horse had to admit it did feel good to be out in the open air.

"Huntress is not the most welcoming planet, but it does have its charm. The sudden changes of terrain can be interesting, and I am even coming to accept the never-ending grayness of the days." Howell squinted up at the sky as if proving his point, then took another pull off the flask. Horse sat down on a nearby rock, sensing that one of Howell's rambling, alcohol-induced speeches was coming on.

"Of course, likes and dislikes are of little import to a true Smoke Jaguar. We warriors are bred to have but one purpose. We are engineered for victory on the battlefield and there can be no greater honor in life. To eliminate our enemies, protect the integrity of our Clan, to die in glory—"

"This man can babble on, can he not, Horse?"

Horse was much less startled than Howell, since he was used to Sentania Buhallin's talent for sudden appearances. This time she swung lightly down from the branch of tree next to where Howell was leaning.

"Who are you?" Howell said, startled and losing his balance for a moment.

"You do not remember me?" Sentania said. "And I thought we had such a good time together." She stood facing Howell in a relaxed but ready posture.

Howell stared at Sentania, struggling to recall.

"I do recognize you. You are a tech, *quiaff*?"

"You thought I was."

"You were in a tech uniform then. Now, what is this? You are wearing Jade Falcon fatigues?"

"I am of the Jade Falcon Clan, aff."

Howell's face flushed. "Horse, take her into custody."

For once in his life, Horse was unsure what to do. He had not expected Sentania to reveal herself yet, although he had suspected she was tracking them from somewhere.

"Forget it," Sentania said. "I am not the only Jade Falcon in the vicinity. We outnumber you. You are not carrying sidearms." She smiled.

"What is your purpose here, freebirth?" Howell sputtered.

"I am not a freebirth. He is a freebir—a freeborn, as you so well know, Galaxy Commander Howell. But, freeborn or not, he is *our* freeborn and I wish to reclaim Horse for the Jade Falcons."

"You cannot do that. He is Smoke Jaguar now. It is—"

Sentania held up her hand. "I know all about that. And I am fully cognizant of Horse's sense of honor, his beliefs about honor. He has taken Smoke Jaguar oaths, after all. He cannot just up and leave. Therefore, Galaxy Commander Howell, I am issuing you a challenge."

"Challenge?"

"Yes. I am Solahma Star Commander Sentania Buhallin—"

"Solahma?"

"Do not interrupt a challenge. Such rudeness is unworthy of you."

Howell gaped at her. "What? You are solahma, and you wish to issue a challenge?"

"Why is that surprising? In a bid or in response to one, you would include the many solahmas in your Galaxy, *quiaff*?"

Howell seemed rattled. "Horse, who is this solahma?"

Horse smiled, happy to see that Sentania's talent for keeping him off balance extended to others as well. "That is an extremely hard question to answer. Trying to pin down this Sentania Buhallin is like clutching at wind gusts."

Howell shook his head to clear it. He seemed disturbed, and the confusion in his eyes amused Horse.

"Do not play word games with me, Horse. Is this some kind of joke? You show up out of nowhere, calling yourself Sentania Buhallin, to issue a challenge when you have no visible support for any bid you might make. You are solahma and I am a Galaxy Commander. What makes you believe you have any right to speak to me, much less issue this impertinent challenge?"

"Let me finish, and you will understand."

"The challenge is absurd."

"You have not heard it yet."

"I do not need to hear it."

"If you do not allow me to issue the challenge, then I automatically win the bid, you know that. That would be easy, I will admit. Too easy. We came to fight you, Russou Howell."

Howell sighed. "Very well. Proceed."

"I am Solahma Star Commander Sentania Buhallin, assigned to the Jade Falcon Research Station, Falcon Eyrie. Who defends the spawn of the freeborn known as Horse?"

Howell's mouth dropped open. "The spawn of Horse? That is a challenge for a genetic legacy! A *trueborn* genetic legacy. Horse is a freebirth. Clan Smoke Jaguar does not store the genetic legacies of any freeborns. The freeborns themselves may have some customs, but they are meaningless to Smoke Jaguar warriors."

"You are interrupting again. Do you Smoke Jaguars have no respect for ritual?"

Howell shook his head. "Go on."

"I consider the legacy to be in Horse's codex. He was once Jade Falcon and now is Smoke Jaguar. Horse is a respected warrior within our Clan. He does not belong in the ranks of any other Clan. It is for the honor of the Jade Falcons that I make this challenge. We honor Horse who, as you point out, is a freeborn warrior. That is how important Horse and his achievements are to the Jade Falcons. He deserves nothing less than a proper fight for his codex, for his legacy. And that is my purpose. I will now bid."

Howell was clearly angry now. "And what will you bid? Tree branches against a pile of rocks?"

"We will ignore your rudeness, Galaxy Commander. I see that you have two BattleMechs in your party."

"Four, actually."

"Two, actually. The other two are too far down the road, clearly on the way to Bagera, and we will not wait for them to be ordered to return. However, you have a *Warhammer* and a *Summoner* and, since we want a full-fledged and fair encounter, we will bid two of our 'Mechs against your pair."

Horse admired Sentania's bluff. He knew she only had the two 'Mechs with her, but she made it sound as if there were larger forces ready to go into the field.

"That is my bid, Galaxy Commander Howell."

Howell stared at the ground for a moment. Then he shook his head as if to clear it. "A Smoke Jaguar is always ready to defend Clan honor," he said loud and clear, "no matter what the circumstances. In what *absurd* circumstances, I might add. And I have a fine motive for vengeance, since you Jade Falcons are responsible for the murder of the Keeper of the Jaguar kin. My own blood longs to avenge that horrific crime. Well bargained and done, Sentania Buhallin."

"Well bargained and done then."

"I will allow you, as challenger, to choose the venue. We can beat you anywhere, I am certain."

"We fight you here. The field on the other side of the road is wide and deep. Good for open combat."

"Produce your 'Mechs then."

"In time, Russou Howell, in time."

With Horse and Sentania close behind, Howell returned to the car and summoned his 'Mechs. Soon the ground was rumbling with their heavy steps. Howell, strangely silent, watched the *Summoner* and *Warhammer* approach. When they were a half kilometer away, he ordered them to stop and explained the challenge to them.

Then Howell crossed from the car back to Sentania.

"We will be ready. I will pilot the *Warhammer* myself."

Sentania nodded. "I will be honored by your participation, and I look forward to contesting this issue with you myself."

"What do you mean? You will pilot one of your 'Mechs?"

"That is correct."

"But you are only a solahma. A solahma against a Galaxy Commander?"

"Aye."

"I protest. You deliberately insult me."

"And you make a good target."

Howell stared at her for a long moment. "Very well then. I vow not only to defeat you, Sentania Buhallin, but I will also kill you. At least somebody will die for the Keeper's murder."

"You waste your vengeance on me. If you kill me in combat, a solahma warrior cannot ask for more. But, solahma or not, I am no less a warrior of the Jade Falcon."

Howell nodded. "You have no right to challenge me, solahma. But that will not stop me from killing you. I have, as you said, a strong thirst for vengeance."

Standing a few paces away, Horse knew that Howell was correct. It was inappropriate for a solahma to fight a commander in a 'Mech battle. Solahmas rarely piloted 'Mechs, and who knew how long it had been since this wild thing named Sentania had last piloted one? Furthermore, it was Horse who had killed the old Keeper in the repository. If Howell wanted to wreak vengeance, it should be against him.

Well, the die was cast, and Horse could do little about it now. There was the rub. He was not used to being passive during a major combat action. There was no skill in being an observer, especially in this situation, where he had become the object of challenge. It was something like being the maiden in a joust between two knights. He had complained of this originally to Sentania, but she had said this was the only way to unfetter him with honor. She said that, any time afterward, there would be a situation where he could get his chance at Howell and his hated warriors. But first priority was his freedom from the Jags, then the freeing of his imprisoned Trinary. She told him to be comfortable as an observer.

"Do you actually have any 'Mechs, Sentania Buhallin?" Howell said impatiently.

"Yes. You will see them any minute."

"Do you have them hidden in the forest?"

"No."

Howell gestured expansively toward the terrain around them. "They must be coming up out of the ground then."

"No."

"I cannot see how—"

"Try looking up."

Appearing above the treeline the Evil Twins flew over and past them. Evil Twin Two dipped its wing toward the two standing Jaguar 'Mechs, an insult Howell could not miss. Taking a long looping path over the road, they turned and came back at a lower altitude toward the 'Mechs.

"You did not bid aerofighters," Howell said angrily.

"No, I did not, Galaxy Commander. These are Battle-Mechs configured in the Land-Air mode."

"LAMs? But they are obsolete."

"In some places, yes. But do not assume that this pair fits that category. They have been under study and development and are high-order BattleMechs."

Sentania briefly explained to the astonished Howell about the two-pilot version of the LAM.

"But are they not lighter than our two 'Mechs?"

"That is not your concern. You have accepted the challenge. Let us begin."

At a signal from Sentania, the Evil Twins descended. Horse was impressed by the smoothness of their switch from aerofighter to 'Mech as each landed gently, their jump jets barely stirring up the ground beneath them.

"Sentania Buhallin," Howell said, "your challenge is mad, insane. I wish to re-bid. To make the challenge at least fair, I will take on both your LAMs with my *Warhammer*."

"Your protest, with its implied arrogance, is worthy of your Clan, but we have bargained and done. We will fight you for the legacy of the freeborn hero named Horse. Horse, come forward."

Confused, Horse walked to where Sentania and Howell stood. "You understand the challenge, *quiaff*?" she asked.

"Aff," Horse replied.

"And you vow to stand by your oaths to whichever Clan is victorious in this engagement, *quiaff*?"

"Aff."

"That is fair to you also, Galaxy Commander, *quiaff*?"

Howell hesitated. Horse wondered if he felt cornered. "Aff," Howell said.

"Then I think we should assume our places in the cockpits of our 'Mechs."

Howell walked a few steps away.

Horse whispered to Sentania, "I hope you know what you are doing."

Sentania shrugged. "I know a hawk from a handsaw."

"Knowing what you are quoting from does not increase my confidence."

She shrugged again.

"You told me you would confront Howell with a pair of 'Mechs. You did not tell me they would be Land-Air 'Mechs."

"Had you known, you might not have agreed to the plan."

"I would not have."

"See?"

"They have no chance against heavy 'Mechs like the *Summoner* and *Warhammer*."

"That would be the conventional belief, Horse. But these have been retooled. Our techs at Falcon Eyrie have worked on them for half a decade. Changes have been made. Howell will not suspect the changes. He will expect them to act only in the way he has known LAMs to act."

"But, still—"

"Hush. Here he comes."

Howell walked up to Sentania and Horse, and unnervingly satisfied smile on his face.

"Horse," he said quietly. "You will pilot the *Summoner*."

Horse and Sentania looked at each other. For a brief moment both were speechless. Then Sentania said, "This is—it is unorthodox."

"Is it?" Howell said. "To have a warrior fight for his own legacy? Rather than unorthodox, I believe it to be proper. If Horse is to prove his honor, he can do so by winning the challenge for his present Clan, for the far superior Smoke Jaguars. If he is dishonorable, he can lose it and crawl on his stomach back to the Falcons as an abject coward. But Horse is not a coward, are you, Horse?"

"I have never been a coward."

"Then go to the *Summoner*. You have been itching to get back into a 'Mech. You said so yourself. Winning this contest will not only bring honor to your already honorable codex, it will earn you the commission we spoke of earlier."

"Commission?" Sentania asked, confused.

"I have offered Horse the opportunity to become a freeborn Star Commander in the Smoke Jaguars," Howell said. "An unprecedented honor and one only possible in a garrison like this, where we are already understaffed and have to use aging warriors much like yourself, Sentania Buhallin. Besides, this will be an even better trial than the one we spoke of. Horse, we fight side by side instead of against each other. Win, and your legend will grow. Lose, and you prove that everything said about freebirths is true. Worthless scum. Somehow this is all fitting. Come, Horse, your *Summoner* awaits you."

Howell could not stop laughing as he walked away from Sentania and Horse. Horse looked at Sentania, his eyes troubled.

"Do your best, Horse," Sentania said. "I would expect nothing else from a Jade Falcon."

She started walking past him, heading for Evil Twin One, the LAM that she would pilot in its 'Mech mode. Another woman stood at its feet and obviously awaited Sentania. Horse had never seen Peri Watson before, but he recognized the resemblance to Diana, even from a distance.

"Horse!" Howell bellowed and beckoned Horse to come to him. The gesture was arrogant and impatient and, thus, very much Smoke Jaguar.

Horse started toward the *Summoner*. He glanced back toward the Evil Twins. They looked weak. He felt he could dispose of both of them himself. He could win easily, he knew.

And his honor demanded that he do just that.

═══ 32 ═══

Bagera Forest
Huntress
Kerensky Cluster, Clan Homeworlds
9 May 3059

Sentania quickly explained the new developments to Peri Watson, whose face paled as she listened.

"That turns the odds against us," Peri said. "I believe in your skills, Sentania, but against Horse, well—"

"He is a fine warrior, true, but so am I. And, after all, he is only a freebirth. I would be insulted to lose to a freebirth."

"But, Sentania, you are solahma. You have not been in real combat for a decade."

"Horse is no youngster, either."

"But he is fresh from Inner Sphere combat. You, on the other hand—"

"There is no other hand. The contest is engaged. Perhaps I will concentrate on defeating Howell. Wyatt is skilled, relatively young, with a good codex. He can fight Horse."

"Um, Sentania . . . Wyatt is not with us."

Sentania had enthusiastically endorsed Wyatt's selection for this mission, and his absence disoriented her.

"If not Wyatt," she asked, "who?"

"Just me, old woman," Stenis said as he walked around the leg of Evil Twin One. It was Sentania's turn to blanch.

Stenis, after all, looked even older than Sentania and, in battlegear, he seemed like a stick figure who did not even fully inhabit clothing that should be skin-tight. "And if you want to examine my codex for credentials, you are welcome to it. I was so good in a 'Mech that I managed to postpone the solahma assignment for a decade. Can you claim that, Sentania Buhallin?"

"This is no time for your kind of foolishness, Stenis. No matter what you may have done in the past, you are crazy, feeble, and probably blind and deaf."

"None of which disqualifies me from operating a BattleMech. I can do it in my sleep."

Sentania turned toward Peri and shrugged again. "Do we even have a chance?"

"We have issued the challenge, a bit late to take it back. Although . . . well . . ."

"Tell me."

"Well, we are not authorized. I have no right to authorize such a mission as this. Roshak, if we inform him, can smooth things over with the Jaguar commander, and we can just retreat from the field."

"Fat chance. You forget that the Jaguars are out for revenge on us for the repository killing, of which we are guilty—myself and Horse, anyway."

"*You* killed the Keeper?" Stenis said.

"It is a long story, Stenis. Anyway, Peri, Howell will still be in the mood for vengeance, whatever we do. There is no way out and it is not the Jade Falcon way to seek one, after all."

"The way of the Clans is the way of our warriors, and theirs. I am a scientist, not a warrior, and I would like to find a way to scrub the mission."

Sentania laughed. "Come, we both know you would be a warrior, given half a chance. Stop thinking like a freebirth."

Some fire came into Peri's eyes. "Aye. Let us get this fight started."

Sentania clapped Peri's shoulder. "You are all right—for a scientist."

"Step into the Circle of Equals with me, Sentania Buhallin, and I will show you what a scientist can do."

"Whenever you say. But not just now. I expect to be busy for a few minutes."

Peri nodded.

"Just tell me one thing, Peri Watson."

"What?"

"The alterations you and your crew made to these LAMs—they can do the job, *quiaff*?"

"How could you think otherwise?"

"I do not know. I really do not know. One more thing. There is a jump seat in the LAM cockpit, behind the air pilot's seat."

"Yes, well, we put it there for observation on specific tests."

"Exactly what we need it for now. You should be in Evil Twin Two, to observe Stenis. I would feel better having someone there I can trust. Make sure that Stenis knows what he is doing and that he does not suddenly go crazy, which he can do without much notice, as you know. If he flips, I'll need to know right away, so have Geoff patch you into the commline, *quiaff*?"

"Aff."

Peri could not have expressed to this aging solahma warrior how excited she was to be in the cockpit of one of the experimental Land-Air 'Mechs, even in a passenger seat. And, if it failed, she longed to go down with it.

Inside the Evil Twin Two cockpit, Peri greeted Stenis and Geoff with a quick explanation of her presence as an observer. She did not mention what Sentania had said about Stenis and his craziness.

"That loony surat, Sentania Buhallin," Stenis muttered. "Will she ever do anything that is orthodox?"

Geoff, who was famous for remaining silent through most activities, spoke up suddenly. "You are crazy, all of you. Challenging 'Mechs in these rattletraps. Thinking you can do it. Thinking you can do anything."

Stenis turned toward Geoff and snarled, "You do not speak like a warrior. We can do this. We can win. We are Jade Falcons."

Peri was impressed by Stenis' firmness and the authority in his voice.

"Of course we can win," Geoff said. "But you are all crazy anyway."

"That is better."

The signal to start moving came from Sentania through the commline. Peri thought Sentania sounded confident, ready. In the distance the *Summoner* and the *Warhammer* had begun to move also. They looked like giants. Even high in this cockpit, Peri had to look up at them.

Geoff might just be on target, she thought. *Crazy does seem the operative word here.*

Stenis' handling of the controls was sure, and Evil Twin Two moved ahead steadily. Geoff sat in his seat, his hands on the controls, ready to take over and lift the LAM immediately into the sky if need be. Peri's hands moved nervously, wanting something to do.

The *Summoner* and the *Warhammer* kept coming.

"They sure are big damn things," Stenis muttered.

Bagera Forest
Huntress
Kerensky Cluster, Clan Homeworlds
9 May 3059

Feels good to be back in a cockpit, even if the Jags have redone it according to their designs. This scanner is newly installed. Good—the old one glitched too often. Viewport has new plexiglass—I don't see the old shrapnel scars. Joystick's positioned too high, but its action has been eased. It'll take me a few minutes to get used to this new control panel. Too many buttons, levers, all that. Simpler is better. The Jags gussy things up too much. Have to hand it to them, though. They have obviously taken great care reconditioning this Summoner. *Listen to that rumble, the noise of a 'Mech ready to go—steady and smooth. The controls, lubricated to perfection, they respond to my touch like it was not redone for some other pilot, some Jag pilot. Like they remember me. All right, Mech, let's see what we can do. You're ready to roll, to smash anything that gets in your way.*

Howell's voice came over the commline. "They are allowing us a five-minute pause while you check out your 'Mech. Look at theirs. LAMs? Pitiful. What do they think they are doing? Perhaps they want you to remain a Smoke Jaguar, Horse, by offering such a feeble challenge. Maybe this is only symbolic—to fulfill some ritual, then say at least they made the effort."

"Jade Falcons would do nothing of the sort," Horse replied. "They are not deceptive." It sounded so odd to speak as though he were really no longer a Jade Falcon. "I can tell you something else too, Galaxy Commander."

"What is that, Horse?"

"They are offering this bid because it is the only one they can make. Falcon Eyrie is, first, a research station and, second, it has no use for BattleMechs in its strongly defended placement."

"I knew that, yes. We knew there was little or no BattleMech presence on Falcon Eyrie. This is the first I have heard about the Land-Air 'Mechs. I am surprised they would actually use them in a vital combat situation. An interesting development. But LAMs are notorious for their ineffectiveness in combat. Why deploy them here now?"

"The way of the Clans is to fight with the best one has to offer. Face it, you would do the same. We do not retreat because we are outnumbered or not properly outfitted—unless, of course, the retreat is part of an attack strategy."

"You speak nobly, freebirth. Are you sure you are not a trueborn in disguise?"

The savrashri. He wishes to provoke me. And why not? He knows my predicament and seeks every opportunity to remind me of it.

He seems to think I have a dilemma. But there is no choice. I must fight honorably, Howell is right in anticipating that. All my life, everything I have won, would be brought to disgrace if it looks like I am holding back, losing in order to be a Jade Falcon again. I must be the best Smoke Jaguar possible. I must show myself a true warrior to Smoke Jaguar eyes. I will have to destroy Sentania, maybe Peri, all their team. It is best if I do it myself and not let Howell take the advantage. It would seem just as cowardly if I let him gain the win. There will be long weeks of insults from Jag warriors and words of hidden meaning from Howell. I could bear that, but I might as well acquit myself the way a warrior should—I am doomed, I can see that! Sentania's led me like a blind man to—to what?

"Time is up, Horse, let us begin."

* * *

Sentania felt a momentary scare as she watched the *Warhammer* and the *Summoner* swing into action. It was, however, not the first battle she had fought with the odds against her, and she actually welcomed the underdog role.

Maneuvering Evil Twin One, she turned it toward Horse and his *Summoner*. She knew that he would go after her first. It was only logical. Her LAM had more tonnage and represented a greater threat. He had to attack fiercely, in order to maintain his honor and impress Howell. With Stenis piloting Evil Twin Two, the responsibility for the battle fell upon her. If she did not succeed, they would not succeed. Evil Twin Two was the less reliable of the LAMs, and also the lighter. The two Jag 'Mechs would just roll over it if it were the only Falcon 'Mech left on the field.

Sentania, always a quick thinker, had reconsidered her plan of attack to include the presence of Horse as an opponent. It was true he was between a rock and a hard place, as the ancient warrior saying went, and it was true that he had to fight honestly, but—to Sentania—it made him even more vulnerable. He was in the same situation as Howell, since neither, presumably, had gone up against a LAM before. They would be basing their attack on old, vaguely remembered manuals regarding Land-Air 'Mechs. They could be thrown off easily, and Sentania could press unsuspected advantages.

Beside her, the usually nervous Gerri was unusually taciturn.

"You are ready, *quiaff*?" she asked him.

"Ready as I can ever be."

"Do not be so tentative. You will have to take over in AirMech mode as soon as I utter the words. We must work together, as we have done in previous tests. We must be as one, that is the key to the Land-Air 'Mech."

"You know I understand, Sentania Buhallin, and you know I will follow your lead, *quiaff*?"

"Aff. Let us test our opponents with a bit of unorthodox strategy right away. I am engaging jump jets."

Evil Twin One jumped into the air, straight up, and soared above the scene. She could tell that Howell was having a hard time adjusting to the move. The use of jump jets was not considered a Clanlike advantage. However,

Peri had given this 'Mech extra jump jet power and ability. The jets would last longer and could be used more often. Where the use of jump jets was normally limited, Evil Twin One had more jumps in it than it knew what to do with. Evil Twin Two was not similarly fitted because it could not sacrifice any of its firepower weight.

"All right. Gerri, prepare to engage AirMech mode. Engage!"

The 'Mech's wings eased out as smoothly as its legs retracted.

"Let us ignore Horse and his *Summoner*. Make him sweat—dive at the *Warhammer,* and fire!"

In Evil Twin Two, Stenis watched Sentania's jump and switch to air mode with astonishment.

"What is she up to?"

Peri did not know how to respond, and Geoff said nothing. Peri noticed how old Stenis looked, with his mouth wide open and his eyes showing amazement. He had all his teeth but looked strangely toothless, a phenomenon that often seemed to accompany those who'd reached his age.

"She's jumping right off," Peri responded. "That is in the design. She does not have to conserve her jumps."

"That is wrong. It gives the LAM an unfair advantage."

"Perceptive of you. But not an advantage really, unless you count that of surprise. We have few advantages here, believe me. And what is wrong with an advant—Look at that!"

Gerri had put the Evil Twin One into a sharp dive. Just before coming out of the dive and soaring upward, he fired two pulses from the large laser at the *Warhammer*. The shots were just off the mark but knocked several pieces of side armor off the Jag 'Mech. Evil Twin One reached an apex high above the scene, then soared over its opponents while heading to a point behind them, not far from the road, and quickly landing. The *Warhammer* torso twisted around, then with some laboriousness, Howell got the legs around too, so that the whole 'Mech faced Sentania's LAM, which was now running toward it. The run was considerably more graceful than anyone would have expected.

* * *

Peri was thrilled by the running ability of Evil Twin One. She knew that the LAM she was in could not manage such grace and, in fact, could not move very smoothly at all—at least during its several tests. But the refinements of Evil Twin One's jumping ability gratified her.

"The witch!" Stenis yelled. "By going behind them, she has made us vulnerable. We would fight better if we stayed together."

"Do not be too sure of that. None of our tests have been successful with LAMs working in unison."

"Well, tell your friend in the *Summoner* that!"

Horse had turned away from the sudden flight of Sentania's LAM, and his *Summoner* was heading, ominously in Peri's eyes, toward her own Evil Twin Two. It seemed all the scarier because it walked slowly and had not yet made any move to attack.

Howell felt like a giant being annoyed by a gnat, an effect heightened by the insectoid look of the Falcon 'Mech. The LAM had made him look foolish as it rose up, then dove down at him, while landing a couple of close shots. The lost armor did not amount to much damage, but his inability to inflict at least equal damage irritated him. He fired his PPC, which the LAM managed to dodge with a dancing kind of sidestep that Howell had never seen before in any type of 'Mech. And it performed the maneuver with such ease that it did not once break its attacking stride.

Howell cursed and vowed to annihilate the ugly slug before it embarrassed him further. He only wished he could stop to have a drink.

Sentania whooped when she avoided Howell's first shot. This was the way a LAM was intended to be used in combat, making quick little assaults, then getting out of the way of counterattack.

The usually silent Gerri could not keep from giving Sentania a bit of praise. "You think fast, Sentania, 'specially for an old woman."

"Shut your mouth about old age or you will never reach it, *surat*!"

* * *

Horse wanted Evil Twin Two to make some move, not just stand there as if it was a repository statue. He intended to crush it, but he did not want to overwhelm it without a fight. He slowed the *Summoner*'s pace to a crawl.

He told himself that the LAMs were the enemy, whether piloted by Jade Falcons or not. He must not make any exception to his urge to kill an enemy. Thinking any other way would show him to be weak, not really a warrior with a falcon's heart. And when they called him a slimy freebirth, they would be right. *I have to kill,* he told himself. *I must kill. I can and will kill.*

Peri could not help speaking out, even if she was only an observer in the LAM.

"What is wrong, Stenis?"

"I am looking for a good shot."

"A good shot? He is practically standing still. I have provided a targeting device that is nearly perfect. Just trigger and fire off something!"

He thumbed the trigger, and the only thing that happened was a red warning signal lighting up on the control panel.

"Malfunction!" Stenis cried. "Hold on!"

He walked the Evil Twin one step forward, then quickly sidestepped it between two trees and into the forest.

"I still have control of the steering," he said, as they crashed through the brush. "We will do a weapons systems check while Horse decides whether or not to try to chase us into the forest, where our smaller size becomes a definite advantage."

Stenis took the LAM deeper into the forest.

For a moment Horse did not know what to do. The forest here was fairly dense. A big *Summoner* would have a hard time maneuvering among the trees.

But why did they retreat into the forest in the first place? They were not firing at him from cover, which would be a cowardly tactic, at any rate. Something had to be wrong.

He decided to wait a bit longer, not willing to waste shots fired into the forest based on flickers of light that might or might not come from the LAM. Patience more often won the day than force.

And there was the other LAM.

He turned his 'Mech around and saw that Sentania's LAM was heading toward the *Warhammer*. It had just opened fire with its medium lasers and had apparently locked on target well. More pieces of the *Warhammer*'s armor were creating a falling cloud.

Horse accelerated the *Summoner* to give aid to Howell. Before he got within range, the shoulder of the *Summoner* was severely nudged by shots from the other LAM's medium lasers as it rose above the forest in its air mode.

Stenis enjoyed weaving the Evil Twin Two among the trees. It made him feel young.

"Done," Geoff yelled after fiddling around with some loose wires and rearranging them.

"Jump jets engaging," Stenis said, and Geoff nodded. "As soon as we clear the treetops, go into AirMech mode. When you get a bead on that *Summ*—"

"I know what to do, old man."

Stenis took the LAM over the trees, and right on cue, Geoff eased the 'Mech into air mode. Thrusting forward toward the *Summoner*, Geoff yelped with joy as he began firing the lasers.

Peri found her hands moving in imitation of the required operations in both modes. She cheered when the *Summoner* staggered from the shoulder hit.

"We can do it!" she yelled.

Aidan would have loved this, she thought. *He liked taking impossible risks.*

For a moment it looked to Horse as if the other LAM was coming right at him, then it swooped upward and made a tight reverse loop that took the LAM up over the treetops. After a compact narrow turn, it headed back toward his *Summoner*.

If that's the game you want to play, all right. I can't fly, but I can get into the air.

Engaging his jump jets, Horse sent the *Summoner* on a straight-up jump, timing the move so that he could reach the LAM's altitude, just as it came within close range. He fired off a round from his autocannon, figuring that it was best to damage the LAM in its air mode.

The *Summoner* continued to rise.

Peri sensed Horse's maneuver and shouted to Geoff as the *Summoner* began its upward flight, "Get out of his damn way! He's going to blast us."

Geoff responded as quickly as he could, veering the aircraft to the right, but his move only partially succeeded. Some of the autocannon fire hit the Evil Twin and rocked it. The aircraft went out of control for a moment, and Peri thought it might suddenly be ejection time. Geoff struggled with the controls, regained a level flight, and swept under the *Summoner*'s feet.

"Good job, Geoff!" Peri shouted, then looked at him closely.

His eyes were vague.

"I . . . I hit my head against something, I don't know—"

Then his look went blank and he went unconscious.

Peri started to shake him.

"You won't wake him that way," Stenis said, with almost too much calm.

The Evil Twin began to lose altitude and tip downward.

"I am putting us back into 'Mech mode, Peri," Stenis said as his hands reached for the 'Mech controls. "You work on Geoff. See if you can revive him."

Stenis flipped the mode-changing switch, and Peri felt a bump as the 'Mech's legs began to extend, then her stomach jolted as the jump jets slowed down the LAM's speed and Stenis began to work the controls.

Peri began to shake Geoff, but his body remained limp. If only she could pull him out and take his place, but the cockpit was much too small for such a maneuver.

"Cheer up," Stenis yelled, "we may not even need to go back into air mode."

Peri stared over Geoff's shoulder at the control panel and tried to make sense of the digital information on the secondary display. Nothing made sense to her now, not even her own design mods.

She made a fist and brought it down on the back of the pilot seat. Pain surged through her hand and, as if in sympathy with her, Geoff moaned. Ignoring the pain in her hand, she reached around the seat and began to shake the apparently woozy pilot.

Stenis chuckled to himself, and Peri felt as if she were in a nightmare, depending on the skills of a solahma so old that he seemed truly senile and an unconscious pilot. She might have prayed, but no one had ever taught her the meaning of prayer and she knew of no god who would hear her.

=== 34 ===

Bagera Forest
Huntress
Kerensky Cluster, Clan Homeworlds
9 May 3059

Horse sent a stream of laserfire toward the LAM as it
settled onto the ground. It grazed the LAM's left side,
making a shallow gouge.

*Well, the Jag techs aren't perfect. Something's wrong
with my weapon alignment. I can compensate. I've done
that enough before. No matter. I've got sufficient firepower to pick that thing apart, bit by bit. Or I could just
blow it away. Which'd be more merciful, I wonder?*

Demolishing the LAM might have been easier if it had
not turned and started dashing for the forest again. What
fascination did the depths of that forest hold for these
stravags?

" . . . live to fight another day," Stenis finished.

"What does that have to do with it?" Peri demanded.
"We will not have another day. This is the day."

"I only meant it comparatively. We need a moment's
respite. I am not certain that, just because weapons
worked in the AirMech mode, that they will operate in the
BattleMech mode."

"You are too cautious, Stenis."

"And I am still here after decades of combat, *quaiff*?"

Peri was astonished by the firmness in the old man's voice. He had always seemed so feeble before.

"Aff. You come alive for combat, don't you?"

"That is correct. But do not abuse me with your use of contractions."

"Sorry, old man."

"And stop calling me—"

"I will, I will."

Sentania had given up trying to discern Stenis' movements. He was not responding to her call over the comm-line either.

She bore down on the *Warhammer*, keeping careful note of the direction its extended-range PPCs were pointing. They could do her the most damage, even end the battle for her in an instant. Though she had already discovered that the Evil Twin was supremely maneuverable, she could not perform fancy stratagems forever.

Abruptly halting the 'Mech, she stood her ground for a second, then fired off the first of her short-range missiles, knowing it might catch Howell off-guard. An SRM was not one of the usual armaments for the light-weaponed LAM.

It was a good shot, one of the best she'd ever made. Sailing in toward the head of the *Warhammer*, the missile changed direction slightly to zero in on the 'Mech's center torso. Sentania, using the enhancements in targeting control provided by Peri's research team, had been able to lock onto the torso of her target while programming the slight misdirection of the missile path.

The explosion staggered the *Warhammer*. It teetered backward, but then regained balance.

"Score another point for David, Goliath," Sentania muttered.

Howell was furious. He had begun to wonder if it was harder to deal with one of these annoying little craft than with a heavy BattleMech. It should not be.

How can this warrior be a mere solahma? Her instincts seem too quick for that. It does not make sense. But nothing makes sense about this battle. I could crush her if I could get close enough.

A quick check of his display showed that Sentania's

attack had caused severe torso damage but no internal damage.

Time to put this one away.

He leveled the extended-range PPC and aimed it in the general direction of the LAM cockpit.

Through the trees and the sputtering licks of fire, Peri could see a thin portion of Horse's BattleMech. After Horse had ignited a pair of trees guarding the opening that Evil Twin Two had narrowly passed through, he held his fire. While she watched, the *Summoner* stepped closer to the forest.

"Get Sentania on the commline," Peri told Stenis. "Let her know we are temporarily inoperative."

"Impossible. I have tried several times. The line is dead, not even static. Just one of the many things wrong with your blasted experiment, Peri. And that is not all. The cross hairs mechanism seems to be off-center or something."

Peri just listened. How could she have ever thought it possible to improve the LAM for combat?

Geoff was coming around slowly. He had asked her, in a vague voice, what was wrong with the simulator. Not a great sign, but he was at least semi-conscious. Her body was tense. Her back hurt. Her legs hurt. Her head hurt.

She saw that she could not suddenly become a warrior again. She had failed once, and there had been reasons for it. Now she was also wondering how well she had succeeded in her role as a scientist. With a carefully designed research program she had apparently turned a machine that was regarded by some as a pile of junk into an enhanced pile of junk.

"All right," Stenis said suddenly. "We can fight again."

"Something is working?" Peri could not keep the surprise out of her voice.

"Not everything. The laser system is down, but the machine guns are green-light."

"Machine guns? That is a *Summoner* out there. What will we do? Riddle it with holes and make it fall over from too much ventilation?"

"Maybe. All I know is that a Jade Falcon does not surrender."

"Are you crazy, Stenis?"

"You know very well that I am."

"That is the famous Horse out there. He will chew you up."

"Sometimes you win, sometimes—"

"Oh, shut up," she grumbled. "Just get us out of these woods."

Horse saw that Howell's attack on Sentania's LAM was succeeding. Yes, Sentania showed skill in her erratic defensive maneuvers. She forced Howell to waste many of his shots, but enough hit the mark to cause extensive damage.

If the other LAM is going to hide out, there is no sense in my remaining here. I'll help Howell finish off Sentania. What a joke! I kill the one person who made a vow to save me.

Thinking these dark thoughts, Horse made the laborious turn that took him in the direction of the conflict between Howell and Sentania. Before completing the turn he fired his lasers once more at the part of the forest where the cowardly LAM hid. He aimed high and ignited the leaves and branches of several trees in the area around the LAM.

As his *Summoner* took a step toward the *Warhammer* and Sentania's LAM, the other LAM came through the flames out of the forest. Some licks of flame were briefly ignited by apparent oil patches on the LAM's surface, and it looked something like a devil emerging from hell.

Although the damage display showed that the LAM was scoring hits against his *Summoner,* Horse felt no sense of impact. He decided his attacker was no more than an insect, after all. He would help Howell first, then swat this one.

"He is going to demolish us, Sentania," Gerri cried. "Let us go to AirMech mode."

In spite of Sentania's expert piloting, pulses from the *Warhammer*'s medium laser hit Evil Twin Two again and again. The 'Mech was clearly reeling from the attack.

"Not yet, Gerri. Remember I am in charge when we are in BattleMech mode."

"I know that. I feel helpless. I want a shot at this guy!"

"And you will. All right. Another few meters and I'm

going to fire another SRM. In a moment. A moment. Now!"

Sentania triggered the missiles. Almost simultaneously, she initiated a jump.

"Okay, Gerri, you get your wish. I am switching to AirMech mode."

Below, she saw that the missile had hit just below the *Warhammer*'s cockpit.

Howell's got to be screaming with frustration, she thought as Gerri accelerated Evil Twin Two so that it passed directly over, and not too far from the *Warhammer*'s head.

Howell was not screaming, but he was cursing. While damage from the missile fire was not disabling, it had left that area of the *Warhammer*'s torso extremely vulnerable to further attack.

"Horse!" he shouted over the commline.

"Aye?"

"What in Kerensky's name are you doing? These LAMs should not even touch us. Is this some sort of conspiracy? Are you in it? You can go back to the Falcons, if you wish, but I will advertise your cowardice to the limits of the homeworlds and beyond into the Inner Sphere."

Horse did not reply.

"Horse?"

"You rest or something. I will take care of both of these LAMs for you."

"You insolent—"

The line went dead. Horse had obviously cut off communication.

If that is the way you want it, Horse, fine. But you will not count me out of this battle either. I mean to demolish these Jade Falcon stravags. And when I get done with them, I will take care of you, hero!

35

Bagera Forest
Huntress
Kerensky Cluster, Clan Homeworlds
9 May 3059

Howell's verbal attacks were like explosions destroying
Horse's personal armor.

*I am meant to be Smoke Jaguar now. All deceptions are
over. All lying words. There may be some kind of destiny
in this. The only word that means anything now is honor.*

Tracking the flight of Sentania's LAM, he anticipated
that it would come down a few meters on the other side of
the *Warhammer*. Then he would take it out of the action
for good.

The other LAM kept coming on, its machine guns firing
wildly. Horse put the *Summoner* into a brisk run. He did
not care that someone watching might have thought his
'Mech looked like a giant frightened by a toad.

"Our best chance is to get to ground again and assault
Howell from his other side before he can turn his 'Mech
toward us," Sentania told Gerri.

"We already did that. I am going to strafe him."

"You are not in charge. I am. We are going to Battle-
Mech mode." Sentania flicked the proper switch. Nothing
happened. They were still in air mode. "What did you do,
Gerri?"

"Geoff and I, we foresaw arguments over command, so we added an override for the transition switch, similar to the override you already have. You cannot make the switch without my cooperation. Sentania."

"You idiots! The BattleMech pilot is in command of the operation during a battle. You serve me!"

"That is what you think," Gerri cried, as he headed the 'Mech in an arc toward the *Warhammer*. He began shooting at its legs, but most of the fire hit the ground on either side or between the 'Mech's knees. Pieces of dirt flew upward, with such velocity they looked like missiles themselves.

As Gerri swooped by, the *Warhammer* fired at the LAM's underside, sending it into a spin. Evil Twin One flipped over and began to plummet toward the ground. Cursing, Gerri worked the controls until, just as the LAM seemed about to crash, he pulled it out and back up again.

When they had leveled out, high above the fray, Sentania muttered. "Well, that was certainly impressive."

"I am going after him again."

"No. You are not."

"What are—"

As Gerri turned toward Sentania, she dealt him a quick left jab to the sharp point of his jaw, then followed with an arcing right to his throat that made him choke as he slid into unconsciousness.

"You two were never worth anything anyway," she said, as she reached over and released his mode lock. The craft began to spiral downward. She switched into Air-Mech mode, engaging it just before the LAM would have crashed. The jump jets engaged at the last possible safe moment and the LAM landed, if a bit unsteadily, on both feet, swaying slightly before Sentania regained complete control.

It was also some struggle for Sentania to regain control of her breathing.

Maybe the age is showing, after all. Or is it just this damn machine? Too many variables to be much use in a fight. If one mode is damaged, the other has to take on full responsibility in combat. And then you get a hard-headed aeropilot like Gerri, and suddenly everything goes out the hatch. Somebody has to be in charge. It can't just be each man for himself in the same cockpit.

In the meantime, she saw that she was in real trouble now. She could no longer attack the *Warhammer* because the *Summoner* had passed it and was heading straight for her.

She triggered another SRM, targeting the *Summoner*'s torso. Horse's quick response in twisting the torso sideways resulted in the missile just grazing it, and then exploding a few meters on the other side of the 'Mech.

Hoping for the advantage of surprise, Sentania put Evil Twin Two into a flat-out run at the *Summoner*. She had most of the 'Mech's weapons firing as she charged.

Horse steadied the *Summoner* after the SRM hit and turned it back toward Sentania's LAM. Some of his anger had subsided, and he was again the cooler-headed warrior who had lived through much worse than this.

The LAM, now coming right at him, looked damaged enough that he thought he could polish it off with a steady barrage of laserfire.

A few steps, Sentania, and you'll get your wish of ending your life in combat . . .

Horse saw on his secondary display that the damage Sentania was doing was relatively insignificant. The LAM's firepower was clearly insufficient.

He responded with laserfire concentrated against the LAM's running legs, severely damaging the left knee.

The LAM, a bit unsteadily, began to rise.

Jump jets again? Sentania, you do like to bounce around, don't you?

Continuing to fire his lasers, Horse was able to shear off both legs of the LAM, one near the hip, and the other at the knee, before it had gone very far off the ground.

Peri, in Evil Twin Two as it pursued the faster *Summoner*, watched the fate of Evil Twin One with mixed anger and sadness. With all of her own LAM's troubles, she realized she had been depending on Sentania to turn the tide of battle. Now, Sentania was spiraling crazily in the sky in Evil Twin One, clearly out of control.

"Stenis, why doesn't she go to AirMech mode?"

"Not sure. Maybe Gerri's been taken out of action, too."

"Impossible! How could that happen, both pilots injured?"

"Beats me. But it looks to me like Gerri must be all right. Look at the LAM. Flying smoothly now."

Peri breathed a sigh of relief.

"Good. What now?"

"We have to see what we can do by way of a diversion, especially with that *Warhammer* directly in our path."

In an almost graceful move, Stenis diverted Evil Twin Two to the right, and the *Warhammer* rocked the LAM as it fired its lasers, just narrowly missing hits that might have disabled the LAM.

"What are you doing now, Stenis?" Peri cried.

"Call it evasive action—until I think of something."

The *Warhammer,* now in pursuit, hit Evil Twin Two at hip level, shattering armor and exposing clumps of myomer fiber.

"Curious," Stenis said as he struggled to keep the LAM upright.

"Our damage is curious?" Peri shouted.

"No, our plight. Sentania has a LAM that is now inoperative in its land mode, while we are essentially inoperative in air mode, unless Geoff wakes up and—"

As if in response to hearing his name, Geoff groaned. "Where are we?" he mumbled, without opening his eyes.

"Still in the thick of battle, strangely enough," Stenis replied.

Geoff came suddenly awake. He seemed ready to take over the controls if needed. Peri tried to make sense out of any move *anybody* made in this skirmish.

Evil Twin Two reeled from another burst of PPC fire that made metallic mincemeat out of its left arm.

"That hit takes away half our working weaponry," Stenis said, checking the damage display. Evil Twin Two then took another hit, this one so hard that the LAM jerked forward, then bounced off a tree at the edge of the forest.

"There goes the other half," Stenis yelled.

Without looking, Peri could envision the *Warhammer* picking up speed and moving in for the kill on a *Stinger*-type LAM that had now lost all of its sting.

"Our jump jets are still operative," Stenis said, looking over at Peri. His face had suddenly aged beyond any years

it had ever showed before. He looked to Peri as if he
would fold in on himself and collapse into dust. He
engaged the jump jets, and the LAM rose on a slanted
path that carried it narrowly past the *Warhammer*'s head
and above it.

"Your move, Geoff," Stenis shouted.

Evil Twin Two seemed to groan as Geoff made the
switch.

It sounds like the throes of death, Peri thought.

"Now, Geoff!" Stenis shouted.

"Now what, old man?" Geoff returned, shaking his
head to clear it even as he spoke. He winced in pain several times. Peri's doubts grew.

"We have to get far enough away from the *Warhammer,*" Stenis said firmly. "Get it chasing after us, lure
it into the trap, so to speak."

Peri swallowed hard. "You mean you have a plan, old
man?"

"Stop calling me that! I am a warrior and I do have a
plan. Of sorts. The odds are that it will kill us."

"Comforting."

"Then again, it may not."

"And you are crazy."

"That, my dear Peri Watson, is our present advantage. Slow down a bit, will you, Geoff? Gentle with
the joystick, and take a wide turn and go back for the
Warhammer."

"We are attacking?" Peri yelled.

"Why not?"

Peri nodded. "Aff. Why not?"

The LAM felt surprisingly smooth as Geoff worked the
LAM's joystick to make the wide-arcing turn Stenis had
commanded.

═══ 36 ═══

Bagera Forest
Huntress
Kerensky Cluster, Clan Homeworlds
9 May 3059

Gerri looked sullen as he piloted the LAM in air mode. Sentania spoke to him as quietly as the noise inside the cockpit would allow. He flinched a few times at her insults.

"Well, Gerri, my fine feathered falcon idiot, the string is running out. We are legless and therefore stuck in AirMech mode. You get your wish. Control of the craft. Except you will listen to me and do what I say, *quiaff*? *QUIAFF*?"

"Aff," Gerri said, his eyes now focused ahead, so that he would not have to look at her.

"You two really did it, with your stupid override of the override. What were you thinking? No, don't answer that. Let me see what we've got left in terms of weapons—not bad, not bad. Still a lot to send Horse's way. Zero in on him now."

Even though Horse was in the *Summoner* and there was no commline between them, Sentania began addressing Horse. Gerri looked at her sideways, probably wondering if she had really gone beyond the Periphery this time.

"Horse, old friend, you old *stravag surat* freebirth— and I can now call you freebirth because you cannot hear it—I guess I'm not as smart as I thought. I thought I had a plan to save you and I thought it would work. I thought I could—Oops, nice shot, Horse. How did you like our evasive maneuver? Good move, Gerri."

She told Gerri to take Evil Twin One on a sweep to the right to evade Horse's laserfire. Even then, some of the scarlet beams got through and sheared away the edge of a wing. The LAM became even harder to handle.

Sentania, glancing toward Geoff, saw the worry on his face and knew it came from her talking aloud to Horse.

Maybe I am crazy, after all. I mean, really crazy. I better stop talking to myself. She watched fragments of the LAM wing fall. *Maybe you can drop us from the sky piece by piece, Horse. Colorful, quiaff? Where was I? The mission. The rescue mission. I thought it would work out. Once, it might have, years ago. I had pride then, and ability—and youth. I guess now I just have pride. My plan was sound though. It was based on fighting normal Jag warriors, but no one like you, Horse. There is no Smoke Jaguar on Huntress that could have won this fight— including Russou Howell—who, after all, is almost as crazy as I am. These Jags are over-the-hill warriors and solahmas and I could have beaten any of them, even in one of these LAMs. Hell, even in a farm wagon. But not you, Horse. You were the unconsidered variable. And, even though you will have to remain a Smoke Jaguar and the Falcons will lose a fine warrior, I am oddly glad for you. In the annals, in somebody's annals, you have again proven yourself a hero. Oops, here you come again.*

Evil Twin One was rocked by Horse's fire. Red lights flashed in several places on its command console.

"We are going down fighting," Sentania shouted. "Agreed?"

"Agreed, old woman."

"Sentania Buhallin goes down fighting, Horse. Back at you, freebirth!"

At Sentania's order, Gerri triggered all the LAM's lasers. At the same time he fired an SRM, and leveled off Evil Twin One. Coming in under Horse's fire, he headed straight for the *Summoner*'s torso, intending to sweep up at the last split second and crash into Horse's cockpit.

With any luck, Horse, both of us will go out in a blaze of glory, Sentania thought. *Here's to death, freebirth!*

* * *

Howell perceived quickly that both LAMs seemed to be engaged in the same maneuver. Both were in air mode and both were heading toward a standing BattleMech. One bearing down on him, one going straight for Horse. It was a sacrifice mission. The LAM coming at him would hit first. Only one of his arm lasers was currently operating. He raised the 'Mech's left arm with the intention of blowing the LAM out of the skies once and for all.

He watched it come, awaiting the good shot. It was confusing, though, that the LAM pilot was not firing his weapons and that his flight path was awkward. Very awkward.

"I cannot control this *stravag* thing," Geoff screamed, as Evil Twin Two first pointed nose down, then nose up, then began to shake all over.

"You are doing fine," Stenis said. "Do not try for the head or the cockpit. He may expect that. Our best shot is at the legs. Crash into the legs. Make him think you are going to fly between them. You may disable him. Not on this pass, though. Veer to the right. Now!"

Stiff with tension, Geoff obeyed Stenis' instructions. The moment was well chosen, for Howell fired again, and just missed Evil Twin Two.

Not a suicide ploy, then, Howell thought. *There is no logic to this 'Mech's fight. No firing, erratic flight pattern, illogical moves. Time to finish it off.*

Howell tried to reposition the left arm to take aim, but he was too late. The LAM was heading straight at him, and going into a dive. It would crash somewhere into the lower part of the *Warhammer*. Reacting instantly, he lowered the 'Mech's left arm and swung at the incoming LAM with a back-handed motion.

"Watch out!" Stenis shouted.

The *Warhammer's* arm and the autocannon barrel on the end of it seemed gigantic, and it was all coming straight at the cockpit of Evil Twin Two.

Geoff managed to raise the fuselage enough to attempt to fly over the *Warhammer's* arm. He almost made it, except that the *'Hammer* reacted to Geoff's new maneuver, its arm raised to block the LAM's path. Geoff pushed the joystick upward and to the left. At first it looked as if Evil Twin Two would smash into the arm. Then, thanks to Geoff's quick reaction, it flew over it. The maneuver did send the LAM spinning out of control, however. The controls seemed to jump out of Geoff's hands as he tried to recover and pull the LAM out of its dive. His head slammed back against the pilot seat and his eyes glazed as Evil Twin Two continued to spiral downward.

An insect, after all, Howell thought, *almost like swatting a fly!*

He started to smile, then he saw that the rapidly spiraling LAM was on a direct path toward the back of the *Summoner*'s upper torso. He would have warned Horse over the commline if there had been time.

Horse could not adjust to the incoming SRM from Sentania's 'Mech. It hit dead center, where there was already extensive damage. On his display, the red light indicating gyro damage went on. Even as it lighted, Horse felt the *Summoner* begin to totter. He had to struggle to regain balance.

The hit was damaging, but the gyro was still operational.

Good try. Now, my turn.

He could see that the LAM was being guided to come in under his laserfire, but his weapons were scoring massive pieces off its light armor. Even before the LAM could nose up toward his cockpit, Horse could discern its goal.

No, Sentania, we won't go down together. I can blow you to pieces before that.

He was just about to fire the fatal shots, when the other LAM crashed into the *Summoner*'s back with an impact that knocked it off its feet and sent it plunging toward the ground.

Sentania saw the big 'Mech begin to fall toward them, and she immediately ordered Geoff to point the fuselage upward and perform a beautifully executed reverse loop. The underside of the LAM nearly brushed the top of the falling *Summoner* but did manage to get out of the way, even though just barely.

When the craft was again level and sailing back again toward where the *Summoner* had stood, she saw that the prone BattleMech, still reverberating from hitting the ground, was afflicted with Evil Twin Two on its back.

Howell was stunned by the events.

But mine is the only 'Mech on this battlefield that is still intact. I guess we win the challenge, after all.

He had not yet noticed that the accelerating Evil Twin One had, without apparent interruption to its attack on the *Summoner,* switched to the *Warhammer* as its target and was barreling toward Howell's cockpit at high speed.

Howell could not adjust his position to get off a good shot, but he managed to turn the 'Mech's torso sideways so that it took the LAM's charge just below the cockpit. The crash resounded through the 'Mech and deafened Howell for a moment. He fought the controls, but could not stop the *Warhammer* from suddenly toppling backward.

Howell hit the eject button, but it jammed. He could not escape. But maybe the pilot of the LAM crashing into him would also die in the crash. What did she say her name was, that solahma?

= 37 =

Bagera Forest
Huntress
Kerensky Cluster, Clan Homeworlds
9 May 3059

"Sentania Buhallin."

She was sure Howell could barely see who was peering in through the cockpit glass at him, but he recognized her voice.

"You? After that crash, in that light craft, you should be dead," he said.

"Right. I should be. We ejected, my aeropilot and I, at the last second, felt like the last nanosecond. Got wrapped up in the flames and smoke from the explosion and damn near burned to death. For now, I can claim a good suntan."

"What are you doing?"

Sentania looked briefly over her shoulder at the *Summoner*. Horse was trying to get the BattleMech to function, but it looked as if the weight of the Evil Twin Two on its back and some malfunctions within the 'Mech were giving him difficulty. He looked surely done, but he was Horse and she could not count on that.

"Galaxy Commander Russou Howell," she said, looking back down at the Smoke Jaguar wrapped in cockpit wreckage. "I have challenged you, successfully executed the challenge, and request your submission."

Howell growled his response. "Kill me first."

"If I have to, but I would prefer for you to act rationally. If you wish, we may fight to the end in hand-to-hand combat."

Howell seemed willing, but when he tried to move, intense pain made him grimace.

"As I thought," Sentania said, "your arm is broken. It looked it. Any other injuries?"

"Something is pinning this leg," he said. "I cannot move."

"It is irrelevant, then, for me to say submit or die, *quiaff*?"

"All right," he said weakly. "Submit. But, when I recover, Sent—"

"You may have your own opportunity for challenge. Now, with the challenge fulfilled, I will help you out of that wreckage. Then we will see how the others made out."

Before starting to remove pieces of metal from the cockpit in order to free Howell, she glanced again at the *Summoner*. Horse had raised it to its knees. It was a good thing she had talked Howell into submission. If Horse had managed to get the *Summoner* upright, he could have claimed the win and, ironically, remained a Smoke Jaguar.

Turning back to work at the wreckage, she saw quickly that its tangle was too complicated. Howell could not be extracted from it.

"There are some things even I cannot do," Sentania said. "We will have to get help."

As she jumped off the *Warhammer,* the two warriors who Howell had left behind came running up to the 'Mech. Sentania told them the fight was over, and they should attend to their commander.

Walking toward the *Summoner,* she breathed a sigh of relief when she saw Peri and Stenis lifting the apparently unconscious Geoff from the remains of Evil Twin Two and descending from the *Summoner* to the ground.

When Sentania signaled to him that Howell had submitted and the battle was ended, Horse stopped trying to get the *Summoner* upright. First hanging from the cockpit hatch opening, then dropping to the ground, he landed on his feet and ran over to Sentania, who told him the parts of the battle he had not seen and of her confrontation with Howell.

"You are a Jade Falcon again, Horse."

"For a moment there, I was certain of being a Smoke Jaguar forever."

"For a moment there, probably the same moment, I would have agreed."

"What now?"

"That pair of warriors Howell ordered out of these 'Mechs are contacting one of Howell's other 'Mechs via commline, to come with the equipment to extract him. There was too much heavy stuff on top of him for us to get him out of the wreckage. I expect we better get out of here before they arrive. They might be in a bad mood. Howell is, certainly. I know a way out through the forest. It is a long walk, but we are too vulnerable on the open road. We could contact someone at Falcon Eyrie, but the communication systems in both LAMs are out."

"All right. I just have one more thing to accomplish."

Horse started walking toward the fallen *Warhammer*. Sentania followed.

"So, Peri Watson, what do you think of your precious Land-Air 'Mechs now?" Stenis asked with heavy sarcasm.

"Well, the test worked, that much is for sure," she said. "We have successfully proven that LAMs are too dangerous to use in combat situations. The two-pilot concept depends on the abilities of the pilots to work together—a major obstacle for Jade Falcon warriors. We are too aggressive, too independent. The bidding system allows for some use of strategy, but success in battle tends to depend on individual efforts. The LAM itself is too erratic. Shifting from mode to mode seems to be its advantage, but it is more likely its downfall. It simply puts too much stress on the 'Mech itself."

"You seem too negative. We won the engagement, after all."

Stenis' comment drew a huge laugh from Peri. "Talk about winning a battle but losing the war," she said. "We won because some kind of fate was on our side today. The *Summoner* and *Warhammer,* the losers if you want to call them that, need repair, but they will fight again. However, the Evil Twins are unsalvageable rubble. A tainted victory, at the very least, Stenis."

"Your report about the LAMs?"

"I will recommend that the project be totally scrapped, especially since Land-Air 'Mechs are outmoded in all their other roles. I consider the grand experiment to be ended and will inform my superiors of its failure. I will also recommend that the whole project be purged from the Falcon Eyrie database, so that no one will ever be able to capture data on it. The remaining experimental LAMs can be shipped out for whatever disposal is deemed necessary. Or we may have to dismantle them here, for parts or some other use. At any rate, Falcon Eyrie will get a new project and, with any luck, I will be reassigned elsewhere. Besides, there is another—"

"Another what?"

"I cannot talk about that with you."

"After what we just went through, you do not trust me?"

"I did not mean that, I meant—"

Stenis whirled around and walked away, to join Sentania and Horse, who were heading for the *Warhammer*. All three climbed toward the cockpit. Peri sighed and followed them.

"You are still Smoke Jaguar, Horse. All I saw on your part was cowardice."

Hearing those words, Horse wanted to climb into the *Warhammer* cockpit and start pummeling the injured Galaxy Commander.

"You submitted," Horse said. "The Falcons fulfilled the challenge."

"And what credit do you claim, coward? Did you actually defeat even one of these infernal LAMs?"

"I do not have to explain anything to you. Sentania admits she would have been blown up if the other LAM had not crashed into me."

"Small excuse for cowardice."

"You stravag—if you had forced that LAM out of position and blown it out of the skies, as you should have, it would not have been sent spinning into the *Summoner*'s back. If anyone lost the battle, it was you in that action. What honor does that bring you, Russou Howell?"

Howell's anger suddenly seemed to drain away. "None," he said finally. "You are right. We were beaten fair and square, if not in an orthodox fashion with orthodox 'Mechs. I will have to live with that. If I was not trapped in here, with one arm and probably two legs useless, we could fight this out."

"Perhaps some other day. But I intend to return to my Clan, to the Jade Falcons."

"You will never be anything more than a freebirth."

Horse let out a loud guffaw, the laugh that had given him his name. "They will get you out of this cockpit soon, but I must bid you farewell now, Russou Howell."

Horse and the others started off the 'Mech, then Horse turned back.

"Oh, and there is one more thing, Galaxy Commander," he said, leaning down to get closer to Howell's face. "It was I who killed the Keeper of the Jaguar kin."

Howell screamed in rage and began flailing his arms desperately, trying to free himself from the wreckage. Horse slipped away from the cockpit opening.

"It is not over yet, Horse!" Howell shouted.

By now, Horse was swallowed up by the trees and never heard a word Howell said.

Epilogue

It is unusual in anybody's universe for people to get what they want. But occasionally they do, although sometimes in costly ways.

Horse and Sentania, both preferring the outdoors to the dark and sometimes unpleasantly cavernous Falcon Eyrie interiors, often sat outside for long discussions, occasionally enduring the fierce storms that passed briefly over the station. Since warriors were there mainly to defend a normally indefensible area, there was not much for them to do on Falcon Eyrie except wait for the next DropShip that would take them away from the world of Huntress.

One afternoon, the two of them were sitting on a mossy spot near the main station. The silence between them was rare, but Horse barely noticed. He was thinking how good it was to be back among Jade Falcons, even if they were mostly solahmas and this was an otherwise unremarkable scientific outpost perched on the homeworld of another Clan.

Early on, he, Sentania, and Stenis had bid goodbye to the departing Peri Watson. That had happened after the arrival of the last DropShip.

"You have to go?" Sentania had asked Peri.

"Yes. Etienne Balzac has decreed it. He does not care much for me, and I suppose he has some other depressing backwater assignment in mind—in some deeper backwater, so to speak."

They all knew the other reason for her departure, however. Sentania had informed Peri of what she and Horse had discovered in the Smoke Jaguar genetic repository. Peri was furious to learn that the Jags had a copy of Aidan Pryde's genetic legacy and might be experimenting with it, developing some revolting combinations of Aidan Pryde and Smoke Jaguar genes. She had taken the copy of Aidan's genetic legacy lodged at Falcon Eyrie and secreted it in one of the equipment cases leaving Huntress with her. She wanted to know more about it, perhaps to confront Etienne Balzac and discover what kind of genetic meddling was going on among the scientists of the two Clans. She knew that these secret experiments were not rightful, and that no good could come of it. It was unClanlike, and someone had to stand for the way of the Clans, even among the scientist caste. She would do that.

The remaining three LAMs were also loaded onto the DropShip, which would carry them to some other unknown fate. The geneticists and the naturalists were overjoyed to see the doomed vehicles go. More of the station's resources would now turn toward their work.

Roshak was happy, too. The change in program meant more attention to falconry. He asked for falcons with even more skills than Jade Rogue.

"Peri had a little LAM," Stenis said, "and now it is gone."

Peri stared at Stenis quizzically, trying to work out his sarcasm. It seemed to her that he made even less sense these days than ever before. What happened to the lucidity he had shown during the battle at Bagera Forest?

After saying their goodbyes, Sentania and Stenis had walked away, still arguing with each other. Peri smiled after them, then turned to Horse.

"Goodbye then, Horse. I am very glad we met."

"Will you see Diana on Ironhold?"

"I will try, if I can find her there."

"I wonder what has become of her hopes of winning a bloodname."

"I cannot believe she would be allowed to compete."

"She had full sponsorship," Horse said.

"I cannot believe that either."

Peri touched Horse's arm. Had Horse been a trueborn, her touch would have been offensive, coming from a member of a lower caste. But he was only—as so many had reminded him so often in recent months—a freebirth. The lowest trueborn could casually touch a freebirth, even if he was a warrior.

"Horse, your work is done here on Huntress. You should be leaving too."

Horse shook his head firmly. "Neg. Not with my Trinary still in Jaguar chains."

"No," Peri said. "Of course not. What was I thinking?" Then, "So, this is goodbye. I wish you success in freeing them, Horse."

She had left, and he was sorry to see her go. He was, after all, being left at a station run by a commander who cared more about falcons than his command. Not long after Peri's departure, he and Sentania had traveled to Lootera to liberate his Trinary. That was all that remained and his mission on Huntress would be complete.

They had sneaked back into the city dressed as techs and slipped into the prisoner detention center. The Trinary members had not heard about the battle of Bagera Forest and Horse's return to the Jade Falcons, and they were hostile at first. Their anger vanished after Horse brought them up to date. Their imprisonment and the thought that their commander had abandoned them for the Jaguars seemed to have turned them into a tightly knit group, and Horse was glad at least something good had come of it.

While he was telling the tale, Sentania interrupted now and then with explanations of how she had persuaded Horse to deceive the Smoke Jaguars in hopes of finding a way for him to return to his rightful Clan. When the tale was told, the Trinary members clapped both Horse and Sentania on the back and threw up their fists in silent victory salutes. They would probably have liked to send up a mighty cheer, but they dared not attract the attention of the guards.

Though Horse knew he could have led them out of Lootera through one of Sentania's many secret routes, he also wanted to reclaim the 'Mechs Howell had so brazenly stolen. Horse had decided that the best plan was to seize both 'Mechs and prisoners in a single swoop.

Once the Jaguars realized their prisoners had escaped, they would probably increase security at the 'Mech bay. The site was within Mount Szabo, like just about everything else on Huntress that the Jaguars held dear. Rescuing the 'Mechs would require a clever and daring plan.

Sentania, of course, had one. And it was clever. And it was daring. But it only partially succeeded.

The whole group headed for Mount Szabo in the dead of night, killing a pair of sentries along the way. Normally, no one could have gotten the storage doors open without alerting guards, but of course Sentania had a way. Sneaking through a guard post, and then disposing of the guard, she led the others to a platform that served as an elevator down into the area.

But, waiting for them below were some Jaguar guards. These must have spotted them earlier and taken another route to catch them by surprise at the bay. For a moment the Jags had the drop on them, but Andera, a member of Horse's Trinary, gave her life by leaping at, and distracting, the Jag warriors. One of them nearly sliced her body in two with the beam from a laser pistol, but Andera's action surprised the ambushers enough that her comrades could engage them in a fierce fight.

Then Horse ordered a retreat, not wanting to ruin the entire mission. The Jag warriors pursued them among the standing BattleMechs, but a trio of Horse's people diverted them while the others found their various 'Mechs. In two cases they had to settle for Jag machines, a *Glass Spider* and a *Bane,* but Horse regarded that as small enough compensation for Howell's treachery in confiscating the Trinary's 'Mechs in the first place.

Sentania had discovered and copied the code that would open the great doors of the bay. Once inside a 'Mech, she used a short-range codebox to key in the code, and told Horse and the others to head for the doors as soon as they began to open.

Watching from his *Summoner,* now rebuilt since its encounter with the LAMs, Horse saw two of the trio holding off the Jag ambushers fall. The third did manage to make it up into the cockpit of a *Howler* and was the last one out of the bay.

Horse felt triumphant as he cleared the great doors, and he quickly took the lead as they charged out of Lootera.

He let his *Summoner* thunder through the pristine Looteran streets with an almost perverse joy. He envisioned all the scars and gouges the 'Mechs would leave in their wake as they passed through the city.

Alarms were sounded, and the Trinary was attacked from several different positions. Four of the ambushers had managed to mount 'Mechs and pursue them. This rear-guard action resulted in the disabling of the final 'Mech in Horse's line, the *Howler* piloted by the warrior who had held off the Jags while her comrades got their 'Mechs powered up and moving. She was killed fighting, and managed—Horse found out later—to take a few Jag warriors with her.

One more of the Trinary was killed during the escape, slain by a Jag warrior who jumped down onto his *Bane* from the roof of a building several stories tall near the outskirts of Lootera. Somehow the Jag warrior had fought her way into the *Bane*'s cockpit and cut the throat of the Falcon pilot. Taking control of the 'Mech, the Jag warrior turned it around and headed it back the way it had come. Unfortunately for her, one of her fellow Jag pursuers, piloting a *Stone Rhino*, fired a missile at the cockpit and turned both killer and victim into burning flesh.

The rest of the escape was easier. Once they were out of Lootera proper, Sentania led Horse and his Trinary down an intricate route through the forest, until they finally confused their pursuers enough to lose them.

In response, Russou Howell had launched an attack on Falcon Eyrie, although, ironically, both Horse and Sentania were away overseeing the rescued BattleMechs, which had been camouflaged and hidden away in a nearby valley. Horse suspected that the retaliation was as much for the killing of the Keeper as it was for the 'Mech raid. In a way, the action against Falcon Eyrie was surely intended as an attack on Horse, and he wondered if Howell was aware of the irony of his absence.

The attack had been relatively futile. Howell had not been able to bring BattleMechs up the steep mountain slopes to Falcon Eyrie. Even if he had, the Eyrie's artillery would have hurt too much to get into position to fight. Therefore, Howell had to rely on infantry and the few aerofighters of his command, along with some long-range missile fire from the foot of the mountain. Only one of the missiles actually reached its target of Falcon Eyrie, and it succeeded only in demolishing one of the makeshift buildings on the surface of the installation, most of which was below-ground anyway.

The infantry, by attacking first from undetected positions, had at first been successful in shooting down a few of the unsuspecting guards below their high vantage points, but the Falcon counterattack was furious enough that they had to retreat. The aerofighters were brought into the attack too late for tactical purposes, and their barrages were ineffective, despite the impressive number of small fires they left behind before swooping away for the last time.

In only one way was the attack a success. One of the wounded warriors was the Eyrie's commander, Star Colonel Bren Roshak. When the attack came, he had been on his way down the mountainside for his favorite sport, falconry. The falcon named Jade Rogue had been killed immediately, Roshak's arm shot away along with it. Even now, Roshak was bedridden, still being cared for by the medtechs. He would be lifted out to one of the Jade Falcon worlds by the next Falcon DropShip that came to Huntress. Sentania had commented more than once that Roshak seemed more injured by the loss of his beloved falcon than by his actual physical injuries.

The failure of the raid must have incensed Howell even more, Horse thought, and he wondered what new plots the Galaxy Commander might be hatching even now.

The rescue of his own troops and their 'Mechs had exhilarated Horse, but then life suddenly became quieter, almost lethargic, as he too awaited the next DropShip. Sentania had suggested a raid or two—"just to stay in shape"—but Horse rejected the idea. He saw no value in running raids just to fill idle days. Nor did he wish to lose more warriors or more 'Mechs. He had done what he was supposed to do here, though he had surely taken a round-about path in doing it. Now, he merely wanted to get off Huntress and back to other missions the Khan might have in mind.

"You and I, we are becoming too serious," Sentania said suddenly.

Horse shrugged. In the distance some high, dark clouds were moving toward them.

"I am not serious. Just numb."

"Even closer to what I was thinking. You know, Horse, one of the consequences of becoming a solahma is a tendency to give up, well, certain parts of life. I almost immediately became a, well, loner here. Urges that were once, well, quite active became nonexistent. Lately they have returned and, well, I would like to do something about them."

"Sentania, you are adept at speaking in odd tongues. What are you talking about?"

"Come to my quarters. What I am talking about is what we warriors so delicately refer to as coupling. I feel the, well, whatever you would call it—the urge, the need—right now."

"You, a trueborn, would invite a free—"

"Damn, Horse, you make everything too complicated. This is already complicated enough. There are feelings, well, some unwarriorlike, well—Horse, let me shut up now."

She stood up and extended her hand toward him. In the still bright daylight that was beginning to darken with the coming clouds, he could see some of her age in her face, but only some. She looked no older than many active warriors. She definitely looked younger than Joanna. She closed and opened her hand as a gesture for him to take it. He did. She pulled him up and they stood, facing each other, each one ready to smile at the slight absurdity of their present situation. The invitation to coupling usually felt more casual, more perfunctory, than this.

Sentania let her smile happen and said, "Come to my quarters, freebirth—and I mean the word, well, in all kindness."

Horse smiled in response and they started to walk down the hillside as the first drops of rain came.

Russou Howell stood on a hill near the outskirts of Lootera, watching his warriors drill. In recent weeks he had initiated a complex series of physical training exercises and BattleMech field maneuvers. At first some of the warriors still seemed to resent him, but he was gradually, through strong discipline and no-nonsense regulations, gaining their respect. The evidence of that was there on the field below. The warriors' moves were crisply executed and their enthusiasm was clear. Howell was confident that should Huntress ever be attacked while he was its commander, he and his two galaxies of warriors would be ready for it.

He walked a few steps down the hill, satisfied that the limp that had afflicted him since the LAM battle was now gone. He flexed his arm and felt no pain there, either.

Healed now, it seems. I feel better than I have in some time. Better than I have since that day on Maldonado. I can put all that behind me now.

Logan thought I was crazy, my behavior unClanlike. Maybe I was, for a time. I cannot judge. I can hardly remember the last few months. I only remember Horse and his treachery.

Well, Horse, we are not finished with each other. I sense that. I know that. I do not know what will happen, or when, but we will fight again. I do not know which of us can best the other, but I would rather lose to you than never resolve our quarrel.

Glancing toward the skies, seeing the same bank of dark clouds that Horse and Sentania had viewed earlier, his mind racing with thoughts of Horse and one day challenging him, Russou Howell did not suspect that the real danger of attack on the Smoke Jaguar homeworld of Huntress was not from Horse and his Jade Falcons, but from something that was presently beyond those storm clouds, and coming closer and closer.

Howell looked back toward the smoke jaguar carved out from the side of Mount Szabo. As so often happened, he felt its power, the power of his Clan. It seemed to emanate from the sculpture.

Yes, he thought, *I feel better than I have felt in a long time. In control. Even more, in command.*

About the Author

Freebirth is Robert Thurston's fifth novel for BattleTech®
and his twentieth overall. His previous novels in the line
were the Legend of the *Jade Phoenix Trilogy* and *I Am
Jade Falcon*. His published work also includes eight
books in the Battlestar Galactica series, *Alicia II, A Set of
Wheels, Q Colony,* plus novelizations of the movies *1492:
Conquest of Paradise* and *Robot Jox*. His career in science fiction dates from his attendance at the Clarion
Science Fiction Writers Workshop, where he won first
Clarion Award for best story. He has published more than
40 short stories, several critical essays, and historical
articles for a volume in the Reader's Digest Books series.
He lives with his wife and daughter in New Jersey, where
he works as a college administrator and instructor of
Humanities.

Next in the Twilight of the Clans series

Sword and Fire

by Thomas S. Gressman

Frigate ISS Haruna, *Task Force Serpent*
Huntress
Kerensky Cluster
19 February 3060

After almost a year of heading secretly for the Smoke Jaguar homeworld of Huntress, the WarShips of Task Force Serpent have finally arrived. Under the command of General Ariana Winston, the Inner Sphere forces intend to wipe out the planet's 'Mech and munitions factories and annihilate the many warrior sibkos, thereby destroying the Jaguars' ability to make war. All part of a plan to eliminate the Clan threat forever.

The first wave of the operation begins as a team of commandos led by DEST Commander Major Michael Ryan ready themselves to drop onto the planet Huntress.

As Ryan settled the helmet of his Kage suit over his head, a quartet of ship's crewmen scuttled around him, erecting a drop pod. This thick, heavy egg of ceramic and steel would protect him during his long fall through Huntress's upper atmosphere. To prevent their detection on enemy radar, the pods were given two layers of Radar Absorbent Material. In theory, the outer layer RAM would protect the pods during their fall into Huntress's upper atmosphere. That thick coating of high-tech paint would be burned away by the entry heating, along with the pod's ablative shell. The inner layer of RAM would continue to hide the pod until it split apart deep inside Huntress's atmosphere. If everything went according to plan, the DEST teams would be "below" the Jaguars' radar net by the time that happened. In some ways this was the ultimate in High-Altitude-Low-Opening drops.

To cover the disappearance of the DropShip, Captain Ge would broadcast a weak, purposefully broken distress signal, claiming that his vessel was in trouble, and was about to crash. The subterfuge had the added effect of explaining any faint radar traces the Jaguars might get off the descending pods. As small as their radar cross-section would be on the enemy's sensors, the pods would in all likelihood be mistaken for debris falling from a supposedly stricken ship.

At various places around the bay other techs were likewise cocooning the rest of his unit.

As soon as the last drop pod panel had been bolted in place, Ryan's egg-like container rocked heavily. Ryan knew that the motion was caused by a crewman wearing a heavy industrial exoskeleton lifting the pod and placing it in the ship's drop chute. Locked in the capsule, Ryan tried to anticipate the moment when Maeda Ge would give the command to eject the pods. He knew approximately how long it took to load the pods, and to seal the chutes, and watched the chronometer set into the Kage suit's viewscreen, counting down the seconds until . . .

Unexpectedly, the world dropped out from underneath him. His count had been off by nearly ten seconds. For several long seconds, the pod fell free, buffeted by the wake of the *Stiletto*'s passing. Dimly through the thick shell, Ryan began to hear the roar of the wind as his pod punched through the air like a rifle bullet. Despite the heavy insulation of the pod, and the environmental protection of his suit, heat began to creep up Ryan's legs and back. His pod, and he prayed those of his men, was entering Huntress's upper atmosphere, where air friction heated the capsule's ablative covering to a hellish temperature. Ryan hoped that any Smoke Jaguar seeing the fiery streaks of the drop pods scoring across the night sky would assume they were shooting stars.

I know what I'd wish for. Ryan snorted a bitter laugh. *I'd wish that the Jaguars just stay fat, dumb and happy.*

Looking again at his chronometer Ryan estimated the time remaining until the pod entered the lower atmosphere. This time he was right on the mark.

Just as his count reached zero, the pod split into six narrow sections and peeled away, leaving the commando leader falling through space. Arching his back as far as his armored suit permitted, Ryan fought to bring himself under control. As he settled into the spread-eagle position dictated for High-Altitude-Low-Opening jumps, he searched the sky for the rest of his team. At first, the black-armored troopers were invisible. Switching on his visor's built-in thermal imager allowed him to pick out the falling commandos as barely lighter patches against the cool darkness of the sky. Not far away was the robot-controlled cargo pod. Not known for being reliable, amazingly enough it seemed this cargo pod was working correctly.

With outstretched arms and legs, the troopers maneuvered into a rough aerial formation, falling into place behind their leader. Following the discretes generated by his suit's Heads-Up Display, Ryan angled off into the night sky, aiming for an unseen point on the planet below. Like a flock of silent predatory birds, the twenty-three men and women under his command followed his lead.

Making the drop itself wasn't particulary difficult. Finding the right drop zone was. With no navigation aids, or drop beacon, the DEST commandos had to drop almost blind, trusting the data loaded into their suits' on-board computers to locate the out-of-the-way plateau that was their zone in the mountains west of Lootera, the planetary capital. Ryan prayed that Trent, the spy that had provided the Task Force with a wealth of intelligence on the Smoke Jaguars, had given them accurate information. If it wasn't, the commandos might be in for a very hard landing indeed.

Ryan's altimeter clicked over to five hundred meters. A second later at two hundred meters, his drop chute deployed with a muted pop, the black nylon main canopy slowing his fall. A careful look upward assured Ryan that the air-foil parachute had opened properly. With grim purpose, he aimed his chute toward the now-visible drop zone. The relatively level area designated as his insertion point was narrower than he had been led to believe, and appeared to be strewn with low thorny bushes.

As the ground rushed up to meet him, Ryan wheeled into the wind, bringing himself to a gentle, upright landing. No sooner had he touched down, than he slapped the quick release harness, freeing himself from the now limply flapping parachute. All around him, the rest of his troopers were doing the same.

Silently, by means of hand signals, his team checked in. All had made the HALO drop safely.

High above, as the DEST troopers got themselves organized to begin their mission, the *Stiletto* swung away from the drop zone, turning her nose for her own landing place on Huntress.

"What do you mean they have disappeared?" Smoke Jaguar Galaxy Commander Russou Howell hissed to the lower-caste sensor operator.

Howell was unhappy at being awakened in the middle of the night by what he considered a routine matter, the unscheduled arrival of a DropShip. He had only gotten an hour-or-so's worth of fitful sleep when the officer of the deck awakened him. All the drink he'd consumed the evening before had yet to pass out of his system, leaving him with a sick, pounding headache. Of late, Howell felt the increasing need to bludgeon his senses and emotions into oblivion in order to sleep. The death of his one-time friend, Star Captain Trent, at Howell's own hands still haunted the Clan officer. Sometimes even the liquor could not bring sleep. Predictably, it was one of those nights when a trivial problem that demanded his personal attention arose.

When questioned, the technician-caste sensor operator informed his commander that the ship, a *Broadsword* identified as *Tracker* had arrived in-system, claiming that they carried parts and technical personnel for the 'Mech factory complex at Pahn City. When the cargo was delivered, the *Tracker* was to take on a star of OmniMechs for transport to the Occupation Zone. Though the arrival of an unscheduled flight was rare, it was by no means unheard of. The ship's captain would be reprimanded for breach of normal operating procedures, as would the merchant caste administrator who failed to arrange the proper scheduling. No, it wasn't the arrival of unexpected cargo that bothered him. It was the second part of the *Tracker*'s supposed mission, the transfer of a star of 'Mechs to the Occupation Zone. He had believed himself familiar with the shipping schedule. To the best of his knowledge, there was no shipment of 'Mechs, or any other military asset for that matter, due to leave Huntress for at least a month. If what the *Tracker*'s pilot said was correct, then someone would receive more than a reprimand for his failure to keep the proper records.

By the time Howell reached the command center, something new had developed.

"I am sorry, Galaxy Commander," the technician said with confusion. "One minute the *Tracker* was on my scopes just as it should have been. The next it vanished."

"Confirm her cargo and destination."

"Yes, Galaxy Commander."

It took a few seconds for the tech to locate the proper section of the automatic communications log and play it back.

"Cargo and destination confirmed, Galaxy Commander."

For a few minutes Howell stared at the computer-generated map of Huntress hanging in the air at one end of the communications center. He knew that the sensor techs and aerospace controllers used the map to keep track of all traffic arriving or departing from the planet. High-speed computer links from similar tracking stations all over the planet kept the data current.

"Where did she disappear from your sensors?" Howell demanded. "Show me."

The tech manipulated the proper controls to draw a glowing line across the face of the map. The track began over the Dhundh Ocean, just to the west of the Path of the Warrior Peninsula. From there, it extended across the north western portion of the continent of Jaguar Prime, and ended abruptly just before it reached the edges of the Shikari Jungles.

Howell stroked his chin, gazing thoughtfully at the band of dark green rain-forest which ran at a slight angle across the larger of the two continents making up Huntress's land mass. At the western end of the jungles was an expanse of fetid water-logged marshes, called the Dhuan

Swamps. It was just to the north of these marshes that the *Tracker*'s flight path came to an abrupt end.

"Did he send out any kind of a distress call before he disappeared?" the Jaguar officer asked.

"Yes, Galaxy Commander, but the message was so faint and broken up that we could barely read it. Sensor tracks suggest that the ship may have broken up in flight."

"This is most peculiar," Howell mused tapping his cheekbone with his forefinger. "Most peculiar indeed."

"Very well," Howell said crisply. "We can only assume that the *Tracker* has crashed, probably in the vicinity of the Dhuan swamps. Initiate a search. When you find her, bring me the captain, the shipping manifests and the flight-data recorders. Notify me if there are any further developments."

Russou barely heard the technician's acknowledgment. The Clan warrior felt an odd shiver along his spine, a sensation he'd not felt since Tukayyid. Would his Jaguar pride permit it, he would have called the feeling a premonition of impending disaster.

Stop it. You are beginning to sound like a Nova Cat mystic, rather than a Jaguar warrior.

The Galaxy Commander glanced at the chronometer fixed to the room's north wall.

"Freebirth!" he cursed. *0335. I have to be up in less than three hours. It is hardly worth even trying to go back to sleep.*

With a wordless snort of disgust, he stalked out of the communications center, heading down the corridor for his quarters. Something told him he was going to need all the sleep he could get.

Mackie

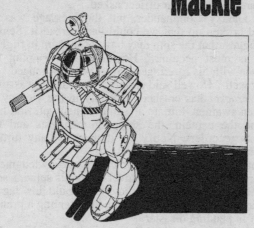

Mad Dog

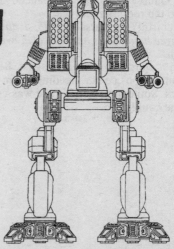

Night Gyr

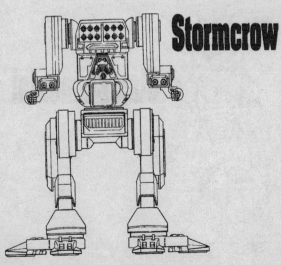

Stormcrow

Summoner

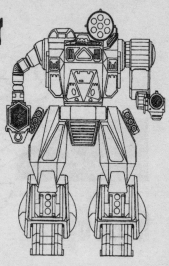

Clan Elemental

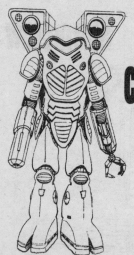

Clan Scout
Class Jumpship

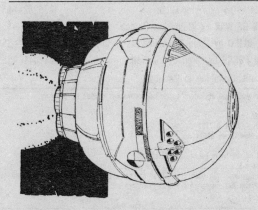

Clan Union-C Dropship